LEGACY OF SHADOWS

LEGACY OF SHADOWS

CAMBRIDGE GOTHIC – BOOK 3

Mark Wells

A CAMBRIDGE TALES BOOK

First published in Great Britain in 2023 by Cambridge Tales Ltd

A catalogue record for this book is available from the British Library.
ISBN: 978-1-9160284-5-6

Formatting by Polgarus Studio

Cambridge Tales Ltd
115c Milton Road
Cambridge CB4 1XE
www.marknwells.com

To Karina and Michael
I couldn't have done this without you

Prologue

Some journeys stay with you forever.

At least that's what Alfonso thought, clinging to Katya's feathers as the harpy bore him over Gemini's alien landscape. Her mighty wings beat a steady rhythm, keeping pace with those of her older sister, Olga, flying ahead of them.

The two creatures, part harpy and part human, had the azure sky to themselves, their mother's DNA making them immune to the calcifying effect of the twin suns. They soared over the valley far below, free from threat or interference, as they carried him and their mother to the distant uplands.

Alfonso glanced over at Mary, riding proud and erect on Olga's back. The woman was unrecognisable from the gnarled old crone who had captured him emerging from the portal all those months ago. Gone were the wrinkled features and white hair, replaced by the glowing skin and flowing locks of someone half her age.

Restored to health by a Matriarch's egg, her hunched posture was also a thing of the past. The broken staff Mary had once used as a crutch had been replaced with one wielded as a weapon. And there was no mistaking the intensity in those piercing blue eyes as she glared back at him from her daughter's back.

"Alfonso!" Katya hissed. "Answer her!"

"What?"

"Mother was calling you!"

"I didn't hear her."

"For goodness' sake," she muttered, beating her wings faster to draw level with her sister.

"Are you deaf?" Mary bellowed.

"I'm sorry."

She pointed with her staff at the ragged line of stone pillars rising high above the valley floor.

"Tell me what you see."

Columns stood in the middle of the river, water flowing around their base and leaving a foaming trail in their wake. The red rock surfaces were scarred and pitted with fissures, and though some pillars had borne the ravages of time better than others, there was little difference between these and the others they had flown over that day.

Keeping his voice low, he whispered to Katya, "What am I looking for?"

"The last one," she replied.

The flat-topped peak was high above the valley and exposed to the unrelenting glare of the twin suns. Alfonso expected to see nothing but dust on the summit. Instead, there was a pale circle of what might have been dried vegetation. As they drew closer, this morphed into a tangle of bleached ribcages and bones. He remembered standing in a similar structure within a vast colony of harpies, a shaft of moonlight illuminating an egg in its centre. The egg he and Katya had stolen to restore her mother to life.

"A nest," he murmured.

"What was that?" Mary's voice was becoming harder to hear over the growing rumble of the river, but her eyes were eager.

"A nest," he shouted.

"An abandoned nest!" She laughed, and something in that sound made even Katya flinch. "Alone, even the strongest harpy is vulnerable. Now, let me show you where true strength lies."

She leaned forwards and issued a command to her mount. Olga dipped her head and accelerated, her mother's hair streaming back. Before Alfonso could ask Katya what Mary meant, his stomach lurched as she set off after her sister.

They swept into the valley, the harpies following the course of the river as it ran between the terracotta cliffs. As each mile passed, the walls drew closer together, funnelling the meandering stream into a fast-flowing torrent. Trees began to appear, the green borders becoming denser the further they flew.

Alfonso wondered what other life could be eking out an existence beneath the protective shade of the leafy canopy. Not that Mary and her daughters showed any interest, racing onwards with barely a downward glance.

"Hold tight," Katya called over the sound of the wind.

Alfonso clung on as the walls rushed past on either side, the siblings twisting and turning around the buttresses of rock in a dizzying display of skill. Below him, the thunder of the river grew in intensity, the air damp with spray thrown up by the crash of waves against rocks.

With a final, gut-wrenching swerve, Katya swept around a wall, and Alfonso saw the source of the roar. A towering waterfall rose above them, cascading white water throwing up a cloud of mist that filled the cauldron of encircling cliffs. The water's percussive force battered his eardrums and pummelled his senses, leaving him dazed and dull-witted.

Ahead of him, he was vaguely aware of a dark object swooping up before the vertical wall of water. Wings swept back, Olga rode the rising column of air that propelled her dart-like form skywards. Alfonso just had time to grip Katya's feathers before she angled her wings and did the same.

Flattened against her back, his breath was squeezed from him as they soared upwards. Spray stung his face, and he closed his eyes, hoping Katya hadn't misjudged her angle of climb. A split second later, they shot clear of the cliffs, Alfonso coughing and spluttering as they left the sound of the waterfall below them.

"Stop whining. It was just a little water!" Katya said.

"You could have warned me."

"You needed a shower. You were beginning to smell like a molevin's latrine."

Perhaps it was the adrenaline rush or simply relief, but Alfonso laughed for the first time since arriving on Gemini. The sound died when he saw Mary staring at them, her expression anything but cheerful.

"To the Citadel, Olga," Mary ordered.

Her mount didn't respond; she was glaring at her sister.

"Olga!" Mary repeated.

With an angry jerk of her head, Olga banked away towards the mountains. Katya followed, leaving Alfonso to wonder what had passed between the sisters. However, these thoughts were swept from his mind by the landscape beneath him. A vast lake filled the valley above the waterfall, its dark green waters spreading out to the lower slopes of the nearby mountains.

After months in the dusty, dry confines of the lowlands, it was a shock to see such an expanse of water glittering in the light of the twin suns. For a moment, he was transported back to the balcony of his parents' villa in Mallorca, gazing out over the gently lapping waters of the bay towards the distant headland of Alcudia.

The image faded as he noticed the differences. They were flying towards a barren peninsula jutting out into the lake rather than a crescent-shaped beach curving into the distance. And what he might have mistaken for clusters of folded parasols dotted along the shoreline were clumps of pale tree stumps offering nothing in the way of shade from the relentless suns.

The most striking contrast was the towering columns rising from the headland. These stone giants had the same ruddy hue as those they had flown over earlier, though they were far more extensive in scale and height. Each one would have dwarfed even the Hive, the massive rock housing an entire colony of harpies from which he and Katya had managed to escape. That mountainous rock had stood on its own, but Alfonso counted six in front of them.

Mary's daughters were headed for the largest of these, their twin shadows racing across the lake's surface. The looming monolith's unnaturally straight walls had rectangular openings at regular intervals, and the summit looked like it had been levelled by one swift stroke from a giant craftsman's blade.

Olga and Katya soared towards this flat-topped peak, spreading their wings at the last minute to land with barely a tremor. Mary alighted at once and strode across the rock platform. Alfonso eased himself from Katya's back and waited for his legs to adjust to the strange sensation of standing on solid ground.

"Come here!" Mary commanded. "I have something to show you."

The woman stood at the tower's edge, staff in hand, staring out. Olga was watching him, wings folded, and Katya's face was once again a mask. So he did as he was told, stopping a few feet from their mother.

"I said I would show you what strength looks like."

She lifted her staff and pointed at the nearest column, and Alfonso gasped.

The bare red rock had been transformed into a honeycomb of alcoves, reminiscent of the Valle de Los Caídos, the mausoleum cut into the mountain north of Madrid – except that the inhabitants of this tower were far from dead. In the shadows cast by the arches were thousands of nests, their pale tangle of discarded bones similar to the remnants he had seen on the columns in the river valley. And on each sat a harpy, its wings stretched protectively over its precious contents.

"So many," he whispered.

"That's why we needed the lake."

"Sorry?"

"A food source to sustain the colony. The river alone could not provide enough. But creating a spawning lake made all this possible."

The waters far below suddenly seemed darker. "You built that?"

"You've seen dams before, haven't you?" Mary pointed at the distant waterfall. Despite the rising mist, he could make out tops of the boulders heaped across the entrance to the valley. The task of shifting that amount of stone into place must have been monumental, not to say fraught with danger.

"How?"

"It turns out male harpies have their uses after all." She indicated the statues lining the banks of the lake. "Subject to certain… constraints."

A strange hissing noise made Alfonso turn. Olga was grinning at her mother as if they had shared a private joke. Though not one that Katya found amusing, given the grim expression on her face.

"Speaking of uses," Mary continued, "what are we to do with you?"

Alfonso's stomach shifted as she considered him.

"Too scrawny to lift boulders. And far too pale to stand in the sun, of course." She paused, clearly enjoying his discomfort. "How about the Tower of Skulls?"

Olga snorted. "He wouldn't last a night."

"And yet somehow he has survived so far."

"Luck is a fickle friend."

"True." The woman leant on her staff. "Still, it could be amusing to watch."

"Mother, is that wise?" said Katya. "He will be torn apart."

"You sound concerned, Daughter." There was a dangerous edge to Mary's voice. "You've not become overly attached to this one, have you?"

"I don't know what you mean."

"Oh, but I think you do. Bearing him on your back, hushed conversations, shared confidences… Why, anyone would think you two have imprinted."

Katya flinched. "That did not happen."

"I hope not, for your sake." There was no doubt about the warning note now. "Let me give you a bit of advice, Daughter. Never let one of these" – she smacked her staff into Alfonso's groin, and he dropped to his knees in agony – "take advantage of your good nature. Never, you hear me?"

"No, Mother."

Despite Katya's acquiescence, Olga eyed her with undisguised suspicion.

Frowning, Mary said, "I think it is time we broke up the dream team. Olga, you take charge of the boy. He requires a minder who is sufficiently… detached."

"With pleasure, Mother." Olga gave Alfonso a murderous look.

"As for you, my dear…" Mary considered her younger daughter. "Our forces remain scattered after the raid on the Hive. I need you to gather and return them here. I want the entire colony back for the solstice."

"That is less than a week. What about the injured?" Katya asked.

"We cannot wait for them."

Katya went very still.

"Well, you have your orders," said Mary. "What are you waiting for?"

Alfonso thought Katya might say something. But then she turned and, casting him a fleeting look, launched herself into the air. Her broad wings beat furiously, throwing up a cloud of dust that forced him to avert his gaze. When he raised his head again, her graceful outline was heading for the distant falls.

Alfonso suddenly felt very alone. Then, a jab to the ribs made him look up. Mary was standing over him.

"Get up. Playtime is over."

Gingerly, Alfonso eased himself to his feet.

"Take him to his cell."

"As you wish, Mother."

Olga leapt into the air, dug her claws into his shoulders and swept him out over the lake. The landscape hundreds of feet below was dizzying, and Alfonso gasped.

"Stop whinging!" Olga hissed, banking around and returning to the lowest rectangular opening. As they swooped, he braced himself for landing. But rather than lowering him into the space, Olga let go.

Alfonso dropped, his arms and legs flailing. Then, his feet hit the outlying edge, pitching him forwards, and he fell onto a crude mattress of compacted feathers and bone. Olga hovered outside the opening, leering at him. Then, with a sweep of her wings, she was gone.

For a few seconds, he lay there, his heart still racing. Only when his breathing slowed did he hear the clicking sound. Twisting, Alfonso saw an articulated shape worming its way from under the pile of bones. A giant cockroach-like creature emerged, almost two feet in length, its glossy red carapace mottled with dust. Extending two antennae, it probed the ground around the nest, searching.

Scarcely daring to breathe, he moved his hand very slowly towards the pocket of his tattered trousers. There, pressed against his leg, was the sliver of bone he'd used to carve his days of captivity into the wall of his last cave. Those long hours of painstaking work had worn the tip of this makeshift stylus to a point as sharp and deadly as a dagger.

Eyes never leaving the creature, he shifted his weight – just a fraction, but that was all the monster needed. It paused, its blunt head turning towards him.

"*Merda*," he murmured, scrambling backwards.

In a blur of legs, it skittered after him. Its speed was incredible, covering the ground in a heartbeat. But Alfonso was no longer the hapless waiter who had stumbled, blinking and unsuspecting, into this harsh world. Weeks hunting molevin in the tunnels below the river valley had sharpened his reflexes to those of an assassin.

Even as the monster lunged, its mandibles opening wide, he brought the stylus up, driving the point into the vulnerable underside of its head. The articulated body convulsed, its needle-sharp legs clamping around his arm.

Ignoring the pain, he used the creature's momentum to slam it onto the cave floor, burying the spike into its skull. He pinned it there, gritting his teeth as the legs thrashed back and forth until, with a final juddering spasm, they went still.

Only then did he pull his bleeding arm free. He leant against the wall of his cell for some time, remembering the monstrous centipede that had stalked him through the Underhive. To find something like that here made him wonder what other horrors Olga had waiting for him.

How long would it be before Katya returned? Two, maybe three, days? Until then, he was on his own.

Alfonso dug in his pocket for the leather pouch of flints. It wasn't long before he had a small fire going in the entrance to his cell, just as his mentor had taught him. Thrusting the cockroach carcass into the flames, he listened to the sizzling of his evening meal and waited for the night.

Chapter One

The sun was already dipping behind the College Library when a stooped man in a crumpled summer jacket walked around the tree-lined square of St John's College Chapel Court before disappearing through an archway in its north-east corner. Emerging from the short passageway, he continued along the sandy path past the Master's Garden and through a discreet side gate to the Master's Lodge entrance.

Professor Ravi Gupta pressed the brass doorbell of the imposing Victorian manor house. The benefactor's crest was carved above the door; a pair of stone Yales, the mythical horned creatures flanking the Beaufort coat of arms, stared down at the new arrival. Ravi wondered about the many visitors that had been subject to their scrutiny over the years. How many had as much to conceal as he did?

He had been putting off the upcoming meeting for most of the vacation. Thanks to his hospital appointments, the Easter bank holidays and some lengthy but inconsequential trips to the Mullard Radio Observatory, he'd managed to avoid responding to the Master's open invitation until now. But with term about to start, he'd finally run out of time and excuses.

An electronic buzz interrupted his thoughts, and the tinny voice of the Master's Secretary came over the intercom.

"Yes?"

"Helen, it's Professor Ravi Gupta to see the Master."

"Ah, yes, Professor. Would you make your way up to the Oak Room? He'll be with you shortly."

"Of course."

The intercom emitted a continuous buzzing noise, and Ravi pushed open the door. Entering the lobby with its racks of hats, gowns and cloaks, he made his way to the entrance hall, the large fireplace now filled with tastefully arranged pine cones rather than glowing coals.

As a further reminder of the College's founder, a portrait of Lady Margaret hung on one wall, her long, pale hands clasped before her as she knelt in prayer. Ravi felt her pious gaze on him while he crossed the carpeted hall and ascended the stairs to the first-floor drawing room.

Taking its name from the wood-panelled walls, the Oak Room sat on a landing that ran the entire length of the building, connecting the Master's private quarters at one end with the state bedrooms at the other. Like the entrance hall, it was graced by a large fireplace and a portrait – not of the founder but of her long-time adviser and confidant, Bishop Fisher: the same cleric who had later lost his head for opposing her son's divorce from Catherine of Aragon.

The significance of hanging the painting of a man executed for standing up to Henry VIII in the Master's waiting room was not lost on Ravi. It was the sort of subliminal message the former intelligence officer would have enjoyed sending to those sitting here. For Ravi, though, the portrait did nothing more than stiffen his resolve.

After all, he thought, *some principles are worth dying for.*

"A striking portrait, don't you think?"

Lester was standing behind him.

How does he keep doing that? Ravi thought, marvelling at the man's ability to appear out of thin air.

"Indeed, Master, as befits the man."

"You're an admirer, then?" Lester raised an eyebrow.

"Of the subject or the artist?"

"Both, perhaps?"

"I know little about art, but for Bishop Fisher I have the highest regard."

Lester nodded. "Well, come through. I've ordered some tea. Earl Grey, if I remember rightly?"

"Quite so, Master."

Ravi wasn't fooled by Lester's pleasant demeanour, which had won him many friends in College. The man had a sharp and perceptive mind, and Ravi had witnessed him undermine an obstructive Fellow's most well-prepared defences on more than one occasion.

During his time at John's, the Master had also established an extensive network of sources that spread far beyond the College's walls. Like any network, its many strands led back to the centre. As Lester opened a wood-panelled door and indicated that his guest should enter, Ravi couldn't help but feel like the proverbial fly being drawn into the heart of a spider's web.

"So, Ravi," said Lester, as they entered the study, "make yourself comfortable while I ask my Secretary to divert my calls. We don't want to be disturbed now, do we?"

Ravi thought a timely disturbance might prove helpful but decided not to share this with his host. Instead, he chose a seat at the small table facing the desk while the Master pressed a button on his phone.

"Helen, would you make sure we are not disturbed?"

"The Vice-Chancellor was hoping to have a word with you, Master."

"It'll be about the Royal Visit. Tell him they are welcome to use the Playing Fields for the helicopter. Just make sure they avoid the cricket square. The Head Groundsman is rather protective of his grass, and while the Royal security officers are armed, I don't want them to get injured unnecessarily."

"Of course, Master. I'll ask him to let the Palace know."

Lester gave Ravi a wink and joined him at the head of the table.

"Now then, where were we?" he said, easing himself into a chair. "Ah yes, you were going to tell me about the nasty fall you had in the New Court cellars last term. How is the shoulder, by the way?"

"Much better, thank you, Master." Ravi lifted his arm to indicate how much movement had returned. "I seem to have made a full recovery."

"Excellent. And I see your smile is back."

If anything, his new front teeth were a good deal better than the stained and crooked originals, smashed from his gums by the stone fist of his attacker.

"The implants take some getting used to, but I'm sure I'll cope."

"Well, I'm glad you're on the mend, as we have much to discuss."

"I'm not sure there is much to say, Master. An unfortunate accident, that's all."

The smile on Lester's face was at odds with the steel in his eye.

"I think we both know that the injuries you suffered, Ravi, were not caused by a tumble down the stairs. Modern-day interrogation techniques have come a long way, but I am old enough to recognise the results of a more primitive approach."

Ravi expected that Lester had seen some pretty grim things in his time. However, he doubted the man could imagine the full horror of the creature that had tried to bludgeon him into opening the portal. He closed his eyes briefly to banish the memory.

"Bad, was it?" The Master's smile had gone, and his voice held genuine concern.

"Yes."

They shared a moment of silence.

"I have to ask, Ravi. The… perpetrator?"

Ravi pictured the thrashing, burning figure in the cellar, its foot pinned to the ground by the metal ruler now tucked into the breast pocket of his jacket.

"Has been dealt with."

Lester's intense gaze intimated that he wanted to know more. But Ravi had no intention of divulging that the intruder stalking the College last term had come from another world. Or that the arcane portal through which it had travelled was located beneath New Court.

Lester's eyes hardened. "So, you're saying we are secure?"

Ravi thought back to the closing ritual he'd performed before the creature had ambushed him.

"We are."

"Hmm." The Master frowned. "But for how long?"

Ravi wasn't sure what he meant, but he was saved from replying by a knock at the door. Lester stirred.

"Ah, that will be the tea. I'm not sure about you, but I'd welcome a cuppa about now. Besides, it's someone who is rather keen to see you again." He spoke to the door. "Come in!"

Ravi half expected Aurelia to enter. Instead, an elegant young woman carried the tray into the room and set it down on the table.

"Hello, Professor," she said. "Long time, no see."

It took him a moment to recognise who it was.

"Jane?"

"And there was me thinking you wouldn't remember me."

The peroxide blonde hair and goth make-up were gone, but there was no mistaking the sharp, intelligent eyes of the undercover agent who had worked as a College waitress last year.

"You are not easy to forget."

"I'll take that as a compliment." She began pouring the tea. "Milk, Professor?"

"Just a dash."

"And you, Dominic?"

Her reference to the Master by his first name was almost as surprising as her voice. It was deeper and more mellow than the cheeky Essex accent he remembered.

"Please, my dear," said Lester, watching Ravi. "Your timing, as always, is impeccable. We were just about to talk about our mole problem."

"I take it we're not talking about College lawns," she said, sitting opposite Ravi.

"Heaven forbid, no. Things are serious but not catastrophic." He took a sip of tea, and when he replaced his cup, his expression darkened. "No, I am referring to one of our Fellows, Dr Gabrielle Dutour. Thanks to Ravi, we have evidence to suggest she may work for our friend, Julian Schiller."

"And what evidence might that be?"

"I found photographs on Gabrielle's computer of her with Schiller," Ravi explained.

"A coincidence, perhaps?"

"The Schiller Foundation has also been funding her research," the Master added.

"What research might that be?"

Ravi glanced across at Lester, who nodded. "The work that Robert Mackenzie and I were doing in the 1960s."

"So, Dutour knows your interest in interdimensional travel?"

Ravi tried not to flinch at her speaking so matter-of-factly about what they had discovered.

"I don't know. I saw a reference in Gabrielle's work that suggested she might. Specifically, there had been a reference to the Gemini Passage in the margin of one of her research papers. But I believe she may have reached a dead end."

"What makes you say that?"

"Because she came to me for help."

Lester chuckled. "Ravi spent most of the last term trying to avoid Gabrielle. Finally, it got to the point where the poor man could barely dine in Hall without her ambushing him."

"She was very… persistent," Ravi conceded.

"And what did she discover?" Jane asked.

"From me, nothing."

"And from Robert?" Lester asked.

"Nothing from his published papers, from what I could see."

"And from his unpublished papers?" Lester's cup hovered near his mouth, but he didn't drink.

"As you know, Master, I went through his effects following his death and found nothing. After I warned him about Schiller, Robert assured me that he had taken measures to keep our secret safe. Exactly how, he never said, but we found nothing in his rooms here or at the Faculty."

The room had become very quiet.

"However, at the end of last term," he continued, "a trunk with Robert's initials was discovered in the New Court cellars."

Lester put his cup down and leaned forwards, eyes bright.

"You have it?"

"In my room."

"And?"

"I haven't finished reviewing all the contents, but they

include Robert's journals from 1969 and last year." Ravi paused. He'd spent hours over Easter reading Robert's handwritten notes and diagrams of their heretical discoveries. "They are, I'm afraid, revelatory."

For a moment, no one said anything.

"This trunk, Professor, who else knows about it?" Jane asked.

"Let me guess," Lester said. "The usual suspects: Chamberlain, Wood and Hamilton."

Ravi bristled. "I... We owe Giles, Nick and Annabel a huge debt of gratitude. Without them, things could have been a good deal worse."

Too late, Ravi realised the jibe had been deliberate, goading him into revealing their involvement. Annoyed with himself, he took a sip of tea to recover his composure.

"Do they know what is in the trunk?" Jane asked.

"If Chamberlain's involved, I think that's a fair assumption," Lester said.

This time, Ravi didn't take the bait. He suspected the students had seen what it contained. Giles had practically said as much in the note with the keys to the trunk. But he didn't want to implicate the students more than he had to.

"They, more than anyone, know what is at stake here," he said. "I suspect that is why they moved the trunk to my room."

"You may be right, Ravi," said the Master. "The question remains, what are we to do with it?"

Ravi had been wondering the same thing these past weeks.

"For now, I suggest we keep it in my room until I have finished reviewing the journals. I hope to discover more about Schiller's involvement in Robert's research."

"I'm not sure your room is safe, Professor," Jane said. "It has been broken into before."

This was true, and Ravi knew it. But his terraced house in Newnham was even less secure. Perhaps sensing his hesitation, Lester spoke up.

"Might I suggest an alternative?"

"Not if it involves having the trunk here in the lodge," Ravi said before he could help himself. The thought of the Master knowing his and Robert's secrets was unconscionable. Jane's face betrayed her surprise, and Ravi added, "I mean, with all the visitors here. Well, the risk would be too great."

Lester studied him. "Believe me, Ravi, security here is much tighter than it appears." Then, he smiled and held up his hands. "But I was going to suggest the School of Pythagoras."

Ravi blinked.

"Where's that?" Jane asked.

"It's a rather obscure building at the back of College," Lester continued. "Dates back to the twelfth century. Isn't that right, Ravi?"

"I believe so, Master." He was still processing this unexpected suggestion.

"So, why there?"

Lester nodded at Ravi, who explained, "Some years ago, the College decided it needed a secure storage facility for our most treasured archive material: ancient deeds, founding documents, scrolls, that sort of thing. As you can imagine, many of these priceless artefacts require specific temperature and humidity-controlled conditions."

Lester added, "We needed a building away from the river that could be hermetically sealed and safe from fire, theft and natural disasters. What better than a stone building that had survived largely intact since Anglo-Saxon times?"

"It's a storage bunker, then?"

"Ooh, I think that's a bit harsh," said Lester. "Outwardly, it is one of the most historic and characterful buildings in College. Though few people ever see it, tucked away as it is behind Cripps."

"However, you are correct, Jane," Ravi said. "Within its ancient walls, you have one of the most secure facilities in Cambridge, with a state-of-the-art security system linked to the Porters' Lodge."

"I take it, Ravi, you approve of my suggestion?"

Ravi had to admit it was an inspired choice. Not only would the trunk and its contents be stored in a safe environment, but Mr Weston, the College Librarian, strictly controlled access to the building.

"I do, Master."

"Excellent. That's settled, then. When can you have the trunk moved?"

"Once its contents are in order, I shall make an appointment with the College Archivist to have it admitted."

"With an appropriately obscure reference, I suggest, to avoid attracting the attention of our mole."

"Of course, Master," Ravi agreed, though he doubted

Gabrielle would consider consulting that part of the College's collection.

"In that case, I don't need to detain either of you any longer." Lester leaned back in his chair. "And many thanks for the tea."

"You're welcome," Jane said, tidying the cups away.

Ravi rose from his chair and held the door open for her. As she stepped outside, Lester said, "Oh, Ravi, one other thing."

He paused in the doorway. The Master was consulting some papers on his desk.

"As you probably know, Schiller's trial has been scheduled for later this summer."

Ravi's stomach tightened. "I knew it might be some time this year."

"Naturally, we'd all like to avoid a media circus surrounding the College."

"Of course."

"We don't want Dr Dutour providing Schiller with anything that might cast a shadow over our... involvement."

Their eyes met.

"Understood, Master."

"Good man." He smiled. "You can leave it open. It gets very stuffy in here."

Ravi left the study and descended the stairs, his mind whirling. The news about Schiller's trial had caught him off-guard. Though he had already given a statement regarding the attempt on his life by Schiller's associates, he would still be called as a witness. The thought of coming face to face with the man who was almost certainly responsible for Robert's death was deeply unsettling. So much so that he barely registered the person waiting for him at the bottom of the steps.

"You all right?" Jane asked, tray in hand.

"Me? Fine. Just lots to think about."

She nodded. "I wanted to ask you something."

"Of course."

"I was wondering when you'd last seen Giles Chamberlain."

"Giles?" he said, surprised. "Not since last term, when he visited me in hospital."

"With Raquel?"

"Yes, as it happens. They were about to go away together."

"Did they say where?"

"Mallorca."

"You're sure?"

Ravi frowned.

"I see."

"Is anything wrong?"

"Probably not," she said, balancing the tray on one arm. "But if you happen to see him, or Raquel for that matter, would you let me know?" She handed him a plain white card, blank except for a mobile number. "Day or night, Professor."

"Of course."

She gave him a brief smile and disappeared into the kitchen. Ravi watched her go and wondered how Jane, with all the intelligence resources available to her, was unable to locate Giles Chamberlain. And why would she ask him, of all people? He wasn't even the boy's Tutor.

As he slipped the card into his pocket under the ever-watchful gaze of Lady Margaret, an uncomfortable thought formed in his head. Did Jane think Giles was somewhere only Ravi had visited before?

"Impossible," he said to himself. "He wouldn't know how."

But as he left the Master's Lodge, Ravi felt even more unsettled than when he'd arrived.

Chapter Two

Nick shared a companionable silence with Annabel as their taxi from the station pulled into the Forecourt of St John's College. The cobbled courtyard, with its racks of student bikes nestled alongside the imposing Victorian Chapel, was a far cry from the quiet hillside village on the edge of the Yorkshire moors where they'd spent Easter with Annabel's grandmother.

"Here you are, folks," said the driver as he pulled up outside the Porters' Lodge. "Cash or card?"

Nick glanced at the digital meter and winced.

"I've got this," Annabel said, offering the driver her credit card. "You get the bags."

"You sure?"

"Definitely. Mine weighs a ton. Gran packed enough chocolate to feed a small country."

While Annabel paid the driver, Nick retrieved their bags from the trunk, though he noticed hers was much lighter than she'd made out.

"All good?" he asked as the taxi pulled away.

"Yep," she said, looking around the square. "It's great to

be back, isn't it? Come on, let's see who's in."

In the Porters' Lodge, they found a familiar face behind a bank of new security screens.

"Ah, Miss Hamilton and Mr Wood. Did you have a good Easter?"

"Revising, you mean?" Nick said and received a shove from Annabel.

"Yes, thanks, Bert," she said, "it was great. Gran sends her best, by the way."

"Oh yes, how is Mrs Hamilton?"

"Fit as a flea, isn't she, Nick?"

"Mountain goat, more like. I've had easier pre-seasons."

The Porter chuckled. "Still, good you had a break. Some of your lot spent all holiday in the Library."

"That's not making me feel any better," Nick said. "I may have to go over and bag myself a space."

"Yes, well, don't overdo it. You can't work all the time. I take it you'll be rowing, Annabel?"

"That's the plan. May Bumps and all."

"What about you, Nick? No rugby this term, of course."

"Not sure. I'll think of something."

"Well, all work and no play never did anyone any good," said the Porter. "And if it's getting too much, you can always pop in here for a cup of tea. We make a good one, don't we, Shirley?"

A sturdy Porter appeared from the back office.

"What was that?"

"I said we make a good cup of tea."

"Certainly do."

A voice behind Nick said, "That's what I tell all my Tutees."

"Professor Gupta!" Annabel cried, hurrying over to her Tutor. "How are you?"

"Oh, I'm on the mend."

"It looks like it!"

Nick had to agree. The old academic had made a remarkable recovery from his injuries last term.

"Of course, I have you both to thank for that."

"And Giles," Nick added.

"Indeed. Tell me, have you heard from him at all?"

"Not since last term."

"I may be able to help you there, Professor," said Bert, heading over to the Fellows' pigeonholes and returning with a card. "This arrived for you the other day."

It was a cheap holiday postcard of a crescent-shaped beach against a spectacular rocky backdrop. The Professor read the message.

"Dear Professor Gupta, hope you are well. Having a great time. Plenty of sun, sea and… sangria! Much love, Giles and Raquel. XXX"

"Three kisses, Professor."

But rather than smile, he almost looked relieved. "Well, it would appear he's in good spirits."

"It's certainly a lot quieter without him," Bert said. "So I'm not complaining."

"Anyway, I'd best be off," the Professor said, pocketing the card. "I have cakes to order for your Tutorial, Annabel."

"No Pimm's then? It is the summer term, after all."

"I suggest we save that for after exams, don't you? Best to keep a clear head for now."

"Fair enough. Goodnight, Professor."

After he left, Nick looked at Annabel. "Pimm's?"

"It's practically mandatory for May Week. You know, all the garden parties?"

"Don't forget the May Ball," Bert said. "I take it you two will be going?"

Nick couldn't hide his shock, and Annabel's smile faltered.

"I... hadn't really thought about it," he stammered, his face colouring.

This wasn't entirely true. He'd thought about it briefly when the tickets had been released, but at £400 a pair, there was no way his budget would stretch to it, even with his bursary. After that, it had slipped his mind – though from the look on Annabel's face, it hadn't left hers. This made him feel worse, but he was saved from saying more by Bert, who had no doubt seen Nick's flushed cheeks.

"Mind you, plenty of Freshers don't go in their first couple of years. Save it for after finals. You know, as something special to look forward to."

"Good idea," Annabel said, a little too brightly. "Anyway. We'd best get off, Bert. Lovely seeing you. And you, Shirley."

Nick nodded at the Porters before setting off after her.

"Don't forget we're here if you ever need a chat," Bert called after them.

Nick found Annabel staring up at the Chapel Tower. Its

pale sandstone surface was turning pink in the late afternoon sun, and there, high in its western wall, was the empty alcove where Lady Margaret's statue had once stood.

"You OK?"

Annabel started. "What? Oh, yes, fine."

Nick knew she wasn't. But he couldn't be sure whether it was disappointment at the May Ball or the memory of that terrifying ordeal.

"Come on," Annabel said. "Let's get back before this chocolate melts."

"Fair enough."

As they made their way across the old courts, though, Nick couldn't think of a way to explain about the tickets without humiliating himself further. In the end, he tried safer ground.

"You're fortunate, you know."

"How so?"

"Having Gupta as your Tutor."

"Oh, right. What's yours like?"

"Dutour? She's OK, I suppose."

"Also an advocate of tea and cake?"

"Hardly. Bordeaux and Brie, more like."

"Really?"

"She's made it her mission to teach us the finer points of French cuisine."

"I take it you don't approve."

"It's not that. It's that Dutour seems to think I'm some sort of expert."

She looked at him. "Whatever gave her that idea?"

"Beats me. But next time, she's threatened us with frog legs."

Annabel stifled a laugh. "Sorry."

But Nick was relieved to see her smile again. "Don't be. I just hope I can keep them down."

"Well, if it's any help, they taste like chicken. Only a bit more springy."

It was his turn to smile. "Thanks. I'll bear that in mind."

As they crossed the Bridge of Sighs, a punt passing underneath them, Nick was about to describe how he'd managed to spill wine over Dutour's carpet when Annabel stopped suddenly.

"That's it!"

"That's what?" he asked.

"Punting!"

"What about it?"

"If you're not playing rugby this term, you can learn to punt instead."

"Me?" He shook his head.

"Why not? Gets you out in the fresh air. And the risk of concussion is low. As long as you remember to duck under bridges."

Nick snorted. "I don't think so."

He continued walking. The truth was that he had never felt comfortable on the water. Last term's midnight assault on the New Court cellars hadn't done anything to improve his feelings on the matter. The memory of leaping from that punt over those murky waters still gave him chills.

Annabel, though, was clearly on a mission. "Go on, Nick.

Join the Punt Society. I'm sure Ash and Brian would love to have you."

It was true that Annabel's oddball friends were always looking for new members. Still, he'd never told anyone about his aquaphobia, and he wasn't going to do so now. "I'll think about it."

"Of course, if you did learn to punt," she continued, "you could take me out to Grantchester once exams were over. You know, picnic on the meadows, in the sunshine, watching the clouds wander overhead..." She smiled at him. "I'm just saying, that's all."

He was saved by the buzz of her phone.

"That's probably Gran," she said, retrieving it from her pocket, "making sure we arrived safely... Oh!"

"I've probably left something behind," he began, but she held up a hand and put the phone to her ear.

"Hello, Brett."

A lump of lead settled in Nick's stomach.

"Yes, I'm... What? Oh, OK, sure... I'm heading there now. Come right over."

She lowered the phone, frowning.

"Brett wants to see me."

The lump gained an extra kilo.

"Why?"

Annabel glanced up at him.

"I mean, why now?" he added. "It's a bit late, isn't it?"

"He wouldn't say. Only that it was important."

What was so important that Brett had to tell her face to face?

"Listen," Annabel said, adjusting the bag on her shoulder. "I'd better go up and put this stuff away."

"Yeah, of course."

They set off for their staircase, Annabel moving faster now. Nick wondered if he should offer to carry her bag upstairs, but it was clear she needed no help. When they arrived at the foot of the steps, she flicked her room indicator to IN and began climbing as quick and sure-footed as her Gran. Nick followed, stopping outside his room on the first-floor landing.

"I'll say goodnight then," he said as she continued up the next flight of steps.

"Oh yes, sorry," she replied, pausing and giving him a distracted smile. "Sleep well. I'll see you in the morning."

"Sure."

He was about to ask what time, but she continued up the stairwell, her footsteps fading. Nick was left alone to run through the possibilities of why Brett wanted to see her. Of course, logic told him it would be something to do with rowing. But the deadweight in his stomach swung towards the unsettling prospect that, unlike himself, the handsome American had obtained May Ball tickets.

Nick unlocked his door with the image of Brett greeting Annabel with that dazzling smile and a fairy-tale invitation she couldn't refuse.

"Just great," he muttered.

Chapter Three

Annabel was halfway through unpacking when she heard the knock at the door.

You've got to be kidding me, she thought, her hands hovering over the assortment of clothes, toiletries and confectionery spread across the bed.

Grabbing her empty laundry bag, she stuffed everything inside and slung it into the wardrobe. Straightening, she saw her flushed face in the mirror.

"Come on, girl," she said, tucking a strand of hair behind her ear. "Pull yourself together."

Lifting her chin, she crossed the room and opened the door.

Brett stood framed in the doorway, dressed like he'd come from a fashion shoot. He was a picture of masculine perfection in chinos, a polo shirt and deck shoes, the faded fabrics accentuating his tanned features.

"Hi." He briefly flashed her his dazzling smile.

"Hi," she replied, hoping her voice wasn't as high as it sounded.

"Can I come in?"

"Of course."

Annabel flattened herself against the wall as he squeezed past. He left a hint of sandalwood and sweat in the air, and the combination made her head spin. She took a moment to compose herself before closing the door.

"Take a seat," she said, following him into her study. Brett chose the sofa, the only chair large enough to accommodate his broad frame. Even so, he had to draw up his legs to avoid knocking his shins against the coffee table.

"Would you like a cup of tea?"

"No, I'm fine, thanks. Some water, maybe?"

"Of course."

When Annabel returned with two glasses, he still looked uncomfortable, perched on the edge of the seat, his hands clasped over his knees.

"Here you go." She set the glasses down and drew up her desk chair. "So, how was your Easter?"

"What? Oh, great, thanks." He smiled. "Decided to head off to Wales. Do a bit of sightseeing. Great country. Lots of sheep."

"So I hear."

"What about you?"

"Oh, I went home, spent some time with Gran, hit the books, that sort of thing." Then, she added, "And Nick came over. You know, to spend a few days together."

She said it casually, but all he did was smile and say, "Great."

Annabel wasn't sure if she was disappointed or relieved.

"Anyway," she said, "you wanted to speak with me?"

Brett put his glass down, and their surroundings faded into the background as Annabel stared into his deep, dark eyes.

"OK, I'm just going to say it," he said. "I saw the consultant neurologist, and she's passed me fit to row again."

This came as such a surprise it took Annabel a moment to respond.

"Brett, that's great news! I'm so happy for you!"

And she was – in no small part because Annabel felt responsible for the injury. She'd been coxing, after all, when they'd capsized, causing him to fracture his skull.

"Thanks," he said, though he showed none of the enthusiasm she was feeling.

"You don't seem very happy?"

"The thing is," he continued, "the Men's Captain heard about it and asked if I would row for the men's first boat."

"For M1, you mean?"

"Yes, in the May Bumps."

"Well, of course," she said, thinking how thrilled any college captain would be to have an Olympian available to row for his top crew. "That's great, isn't it?"

"Great for M1, maybe," he said. "But not for the women's third boat."

That's when the penny dropped. "Oh."

"They say M1 has a real chance of going Head of the River this year. They've got a new boat, oars and an international coach, all funded by alumni. Apparently, they've been planning this for some time since hearing I was coming to John's."

"I see," she said, her heart sinking. "Makes sense."

"They have a whole programme mapped out. Two sessions a day, seven days a week. It's pretty much full-on."

"Which means you won't have time to coach W3."

"No, not if I agreed to row."

"What do you mean?"

"I told them no."

Annabel froze. "You're kidding, right?"

"No, I'm not."

"But Brett, you can't do that. How many people get a chance to go Head of the River?"

"I made a promise to you all, Annabel. After the Lents, I said I'd help you get your blades."

"I know, but this is different, Brett. You've got to go for it. Besides, once word gets out that you turned down M1 to coach W3, we're not going to be popular at the Boat Club, are we? Scrap that. Half the College will think the same."

"This would be my decision, Annabel, not yours."

"Yes, but others won't see it that way," she said. "Anyway, that's not the point. This is your chance to make a bit of history. You won't get a better one. Whereas the rest of us still have years to get our blades."

"Clarissa doesn't."

He had a point there. This would be the final Bumps regatta for the third years. And Annabel suspected their talented Stroke was only rowing with W3 because the handsome American was coaching them. If he jumped ship now, what would she do?

Brett was silent, his eyes never leaving hers. It struck

Annabel that the real reason he was here wasn't to tell her he was sticking by W3 or even so she could persuade him to reverse his decision. He was giving her the opportunity to convince her crew, including Clarissa, to allow him to row for M1. It was his way of protecting them from the inevitable backlash, transforming them from potential pariahs to selfless heroines, whatever happened to M1 or W3 in the Bumps.

"Why me?" she asked.

"What do you mean?"

"Someone will have to persuade the others. So why did you choose me?"

"Because I trust you. As do your crew."

"To do what?"

"To do what you think is right. Even if it's not easy."

It was a good line. He could be bullshitting her, but Annabel didn't think so.

"You're right," she said. "Convincing Clarissa isn't going to be easy, but I think she'll understand."

She put her glass down and rose from her seat. "You owe me big time, you know that, don't you?"

"I figured as much," he said, getting to his feet.

"Still, I'm glad your head's OK. I've been worried about it."

"You and me both."

She led him back down the hallway and opened the door. This time as he squeezed past, Brett bent down and kissed her on the cheek.

"Thanks, Annabel."

Had he done that ten minutes earlier on entering her room, Annabel wasn't sure how she would have reacted. Now she smiled and waved him on. "Don't be daft. I'm glad you're all right."

As he stepped onto the landing, she asked, "Any thoughts on who could coach us?"

"You could do worse than the College Boatman."

"Blades?"

"Why not? He'll have more time with this new coach they're bringing in."

"You think he'd want to coach a women's third boat?"

"It can't hurt to ask. What's the worst that can happen?"

"What indeed," Annabel said with a smile that faded when she closed the door and returned to her room, deflated.

******

A punt glided beneath Annabel's window as evening shadows stretched across the river. The flat-bottomed vessel sat low in the water, its seats filled with high-spirited passengers passing around bottles of Prosecco as their punt guide looked on.

Jez had been about to knock off for the evening when the party, all wearing matching pink bomber jackets, had arrived at the punt station on the Mill Pond.

The hen party had fallen prey to his colleague, Luca, one of the smooth-talking punt touts who roamed King's Parade like marauding sharks. With the bride-to-be keen to experience a romantic river tour, Jez had agreed to punt them back to their hotel near Jesus Green, tailoring his usual script accordingly.

"So, ladies, on the left is St John's College, home to some of the most eligible bachelors in Cambridge."

"Too late for that, mate, I'm already hitched!" said the woman with a fluffy pink tiara.

"Hold on, Cheryl! Some of us aren't," said one of the others. "Let the man speak."

Jez waited for the laughter to die down.

"On the left, you have New Court, built in 1834. Rather appropriately, the large tower in the middle is known as the Wedding Cake."

"Yay!"

"And the bridge ahead of us," Jez continued, "was featured in *The Theory of Everything*. That iconic scene when Eddie Redmayne proposed to the love of his life, Felicity Jones."

"I loved that film," someone said as heads turned and camera flashlights lit up the structure in the shadowy gloom.

"Known as the Bridge of Sighs, it is said that Queen Victoria–" Something snagged on the punt pole, almost wrenching it from his grasp. "Whoa!" he cried as he tottered on the stern before recovering his balance.

"Are you all right, mate?"

The surface of the river was dark in the shadow of the surrounding buildings, and waves slapped against the bank. His guests' faces were pale and anxious and fixed on him.

"Sorry, my pole got stuck there for a moment."

There was a moment's silence before someone blurted out, "That's what they all say!"

Raucous laughter eased the tension, and Jez got them

underway again with an embarrassed smile. But it wasn't until they were approaching the jetty at Jesus Green that he recovered his composure sufficiently for his final and most important announcement.

"Sadly, our brief time together is coming to an end, ladies. I hope you enjoyed the tour." He removed his straw boater and handed it to one of the guests. "If so, do feel free to leave a tip."

A few minutes later, after the hen party had tottered none too steadily back to their hotel, Jez was left alone in his punt to count his takings. Rifling through the contents of his hat, he found an assortment of ten- and twenty-pound notes and a couple of telephone numbers scribbled on paper napkins.

Not a bad haul, he thought, tucking the napkins in his waistcoat pocket.

"Successful trip, was it?" Luca was on the walkway above him, a sly grin on his face.

"I'll find out later." Jez slipped the tips inside his boater and placed it back on his head. "Don't want a bad review on TripAdvisor, do we?"

The other man snorted. "Well, I hate to break it to you, mate, but you've drawn the short straw tonight."

"What do you mean?"

"We've ended up with too many punts at this station, so you'll have to take yours back to the Mill Pond."

"You're not serious?"

"That's what comes from being the last one in."

"But I was the first one out this morning."

"Yeah, and I'm sure you've done very well out of it, too," Luca said, tipping his boater.

"Oh, come on, Luca."

"Sorry, mate. I'm just the messenger. See you tomorrow. Bright and early, mind you. It promises to be another busy one."

The tout sauntered off as Jez muttered, "Smarmy git!"

Fuming at the injustice of it all, he reached into the cubby hole under the stern and withdrew a small plastic roll wrapped in an elastic band. Thinking mutinous thoughts, he rolled himself a spliff and sat in the bottom of the punt, waiting for the drug's calming effect.

What the hell happened with the pole? he wondered, trying to remember the last time he'd ended up in the river. He could imagine what Luca would have said if he'd returned to the jetty soaking wet.

"Oily toe rag," he murmured, barely noticing the slur in his speech.

Drawing deeply on his joint, he flicked the stub into the air and watched as the glowing dot tumbled end over end before landing in the water with a faint hiss. That was when he noticed he was floating downstream.

"Oh, you've got to be kidding."

The punt had drifted into the middle of the stream, and the pole used to wedge the vessel against the jetty was floating a few yards away.

"Oh, for f…!"

Fumbling, he managed to find the paddle before clambering to the bow to begin to bring the punt around. The heavy wooden vessel was slow to respond, not helped by the difficulty he had coordinating his strokes. But, inch by inch, he drew closer to the gently bobbing pole. Finally, he discarded the paddle and leaned across the water. His groping fingers fell short, the splash nudging the aluminium shaft further away.

"Come on, you b..." But he stopped mid-curse and stared.

A line of bubbles was snaking across the water from the lock above the weir. Jez followed their progress, fascinated, as they curved in a gentle arc towards him. Perhaps it was the weed, but he imagined he could hear them popping as they approached his outstretched hand.

Pop, pop, poppity pop. Pop, pop, poppity pop..., clunk.

The metal pole thudded against the side of the hull, waking him from his reverie. Looking down, he saw it floating there.

"There you are!"

Jez grabbed it and had begun hauling it aboard when a dark shape rose from the water and slammed into the metal shaft. The impact sent the handle swinging back, knocking him back over the passenger seat, sending his boater flying.

"Whoa!" he cried as he landed in the bottom of the punt, his head cracking painfully against the wooden duckboards. For a while, he lay on his back, too dazed to comprehend what had happened. The stars moved back and forth, and he was vaguely aware that the vessel was rocking from side to side.

The familiar sensation evoked a childhood memory buried deep in his subconscious. Jez's eyes began to flutter, as a long-forgotten lullaby replaced the sound of splashing before his world faded into darkness.

The disturbance in the water continued for a few more seconds, sending waves splashing against the riverbank. Eventually, though, the river fell silent. The punt carried its comatose occupant downriver, coming to rest against the barrier above the lock.

A section of the punt pole glided by the hull, its mangled aluminium shaft disappearing over the weir along with a scattering of ten-pound notes. Then, the straw boater, its rim bisected by twin bite marks, passed the bobbing punt and sank beneath the frothing water.

Chapter Four

Giles stared at the back of Raquel's legs, stained red by the dust that clung to her skin, as she tramped ahead of him. They were easily the most eye-catching sight on an otherwise uneventful day.

They had set off early that morning, keeping the fast-flowing river on their left as they hurried towards the distant mountains. Raquel set a relentless pace, as she had done since they first arrived on this alien world.

Giles had done a fair amount of trekking in his time, first at his boarding school in the Scottish Highlands and later with his friends Ying and Trevor. But even he was struggling to keep up with the woman driven by an unwavering determination to find her missing brother.

Her conviction that Alfonso was alive had encouraged Giles to spend all of last term uncovering the truth behind her brother's disappearance. And, after locating the interdimensional portal in a cellar beneath St John's College, he had used its arcane power to cross to Gemini with Raquel to continue their search for her brother.

Days later, Giles was beginning to wonder whether he'd

truly understood the lengths she would go to in order to recover her lost sibling. Honed by their regime of meagre rations and daily hikes under the twin suns, Raquel's athletic physique had been transformed into something close to Amazonian – an impression accentuated by the sweat-soaked bandana that kept her unruly hair in place. And by the fierce look in her eye when she turned to him.

"What?"

"Nothing," he said. "Just admiring the view."

Raquel surveyed the surrounding cliffs. "You see anything?"

The sheer-sided walls still towered overhead, though there was a good deal more vegetation now that the valley had narrowed. Scrubby bushes and trees had formed in the gullies and ravines, undoubtedly benefitting from the patches of shade and proximity to the river.

"Somewhere to rest, perhaps. I don't know about you, but I could do with a break."

And something to eat, he thought, though he didn't say the latter out loud. The subject of their dwindling food supplies had become taboo since leaving the lowlands behind. They'd barely have enough to get them home, even if they found her brother in the next day or two.

Raquel pursed her lips and turned towards the mountains, their jagged profiles visible in the distance. No doubt she was wondering whether they should press on before the shadows started to creep onto this side of the valley floor. They had not seen any harpies since leaving the last columns, but they always laid a fire in the entrance to whatever cliffside hollow they found for the night.

"Why don't we try over there?" Giles pointed to the line of trees at the foot of the sheer-sided cliffs. "At least that will offer some shade. Besides, we need to gather some wood for tonight."

After a moment's hesitation, she nodded. "OK. Is a good place."

"How about some food and a nice cup of Yorkshire tea?"

"Tea, in this heat? Are you serious?"

"What can I say? I'm English."

Raquel rolled her eyes, but he detected a hint of a smile. "OK, but you get the water."

Relieved she'd agreed to a break, Giles doffed an imaginary cap as she made for the trees. He hoped she'd be as receptive when faced with more difficult choices in the days to come.

Reaching the water's edge, he noticed how much faster it flowed this far up the valley, the waves breaking over boulders worn smooth by millennia of rushing water. The splashing and moisture in the air alleviated the oppressive heat of the twin suns.

Dipping his canteen into the stream, he was pleasantly surprised by how cold the water was. He swished his hand back and forth, enjoying the chilling sensation over his fingers. He might have lingered there had it not been for Raquel's call. But hearing her voice, he looked up in time to glimpse a long, dark shape gliding beneath the water's surface a few yards from where he was squatting.

Instincts kicked in as Giles leapt back from the water's edge. The shadow turned sharply and slinked away between half-submerged rocks before disappearing into the turbulent flow of the stream.

For a moment, he stood there, staring at the river. Whatever the shape was, it had come within a few feet of him undetected.

"Giles?" Raquel waved at him from the treeline.

"Coming!" he called back.

She headed into the woods, and he set off after her, mindful that dwindling provisions weren't their only worry in this hostile world.

When he reached the trees, Giles heard the welcoming rattle of a cooking pan and the sound of branches being snapped for firewood. Sitting down even briefly with Raquel for a brew would go a long way to settling his nerves.

Stepping over gnarled and twisted tree roots, he emerged into a small clearing where thin shafts of sunlight filtered through the canopy of leaves to reveal Raquel's backpack propped against a tree. A small patch of ground had been cleared, and a collection of dried twigs and leaves had been piled up for the fire. Next to these lay the aluminium cooking pan and a packet of tea bags.

Someone's been busy, he thought, easing off his own backpack and laying it next to hers. More branches snapped nearby.

"If you come across a cow," he called out, "a dash of milk wouldn't go amiss."

The woods went silent for a moment. Then, footsteps approached, and Raquel emerged from the trees, her face pale.

"I was just asking, with or without..." But he stopped short when he noticed a trickle of blood running from the corner of her mouth.

"Hey," he said, "have you cut your lip?"

She began to shake her head and then stiffened as a dark outline shifted behind her and a gnarled tree branch rested on her shoulder.

No, not a branch, he thought. *A claw.*

"Giles?" Raquel's voice was strained, and he could see the talons pressed against her skin. But her eyes were steady. "Run!"

He could, of course. Turn and sprint through the trees. Once he reached the safety of the valley floor, no creature would dare to follow him. The suns' calcifying rays would shield him from pursuit. But what of Raquel? What would happen to her while he cowered outside the monster's reach?

Giles couldn't leave her. Besides, he had another idea.

"Now, why would I do that?"

"You... must," she grunted. "Go... on."

"What? When we have a dinner guest? What sort of host would I be?"

Raquel glared at him, but he ignored her.

"We haven't been introduced." He held out a hand to the dark shape behind her and stepped into the patch of sunlight shining through the canopy above him. "My name is Giles Chamberlain. And you are?"

The figure didn't move. It stood in the shadow of the trees and let out a long hiss, which Giles knew only too well. He lowered his hand but continued to smile.

"Shy, clearly. Not to worry. Why don't I get this fire going, and we can talk over a meal."

Reaching in his pocket for Professor Mackenzie's lighter, he turned towards the pile of dried wood and froze.

In the shadow of the trees surrounding the little clearing, a circle of figures had appeared, each careful to remain out of reach of the light as they watched him. It was hard to make out their features, but it was clear to Giles that there was something unnatural about them. Like the trees from which they had emerged, they appeared misshapen, their outlines twisted and lopsided. Perhaps that was why he hadn't noticed them before: they had blended into the background until their trap was sprung.

"Well, well, well," he said. "Quite a gathering. I'm afraid some of you will be disappointed, as I'm not sure we'll have enough to go around."

The menacing hiss from the circle suggested that he and Raquel would provide more than enough sustenance. Fingering the object in his pocket, he faced the creature holding Raquel. Could he use the lighter's flame to release her?

But even if he did, their escape was now blocked. The only thing holding back the surrounding shapes appeared to be the circle of light in which he stood. And that temporary refuge would inevitably disappear when the second sun began its descent. Giles needed time to think.

"Now, listen, this is all very cosy, I grant you, but I wonder if we might have a little chat. Man to man, as it were." He frowned. "I say 'man to man', but I don't know who you are. Would it be too rude of me to ask you to show yourself?"

Raquel gasped as the claw tightened around her neck.

"Steady," Giles said, holding up his hands in a gesture of appeasement, though not before concealing the lighter between the fingers of his left one. "There's no need to come into the light. Just enough that I can see your face."

Giles gave Raquel a smile that he hoped was reassuring, though, in truth, he had no idea what he was going to do next. It wasn't the first time he'd resorted to winging it, and he hoped it wouldn't be his last.

"So, what do you say?" he asked the shadow behind her. "Face to face or not?"

The clearing went very still. Giles felt concealed eyes considering him. He had no idea whether their owners understood his words, but he hoped his conciliatory tone conveyed his meaning.

How long this lasted, he couldn't tell. His arms grew heavy, and sweat formed on his forehead. Finally, when he thought he could hold his hands up no longer, Raquel was thrust forwards, the claw still clasped around her neck, and her captor was revealed.

It was a harpy with the same raptor's head as the one he had seen on the Chapel Tower, only smaller in stature. However, this one had an ugly scar from its head down to its shoulder, the puckered flesh clearly visible through the gaps in its plumage. This wasn't its only disfigurement. One of its wings was missing, replaced by an ugly stump protruding from a thatch of broken feathers. The other was wrapped around Raquel's neck, its taloned claw pressed against her throat.

Giles lowered his arms, conscious of how insulting they must appear to the mutilated creature. There was movement behind him as the others emerged from the shadows.

Even in the dim light of the clearing, it was clear that these too were horribly disfigured. Terrible wounds covered their heads and torsos, some far worse than those suffered by the harpy holding Raquel. But there was one disfigurement they all shared: each creature was missing a wing, suggesting something more sinister than a random battle scar.

"What the hell's been happening here?" he murmured.

The harpy holding Raquel made a strange hissing sound.

"Sorry?"

The harpy glared at him before repeating the sound, pausing long enough for him to make out the words.

"She… did… it!"

Raquel's eyes widened in alarm as a chorus of hisses broke out.

"Now, hold on," Giles said, holding his hands up. "We've only just arrived."

But the creature ignored him.

"She did it!"

The circle began to close in.

"Wait a moment. You've got this all wrong." Giles adjusted his grip on the lighter.

The harpy threw back its head and screeched to the heavens. The next moment, a dark shape appeared over the gap in the canopy, its broad wings blotting out the light.

"Oh, crap," he muttered as the protective circle of light disappeared.

Then, his captors pounced, their misshapen bodies bumping into one another as they lunged for him. Giles ducked beneath a clumsy claw swing but was bowled over as something heavy barrelled into him. He hit the floor, the impact knocking the lighter free from his grip.

Raquel screamed, but her cry was drowned out by a screech that echoed around the clearing, so piercing that Giles raised his head in panic. And he wasn't the only one. The creatures swarming over him flinched and cried out in alarm. They barely had time to move before the winged being fell on them. Those that didn't leap clear were plucked from the ground and hurled against the surrounding trees.

The giant harpy landed, wings fanned out in challenge, and Giles's attackers backed into the shelter of the woods. All save one. The grizzled old veteran remained, glowering at the newcomer, its claw to Raquel's throat.

"Raquel!" Giles cried, struggling to get up.

A heavy claw slammed into his chest, shoving him back down. Gasping, he looked up into the two amber pools glaring at him.

"What did you call her?"

Giles was so surprised that, for a moment, he didn't know what to say. The pressure on his chest increased.

"Well?"

"Raquel," he said. "Don't let him hurt her."

The harpy then spoke to the one holding Raquel. "Father, release her."

The other creature didn't move.

"Father!"

The old harpy's eyes narrowed before he released Raquel with a disgruntled hiss. She stumbled to her knees, hands going to her throat. The pressure on Giles's chest eased as the harpy removed her claw, and he scrambled over to Raquel's side.

"Let me see," he said.

"Is OK," Raquel murmured, lowering her hands.

Her neck was red and sore, but she seemed otherwise unharmed. Their saviour was studying Raquel, but when Giles turned, the harpy's amber eyes fell on him.

"Who are you?"

"Me? I'm Giles. Giles Chamberlain."

As if there were another one here, he thought, too late.

Her expression was unreadable.

"And you?" he asked before he could help himself.

The clearing went ominously quiet. She considered him for a long while before finally speaking.

"My name is Katya."

Chapter Five

Giles sat on the ground next to Raquel, while the two harpies argued on the far side of the clearing. The wizened old male remonstrated with his daughter Katya, his harsh guttural tongue impossible to follow but his anger all too clear in his gestures.

"What do you think is going on?" Raquel asked.

"I don't think he appreciated his daughter's intervention," Giles murmured, though as far as he was concerned, it couldn't have been more timely. The other harpies lingered on the edge of the clearing but were clearly cowed by Katya's presence.

Her response to her father's impassioned tirade was measured but firm, her low utterances interspersed with glances at Raquel. While the old harpy remained unhappy, it was clear to Giles who was in charge. Finally, Katya placed a claw on her father's shoulder and then crossed the clearing to join them.

"Thank you," Giles said.

"For what?"

"For saving our lives."

"Raquel's life was never in danger. You, on the other

hand…" She glanced around at the mutilated creatures skulking in the trees. "Let's just say that among harpies, males have little worth. Beyond the obvious."

Giles didn't like the sound of this, and it was clear Raquel didn't either.

"Giles is with me," she said.

"He is your mate, then?"

Raquel hesitated.

"So, not your mate." She cast him an appraising look. "Not family either. What then?"

"A friend," he said.

"A friend?" The harpy frowned. "You have travelled all this way with this female because you are… friends?"

"That's what friends do where we come from." This probably sounded as lame to her as it did to him, but he held her gaze.

"I see."

Giles had the feeling that this harpy saw a lot more than she was letting on. He changed tack. "You said Raquel was never in danger. Why?"

"Because I asked my father to look out for you."

"Sorry?"

The harpy addressed Raquel. "I thought Alfonso's sister would come looking for him."

Raquel gasped. "You know Alfonso!"

"I do."

"Then, he… is alive?"

"When I left him, yes."

Giles heard the qualification in her response, but Raquel

was deaf to it, flinging her arms around his neck. "I told you, Giles! I knew it!" He wanted to share in her moment of joy, but the look that passed between Katya and her father suggested Alfonso's survival was far from certain.

"That's fantastic, Raquel. Really it is. Now, let's see if they will take us to him."

"Of course." She smiled through her tears, then asked Katya, "Where is he? I need to see my brother now."

"That's not possible, I'm afraid."

"Why not?"

"He is being held in the Citadel by my mother."

"Your mother?"

"She is the Matriarch there."

Giles wasn't sure what this meant, but the muttering among the watchers in the trees suggested she wasn't popular among this company.

"Why is she holding Alfonso?" Raquel persisted. "What has he done?"

"Alfonso has a unique ability among the males here. His resistance to light."

"So?"

"At the annual solstice, female harpies choose a mate. That time is almost upon us."

Raquel stared at Katya. "Your mother wants Alfonso as her mate?"

"Mother?" she scoffed. "She has no need of him for that."

Her father scowled at this, and Giles understood. "Your mother is human," he said. "That's how you can fly in the daylight."

"Yes," she replied, "as can my sister, Olga."

"You have a sister?"

There were more ominous mutterings from the surrounding harpies.

"Then why does your mother need Alfonso?" Raquel pressed.

Katya's expression became grave. "For the colony. I fear she wants Alfonso as a breeding male."

Raquel's gasp was drowned by a chorus of angry cries from the surrounding creatures. Even Katya's father was outraged, and his daughter had to spread her wings to quell the uproar. Raquel was beyond intimidating, though.

"This is crazy!" She turned to Giles. "We can't let this happen!"

"We won't," he said. "Leave it to me, OK?" He needed to calm her down. Tempers were getting short, and there were a lot of angry harpies in and around the clearing. "Katya, why are you telling us this?"

The harpy considered him for a moment.

"Because what Mother is planning is not… natural. What she has done…" She paused. "Olga and I have upset the natural order here. Together, we have helped her to subjugate all of the valley's harpies. I fear what will happen if she, or Olga, command an army of creatures like us. That cannot be allowed to happen."

"Is that what you and your father were arguing about?"

"Yes. We both think she needs to be stopped. We have different views on how that might be accomplished."

Giles was uncomfortable with how closely the old harpy

was watching Raquel. What did he have in mind?

"In that case, maybe we can help you. If you point us in the direction of this Citadel, we can find Alfonso and take him back with us to our world." Her father snorted in derision, but Giles added, "We'd be doing this in daylight, of course, while the harpies are dormant."

It was a long shot, even by Giles's standards, but the daylight element had silenced Katya's father.

"It is too far on foot," Katya said. "You would never make it on time, and I cannot carry both of you. But I could drop one of you close to the tower while I deal with my sister."

"Then it has to be me," said Raquel. "He is my brother."

"Exactly how big is this tower?" Giles asked.

"Four or five times the size of those in the valley."

There was a flicker of doubt in Raquel's eyes.

"What do you think?" Giles asked. "I'll take the ropes and climbing gear. Once I find your brother, I can belay him down like I've done with you. We'll be back here before you know it."

He could see she wanted to object, but they both knew he was the only one who had any chance of making that climb. "You've got to trust me on this, Raquel. I'm Alfonso's best chance of getting out of there alive."

"I can't lose him, Giles. Not now. Not when we are so close."

"I know," he said, "which is why I'm going to bring him back to you."

She searched his face. "Promise me you will."

"I promise," he said – and he meant it.

"OK. But I will follow on foot," she added.

The harpy nodded. "My father will take you." Katya's father looked mutinous, but she ignored him. "Get what you need. We go as soon as you are ready."

"I'll get the climbing gear," Raquel said, crossing to their packs.

Giles was about to follow when Katya picked up a metallic object from the ground. With a shock, he recognised Professor Mackenzie's lighter.

"That'll be mine," he said, holding out his hand. "I must have dropped it."

For a moment, he thought she might refuse. Then, she placed it in his palm.

"You had better check you have everything," she said, but she looked distracted.

"Katya? About your father."

"What about him?"

"He's OK about looking after Raquel, is he?" Her eyes bore into his. "I mean, if we don't make it back…"

"My father will take care of her." The warning note in her voice was clear.

"Fine," he said. "I had to ask."

Giles joined Raquel, and as they sorted through the equipment, Katya conversed with the old harpy in a hushed tone. He couldn't make out what was said, but it didn't matter now. All he could do was get to the Citadel and find Alfonso. He just hoped that Raquel's brother was still alive, for all their sakes.

Chapter Six

Alfonso was squatting by the fire when they came for him. Wrapped in a cape of molevin hide, he watched the dark outline of harpies skimming over the lake for hydra venturing too close to the surface. Now and again, one would pluck an unwary juvenile from the water before soaring upwards with its catch writhing in its claws.

The hunters didn't have it all their own way, though. Occasionally, one of the flyers would misjudge its prey, the hydra's twin heads clamping onto its claws and dragging it into the lake. Then, even if the harpy managed to struggle to the surface, it would be set upon by its avian sisters seizing their chance for an easy kill.

Fascinated by the nightly games of cat and mouse, Alfonso could see why the Citadel was thriving. The food supply was plentiful, and the serried ranks of nesting alcoves had been designed to support a booming population.

Unlike naturally formed caves, each recess had been carved into the sheer-sided cliffs to allow just enough space for a nest and its brooding mother. It reminded him of the factory farms he'd heard of back home. In place of warehouses full of battery-bred chickens, these towering pinnacles of ancient rock had been transformed into a harpy breeding colony on an industrial scale.

Lost in these thoughts, Alfonso only realised he was not alone when a gust of wind guttered the flickering flames beside him. Olga's broad wings blotted out the nearest moon in the sky, and on her back sat a woman with long, dark hair glimmering in the silvery moonlight.

"Get up, boy," Mary said. "It is time."

"Time for what?"

"To see if your luck has finally run out."

Alfonso straightened, annoyed with himself for not having seen them approach. What would Katya have said? Indeed, he was surprised Mary hadn't instructed Olga to punish him for his potentially fatal lapse in concentration. Perhaps they needed him healthy for whatever they were planning.

What would happen if he refused to go with them? The fire still burned in front of him, and his sharpened stylus lay in his pocket. But, unlike the native harpies, Mary's hybrid daughters had little fear of flames. Once cornered in his cell, he'd be no match for Olga's raking claws.

Besides, Alfonso had made his preparations earlier. Beneath his tattered shirt, he had tied sections of blackened insect carapace around his torso. It was crude, but the articulated plates provided protection without restricting his movement. And with the bone stylus polished to a needle-sharp point, he was as ready as he could ever be for what lay ahead. Rising to his feet, he stepped onto the ledge.

"Very good," Mary said. "We don't want to disappoint your audience."

Olga's claws clamped onto his shoulders and hoisted him into the air. They flew over the lake and banked in a wide circle around the Citadel, where most of the nooks lay empty. When Olga flew past, the few harpies remaining in their nests took to the air and fell in line behind her.

"Why are they following us?"

"To get a good seat," said Mary. "They wouldn't want to miss out on all the action."

Alfonso almost wished he hadn't asked, and he kept quiet as they flew on. More dark shapes appeared below them, all converging on the same squat tower at the far end of the lake. This one was very different to the others; it had suffered a catastrophic collapse down one side, allowing water to pour into its hollowed-out centre. It was into this gap that the remaining harpies disappeared.

Mary said, "Time to make an entrance, Olga, my dear."

"Indeed, Mother."

She dived after them, and they shot through the gap and emerged inside a horseshoe-shaped amphitheatre that was hundreds of feet across. The walls were alive with harpies, many jostling and fighting as they clung to the rock face, trying to find the best perch.

"Take us down," Mary commanded above the raucous din.

There was an outcrop below them, its sides circled by a moat of dark water. They plummeted towards it, the air rushing past with dizzying speed. Alfonso just had time to bend his knees before Olga slowed and dropped him none too gently onto the rocky surface.

Gasping, he remained there for several seconds. Then, gradually, he raised his head and took in his new surroundings. He was on a rocky platform some sixty feet across, its dusty surface bare apart from the half-dozen stone cairns dotted around its perimeter.

The noise from the surrounding harpies grew louder when Mary dismounted from Olga's back. The woman strode to the nearest cairn, removed something from her pocket and struck it against her staff's tip. A blue flame spread over the tightly bound molevin gut wrapped around the end of the shaft.

Screeches echoed around the cauldron as the harpies reacted to the sight of the burning torch, many flapping their wings in alarm. Unmoved, Mary held her staff over the cairn and waited until they quietened.

As the colony's Matriarch basked in her audience's undivided attention, the light of her flickering flame revealed that the mounds were not made of stones but of skulls, empty eye sockets and leering grins now visible between strands of leathery skin. Mary lowered her staff, and with an audible whoosh, the grisly stack caught fire.

The response of the harpies was immediate. The cacophony intensified, though there was a change of tone; it wasn't the panic Alfonso had heard in the claustrophobic confines of the Hive when the fire had taken hold there. Why should it be? Here the harpies were free to flee into the night sky. Besides, they were separated by a moat of water from the flames.

No, it was an altogether different clamour from the watching creatures – one that grew as Mary strode around the tower, lighting pyres of skulls. When she had finished, Alfonso stood in a circle of fire before the baying crowd. A memory returned to him of the bullrings in his native Catalonia, and he recognised the sound of blood lust in the air.

"Olga!" Mary's shout could barely be heard above the din. She was standing beside what looked like a pit in the centre of the ring, her burning staff in one hand. Her daughter stood near Alfonso, her wings flared and face rapt as she gazed at the seething wall of harpies.

"Brief him!" her mother yelled.

The flames reflected in Olga's eyes added to her ferocity.

"The trials have three rules," she hissed. "Do not forget them."

"What… What rules?"

"None may leave the circle of fire. To do so is death."

Of this Alfonso had little doubt. The flames were the only things holding the baying spectators back.

"None may yield during the trial. To do so is death."

"Yield?" he asked, but she ignored him.

"None may offer quarter during the trial. To do so is…" Olga paused, enjoying the moment. "Death."

Leaving Alfonso to take in her words, Olga stalked to her mother standing by the pit in the circle's centre. He watched as Mary thrust the end of her staff at something through the wooden grill and leapt on her daughter's back.

Alfonso thought he heard an angry, braying noise, but it

was lost in the howls from the crowd. Olga reached down and hauled the cover free of the pit before taking to the air, the fires flaring under the downdraft of her wings.

Alfonso stood alone, though he doubted he would be for long. His audience sensed it, too: the noise level dropped, and even the flapping wings fell still. Soon, all he could hear over his own hurried breathing was the crackle of flames among the sightless skulls.

He checked the sky for signs of Olga and her mother hovering above, but there were only moons and stars. He focused instead on the dark hole in the centre of the ring.

Something lay within that pit. Why else had Mary thrust her staff inside before Olga removed the cover? The sturdy wooden frame lay a few feet from the hole, and he wondered if he could lift it back in place.

The question became moot when the hidden occupant leapt from the pit and landed on the tower's surface. A roar rose from the watching harpies for the powerful stag-like creature. It was the height of a man, with curved tusks protruding from a lower jaw, and it reminded Alfonso of the wild boar roaming the hills of Barcelona.

But the long, curved, ridged horns on its head set it apart from anything in his world. One swept back, protecting its heavily muscled neck, while the other swung forwards like a cavalry spear, its tip pointing at his chest.

The harpies grew silent as the two protagonists eyed each other. Finally, the creature lowered its head and began pawing the ground. The sound of its cloven hooves scraping the rock sent gooseflesh up his arms.

Alfonso reached under his cape, and the monster charged. Its speed was incredible: it covered the distance between them in a heartbeat. He barely had time to leap to one side as it swept past. Still, it caught him a glancing blow, scoring a deep groove in the carapace armour.

The creature wheeled around and returned for another pass. Alfonso feinted right before diving left. Again, it thundered past, but a gust of wind parted his hair as something whipped over his head.

As his opponent veered away from the burning pyres, the glow of the flames illuminated the horns on the creature's crown. They swivelled, one towards him and the other angled back along its neck.

The beast could manoeuvre its horns!

"*Merda*!" he breathed. It wasn't enough to avoid the lead horn. The trailing one was the real menace, twisting in its socket to rake him as the beast barrelled past.

In the bullfights he had witnessed as a youth, the matador with his red muleta had pirouetted to avoid the charge of the enraged bull. A creature like this would have sliced the bullfighter open before he was even aware of the threat.

Nonetheless, that childhood memory sparked an idea. Slipping the molevin cape from his shoulders, Alfonso backed towards the centre of the ring. As the creature turned, he began to flap his cape. It hesitated for a moment, eyeing the billowing hide warily.

"Come on!" he hissed, giving the hide a vigorous shake as he took another step back and glanced over his shoulder.

The moment he looked away, it charged. But the clatter

of hooves was warning enough. With a final flap of his cloak, Alfonso stepped back and dropped into the pit. Too late to stop, his attacker sprang over the gap. The sound of its hooves clattering on the rocky ground on the far side of the hole was followed by a splintering crash.

Alfonso hurried up the stone ramp. Beyond the opening was the monster, rolling on the ground, struggling to disentangle itself from the shattered remains of the wooden hatch.

Was this his chance to get close and stab the creature with his stylus? Perhaps not. It was unlikely he'd be able to get near enough to inflict any significant damage before its flailing hooves and thrashing horns tore him to shreds.

With a bellow, the monster staggered upright and began stamping on the broken poles until they were little more than matchsticks.

While it vented its rage, Alfonso retreated to the nearest pyre, the cape held ready. He could feel the prickle of heat on his neck by the time the monstrous head turned.

Though they stood thirty feet apart, the creature's hostility was palpable.

"*Si,* I am here," he breathed, squaring his shoulders and lifting the cape.

The creature took a step forwards, eyes never leaving his. Alfonso didn't move, all too aware of the burning skulls behind him as he continued to flap the molevin hide.

It lowered its head again, both horns pointing at him.

"Mad, are you?" He shook the cape. "Come on then!"

The creature charged. It moved so fast that Alfonso only

had time for one final flourish before it was on him.

Focused on the billowing molevin skin, the monster never saw him roll out of its path. Instead, its horns punched clean through the leathery hide flopping over its head. Momentarily blinded, it ploughed into the burning pyre, sending blazing skulls cascading off the tower. Bellowing, it reared up, but the damage was done. The debris ignited the flammable molevin gut, setting the pinned mask ablaze.

Alfonso scrambled back as it thrashed, its bellows turning to screams as the fire took hold. Then, mad with terror, the beast leapt forwards, crashing into another pyre before disappearing over the circle's edge.

The long, keening scream was interrupted by a series of sickening thumps. Clambering over the embers of the two crumpled pyres, Alfonso saw a rolling ball of flame reach the bottom of the slope and bounce into the water. The splash sent a hissing cloud of steam rising into the air.

A few seconds later, the creature emerged, struggling towards the bank. One of its horns was gone, snapped off in the slippery tumble. The other had flaps of tattered cape hanging from its end.

When it reached the shore, the creature gave a mewling bellow. It was one of the most pitiful sounds Alfonso had ever heard. But it was answered almost immediately by a chorus of screeches from the watching harpies. Whole sections of the far wall took flight, and soon the air was filled with scores of predators clawing at one another to be the first to reach the stricken beast.

They needn't have bothered.

Lines of bubbles broke the surface of the water and converged on the struggling form. A writhing mass of sinewy shapes burst from the surface, glistening bodies wrapping around the doomed creature. Long before the first squabbling harpies made it to the scene, the hydra had dragged its victim into the depths, silencing its desperate cries.

Within a few short minutes, the spectacle was over. The only sign of Alfonso's adversary was a set of concentric ripples spreading across the lake. Around the Tower of Skulls, the harpies took to the air. As the cloud of swirling bodies circled the tower, many looked his way, but none attempted to approach him. He wondered if they were afraid of the remaining pyres, but then he heard the flap of wings behind him.

Olga stood in the centre of the tower, glowering at the circling flyers, none of whom were foolish enough to risk her wrath. Soon the cloud dispersed, unwinding like a dark shadow towards the distant colony.

Mary was sat astride her daughter's back, studying him with a strange half-smile.

"My, my, you are full of surprises."

Her daughter glanced down at the empty pit with its shattered cover. When the harpy lifted her gaze, he saw a hunger there that made him flinch.

"What now, Mother?"

"Take him with us. He'll need all his strength for tomorrow."

Alfonso was too numb from what had happened to ask

why. Instead, he remained still as Olga leapt into the air and plucked him from the summit. Seconds later, they were speeding towards the distant towers, the dark waters and their hidden menace rushing below them.

Chapter Seven

Outside the Buttery window, horned statues stood guard over the Kitchen Bridge. The twin Yales, their pale stonework glowing in the morning sunshine, peered down at the students filing out towards the Backs. Ravi followed their gaze, the bleary-eyed exodus a reminder that term was about to start.

Since leaving the Master's Lodge, Ravi had been busy completing his review of the contents of Robert's trunk before it was "archived" away from prying eyes. The exercise had proven more troubling than he had anticipated.

Robert's final journals revealed his friend's increasing despair over finding a scientific explanation for the portal. That, and Robert's need to provide hard evidence to secure continued funding from the Schiller Foundation, made it depressing reading. At times, Ravi felt like the witness to a Greek tragedy, watching the hero sow the seeds of his own destruction and being unable to do anything to avert the dreadful outcome. The sooner he buried the prophetic record in the dusty depths of the School of Pythagoras, the better.

"You have finished, Professor?"

Startled, Ravi jerked his head around. The waitress Aurelia stood frowning at the plate he'd barely touched. "May I take your tray? I have to clear the tables."

"What? Oh, yes, of course."

Ravi leant back and, as she reached across him, caught a heady mix of perfume and cooking oil.

"You don't like your food?" she asked.

"What? Oh, no. I mean, yes, it's just… I have a lot on my mind."

"If you are not hungry, why come here, Professor?"

When else will I see you? he thought.

"I'm sure I'll feel better tomorrow," he said with a reassuring smile.

"OK. Have a good day, Professor." She headed for the servery.

"And you, Aurelia," he replied, but the waitress gave no indication she'd heard him.

Ravi made his way to his staircase in Second Court. Unsettled by his encounter with Aurelia, he barely glanced at the Old Library entrance as he tramped up the stairs to his sixteenth-century room. By the time he closed the oak-panelled door, the warm glow he'd experienced from their brief interaction had faded, and his mind had turned to this morning's task: the trunk sat next to his desk. Its ominous presence cast a shadow over his mood that even the sunshine streaming through the leaded windows couldn't dispel.

"Come on, Ravi," he said to himself. "One last effort."

He deposited his satchel by the desk and drew up his old

leather chair, which creaked as he settled into it. Then, like a surgeon about to perform an operation, he considered the trunk lying before him.

Robert's faded initials were clearly visible on its scuffed and battered surface, as were the mildew patches from its time in storage. The stale and musty smell that now lingered in his third-floor room spoke of the dark and damp New Court cellars that Ravi remembered all too well.

He unlocked the lid, revealing the contents that had occupied his mind for most of his waking hours – and some sleepless ones too in recent weeks.

His friend's leather-bound journals filled almost a third of the storage area, neatly arranged in date order. Within these were Robert's faithful transcriptions of the arcane glyphs and the incantation that had opened the Gemini Passage to the other world. Robert had once described these scrawlings – initially penned by John Dee, former Fellow and Astronomer to Elizabeth I – as mystical mumbo-jumbo. Still, it was clear from the journals that his friend had spent decades searching for a scientific explanation of the phenomenon before he had ultimately accepted funding from the Schiller Foundation.

The cardboard boxes that filled the central section of the trunk contained the powdered remains of samples from Gemini. Robert must have collected them when they'd first used the portal in 1969. But there were more recent boxes too, suggesting that Robert had returned to collect additional samples. Ravi suspected these were to persuade Schiller to continue funding his clandestine research.

However, it was clear from the journal entries that the fragments of bone and organic matter had crumbled to dust before they could be offered as evidence. His friend's desperation must have driven him to make the fateful decision last summer to bring back a living sample. One that he could be confident would retain its form long enough to demonstrate his discovery. A living egg. More specifically, the harpy egg they had later found on the Chapel Tower, and which Nick had smashed on the court below.

Perhaps Robert had stored it in the protective warmth of the tartan blanket that was now neatly folded in the bottom of the trunk – the egg would have been too big to fit in one of the boxes. No doubt he had planned on showing his prize specimen to Schiller before Ravi had forbidden him from revealing their long-kept secret.

Had the egg been in Robert's room when Schiller visited him on the night of his friend's death? If so, his guest hadn't removed it. Giles had seen Schiller leave empty-handed, lighting a cigarette on the way out.

So how did the egg end up on the Chapel Tower? It couldn't have been Robert. He was lying dead some twenty feet below his open window. Had someone else removed it?

Or something, he thought.

Schiller and the night climbers weren't the only ones prowling New Court that night. Giles had encountered a harpy over the rooftops of New Court. Could the creature sense the presence of her egg?

Ravi considered the sequence of events. Robert had

invited Schiller to his room to end their association. The conversation had got heated – unsurprising given his guest's fiery temper. After showing him the door, the flustered Scot might well have wanted to clear the air. Once open, those magnificent bay windows overlooking the Backs were easily big enough for a harpy to slip through.

Closing his eyes, Ravi imagined his friend's horror on finding the creature hovering there. Caught between a mother and her offspring, he would have had no chance.

"Oh, Robert," he murmured, gripping the blanket.

The rustle of paper within the soft fabric brought him back to the present. Frowning, Ravi reached inside its folds and withdrew a crumpled envelope.

There was no address, but in faded ink on the cover were the words "*To Robert*".

Retrieving the neatly folded sheet of paper concealed within, Ravi read the message written in the same flowing hand.

7 July 1969
My darling Robert,

Thank you once again for a sublime day yesterday. The Grantchester Meadows were glorious, and the cream tea delicious – though I have to confess, I keep finding crumbs everywhere! So, you may need to shake out the blanket before next time.

I was wondering what your plans are this week? Our mutual friend has invited me to stargaze with him on Tuesday at the Cavendish. Still, I'm free on

Wednesday if you have time to resume our own heavenly studies.

Leave me a note in the usual place.

Yours always,

Mary

Ravi held the letter for some time. He remembered that heady summer they had shared all those years ago, his nervousness at introducing Mary to his friend and his relief at how well they had got on together. But then there had been the glances across the table he'd tried not to notice. And the shared laughter at some obscure comment he'd pretended to understand. And the murmur of conversation after he'd left the room. The signs of his friends' betrayal were there for anyone to see, but he had chosen to ignore them.

"You fool," he muttered, crunching the paper.

The sharp knock at the door made him jump.

"Ravi?"

He usually shut the outer door to ensure he wasn't disturbed, but today he'd been flustered after leaving the Buttery.

"Allo, Ravi? Are you in?"

The French accent was unmistakable.

"One minute!" he called, stuffing the letter in his pocket and grabbing the blanket.

He'd just managed to slam the lid shut and fling the tartan blanket over the trunk when the door swung open. A tall woman dressed in a jet-black trench coat and sporting a severe French bob stepped inside.

"Why, Gabrielle," he said, rising from his chair and affecting a welcome smile. "How lovely to see you."

Dr Gabrielle Dutour strode across the room and, extending a long, elegant hand, gave him a perfunctory Parisienne handshake.

"Ravi. 'Ow are you?"

Her intense eyes were magnified by her large, black-rimmed glasses.

"I… I'm well, thank you."

"I heard you had an accident last term."

"Oh, that." He rolled his eyes, wondering how much she knew. "Just a tumble down some stairs."

"But you were in the hospital, no?"

"For a while," he said, smiling. "But I'm feeling a good deal better now."

"I see you have new teeth." Her enlarged eyes focused on them, and he self-consciously covered his mouth.

"Oh, those. Yes, I managed to chip a couple."

"Well, the new ones are much better. Not so yellow and crooked."

"Right," he said, unsure how to respond to what he assumed was intended as a compliment. "Thank you."

"So, this is your room." Gabrielle surveyed his comfortable, though admittedly shabby, study. "You have a lot of bookshelves compared to mine."

Her room in Chapel Court was minimalist, with chic mid-century furniture and carefully curated art objects.

"Oh, quite a few, I suppose. It pays to keep abreast of developments in other fields when dining with one's colleagues."

"But I do not see you in Hall very often," she said, examining one of the bookcases.

A good deal less since you arrived, Ravi thought. "During the winter months, I spend most evenings at the observatory. Astronomers are often referred to as night owls, after all."

She faced him. "So, I can expect to see you at dinner more often during this term?"

Too late, Ravi realised his mistake. "I suppose so, yes."

"Good. I will enjoy that. And perhaps you can show me your telescope afterwards."

"Sorry?"

"The Thorrowood, is it not?"

"Why, yes," he said. "How did you know I prefer that particular device?"

"Robert Mackenzie told me. He said it was your favourite."

The ground seemed to shift. "Robert told you that? When?"

"In Geneva. We were at a conference." She shrugged. "He said it was ancient and kept in a shed."

"An observation hut," he corrected her.

"*Alors*, he said it was freezing there at night. Not good for brass monkeys, is that the expression?"

"Something like that," said Ravi, hoping she wouldn't press him for the anatomical explanation. Still, he was interested in what else Robert might have confided in her. "Tell me, Gabrielle, would you like a cup of tea? I was about to make one for myself."

"Do you have coffee?"

"I think I could stretch to that."

"In that case, *oui*, why not?"

"Excellent."

As he put the kettle on in the sanctuary of his kitchen, he gathered his thoughts. What had transpired at this conference in Geneva? He could well imagine his friend trying to impress her, particularly given her interest in his research on dark matter.

Reaching for the jar of instant coffee, Ravi asked, "How do you take it?"

There was a brief pause followed by a creak from his study. Ravi walked through the connecting door in time to see her straighten from his desk.

"Sorry, Ravi?"

Holding up the jar, he said, "I wondered how you like your coffee?"

"Is that instant?"

"Yes, it is."

"In that case, don't worry." She indicated the desk. "You don't have a computer, Ravi. Why not?"

"I prefer the one at the Cavendish." He did not mention the state-of-the-art laptop locked away in his top drawer. "Besides, I like to keep surfaces clear for Tutorials."

"Ah, yes," she said. "I must organise one of those."

"It's the Law students you look after, isn't it?"

"*Oui*, but they are hopeless. Apart from young *Nichola*, they have no idea about wine."

"Nicholas Wood?" he asked, surprised.

"You know him?"

"He and I may have bumped into each other. A rugby player, I believe."

"Possibly," she said dismissively. "Tell me, have you ever ordered canapés from the College kitchen? Last time their selection was barely adequate."

"Err, no. I can't say I have."

"Well, I have some new dishes I would like them to try."

Ravi couldn't imagine the Head Chef would take too kindly to Gabrielle instructing him on *hors d'oeuvres*. Then again, who was he to interfere? He checked his watch. "The Catering Office should be open by now, I believe."

"*Bon*. In that case, I shall pay them a visit." She headed for the door. "I'm glad you are well, Ravi."

"Thank you for coming to see me."

"It is what colleagues do, is it not?"

"Indeed, but it is much appreciated."

In the doorway, she paused. "Perhaps you can show me your observatory after dinner sometime."

"I'd be delighted," he said. "I shall keep an eye on the weather forecast."

"As will I," she replied. "*A bientôt*." And with the briefest of smiles, she pulled the door closed.

At first, Ravi couldn't see anything out of place on his desk. The heavy-duty padlock was there with the key still inserted in the lock. But the tartan blanket he'd hastily thrown over the trunk had been smoothed flat, its edges straightened. Visible under the tasselled edge were the initials RTFM, which would be well known to anyone working in the Physics Faculty.

"Robert Thomas Findlay Mackenzie," he muttered.

Chapter Eight

After breakfast, Annabel left Cripps and made her way along the narrow streets of Victorian terraces that led down to Jesus Green. Many of the properties here were owned by the College, the hostels proving popular with third years – particularly rowers, given their proximity to the College Boathouse.

Entering Richmond Terrace, Annabel counted down the identically painted doors until she found the one she was looking for. After ringing the bell, she waited for the thump of footsteps descending the stairs. Moments later, the door creaked open to reveal a tall, bleary-eyed girl wearing a tee shirt, baggy tracksuit bottoms and flip-flops.

"Hi, Clarissa. Did I wake you?"

The girl blinked. "Annabel? What are you doing here?"

"I came over for a chat. Well, to share some bad news, really."

"About Brett, you mean?"

"You've heard then?"

"One of my housemates rows in M1."

"Oh, of course."

Clarissa yawned. "Do you want a cup of tea?"

"No, I've just had one, thanks."

"Yeah, a bit of a bummer. Heard yesterday. Everyone's talking about it."

"I can imagine. Anyway, I was off to the Boathouse and wondered if you wanted to join me?"

"What for?"

"I was going to ask Blades about coaching us."

"What, W3, you mean?"

"Brett thinks Blades might be up for it."

"You spoke to Brett, did you?"

"Yeah, last night."

Annabel decided not to mention he'd come to her room, unsure how Clarissa would take it. In the end, it made little difference.

"Listen, Annabel. I hate to disappoint you, but I'm not sure I will be rowing this term."

"Because Brett won't be coaching us?"

Clarissa shrugged. "His leggings did make those early-morning outings more bearable."

"How about if we row in the evenings?"

"Evenings? Blades would never allow it."

"What if we could persuade him?"

"Even if we did, I'm not sure the rest of the crew would be up for it."

"They would if you were."

"What makes you say that?"

"Because you're our Stroke, and they follow your lead – on and off the water. If you told the crew we're rowing in the evenings, they'd do it."

Clarissa smiled. "You rehearsed that speech, didn't you?"

"Multiple times, in front of the mirror."

"It wasn't bad."

"Thanks. It's also true." She sighed. "Come on, Clarissa. You and I both know W3 deserved an oar last term. This is our best chance of getting one, with or without Brett."

"OK, OK," Clarissa said. "Don't push it; you had me at evening outings."

Annabel gestured at her tangled hair. "Shall I give you a minute?"

"I don't think that's going to make much difference to Blades, do you?"

Annabel thought about the dour ex-mariner. "Probably not."

Clarissa grabbed an LMBC hoodie from the ones hanging in the hall. "Well then, let's go and see if that speech of yours does the trick on him."

"I've been practising another one for that."

"I thought you might have."

Ten minutes later, they walked down the ramp to the College Boathouse, where the red double doors were already open.

"Someone's out early," Clarissa said, looking at eight pairs of trainers lined along the bank.

"Nice morning for it." Annabel remembered the freezing conditions they'd endured last term.

Clarissa peered through the workshop window. "Looks like we're in luck," she said, pulling open the door.

The pungent smell of resin and glue wafted out, making Annabel blink. The College Boatman was bending over his tool bench, working on what looked like an aluminium oar.

"Morning, Blades!" Annabel called.

His head jerked around.

"Hope we're not disturbing you. We were wondering if we might have a chat?"

"Oh, morning, ladies." He pulled an old sailcloth over the workbench before facing them. "How can I help you?"

"We wanted to talk to you about W3."

"Oh, yes?" He wiped his hands with a rag. "I was about to make a brew. Can I get you one?"

The Boatman's tea was infamous among the crews. Some said he used the dark, oily liquid to varnish the club's old wooden clinker.

"No, I'm good," Clarissa said quickly.

"Just had breakfast," Annabel agreed.

"Oh, OK. In that case, go and pull up a berth in the office. I'll be with you in a minute."

Clarissa led Annabel into the cramped room with windows overlooking the slipway. They squeezed past the row of hooks on the wall, overflowing with wet-weather gear and LMBC tops, and perched on the narrow sofa tucked in the corner.

It was little more than a cabin, though one that was well-ordered and shipshape. A corkboard hung along one wall, displaying crew photos, maintenance schedules, river regulations and a calendar listing upcoming races. The desk was stacked high with training rosters and invoices, arranged in neat piles and weighed down by nautical brass items and a well-worn whetstone.

"Officer on deck," Clarissa murmured as footsteps approached. "Good luck."

The Boatman entered the room holding a tannin-stained mug in his heavily tattooed fist and sat at his desk.

"What's this all about then?"

"You know Brett's been offered a seat in M1?" Annabel began.

"I had heard, yes."

"Which means he won't be able to coach us."

The Boatman frowned. "You sure? It sounded to me like he still planned to."

"I know. But we couldn't hold him to it. It wouldn't be fair to him or the club."

"I see," he said, putting down his mug. "Well, that's good of you. I'm sure the Men's Captain will be cock a hoop."

"You're not kidding," Clarissa muttered. "I have a houseful of rowers convinced Maggie's going Head of the River."

"We'll see. Anything can happen in the Bumps, as you well know." He glanced at Annabel. "So, you're looking for a new coach."

"That's right."

"Anyone you had in mind?"

"We were wondering if you would do it?"

"Me?" He indicated the stack of rosters on his desk. "I'm not sure I can, I'm afraid. My mornings are busy getting the boats ready."

"We weren't thinking about going out then. How about later?"

"What, after lunch?"

"After dinner, before it gets dark. We'll have the river to ourselves."

The Boatman snorted. "And you think your lot will want to go out then?"

"Faced with a choice between early morning or early evening," Clarissa said, "I don't think there'll be many objecting."

"I don't know," Blades said. "The University doesn't like crews going out in the evening. They get enough complaints from the houseboats as it is."

"It won't be every evening," Annabel countered. "We can intersperse it with Erg sessions."

"Tell us what drills you want us to do, and I'll lead them," Clarissa added.

"What about the rest of the crew?"

"Never missed a session, did they, Annabel?"

"Certainly didn't," she replied.

The Boatman took a sip of tea. "Sounds like you've got this all worked out."

Annabel smiled at Clarissa. "Not yet, but we will."

Blades put down his mug.

"That's good because a winning crew needs this" – he tapped his heart – "more than this." He flexed a heavily tattooed forearm.

"You'll do it then?" Annabel asked.

"Yes, I'll do it."

"Thank you!"

Clarissa gave her an approving nod.

"You can thank me by bumping the boats ahead of you. I don't want M1 hogging all the glory this term. Speaking of which, that looks like them now."

"What?" Clarissa rose to her feet. Outside the window, a red-bladed boat had just rounded the bend in the river. She pulled the hoodie over her wayward hair and headed for the door. "In that case, I'll be off. Thanks, Blades."

"I'll let the others know, shall I?" Annabel called after her. But the other girl was already hurrying from the Boathouse, the smack of her flip-flops fading up the ramp.

Annabel turned back to the Boatman. "I guess that's us done."

Blades nodded, wearing a curious expression. Annabel was about to get to her feet when he spoke.

"Last term, Annabel. What happened?"

She paused. "Sorry?"

"In the Lents. The accident."

Her stomach tightened at the memory of that final day of the Bumps. The crowd's noise, the whistles, her urging the crew on as they gained on Newnham... And then that awful sensation as she lost control, and the boat began slewing across the river.

"I... I don't know, Blades. I can't explain it. One minute we were about to bump, and the next... we were slamming into the bank."

"You know it was the rudder," he said.

"Clarissa said something about that after the race. Unlucky, I guess."

"You think?"

Was he remembering her accident with Brett? If not, she certainly was. Along with all the other near-fatal encounters that kept happening to anyone she cared about.

"Some people attract bad luck, I guess."

Blades frowned. "What, like a Jonah, you mean?"

"I suppose so."

The old sailor shook his head. "Ain't never believed in that sort of thing." He leaned forwards and looked her square in the eye. "You lost control of the boat because your rudder sheared off. Don't ask me how. Those things are made of stainless steel. But something sliced through a shaft as thick as my finger."

He held up a digit for emphasis.

"Now, think carefully. You're sure you don't remember hitting anything?"

As they'd closed with the other crew, W3 had been rowing smoothly and powerfully, Clarissa maintaining a high but steady rating and the fibreglass hull gliding through the choppy waters with barely a tremor.

"No, Blades, nothing."

"Well, if anything occurs to you, let me know. Anything, you hear?"

"Of course."

A call of "Easy Oars" told them the eight had arrived at the Boathouse.

"Right, well, I'd better see how this lot got on. Keep this between us for now, OK?"

"Sure."

He got to his feet, the tense atmosphere lifting. "And

you'll let me know when W3 want their first outing?" He grabbed a faded cap from the hook. "Not too late, mind. I don't want our boats out on the river after dark. Is that clear?"

"Right," she said, a little startled by his intense stare.

His expression softened. "Yes, well, don't want the University on our back, do we?"

"No, of course not."

The Boatman looked like he might say something more, but then the scrape of an oar blade over the concrete slipway made him wince.

"Ruddy hell!" he growled before heading outside. "Call yourself a first boat! I've had novices keelhauled for less!"

Annabel listened as he let rip at the pride of the Lady Margaret Boat Club, glad she wasn't on the receiving end of that broadside. Still bemused by their conversation, she wandered out of the office. The sailcloth had fallen from his workbench and lay in a crumpled heap on the floor. She went over to pick up the oiled canvas and stared at the object it had covered. What she had mistaken for a metal oar wasn't that at all. It was an aluminium punt pole that had been torn in half, the jagged shards glinting beneath the overhead strip light.

Why would the Boatman have one of those here? An idea came to her, and, after covering the workbench, she passed through the access door into the boat shed and walked between the racks until she reached the red prow of the eight they had rowed in last term.

The new bow section had been beautifully restored so the

join was barely noticeable. She moved down to the stern of the boat to the gleaming new rudder plate. Around the rudder housing, there were distinctive markings on the fibreglass. And though the surface had been expertly filled, sanded and polished to a high sheen, a pair of crescent shapes were still visible and clearly identifiable to someone studying zoology.

They were teeth marks. The sort marine predators made in the flanks of their victims. Only these were like nothing she had ever seen before.

Footsteps made Annabel turn, and she saw the sleek nose of M1 edging its way through the Boathouse doors. Before Blades, Brett or any crew could spot her, she slipped through the side door and made her way out of the deserted workshop.

Climbing the ramp, Annabel crossed the bridge and glanced down at the river. In the balmy morning sunshine, its waters were a picture of peace and serenity.

"Come on, girl," she said, breaking into a run, "you're imagining things."

But a few minutes later, when she passed through the College gates, Annabel couldn't ignore her relief at having its protective walls around her once more.

Chapter Nine

Chest heaving, muscles burning, Nick slumped against the wall of the College fitness room. The sweat dripped off the end of his nose and splattered on the rubber mat between the dumb-bells he'd been using. An hour into his workout, the pain was almost as bad as last term's Redboy training sessions on the snow-covered pitches. This time, though, he was the one setting the brutal pace.

After a restless night imagining Annabel with Brett at the May Ball, he'd come here to clear his head and, if he was honest, punish himself for not asking her first.

"Idiot," he muttered, pushing himself off the wall and heading to the bench press.

There was a heavy thump against the gym door, followed by another and then an expletive.

"Hold on!" Nick called, heading to the entrance and pushing open the door.

"Woody!" Aden, a fellow first-year rugby player, stood in the corridor, decked out in Redboy training top and shorts. "Fricking thing wouldn't open."

"They've changed the combination."

"What did they do that for?"

"It's 1511. The College's founding."

Aden sighed. "Come on, make way and let this bad boy show you how it's done." The burly prop strolled into the room, waving a hand in front of his nose. "Phew, it's humming in here. How long have you been at it?"

"Long enough. I'm about done."

"You look it. Been doing much over the holidays?"

"Couldn't really." Nick tapped his skull. "Doctor's orders, remember."

"Ah, yes. Sadly, I don't have that excuse." Aden patted a stomach that stretched the fabric of his top. "I'm not looking forward to this one bit."

"You want me to hang around?"

"No, you're all right. I was just going to do a few stretches. Don't want to overdo it."

Nick didn't believe that for a minute. When it came to the weights room, Aden was a beast. Sure enough, as he went to retrieve his towel, he saw the big prop doubling the weights on the bench press Nick had been using.

"So, Woody, had a good break?"

"Great, thanks."

"Weren't you going to see Annabel?"

"Yep, stayed with her over Easter."

"How'd that go?"

"Good."

"And her gran?"

"Yeah, we get on well."

"Damn. That was my last hope."

"What do you mean?"

"I was hoping you'd mess up there. You know, witter on as you do. Set the old girl against you. Anything to give Annabel a chance to come to her senses and dump you for me."

"Sorry to disappoint you."

"Yeah, well, like I've told you before, you struck lucky there, Woody mate. That girl's way out of your league."

"You're not wrong."

Aden smiled. "Don't worry, bro. You two are going to turn heads at the Ball for sure."

"Annabel, maybe," Nick said, imagining her arriving on Brett's arm.

"What do you mean?"

"I'm not going."

"Why not?"

"I couldn't afford it."

"But what about Annabel?"

"I think Brett invited her."

"Brett? As in, tall, good-looking, I-rowed-for-Yale Brett?"

"That's the one."

"Bro, you're killing me here. What were you thinking?"

"Have I messed up?"

"Messed up? Er, yes. Big time. Huge in fact." He lay back down on the bench and shook his head. "Man, Woody, you really are the best."

Nick stared at his feet, wondering not for the first time how he could have been so stupid. Aden finished a punishing set of lifts and paused.

"OK, Woody," he panted. "So, you're not going to the Ball. Have you thought about working security?"

"Sorry?"

"At the Ball. Me and some of the Redboys have signed up."

"Like bouncers, you mean?"

"Yeah, but nothing too heavy. Checking tickets and stuff."

Back home, Nick had done something similar at rugby club socials, where things could get pretty lively come closing time. It sounded like an easy gig. But what if he saw Annabel and Brett there?

"I'm not sure."

"We get paid. Good money too." He gave Nick an arched look. "Enough to save up for next year, maybe?"

Nick hesitated as Aden lowered the weights and sat up. His friend was breathing hard but otherwise untroubled by a set that would have wrecked most of their teammates.

"Listen, Woody, there's a briefing at the end of the week. Come along and see what you think. Then you can decide."

Nick figured it couldn't hurt to hear what was involved.

"Sure. Thanks."

"No problem, bro." Aden stood up and ambled over to the squat rack, where he laid another two disks on the stack Nick had been using. "Now, piss off. There's only so much I can take of those puppy eyes."

Nick was halfway out the door when Aden called after him, "And think of something nice to do for Annabel! Dating you, the poor girl deserves it."

Nick left the gym a good deal happier than when he'd arrived. Sure, doing security at the Ball wasn't the same as going with Annabel. But maybe he could invite her next year.

Emerging from the Cripps basement, he was about to head for a shower when he heard splashing from the punt pool. That was odd. Skirting past the Porters' Lodge, he took the steps to the concrete jetty where the College punts were moored.

A diminutive figure stood motionless at the far end, staring at a punt sitting low in the water. Bent over the stern of the sinking vessel, someone else was bailing like a man possessed.

"Brian?"

The student at the end of the jetty looked up.

"Hello, Nick."

"What's going on?" he asked, joining him.

"Number 10 has a leak," Brian replied in his usual monotone. "Ash is trying to find out where it's coming from."

Nick stared at the waterlogged punt, which appeared to be sitting lower in the water now, though not for a lack of effort on Ash's part.

Neither of Annabel's friends struck Nick as particularly athletic. Still, Ash's enthusiasm more than made up for what he might lack in coordination. Up to his ankles in water, the gangly student was scooping litres of the murky brown liquid over the side in a display of perpetual motion that would have done an automaton proud. However, even to

Nick's inexperienced eye, he was clearly fighting a losing battle.

"Does he need a hand?"

"Let's see."

Raising his fingers to his lips, Brian emitted a shrill whistle that would have stopped a sheepdog in its tracks. Ash looked up, his face flushed and shirt soaking, though whether from river water or sweat it was hard to say.

"Nick! Great to see you!"

"You too, Ash. Do you want a hand?"

"That would be great! We tried dragging it out, but it was too heavy for two of us."

Nick could well imagine. "OK, bear with me."

A few minutes later, he returned with Aden, who was only too happy to cut his gym session short. Together, they managed to drag the front half of the punt sufficiently high on the dock to allow most of the water to drain away before levering the stern onto the quayside.

Panting, Aden slapped a breathless Brian on the back, while Nick bent double over the hull.

"Come and help the Punt Society, you said. It will be fun, you said."

Nick gave Aden a weary smile. "I thought you wanted a workout?"

"Pre-season is going to be a doddle after this."

"I wish," Nick replied.

"Hey, come and look at this!"

Ash was squatting in the stern, head bent. Exchanging a look with the others, Nick joined him as the last remnants of bilgewater spread across the jetty's flagstones in an ever-widening puddle. With the bottom of the punt empty, save for a few soggy willow leaves, the source of the leak was obvious.

Two crescent-shaped holes had been gouged in the bottom of the hull, each one large enough to put a fist through.

"What do you make of those?" Ash asked.

"No idea." Nick ran a finger around the inside of each one. The edges were clean, with no splinters that he could detect.

"Well, one thing's for sure," Ash said. "We won't be using this punt for a while. I'd better tell the Porters."

He headed off to the lodge, leaving the others alone. Aden arched his back, while Brian shuffled over to join Nick by the damaged hull.

"Odd, really," he said in his strange nasal voice.

"What is?" Nick asked.

"Number 10. Being at the end of the quay under the willow, it rarely gets used."

Nick could imagine the punt would have been all but obscured by branches.

"That might make it easier to trace who last took it out," Nick suggested. "Have you checked the signing-out book?"

"It won't be in the book."

"Why not?"

Brian lowered his voice. "Because she didn't sign it out."

"You know who it was?"

Brian nodded. "Annabel – this was the punt she took out that night last term."

Nick stared at him for a moment and then down at the two puncture marks in the thick wooden decking. He thought back to that nightmarish journey – Annabel and Giles steering them through the pouring rain towards New Court – the punt lurching and swaying as they leapt for the hidden cellar entrance.

Was that when this happened, he wondered?

He tried to remember, but his memory was still fuzzy from his concussion. Probably for the best, given what they'd found in the cellars.

"All sorted!" Ash's cheery voice made Nick start as his friend returned with the punt key. "The Porter said we can leave the punt there for now. How about we clear some space in the Punt Store before towing it over?"

"You got any biscuits left?" Aden asked.

"I think so," said Brian.

"So, what are we waiting for?"

The others set off, leaving Nick trying to marshal his disjointed thoughts.

"Hey, Woody," Aden called back, "are you coming or what?"

Frustrated, Nick gave up.

"On my way," he replied before stepping over the puddles and hurrying after his friends.

Chapter Ten

"Careful, Professor!"

Bert's warning came just in time. Ravi grabbed the handrail as the trunk lurched down the stairs. Straining, he bore its weight on his shoulder while the Porter steadied himself.

"Sorry about that, Professor. Lost my footing there. Are you all right?"

"Fine, thank you, Bert," Ravi panted, though he could already feel a bruise forming beneath his jacket.

Navigating down the narrow upper flight of his staircase with Robert's bulky trunk had proven more challenging than he had anticipated. In hindsight, it might have been better to ask Housekeeping to move it rather than ask a favour of the old Porter. However, Ravi wanted as few people as possible to know about the trunk's existence, and Bert was someone whose absolute discretion could be relied upon. Besides, after seeing Gabrielle Dutour, Ravi had decided to relocate the trunk to the archive centre that very evening, and almost all of the support staff had already gone home.

"Almost there, Professor," the Porter said as they reached

the landing. "Only two more flights of stairs, and they are a good deal wider here."

"That's a relief."

"I hope there's nothing too valuable inside."

The notebooks and the boxes containing remnants of otherworldly samples had led to the death of at least two people and, without his students, could easily have led to more.

"Nothing breakable," he replied.

"That's good to know. Still, it will be good to get it on the trolley."

They reached the bottom of the staircase, where one of the new electric trolleys was waiting for them.

"That's a relief," the old Porter said once they'd lowered the trunk onto the flatbed. "I'm not as fit as I used to be."

"You and me both, Bert."

They stood there for a moment, gathering their breath. Across the court, the windows of the College Bar were dark. Last orders had been called some time ago, and the square was quiet, save for the sound of muffled conversation from some of the upper rooms.

"Ready, Professor?" Bert asked.

Ravi nodded. "Yes. Let's go."

They set off, the Porter operating the trolley, its electric motor whirring into life. They made their way into Third Court and then crossed the Bridge of Sighs, the pitch of the electric motor rising as it laboured up the slope.

"It's a lot easier since we got one of these," the old Porter remarked. "Remember those coal barrows? Used to rattle over the paving stones like railway carriages?"

"I do indeed, Bert. Came in very handy when moving rooms each year." As they continued down the New Court cloisters, Ravi could almost see his friend Robert as a student, his face creased in a maniacal smile as they raced the trunk across the courts, students and Fellows leaping aside to avoid being mown down.

Smiling at the memory, Ravi entered Cripps in companiable silence with Bert, their footsteps accompanied by the steady hum of the motor. There were plenty of lights on in the surrounding rooms. Still, to his relief, no one emerged from the staircases. Indeed, the only person they saw was Shirley, who watched them from the lodge until they disappeared from view.

Emerging into Merton Court, Ravi looked across the patch of lawn to the dark outline of the School of Pythagoras. The medieval building took up the far side of the square, its ancient stonework repaired and rebuilt countless times. Its most recent renovation had left its characterful aspect relatively untouched, save for the refurbished oak doors in the large arched doorway.

A light was shining from one of the narrow, triple-glazed windows, skilfully inlaid in a period-leaded frame.

"Looks like we are expected, Professor."

"Indeed, Bert. I took the precaution of letting Mr Weston know before we set off."

"The Librarian?"

"I didn't think it right to ask the College Archivist to stay late."

In truth, the only person he'd wanted present was Mr Weston, who guarded the College's secrets as closely as its priceless books.

"I see," said Bert, and Ravi suspected the old Porter did only too well.

They steered the trolley to the side entrance adjacent to the timber-framed Merton Hall. Inside was a simple stone lobby incorporating a lift and disability ramp.

"Would you like me to do it, Professor?" Bert asked.

"No, I've got it."

Ravi pressed the intercom. Almost at once, he heard the thin, reedy voice of the College Librarian. "Good evening, Professor."

Ravi peered up at the discreet security camera set above the door. "Evening, Mr Weston. I have Bert with me and the... deposit."

"Excellent. In that case, take the lift, and I'll meet you on the first floor."

There was a click, and the glass door slid open. Bert wheeled the trunk into the lobby while Ravi called the lift, which was a high-tech affair – all brushed aluminium and digital displays – in sharp contrast to the building it serviced. It was large enough to accommodate them and the trunk, saving them another tricky staircase manoeuvre.

When the doors opened, Mr Weston was waiting for them, the late hour making no difference to his neat, trim appearance. Small and with thinning hair, the College Librarian was the sort of man who might go unnoticed at a social gathering. But Ravi knew that those sharp eyes behind the half-moon glasses missed very little; even now, they briefly flicked down to the trunk before he gave them both a warm smile.

"Welcome, gentlemen. Everything in order?"

"All good, Mr Weston," said Bert, reaching down for the handle. "Though it would have been nice to have had a lift installed in Second Court."

"I can imagine," the Librarian said as Ravi helped the Porter hoist the trunk onto the landing. "Let me open this for you."

He swiped a card against a sensor, and there was an audible sigh as the door to the hermetically sealed room swung open. Ravi backed into the space, immediately aware of the change in air quality; the room was maintained at a constant temperature and humidity, whatever the weather outside.

Three walls sported display cabinets housing a selection of unusual artefacts such as wax seals and tokens. The fourth was made entirely of glass, its partition door leading into a space hidden in darkness.

"Put it on the table there," the Librarian said as he sealed the door behind them. They lowered the trunk onto the sturdy oak top, and Ravi let out a sigh.

"Happy, Professor?" Mr Weston smiled at him.

"Relieved might be a better description."

The Librarian nodded. "I felt the same after we moved the College's copy of the original Magna Carta here a few years ago. Having something of such historical significance stored in the main library, frequented by hundreds of spirited students, had been a source of some concern."

Ravi remembered the animated conversations on the College Council about where the most secure location was for this national treasure. There had been talk about storing it in the silver vault or even the Fellows' wine cellar – until someone had pointed out that the required humidity levels might adversely affect the College port. Repurposing a Grade 1 listed thirteenth-century manor house into a state-of-the-art archive had met with almost unanimous approval.

"I take it this trunk contains something of great significance," Mr Weston said.

"It does." Ravi did not elaborate, and the Librarian knew better than to probe further.

"So, Professor, how would you like the items stored?"

"I was rather hoping they could remain within the trunk. Somewhere out of sight and out of mind, as it were."

"I see. Well, in many ways, that makes things simpler. I had been wondering where best to make space among the shelving units. We have some spare capacity, but the College Archivist likes to be consulted on any changes. If you follow me, gentlemen, perhaps I can show you the place I have in mind."

He crossed the room to the glass partition and, swiping his access card, stepped through the doorway.

Immediately, a set of overhead lights flickered into life, illuminating a cavernous space. The upper Archive occupied the entire first floor. With its restored timber arches, the vaulted ceiling provided ample space for the rows of tall wooden shelves. Along the centre of the room ran a long, low cabinet, its smooth oak top dotted with small linen sacks. At the far end of this lay a roll of parchment, its curled edges weighed down by more of these little sandbags placed strategically along its edges. Ravi's eye was drawn to the ancient Latin text, but before he could decipher it, the Librarian reached over and lifted the nearest sacks.

"Forgive me," Weston said as the document furled like a blind. "Just some research I was doing while waiting for you this evening."

With remarkable dexterity, he removed the scroll, slipped it inside a cardboard tube and tucked it away inside the cabinet.

Out of sight and out of mind, Ravi thought.

"Now then, where were we?" The Librarian straightened. "Ah, yes, of course."

He led them to a door at the back of the room, and they descended several flights of stairs to what must have been a basement corridor, at the end of which was a nondescript door. Removing a set of keys, he unlocked it and stepped inside, turning on the lights.

It was a low-ceilinged room with no windows, timberwork or glass partitions. Instead, a storage system of vertical frames filled the entire length of one wall. The contraption reminded Ravi of a much larger version of the racks they used for feeding slides into a projector in the days before digital film. This impression was reinforced by some of the slots being filled with what appeared to be picture frames.

"So, Professor, what do you think?"

"What exactly is this room used for?"

The Librarian looked uncomfortable. "Some unfortunate bequests."

"Unfortunate?"

"Over the College's history, a number of Fellows have generously donated personal art collections to the College for subsequent generations to enjoy in their rooms." He indicated the racks. "Sadly, certain pieces had few takers and were stored here instead."

Ravi was surprised by the number of hidden canvases. Enough to decorate half a dozen Tutors' sets.

"Couldn't we have loaned them to a gallery?"

"There were concerns about damage to the College's reputation were they ever to see the light of day."

"I see," said Ravi. "I take it disposal wasn't an option."

"I believe some at the time favoured that solution, but the College authorities couldn't bring themselves to destroy original works of art, however problematic they might be."

Ravi nodded. "Which is why they ended up here."

"And shall remain so," Mr Weston agreed, "until tastes change or, as the present Master put it, hell freezes over."

"In that case," Ravi said, "I think this will do very nicely."

"Excellent! If there are no more questions, I suggest we collect your item, Professor, and add it to the Unseen Archive."

Twenty minutes later, with the trunk safely stored away, they emerged with the trolley into Merton Court. Mr Weston swiped a key card over a sensor, and the lobby door slid shut with a reassuring thud.

"Well, I think that concludes our business, gentlemen."

"Thank you, Mr Weston," said Ravi, "and you, Bert."

"Always a pleasure, Professor," the Porter replied. "I only hope..."

Ravi never discovered what that hope was because a blinding light fixed him in its beam.

"What's going on here?"

Raising a hand against the glare, Ravi could just discern the sturdy outline.

"Put that down, Shirley," said Bert. "Can't you see who it is?"

The flashlight went out, and Ravi recognised the Cripps Porter in the fading afterglow.

"Sorry, Bert. You'd been gone so long, I wondered if you needed a hand."

She scrutinised his companions, and Ravi felt like a schoolboy caught playing truant. Mr Weston, though, appeared unfazed.

"No, we're all done now, thank you," the Librarian said as easily as if he'd finished washing up. "Many hands make light work, isn't that right, gentlemen?"

"Indeed," said Ravi. "Always happy to help."

"Well, if that's all, Mr Weston," said Bert, reaching for the trolley, "I'd best be heading back."

"Many thanks, Bert," said the Librarian. "And you, Professor."

"Any time, Mr Weston," Ravi replied. "I'm happy to help."

The Librarian inclined his head before walking towards the Cripps Car Park.

"You coming, Professor?" Bert asked.

"You know what, I think I'll head off this way." Ravi indicated the path that led through the College gardens to the Backs and his terraced house in Newnham. "I'm about done for the evening."

"Right you are, Professor. I'll see you in the morning then."

"Good night, Bert, and you, Shirley."

Ravi left them, wondering what Shirley would make of tonight's encounter. Bert could be trusted to give nothing away, but, whatever the old Porter said, it must have looked odd to her. Still, there was nothing more to be done, and he was glad the trunk was safely tucked away in its secure new home.

The gravel path led through the trees behind Cripps, skirting the back of the College properties on Northampton Street. The night air was cool and fresh after the artificial atmosphere of the Archive, and he caught the occasional fragrance from a flower or tree as he passed between the beds and borders.

It wasn't long before he emerged into the Scholars' Garden, a popular venue for post-exam garden parties among the jubilant students. The pristine lawns were empty, save for a couple of rabbits, their bobbing hindquarters visible in the moonlight as they scampered into the undergrowth.

Ravi passed the nearby Fellows' Garden, taking the path to the Trinity Piece Gate leading onto the Backs. This was lit by a series of old Victorian lamp posts casting a warm orange glow over the gently flowing water of the Bin Brook. Weary from his day's worries and exertions, Ravi almost missed the figure leaning against the final lamp post. But then he spotted the red dot of a cigarette and a long plume of smoke.

"Evening, Professor. I was beginning to wonder if I'd missed you."

"Good evening, Jane. I wondered when I'd be seeing you again."

"I thought I'd wait until the School of Pythagoras business was complete. I didn't want to distract you from that."

"Can it not wait until the morning? I've had rather a tiring day."

"I'm afraid not, Professor, but we can walk and talk if you like."

"Very well, but you'll forgive me if I stick to the walking."

Ravi unlocked the tall, wrought-iron gate and waited while she stepped through. Then, he closed it behind them and led her along the path running behind Trinity, their footsteps crunching on the sandy gravel.

"Professor, I wanted to follow up on our conversation regarding Giles Chamberlain."

"Not that again. I told you, Jane. Giles and Raquel went to Mallorca. I received a postcard from them after we spoke."

She frowned. "Well, according to my sources, they didn't return to Mallorca. In fact, there is no record of Giles or Raquel leaving the UK or even Cambridge."

"I don't know, Jane. Maybe they decided to book into a local hotel. Do you really want to talk about Giles's love life now?"

"Professor. Neither Giles Chamberlain nor Raquel Vidal has been seen for weeks."

"How can you be sure?"

"Because I was the last person to see them alive."

He stopped walking.

"I saw them enter the Great Gate that night, and after that..." She shrugged. "Poof! Nothing."

"Are you saying they're hiding somewhere in College?"

"You tell me, Professor. One night they're here, and the next, they've disappeared off the face of the earth. Just like Alfonso Vidal."

And there it was. Not ten minutes ago, Ravi had stored away any records of the Gemini Passage in the College Archives. And here was Jane wanting to reopen the vexing saga again.

"I'm sorry, Jane. I can't think about it now. I need to clear my head, and that is best done after a good night's sleep."

"Very well, Professor. In that case, I'll see you in the morning."

"Good night, Jane." Ravi set off again, keen to put as much distance between himself and the spectre she had raised. As he strode along the path, a thought came to him, and he paused. Jane was still standing where he'd left her, watching him.

"I think you're wrong," he said. "About one thing at least."

"What was that?"

"I don't think you were the last person to see Giles."

She frowned. "No? Who then?"

"I'm sure you can work it out."

"Professor, I…"

"Bed, Jane," he said, turning for home.

"Ying?" she called out. "Or Trevor?"

"Good night, Jane."

Ravi set off through the trees, wondering how long it would take her. Not long, he decided. In many ways, Jane was very much like Giles. Too bright, brave and bloody-minded for her own good.

If those two ever got together…

Ravi tried to banish the thought. There was more than enough to worry about without that daunting prospect. What he needed now was a good night's sleep. Tomorrow, he would track down his source to allay Jane's concerns about Giles's whereabouts – and quieten his own too.

Chapter Eleven

The lake was still and serene in the early-morning light, a thin mist laying over the water's surface a few yards from where Giles crouched. It was a far cry from the dank and dingy cavern where he and Katya had sheltered overnight.

They had arrived at the falls just before nightfall, Giles clinging to the harpy's back as she raced between the steep-sided valley walls. Then, landing at the base of the cliff, she had led him to a naturally formed cavern concealed behind the wall of water.

Hidden from patrolling harpies, they had spent an uncomfortable night recovering from the journey. Though tired, Giles had found sleep elusive, his thoughts returning to Raquel. He'd been uncomfortable leaving her with Katya's father after seeing the ill-matched pair eyeing each other with undisguised hostility before he departed. While Katya had been adamant that the old harpy would keep Raquel safe, Giles tried not to think about what would happen if he failed to return with her brother.

But that hadn't been the only thing keeping him awake. As he'd lain in the darkness, wondering what the next day would bring, something had slapped against the rocks below the entrance. Gripping the ice axe, Giles had crossed the cave to stand in the opening. It had been hard to make out anything in the turbulent, frothing chaos below. But he hadn't been able to shake the feeling that there were more than undercurrents disturbing the surface.

Not that Katya had shown any concern. She had been leaning against the cave wall, watching him.

"I thought I heard something," he'd said.

"Nothing for you to worry about. You're safe here."

From harpies, maybe, he'd thought. *But what's in the water?*

"Get some rest," she'd told him before turning away. "I'll wake you before dawn."

That had been the end of the conversation, and Giles had returned to his damp corner. He'd managed a few hours of fitful sleep before Katya had woken him.

Now, they crouched among the boulders above the falls, the seven distant towers of the Citadel rising from the lake like city skyscrapers, glowing red in the early-morning light. To Giles, who had never seen them before, they were huge, even from afar.

It was hard to believe that somewhere among them, Raquel's brother was holed up in a cave, awaiting his fate. He wondered what sort of state Alfonso was in, if he were still alive.

As if reading his thoughts, Katya said, "There he is. Do you see him?"

"Who? Alfonso?"

"Who else?"

No doubt the harpy's eyes were keener than his; he'd struggle to make out anything smaller than a London Bus at this distance. He retrieved Mackenzie's binoculars from among the climbing gear in his backpack.

"Where exactly?"

"Follow the smoke."

Adjusting the lenses, he trained them on the columns, throwing the vertical flanks into sharp focus. There were regular lines of tiny openings across their surface.

"Are those caves?" he asked. "Those rows, I mean."

"Not there. Those are the nesting towers. The Matriarchy is the tall one in the centre."

The largest structure had a flat top, and the apertures were more regular and spaced out than those elsewhere. Lower down, the surface of the tower remained in its natural state, and the rock face was pitted with clefts and fissures from millennia of exposure to the elements. From one of these, a trail of smoke rose into the air.

"Got it!"

"That will be Alfonso's cell," she said. "Only he would have lit a fire."

To keep the wolves at bay, he thought. *Or harpies, in this case.*

Giles felt a sudden surge of kinship for the person in that distant tower – a genetic bond that traced its origin all the way back to those early hunter-gatherers sheltering behind the protective glow of a primitive fire as the shadows closed in. Across this lake, halfway up that cliff, sat someone like him, doing what their kind had always done to survive in a strange and hostile world.

It was why he was here. This was his purpose. Not to experience some wild adventure or to impress his girlfriend. But to find a man he'd never met – someone who, despite everything, had managed to stay alive this long – and return him to his family.

"Let's go," he said, getting up.

"Wait!" Katya grabbed his arm and pulled him back. "What are you doing?"

Giles shook her off.

"Going to get him. That's why we're here, isn't it?"

"And how do you propose to get across the lake?"

"I was assuming you were going to carry me. Unless you're expecting me to swim."

"You'd never make it," she said. "Don't let those waters fool you. Harpies are not the only predators here."

Giles thought about the slapping sound in the water the evening before.

"So, what do you propose?"

"The Citadel stands on a peninsula. Follow the shoreline, and you will reach where it joins the land. Go to the base of the Matriarchy and wait for me there."

It would take him most of the morning to walk around the towers to the far end of the lake. "A lift would have been nice."

"I have more pressing things to do."

"Such as?"

"The one person who can prevent you from getting to

Alfonso is my sister. I plan to draw her off."

"How do you intend to do that?"

"Tell her I have imprinted on Alfonso."

"Sorry?"

"It is what harpies do, before we mate with another."

Giles gaped at her. "You haven't, have you?"

Katya snorted a little too readily for his liking. "Of course not! But Olga doesn't know that. And if she thought I was trying to usurp her, she would kill me."

"Your sister?"

The harpy gave him a look that a Fellow might reserve for a foolish question at a Supervision.

"Few harpies allow a younger sibling to live. They're too much of a threat. It was Mother who protected me. She needed both of us alive."

"So, now you're going to give Olga an excuse to kill you?"

"I'm going to give her a reason to chase me."

"What if she doesn't take the bait?"

"She will. Believe me."

"And if she catches you?"

"Then you're on your own."

Their eyes met, and Giles nodded. "Fair enough."

There wasn't anything else to say, so he shouldered his pack. "I'd best be going."

"You have everything you need?"

Giles tapped the strap. "All here."

"Before you go, I wanted to ask you something."

"If it's money you want, I'm all out of cash."

"That object I found in the clearing... the metal box."

"The lighter, you mean?"

"For making fire?"

"That's the one."

"You said it was yours, but I saw it was addressed to Robert?"

"Oh, him. He was the old..." He was about to say Dean but realised that wouldn't mean much. "Someone I used to know."

"Used to?"

"He died last year." She went quiet at this, so he added, "Why do you ask?"

"No reason."

Giles knew deflection. He was, after all, a master of it. Then, he remembered something that had bothered him since he'd first discovered the lighter in the New Court cellars.

"Is the Mary on the lighter your mother?"

Katya stood still, shrouded in the mist from the nearby falls. Giles was reminded of a statue he had seen on an archaeological dig at a cemetery in Rome. They had called it the tombstone of a grieving angel. He doubted the sculptor could have found a better muse than Katya. When she spoke, her voice was sad.

"I think Mary died a long time ago."

Giles didn't know what to say. Then, Katya spread her wings.

"When you arrive at the Citadel, wait for my signal. We have one chance at this, so don't be late."

Before he could ask what that signal would be, she sprang from the rocks and disappeared into the haze.

Chapter Twelve

Alfonso was woken by sunshine pouring through the entrance to his cell. It took him a moment to realise that the second sun had already risen above the horizon and that his overnight fire was no more than a smouldering pile of ash.

He closed his eyes and recalled the horned stag's desperation when it had been dragged beneath the water in the Tower of Skulls. Would that image ever leave him?

A gust of wind blew flecks of warm ash into his face, and, blinking, he saw Olga hovering outside his cell. He struggled upright, the sharp pain in his side a reminder of how close he'd come to being gored during the previous night's trial.

The harpy landed on the ledge as he shuffled backwards, her huge outline blotting out the glare. He half expected to receive an admonishing blow for sleeping so late. Instead, she spoke.

"Show me."

"Is OK," he replied, surprised. "Is nothing."

Olga stepped closer and loomed over him. "Show me!"

The warning note in her voice left him little choice. Alfonso lifted his torn shirt to reveal the sections of cockroach carapace strapped to his torso. Even in the dim light of her shadow, he could make out the deep groove across the surface of his makeshift armour.

For a second or two, Olga stared at the chitinous plates. Then, she extended a talon and pushed roughly at the damaged section. The pain was excruciating, but Alfonso suffered her probing in silence.

"So," she said, straightening. "There was me thinking you were lucky."

"I was."

The harpy snorted but continued to consider him. "Still, few have bested a yalek."

Alfonso assumed she meant the stag with its wickedly twisting horns. He lowered his eyes, not wishing to provoke her.

"Come. Mother wishes to see you," Olga said, striding to the opening and launching herself into the air.

Blinding sunlight filled the cell once more. Squinting against the glare, Alfonso limped out onto the ledge. Moments later, Olga's powerful claws clamped onto his shoulders and hauled him into the air. As they soared upwards, Alfonso wondered what new torments were planned for him today. If Mary were involved, they would be grim indeed.

They made for a large opening on the upper level rather than heading for the summit where their sessions usually took place. He'd only glimpsed this in passing before, but as they drew near, he saw it was a balcony. Olga deposited him onto the wide ledge and hovered above him.

"Inside!" she said. "Well, go on!"

Alfonso stepped across the threshold into the shadowy darkness. This chamber was more extensive than the cell he was used to; it shared the same rectangular shape but was at least four times the size and probably twice the height.

As his eyes adjusted to the darkness, he saw the walls were decorated with the skulls of creatures he'd encountered and overcome since arriving in this world. There were centipedes, molevin boars, hydra and even a yalek, its long horns curving in different directions. Between these hung tapestries of animal hide, more of which were draped over a large mattress in the centre of the room. Alfonso expected Mary to be reclining there, but the bed was empty.

Confused, he turned around and froze. The balcony was empty, his minder gone. Instead, another figure detached itself from the shadows and moved between him and the opening. It was not Mary wielding her staff but something even more intimidating: a male harpy, its feathers bristling. Seeing it had him trapped, it emitted a harsh screech of bloodlust and pounced.

That might have been the end had the creature leapt without warning, but that split second was all Alfonso needed. He reached into his pocket, ducked under an outstretched claw and thrust his stylus into the creature's armpit. The sharp point punched through the soft tissue into the tendon beneath.

The harpy hissed, bringing its wing down to protect its exposed flank. The heavy limb slammed into Alfonso's hand, tearing his fingers free of the handle and leaving the blade wedged in the harpy's side.

Cursing his stupidity, Alfonso pitched forwards into a roll as the wounded creature lunged at him again. A claw raked the ground inches from where he had been, sending shards of red rock flying.

Springing into the air and pivoting, Alfonso narrowly avoided another scything blow that would have taken his legs from under him. If he'd still had his stylus, he might have finished it, stabbing down on his attacker's neck. Instead, he had to duck beneath the return swipe, the razor-sharp talons brushing his hair.

Knowing it was just a matter of time before one of its blows landed, Alfonso scrambled towards the balcony and the sanctuary of sunlight. It was then that Olga returned. The giant harpy dropped onto the ledge and spread her wings to block his escape.

"*Puta*!" he spat, diving to one side as his pursuer's claw narrowly missed raking him from behind. Rolling, he finished up by slamming against the wall. Something rattled, and he saw the yalek skull hanging above him.

Alfonso didn't hesitate. He tore it from its mounting just as the harpy lunged. One of the curved horns glanced off his attacker, but the other disappeared into the creature's gullet with a sickening, wet thud.

Breathless, he stared into the startled face of his attacker, inches from his own. He wasn't sure who was more surprised. Then, flecks of grey appeared deep within the harpy's pupils and spread across his eyes, head and neck.

The pressure against his chest eased, and Alfonso thrust

the body away from him. It toppled backwards and hit the floor, exploding into a billowing cloud that swirled around the room. When it finally settled, all that was left of the harpy was dust.

Alfonso let go of the yalek skull, which fell to the floor with a thud. Olga still stood on the balcony, wings spread, her expression fierce. Not with anger, though, Alfonso thought. Rather, she was exultant, basking in the carnage she had witnessed. When she turned to Alfonso, her look changed to one of hunger that made his skin crawl.

Tap, tap, tap, tap, tap.

Mary stepped from behind her daughter, her staff rapping her applause.

"Very good," she said, surveying the scene. "You trained this one well, my dear."

Olga didn't respond at first. When she did, her voice was husky. "Thank you, Mother."

The woman crossed the room to the pile of dust and bent down to retrieve something. With a start, Alfonso recognised his bone stylus. Wiping it on her sleeve, she examined it.

"Hmm." She ran a finger over the sharp point. "They say the pen is mightier than the sword."

Instead of handing it back to him, she tossed it on the floor and brought the heel of her staff down hard, breaking it in two.

"No!" Alfonso dropped to his knees in shock.

He picked up the splintered shards of bone with his blood-covered hands. How many times had his hidden blade saved him? It had been there in the molevin tunnels, the

Hive and even the river when needed. But it wasn't just a weapon to him. It had been his record keeper during those long nights in the cave, a means of recording his survival and a symbol of his continued existence. And now it was gone, crushed by this woman.

He looked up at her. "Why did you do that?"

"You won't be needing it anymore." She indicated her daughter. "Olga has something else planned for you tonight."

Olga nodded, her voice a low rasp when she said, "I do."

There was something far more frightening in her eyes than hate. He saw in her a deep, feral craving that sent a chill through him. It felt like a shadow had fallen over his world. But as her face darkened, he realised the same shadow had fallen over her.

"Katya," he breathed.

The giant harpy stood on the balcony, her wings spread wide in challenge.

"Alfonso is mine," she declared.

Olga spun around, feathers bristling. "Yours? He is mine! By right of trial."

Katya didn't flinch. "He was never yours to have. Not since the Hive. From then, he was bound to me."

Olga rounded on Alfonso, eyes wild. For a split second, he thought she would leap at him.

"Enough!" said Mary, stepping between them and holding up her staff. "The boy has passed Olga's trial, Katya. He is bound to her now."

"Why? Because you say so?"

"Yes, Daughter, I do."

"And what if you are wrong?"

The chamber went very still. The mother and her two daughters glared at one another, Alfonso's presence forgotten. Mary spoke quietly, but her words were laden with menace.

"Are you challenging my authority?"

"No, Mother," she said firmly. "I am challenging Olga."

A low hiss escaped the other harpy's lips, but Katya didn't back down. Facing her sister, she said, "You are a thief, Sister. You claimed my victory over the Hive. You took the dying Matriarch's head from my grasp. You are not taking a mate that isn't yours. He's coming with me."

Alfonso swallowed. He had never seen Katya utter a word against her sister, though he'd long suspected their mutual hatred. Olga launched herself at her accuser, claws scything through the air. But Katya was ready, springing out of reach and batting the attack aside with her wing.

"Stop!" Mary cried, raising her staff and rushing forwards.

Alfonso reacted instinctively, stretching out his leg and catching her above the ankle. Mary sprawled across the floor, cursing. Distracted, Katya was almost decapitated by a vicious swipe from her sister. Olga redoubled her attacks, screeching as she drove her sibling back towards the ledge.

Desperate to help, Alfonso searched for a weapon. His stylus was ruined, but the yalek skull was nearby. He grabbed one of the horns and swung it against the wall, and the impact smashed the crown apart, freeing up the base of the horn. He lifted his curved weapon and sprang at Olga's exposed back.

The staff hit him in the midriff, knocking all the wind from his body. Alfonso doubled over, collapsing to his knees.

"Stay out of this, boy!" Mary yelled, swinging again.

He raised his makeshift sword, which was knocked from his hand by another stinging blow. Wincing, Alfonso met Katya's eyes. Then, the staff smacked his head, and he went down.

The last thing he remembered was a terrible screech echoing around the chamber.

Chapter Thirteen

Giles hurried along the shoreline, keeping clear of the deceptively calm waters. After Katya had left him, he had made good time, looping around the eastern side of the lake until it joined the peninsula.

His only scare had come when he'd dropped down from the boulders and found himself surrounded by male harpies. But the creatures hadn't flinched, their calcified bodies standing in stony silence beneath the midday suns.

Giles was used to seeing inert harpies high on the cliff walls during the day, but to find them standing in the open had come as a surprise. Like Katya's father, these males had either a limb or sections of wing missing, rendering them flightless. Perhaps that was why they were clustered together, seeking protection in numbers. It was either that, he thought, or take to the forests and live a feral existence on the outskirts of harpy society.

The sight of so many mutilated statues had made him uneasy. There was something profoundly wrong happening here, and the sooner he found Raquel's brother and escaped this place, the better.

Giles had so far kept close to the shore, where the going was more straightforward. But when he reached the peninsula, he cut inland, following the line of a fallen column to obscure his approach.

The towers of the Citadel rose in front of him, their jagged peaks thrusting into the clear sky. The columns had looked tall when he'd first seen them from the top of the waterfall, but the closer he came, the more he appreciated how massive they were. Even though he was an experienced climber, the prospect of scaling the largest one, where Alfonso was kept, was daunting.

Keeping low, he made his way to an outfall of rock that gave him a good view of the Matriarchy. There he squatted, breathing fast. The suns were high overhead, and his bandana and shirt were soaked with sweat. He drank from his canteen as he peered over the ridge at the lines of statues covering the intervening ground.

So, it's not just mad dogs and Englishmen, he thought. He remembered that fateful Christmas morning when he'd told Raquel he would find her brother. Now he was here, in some god-forsaken world, about to make good on that promise.

"The things we do for love."

The Matriarchy dominated the towers around it, its peak standing head and shoulders above the others. It would be one of the longest solo climbs he'd done with no partner to belay for him. The one saving grace was that the column of red stone hadn't endured the ravages of time unscathed. Exposure over millennia to the blistering suns had left its side cracked and scarred by fissures running from base to summit. These offered him a relatively straightforward route up vertical chimneys where he could jam his hands and feet to make the ascent. And he could use the long length of rope to abseil back down. He just hoped Alfonso would be in a fit state to do so.

While Giles was trying to locate the cave where he had seen the smoke earlier, Katya arrived. Her twin shadows passed overhead, racing over the standing statues before shooting up the tower wall. Following their progress, he caught sight of her graceful outline, wings spread wide as she glided down and hovered outside the cave.

Had she changed her mind and was about to rescue Alfonso herself? He expected an alarm or another harpy to sweep out from the tower to intercept her. But then she soared upwards and paused outside a broader opening higher up the tower, dipping her wings from side to side before dropping onto the ledge and disappearing inside.

Cue Giles, he thought. *Enter stage left!*

Scrambling from his hiding place, he sprang from the rocks and landed among the stone harpies.

"Sorry, chaps, can't hang about. Important meeting."

Giles ran between the rows of stationary harpies, the pack with its climbing gear thumping against his back. He'd covered less than half the distance to the tower when he heard her screech.

It was a sound he would never forget, so full of anguish that it brought him skidding to a halt. More screeches followed, bitter and angry now, and what might have been a human cry, high pitched and strident. It didn't sound like the family reunion was going well.

There was a flicker of movement around the opening far above him. Then, Katya erupted from the cave in a cloud of dust and feathers. Moments later, another, larger harpy appeared on the ledge.

Olga, he thought.

Katya's sister emitted a shriek of such deranged hate that Giles felt frozen to the spot. Then, she launched into the air and set off after her sibling, wings beating a frantic rhythm.

"No!"

The desperate cry came from the cave, and a figure appeared on the ledge. But it wasn't Raquel's brother. It was a woman with long, dark hair holding some sort of staff.

Mary, he thought.

For some time, Katya's mother stood at the edge, a diminutive figure against the tower of red rock. Giles didn't move, hidden among the hundreds of stationary harpies spread across the peninsula. After what seemed an age, the Citadel's Matriarch disappeared back inside, and Giles let out a long breath.

"Thanks, fellas," he said to the nearest statues. "I owe you one."

He adjusted the straps on his pack and began to run for the tower's base.

******

Alfonso woke propped against the cave wall, his wrists bound behind him. He ignored the pain pulsing through his temples and opened his eyes.

Mary sat cross-legged in the entrance as one of the suns dipped towards the horizon. With her hood pulled over her head and staff resting across her knees, she looked like a sorceress waiting for the sunset.

"Awake, are you?"

"*Si.*" He wondered how long they had been sitting there. "Why have you tied me?"

"I think that's fairly obvious, don't you?"

Through the drumming in his head, he thought back to the fight between Mary's daughters before his foolish attempt to intervene.

"Where are they?" They weren't in the chamber.

"Halfway to the lowlands by now, I expect. Olga is hunting her sister even as we speak."

"But why?"

Mary's voice became bitter.

"Because of you, fool."

Alfonso struggled to understand.

"Katya said she mated with you, so her sister now sees her as a rival. Had you not interfered, I might have been able to talk sense into them. Now, Olga will hunt down her younger sibling and kill her."

"Can't we do something?"

Mary slammed her staff into his stomach, doubling him over.

"Do? Don't you think you've done enough?"

She struck him again, and his ribs would have broken for sure if not for his carapace armour. He could barely breathe from the pain.

"That's right! Stay quiet while you still can. When Olga returns, peace is the last thing you'll enjoy."

She stomped across the chamber, lifted an animal skin and disappeared through a hidden opening in the wall. Moments later, there was the heavy thud of a concealed door closing.

Alfonso remained motionless, his body wracked with pain and despair, any lingering hope fading with the dipping sun. The tunnels, the raid and the trials had led to this moment. He was beaten and alone, waiting for his nemesis to return and exact her revenge.

The one thing that had kept him going over recent days was a growing conviction that Katya would save him. Now that had been taken from him. Worse, he had all but condemned her to a senseless death.

This knowledge hung over him as he waited for Olga's return and his ultimate humiliation. No doubt she would ensure he could never threaten her line again.

Alfonso tried not to imagine how that end would be, staring into those hateful eyes as she took everything from him. This appalling prospect, more than anything else, awoke something inside him. Not hope. That was gone. No, it was something less worthy but no less motivating.

Spite.

After all they had done to him, now more than ever, Alfonso wanted to hurt Olga – and Mary, for that matter. To deny them this final thing they had planned for him.

The shards of his stylus lay in the dust on the chamber floor. Gritting his teeth, he managed to lever himself onto his front. Then, ignoring the spasms of pain, he shuffled inch by inch over to where they lay. Finally, Alfonso rolled onto his side and, feeling with his fingers, gripped the broken shaft.

The finely crafted tool had once been like an extension of his arm. Now it felt like a shattered limb – one that, thanks to Mary, had a jagged edge. Alfonso began to work at his bindings by pressing the shattered stump against the strands of molevin gut.

It took him a long time to sever the sinewy material, which was as resilient as the creature from which it came. But once it finally gave, his hands were free. Rubbing his wrists, he checked the wall hangings for signs of movement while he listened for the scuff of approaching footsteps. There was only the sound of his own breathing. Alfonso eased himself to his feet, paused for a moment or two to steady himself, then walked towards the sky framed in the cave mouth.

When he reached the ledge, Alfonso stopped. The alien landscape was so familiar to him, with its tall columns, dark lake and distant falls. Though he longed to escape this world, he had to admit it had a certain harsh beauty. Perhaps that is what he would take with him, rather than the bitter memories of all he'd had to endure here.

No. Those wouldn't be his last thoughts. He wouldn't allow anything to displace the precious memories of his family. His mother, his father and, of course, his sister, Raquel.

Closing his eyes, Alfonso let out a long breath and stepped forwards.

A hand grabbed his arm and pulled him back.

"I wouldn't do that if I were you," said a voice in his ear.

Alfonso reacted instinctively, slamming his head back into his assailant's face. He heard a satisfying yelp of pain and felt the grip on his arm loosen. Grabbing the wrist, Alfonso yanked it forwards, swinging its owner towards the ledge. Only when he saw the rope and climbing gear did he hesitate, arresting his momentum to leave his attacker teetering on the edge.

For a moment, they stood there, finely balanced, like two dancers frozen in time. Alfonso stared at his unexpected partner in shock and confusion. The face was hidden by a hand clasped over a bloody lip. But there was no mistaking the hair: not long and dark like Mary's. Instead, it was a wavy, bleached blond. And the voice, though muffled, was indignant rather than fierce.

"What the hell did you do that for?"

"I..." Alfonso stammered. "Who are you?"

"Giles," the man muttered, spitting blood. "Giles Chamberlain. A friend of your sister."

"My sister?"

"You know, Raquel. Drop dead gorgeous and fights like a cat."

Alfonso gasped. But then he remembered Mary knew his sister's name. "I don't believe you!" He loosened his hold on the man's wrist, causing him to sway backwards.

"Whoa, hold on!" The stranger glanced at the drop. "You live on the island of Mallorca. Your parents have a villa with a balcony overlooking the bay."

"And you know this how?"

"I stayed there over Christmas. Well, in the guest room outside, by the kennels."

Alfonso couldn't believe this.

"Yes, I thought it was harsh too. Still, I got to know old Chara. Bit of a softie really, she's..."

Alfonso didn't let him finish. He hauled his would-be rescuer back from the ledge and hugged him, ignoring his bruised ribs.

"*Gracias*, Giles! *Gracias*!"

"No problem, my friend." Giles patted him on the back. "Glad to finally meet you."

Alfonso was reluctant to let his sweat-stained companion go, needing to reassure himself that this was not some vivid dream. But a scornful voice broke them apart.

"How very touching."

From the back of the cave, a hooded figure was watching them.

"Aren't you going to introduce your friend, Alfonso?"

"Stay back!" he said, hands bunching into fists.

"Or what, boy? You really think you can better me?" Mary moved closer, holding her staff to one side.

"I've got this," whispered Giles, thrusting something into Alfonso's hand as he stepped in front of him. "Make sure it's good and tight."

It was a climbing harness.

"Forgive us," Giles raised his voice. "Caught up in the moment. I'm Giles, by the way, and you must be Mary."

Slipping the harness around his waist, Alfonso noted the

surprise in Mary's voice as she replied, "You are well informed, I see. I'll have to teach Alfonso not to be so free with his tongue."

"Alfonso?" Giles smiled, glancing briefly at the harness before facing her again. "Oh, no, it wasn't him who told me to expect you. It was an old friend of yours."

"Really?" Mary's voice was level, but Alfonso could hear her interest.

"I say 'friend'..." Giles reached into his pocket and stepped closer to her. "I suspect he may have been more than that."

There was no mistaking he had her attention now, and Alfonso used the time to adjust the harness around his waist and thighs.

"I have no idea who you are talking about."

"Really? You mean you don't remember Robert Mackenzie?"

Mary stood unnaturally still.

"Ah, so you do remember. In that case, I'm sorry to be the bearer of bad news."

"What do you mean?"

"Robert is dead, Mary. He died last year."

Alfonso thought he heard a small gasp.

"I did, however, find this among his possessions."

Giles held up an old lighter, its tarnished surface stained with soot. Mary's eyes widened in recognition.

"I thought I'd return it to you. It was, after all, your gift."

He tossed it across the room. Mary hesitated for a fraction of a second before doing something Alfonso had never seen before. She dropped her staff and dived for the tumbling lighter.

Whether she caught it or not, he never saw. Because at that moment, Giles turned around and hooked a carabiner into the loop of his harness.

"You trust me, right?"

"What? I..."

Without waiting for an answer, Giles grabbed Alfonso and leapt from the ledge.

Chapter Fourteen

"Hey, come back!"

Ravi chased the little white rabbit as it scampered through the forest of impossibly high towers, all too aware of the dark shapes circling overhead. As with all dreams, every time he lunged for it, the capricious creature kept hopping out of reach, its paws kicking clouds of red dust in his face. Finally, Ravi lost his temper, yelling, "Do you want to get yourself eaten?"

His quarry flashed a toothy smile that didn't belong to a rabbit but to Giles Chamberlain.

"Watch out, Professor," he said. "The Queen is looking for you."

"What Queen?"

"The Queen of hearts, of course." Its nose twitched. "And guess what she wants?"

"What?" Ravi replied.

"Your head, Professor!"

Bright sunlight lit the clearing, and a grey pallor spread over the creature's white fur, turning the cheeky smile into a rictus grin.

"No!" Ravi cried, waking abruptly. His duvet had twisted around his sweat-soaked body, and the sun streamed through his bedroom window. Panting, he glanced at the bedside clock. Before he could stop himself, he gasped, "I'm late!"

Struggling clear of the bedclothes, Ravi climbed out of bed, Lewis Carroll's story buzzing around in his head. It was still there half an hour later as he hurried across the New Court lawns with the Trinity clock striking ten.

"Yes, yes!" he muttered, irritated with the interminable timepiece for reminding him of his missed breakfast appointment with Aurelia. Not that she'd notice. His dark mood was only lightened by the lack of bird droppings on the path. The Canada geese who habitually fouled the lawns along the riverbank were nowhere to be seen.

The early-morning rush-hour of students bound for lectures was long since over. He only encountered a few maintenance staff repairing the cobbles and a small group of tourists appreciating the Shrewsbury Tower.

Skirting past them, Ravi headed for the turreted staircase on the opposite side of the court. Here he hoped to find the last person to have spoken to the white rabbit of his dreams. If he wasn't too late.

He strode up the stairs, passing the room indicator confirming that G.E. Chamberlain was OUT. The old timbers creaked, but other than that, the staircase was silent. Had he missed his opportunity? No: the outer door to Giles's room was open and the inner one ajar.

"Hello?" he called and was rewarded with a yelp of

surprise. Inside the room, a Bedder stood by the desk, duster in hand.

"Oh, you startled me, Professor."

"Forgive me..." – he glanced at the woman's tunic – "Rose. I should have knocked. I was looking for Giles."

"He's not in, Professor."

The wood-panelled room was spotless, the bed linen crisp and the kitchen cupboard lacking the usual unwashed mugs and plates.

"Well, I commend you on your work, Rose. I've rarely seen a student room look so tidy."

"That's because he isn't back yet. Believe me, you'll know when he is."

"Any idea when that will be?"

Her eyes narrowed slightly. "You're not his Tutor, are you?"

"No, I'm not."

"Because that would be Professor Winterbottom, wouldn't it?"

"It would, yes."

"And you're not one of his Supervisors?"

"Again, no. I teach Astronomy."

"So, why do you want to see Giles, if you don't mind me asking, Professor?"

Some Fellows might have baulked at being cross-examined like this. However, Ravi was impressed that the Bedder was so protective of her student.

"Giles has been... assisting me with something."

A creak from the staircase made them both start. Rose

crossed the room and checked outside before closing the outer door.

"Can't be too careful. Sound does tend to travel on these old staircases," she said. "Sorry, Professor, you were saying?"

"What? Oh, yes, I wanted to catch up with Giles about a research project."

"The one in the Old Library? I expect you've come to pick up the camera."

"Sorry?"

"The one he got last term. He was very excited about it. Well, you know how he is."

Ravi wondered where she was going with this.

"I'm relieved you came. I thought I might have damaged it."

"What, the camera?"

"It wasn't my fault, Professor. I was vacuuming under the bed, and then I heard this bump. The next thing I know, it's him talking to that librarian lady."

Something shifted in Ravi's stomach.

"I didn't mean to pry," the Bedder continued. "I was just checking nothing was broken. Anyway, that's when I saw you."

"Me?"

She nodded. "That's how I recognised you just now."

Ravi stared at her.

"Oh no, I've not said too much, have I? I didn't want to get Giles into more trouble. He's good enough at doing that himself, as I'm sure you well know."

"Quite," he said, completely at a loss. "Perhaps if you could show me?"

"As long as you promise not to tell the Dean. Giles is not exactly in her good books."

"I won't tell anyone, Rose."

Perhaps the Bedder sensed his sincerity because she nodded and crossed to the bed. She pulled out a cardboard delivery box from underneath and placed it on the coffee table.

Ravi lifted the flaps. Inside, surrounded by climbing socks and base layers, was a video camera, its heavy-duty plastic cover marbled in a woodland camouflage scheme. It was the type of device he'd seen on nature programmes set up outside a wild animal's warren.

"You can see the ON button there." Rose indicated a knob on the side. "That's what I must have knocked with the vacuum cleaner."

The camera was surprisingly heavy. After examining the controls, Ravi switched it on, and a ghostly blue image appeared on the viewfinder. Given the high angle of the shot, it took him a while to realise what it was. "The Old Library," he said, half to himself.

"I figured as much," the Bedder said over his shoulder. "I went there once on an open day. Thought I should, seeing as I work here. It was like something out of Harry Potter, begging your pardon, Professor."

Ravi was too focused on the screen to reply. A hunched academic had emerged from the hidden office at the far end of the vaulted room. Mesmerised, he watched himself walk along the length of the library and disappear into an alcove near the staircase.

Even with the wide-angle lens, it was impossible to see exactly where he had deposited the leather-bound tome he'd been carrying. Still, it was clear in which section to look. And, of course, Giles had already seen the ancient almanack when he'd found Ravi studying it in the Old Librarian's Office.

"You sly fox," he muttered.

"Professor?"

The Bedder's question reminded Ravi he was not alone.

"Forgive me, Rose. I was... surprised, that's all."

"Well, you won't be the first nor the last when it comes to that young man."

"Of that I have no doubt."

Rose smiled, and Ravi thought Giles was lucky to have this good woman as his Bedder.

"Tell me, Rose, have you spoken to anyone else about this recording? Anyone at all?"

"Of course not, Professor. As I said, I didn't want to get Giles into trouble."

Probably too late for that, he thought. "That's good. We must keep the camera's existence and its contents confidential."

"Mum's the word, Professor. You can trust me. I won't tell a soul."

Ravi believed her.

"Shall we put it back?" she asked.

Giles hadn't erased the disk, which suggested he'd wanted someone to find it – perhaps Nick, Annabel or himself – once they'd realised he had gone missing. And though Ravi wanted to destroy the evidence of where the

Gemini cypher was hidden, the camera was still Giles's property, and Rose would know that.

"Yes, I think that would be best." He handed it to her. "I suggest you put it back as you found it."

While she did so, Ravi reflected on how foolish he'd been not to anticipate all of this. After discovering the location of the Gemini Gate in the New Court cellar, it had been inevitable, given his insatiable curiosity, that Giles would try to open it. To have slipped a surveillance camera past the ever-vigilant Mr Weston and deployed it in the Old Library showed how far he'd been willing to go. Ravi had to hand it to the boy: Giles had the makings of an excellent Research Fellow. If he lived that long.

"There we go." The Bedder finished straightening the duvet to hang over the edge of the frame, hiding the space underneath.

"Thank you, Rose."

She planted her hands on her hips. "So, Professor, if it wasn't about the camera, why did you come up here?"

"Oh, yes," he said, wondering how he had forgotten. "I wanted to ask whether Giles had spoken to you before he left."

"Before the holidays, you mean?"

"Yes. I believe he may have had someone staying with him. A young lady, perhaps?"

The Bedder's expression darkened. "Oh, her!"

"I take it you and Raquel are not on good terms?"

Rose bristled. "I'm civil to all our guests, Professor."

"Of course," he said, surprised by her sudden transformation.

"Whatever my feelings towards the individual," she added, the colour rising on her neck.

Ravi remained silent and was rewarded with an explanation for her outburst that the Bedder was only too keen to share.

"Don't get me wrong, Professor, the young lady was perfectly respectable and all. It's just that..." She paused. "Well, Giles, he's a lovely lad. Cheeky bugger at times, begging your pardon, but his heart's in the right place."

Giles had selflessly rescued Ravi from the creature, first on the Bridge of Sighs and later on the Chapel Tower. As for the New Court cellars, he doubted any of them would have emerged alive had Giles not set the hooded statue on fire.

"I think we can all agree on that."

"I could see in her eyes that she didn't really care for him. Not the way he does for her. You know how it is, Professor, sometimes, you can just tell."

Ravi remembered the first time he'd introduced Mary to Robert. How she had gazed at his friend in a way she had never done with him.

"I mean, we all want to believe that someone loves us, don't we? So we tell ourselves they do, even when it's obvious they don't. That's what I see happening with Giles and this Raquel." She sighed. "I worry, Professor, that he will get himself hurt."

You and me both, he thought. "Did Giles give you any indication about where they were going?"

"Not in so many words, but somewhere high up, I reckon."

"What makes you think that?"

"Because he took all his climbing gear. You know, the ropes and those metal clip things. Oh, and that dreadful-looking axe. She made sure of that."

"Raquel?"

"Said it might come in handy." She pulled a face. "If I'm honest, Professor, she was a bit scary."

Ravi had thought the same when Raquel had buried the axe in the creature's chest on the Chapel Tower.

"Anyway, she didn't look right, Professor. Neither of them did. Not like they were about to go on holiday."

"How do you mean?"

"When I go away with the family, everyone's excited. You know, looking forward to it, like. But those two, they were…" She frowned. "I'm sorry, Professor, I'm not good with words."

"It's all right, Rose," Ravi said. "Take your time."

"I know this is going to sound daft, but they looked like my nephew, Callum. He's in the Army, you see. Anyway, they looked how he did when he went off to Basra those times."

That, more than anything, told him all he needed to know.

"Anyway, that's when he gave me the card."

"Sorry?"

"That postcard he sent you, Professor. The one from Spain."

"He gave that to you?"

"Said he wouldn't have time to post it himself. Asked if

I would pop it in your pigeonhole after the holiday. Seemed a bit odd at the time, seeing as how it already had a stamp. I should have realised then something was going on."

"Of course," Ravi murmured. There had been no postmark.

"Then there's that." She pointed at a thick brown package sitting on the desk.

The large manilla envelope was similar to the one containing the trunk keys Ravi had found in his study. This one was addressed to Professor Jones, Department of Archaeology, Cambridge University. Ravi picked up the package, which contained a weighty document.

"There was this note with it," Rose added, reaching into her tunic pocket and handing over the neatly folded piece of paper.

Dear Rose,

I hope you are well and had a good Easter.

The envelope contains my dissertation, which I've been working on since last summer. Believe it or not, I managed to finish it in the end. (Don't look so surprised! I had it all under control – honest!)

Anyway, it needs to be in by 14 April, so I wonder if you could drop it off at the Porters' Lodge when you have a moment? Thanks ever so much!

Looking forward to seeing you when I'm back.

Hugs and kisses,

Giles xxx

"He wasn't sure he'd be back in time," he murmured, almost to himself.

"That's what I thought, Professor. But why didn't he hand it in before he left?"

So it would appear he was back in Cambridge, Ravi thought, *even when he wasn't.*

Ravi closed his eyes, not wanting to think about what that meant.

"Professor? Are you all right? I've not done something wrong, have I?"

Ravi stirred. "On the contrary, Rose, you did the right thing sharing this with me. I'm glad Giles felt he could trust you." She smiled, her relief obvious. "As you must trust me now."

"Of course, Professor."

"I'm going to see if I can find Giles. Until then, we need to keep his absence secret. The last thing he needs is anyone asking questions about him."

"What about his lectures, Professor?"

"People skip lectures all the time."

She bristled. "Not him. I make sure of that. Get him out of bed every morning. And that's no mean task, I can tell you."

"Well, I doubt many lecturers will mind him missing one or two this term. Some might even be relieved."

"But won't he need to know all that stuff for his exams?"

Ravi was touched by her concern; she must have no idea her wayward student was considered a genius, even by Cambridge standards. "Provided that gets in on time" – he indicated the package on the desk – "Giles should do fine."

"Well, if you're sure, Professor." She didn't sound convinced.

"I am," he said. "So, are we agreed? We keep this quiet until I return?"

"Fair enough. I'll make sure this package gets delivered on time."

Ravi smiled. "Thank you, Rose."

Around the room, photos of a happy-go-lucky Giles grinned back at them, and Ravi felt an overwhelming urge to be out of there.

"In that case, I'd best be going," he said. "I have matters to attend to."

"You take care, Professor," she said, "and bring him home."

Ravi wanted to say he would, but the words refused to come. All he could manage was a nod.

Chapter Fifteen

Nick closed his file and glanced at Katie and Darius sitting on the opposite sofa. Their first Criminal Law Supervision of term had been every bit as tough as he had imagined, despite hitting the books over the holidays. Their Supervisor, Dr Esdee Jones, had been a former prosecutor, and her questioning had exposed his knowledge gaps with forensic precision.

Katie had done her best to cover for him. Still, the only one emerging with any credit after a gruelling hour of cross-examination was Darius. With his mother a practising barrister and his father a solicitor, their friend could recite evidential procedure as easily as his times tables.

As they rose from their seats, Nick made a mental note to consult Darius when it came to revision. That would be a lot less daunting than calling on Dr Jones again.

"Thank you, everyone," their Supervisor said, returning to her desk. "I'll see you in two weeks for what will be our final Supervision this term." She eased into her chair and switched on her computer screen. "Make sure you read through your essays again, particularly my notes in the margins. Some of those may prove valuable come the exam."

"So you're saying some of those will be coming up?" Darius asked, full of himself after his stellar performance.

Dr Jones swivelled in her chair and treated him to a look that would have humbled a grizzled defence attorney.

"Do I need to humour that with a response, Mr Levy?"

Darius's smile faltered under her unflinching stare. "I thought I'd try my luck. You know, he who dares and all that."

Katie glanced at Nick; they could both see the car crash coming.

"First, Mr Levy," Dr Jones said. "I find it disappointing that you think I would show favouritism to one of my students."

"Of course not, I–"

"Second, you can imagine how damning the evidence would appear if students of the Fellow setting the Criminal Law exam outperformed their peers from other colleges across the University."

"No, but–"

"Finally, luck has nothing to do with your ability to perform well at the end-of-year exams. That will be down to how you apply yourself in the coming weeks. Do I make myself clear?"

"Perfectly, Dr Jones."

Nick had to give Darius credit for maintaining eye contact. A lesser person would have quailed under such a brutal summation.

"Excellent," she said, returning to her screen. "Now,

don't you all have things to do? Reviewing the evidential case law, Mr Wood; or Lord Denning's judgement, Miss Price?"

"Of course," Katie said, heading for the door. "Thank you, Dr Jones."

Darius hurried after her, mumbling "Good night" over his shoulder.

Nick almost made it out before she said, "Mr Wood?"

He paused in the doorway. "Yes, Dr Jones."

She appeared absorbed by something on her screen.

"You seem to have grasped the concept of *habeas corpus* that we discussed last term."

"I suppose so," he replied. "I read up on it over the holiday."

"Clearly. Well, keep it up." Her fingers played over the keyboard.

"Was there anything else?" he asked.

"No, that is all, Mr Wood. I'll see you in a fortnight."

"Right," he said and ducked through the doorway.

He found the others waiting for him at the bottom of the stairs.

"There you are!" Katie said. "We were about to send up a rescue party."

"We were worried she might have singled you out for additional feedback," Darius said. "Something involving electrodes or thumbscrews."

Nick shook his head. "Nothing like that." He had no intention of sharing the compliment he'd received, though. "Are we done then?"

"Done in," said Darius as they set off across the court.

"Well, you did ask for it," Katie laughed. "Suggesting she'd do something unethical like throw an exam was never going to go down well, was it?"

"OK, not my best moment, I grant you. But I wasn't being serious. It was just that everything had been going so well."

"I think that's the point," Nick said.

"What do you mean?"

Nick shrugged. "Well, you're both smashing it at Supervisions. I guess she doesn't want you getting overconfident."

They stopped walking.

"Is that what she told you?" Darius asked.

"What? No, of course not," Nick said. "I've been sitting across from you this past year, and it's pretty obvious you're both going to get a first. I expect she's trying to make sure."

"I hope you're right," Darius muttered. "My mum will kill me if I get anything less."

"And you, Nick?" Katie asked.

"What, a first?" He scoffed. "No way – 2.2 tops."

"No, I meant, what did she say to you?"

He thought for a moment, then said, "What was needed."

Katie smiled.

"Well, I know what I need." Darius turned towards the College Bar. "A stiff drink. Who's with me?"

"Sure, why not?" Katie said. "Nick?"

He shook his head. "May Ball meeting."

"Oh yeah?" Darius asked. "Not a drummer of some band, are you?"

"Security."

"Oh, I see. Well, if you finish early, you know where we are."

Nick made his way back through College to an angular building opposite the Cripps Porters' Lodge. Built as a summer conference centre, the Fisher Building was used by students during term time for meetings and JCR social events.

Following the signs, Nick took the stairs to the Castlereagh Room and pulled open a door marked MAY BALL SECURITY BRIEFING. Inside, lots of students were milling around, many of whom he recognised from the rugby team, including Trevor, the Captain. And standing on one of the long rows of seats was Aden, giving a pretty good impression of someone punting.

Spotting Nick over the heads of his laughing audience, he called out "Woody!" before jumping down and edging through the crowd to join him.

"Hey, bro, I thought you were going to be late. How'd the Supervision go?"

"Survived it."

"Can't say fairer than that. I was showing this lot here my punting technique."

As far as Nick was aware, Aden's only experience had been paddling a punt from one side of the punt pool to the other. That his friend hadn't ended up in the water had been nothing short of a miracle.

"Anyway," Aden continued, "we have some familiar faces here, as you can see."

There were several rugby players on the far side of the room, near a cluster of girls, one of whom was attracting a fair number of admiring looks. The tall, long-haired beauty chose that moment to flash Nick a dazzling smile.

"Hello, hello," Aden murmured. "Who's that then?"

"Naomi Clarke," Nick replied. "She's Annabel's neighbour on A staircase."

"What's she doing security for?" Aden asked. "You'd have thought she'd have people queuing up to ask her to the Ball."

"She broke up with her boyfriend last term." Nick remembered his ugly confrontation with Colin outside Naomi's room. "A complete git."

"So, she's unattached?"

"Yeah, but I'd give her space if I were you. It didn't end well."

"OK, noted." Then, Aden murmured, "I think she's coming over. You do the introductions while I stand here looking irresistible."

Nick shook his head and waited as Naomi crossed the room, the crowd parting before her.

"Nick!" she said, smiling. "I didn't expect to see you here. How was your holiday?"

"Great, thanks," he replied, wondering if she knew he'd been staying with Annabel. "You?"

"Oh, so-so. Revision, going to the gym, that sort of thing."

"Another gym-goer, eh?" Aden piped up.

Naomi turned to him, and for the first time since Nick

had known him, his friend started to babble.

"I mean, Nick and I, we go together. You know, stretches, circuits, weights..."

"Oh, I'm not into anything heavy like that. Just a few self-defence classes."

"That's good," Aden said. "Well, I can see how that could be useful, you know, with the May Ball Security and everything."

"Naomi, this is Aden, by the way."

"Rugby player, right?" She extended her hand. "I saw you play in Cuppers last term."

"You did?" His eyes lit up before his composure returned. "Yeah, well, Nick's the real player. I run around the pitch making a nuisance of myself."

She smiled before turning back to Nick. "You're interested in doing security too?"

"I'm not sure yet. Aden suggested I take a look."

"Beats moping in your room," Aden said.

Naomi gave him a quizzical look before a loud voice called out, "OK, everyone! Let's get this show on the road."

Trevor was standing next to the projector screen alongside his girlfriend, Ying.

"Come on," said Aden, "let's grab a good seat."

They sat in the middle of the front row, Naomi choosing the chair next to Nick.

"All right, people, settle down," said Ying as Trevor dimmed the lights and she flicked on the projector.

An image of St John's College appeared, the night sky above New Court lit up with fireworks.

"Right then, for those of you here for the usual Pilates class, you're in the wrong room."

"Oh no, not again!" Aden said, rising from his chair before sitting to a chorus of laughter.

"OK," Ying continued, "hopefully, the rest of you are interested in working on the security detail at this year's Ball. This will be the biggest and best event in the Cambridge calendar."

There were a few cheers at this from the Redboys at the back.

"But that means it will also be the most sought-after ticket in town, and therefore plenty of people will try to crash it. That's where you lot come in."

She had their attention now.

"So, my name is Ying, and for those who don't know me, I'm in my final year. The pretty boy over there is Trevor, and for the past two years, we've been doing May Ball Security together. In that time, we've seen pretty much everything."

She flicked to the next slide, which showed someone wearing a scuba-diving suit, a bowtie visible at the neck, being led across the Kitchen Bridge. The next had a girl in a slightly soiled ballgown sneaking out from under a camouflage net somewhere in the Fellows Garden. The final slide had a couple sprinting between the dodgem cars, a posse of Porters in hot pursuit.

As the laughter died down, she flicked up a slide with the word CONFIDENTIAL across the screen.

"OK, that's the fun stuff over. The reality is that it costs couples a lot of money to go to a May Ball. Our job is to ensure they have a fantastic evening without chancers like those you've seen there spoiling it for them. I'm now going to give you an overview of how we do that. That way, you know what you're signing up for."

A College plan appeared on the screen with a thick red line drawn around the main College site.

"Before the Ball, fencing will be erected around the perimeter of the College, including the riverbank."

A photograph of the Kitchen Bridge appeared with the river filled from bank to bank with punts, their occupants staring skywards. "To be fair, most of these are locals enjoying the fireworks, but we don't want any of them getting ideas, like these two, for example."

Trevor turned the lights on to reveal a couple standing at the front of the room, resplendent in ballgown and black tie. They bowed to their startled audience.

"Here we have two potential guests. Let's call them Charles and Camilla," Ying said, prompting some laughter. "Looking very much the part, I might add. And there lies the problem, as we shall now demonstrate."

The couple stepped forwards.

"Imagine you're May Ball Security, manning one of the key checkpoints at the Bridge of Sighs. Along come this charming couple, eager to cross into New Court to watch the headline act."

Ying scanned the front row.

"Nick! Let's say you're on duty at the bridge with…?"

Naomi supplied her name when Ying pointed at her.

"OK, with Naomi here. How can you tell if these guests are the real deal or gatecrashers?"

"Check their tickets, maybe?"

"Could do, except they won't have tickets. Guests hand them in upon entering the Ball and in return get one of these."

The couple each held up a wrist to show the multicoloured silk bracelet.

"Woven from a pattern exclusive to this year's Ball," Ying continued, "and secured with a one-way clasp, these bracelets ensure that genuine guests are easily identifiable on the night."

"Plus, they're rather fetching," said Charles with a smile.

"If you spot someone without one of these trying to move between the courts, you stop them and call for help. We'll notify the Porters to escort intruders off the premises."

"And what if they don't want to be stopped?" Nick asked.

"That's why you work in pairs. One of you follows the couple in question while the other calls for back-up. We don't want any incidents spoiling it for other guests, OK?"

"And remember, you're not alone," said Trevor, holding up brightly coloured sashes. "Everyone working on the night will be wearing one of these: green for security and red for those of us on the committee." He handed them to Charles and Camilla, who slipped them over their shoulders.

"Now that's what I'm talking about," murmured Aden, nodding appreciatively.

"So, there you have it," Ying said. "That gives you an overview of what's involved. Obviously, you'll get a detailed briefing once you sign up."

She turned to Trevor. "Anything I've forgotten?"

"Just that you get paid a basic hourly rate and have priority on ticket allocations next year. Everything's on the application form." He held up a stack of papers. "And if you know anyone who might be interested but couldn't make it this evening, please take more."

"Thanks, babe," Ying said. "If you have questions, we'll be around for the next twenty minutes."

Everyone got to their feet, and Naomi went to consult with her friends.

"You up for it?" Aden asked Nick.

He had to admit it was more organised than he'd expected, and the pay and priority tickets for next year sounded good. "Why not?"

"There you go! Come on, let's go and get some forms."

"Surprised to see you here, Woody," Trevor said. "Not going with Annabel?"

"Not this year," he said as Aden wrapped an arm around him.

"Romeo here forgot to ask her, and someone else beat him to it."

"Oh yeah?"

Nick nodded. "She's going with her rowing coach, Brett."

Trevor frowned. "Brett Davis?"

"Yeah."

"I don't think so."

"What do you mean?"

"Ying and I were going through the ticket allocation. I saw Brett's, and it's not Annabel he's taking."

"Who then?"

"Gareth."

"Gareth?" Nick repeated. "As in the rugby Blue."

"Yeah, didn't you know?"

"I…?"

Then, he stopped, remembering the two giants at the Punt Society gathering last term. And then cycling along the towpath together during the Bumps.

Aden shrugged. "Didn't see that one coming. Still, sort of makes sense now you say it." Then, he clapped Nick's arm. "Hey, you think Annabel would be interested in doing security?"

"I don't know."

"Why don't you go and ask her?" He handed him another form. "Before someone else does."

"Maybe I will," he replied.

"That's good, because I hate to say it, bro, but Naomi and me… You never had a chance, mate."

Chapter Sixteen

"Easy oar!" At Annabel's command, the eight blades of W3 left the water and fanned out either side of the hull. The crew paused, keeping their oars perfectly level as the boat glided towards the Boathouse.

Adjusting the rudder, Annabel brought them alongside the bank. The bow-side riggers came to rest on the slipway with barely a bump. In the Stroke seat, Clarissa gave her a nod of approval before tucking a strand of stray hair away from her sweating face.

"How did we look?"

"Better than I expected for a first outing," Annabel replied. "You were pretty much together on the way out. A bit ragged on the way back, but there was that headwind."

"Yeah, I thought Blades might go easy on us then. But he was really pushing it."

The Boatman had instructed her to keep them going at a steady pace with barely a pause on the return leg.

"He did seem in a hurry to get back." Annabel remembered his terse commands.

"Yeah, well, a few of us were feeling it then. I know I was."

Behind Clarissa, hot and weary faces lined the length of the boat.

"Let's see what our new coach thinks," Annabel said as his bike swept around the corner of the Boathouse before skidding to a stop at the bottom of the ramp.

"Look lively, there!" Blades said, none too kindly. "I want that boat out of the water and stored away."

Surprised by his sharp tone, she exchanged a look with Clarissa, who shrugged.

"OK, ladies," Annabel said. "You heard Blades. Let's get this show on the road."

This was an operation they had performed many times, and it didn't take long to ship the oars and lift the boat out of the water. But, by then, the dipping sun had already disappeared behind Victoria Bridge, its fading glow casting long shadows over the river.

The Boatman remained on the slipway throughout the exercise, glancing across the water. When they finally slid the sleek fibreglass hull back onto its storage rack, he removed his faded cap and sighed. His weathered features looked drawn.

"That'll do, ladies. Though we were slow getting back. Next time, Cox, can we make sure the boat's on the water, shipshape and ready to go?"

"Sure," Annabel said, surprised to be singled out.

"Any pointers on what the rest of us need to work on?" Clarissa asked, frowning.

"The catch was ragged, and the timing was off on those bends, but we'll work on those next time."

The crew were accustomed to individual feedback from

Brett, and this cursory assessment hung in the air above their blank faces.

"Are we done then?" he asked.

"I guess we are," Clarissa said.

"Right then. I'll see you tomorrow. Make sure you turn the lights off upstairs when you're done."

And with that, he headed back to his workshop. The others stood for a moment, looking at one another.

"That's a wrap, ladies," said Clarissa. "I don't know about you, but I've got a stack of revision to do."

There were groans of agreement, and the others began filing out. Clarissa turned to Annabel.

"Not exactly communicative, is he?"

"Not really."

"Do you think we should have a word?"

"Not sure now is a good time," Annabel said. "Seems in a hurry to be off."

"True. Tomorrow, before the outing?"

"As long as we're shipshape and ready to go," she said, mimicking his rebuke.

"Aye, aye, Captain!" Clarissa rolled her eyes. "Listen, I wasn't kidding about revision. Shall we head off?"

"No, I'm going to drop this stuff off upstairs," she said, gesturing at the Cox's equipment and life vest.

"Do you want me to wait?"

"No, I'll probably do a bit on the bike. All that chocolate at Easter."

"I hear you, sister. OK, I'll see you tomorrow then. Have a good one."

"And you."

Annabel trudged upstairs to the first-floor strength and conditioning suite and made her way to the Cox's Room at the back. She hung up her lifejacket, microphone and headset, plugging in her equipment to charge overnight. Then, turning off the lights, she crossed the gym to a spinning bike in the corner and was about to lower the saddle when she heard the squeal of a boat trolley rolling down the slipway. Then, there was the unmistakable slosh of a boat sliding into the water.

Heading to a set of doors between the racks, Annabel stepped onto the balcony. Sure enough, there was the empty trolley at the water's edge.

Who would be going out at this time? Annabel thought. *Blades will do his nut.*

At first, everything appeared peaceful, the dark ribbon of water reflecting the first pinpricks of stars overhead. Then, Annabel heard the splash of an oar and spotted ripples fanning out from somewhere under the bridge. Unable to get a clear view, she hurried inside and down the stairs. The Boatman's workshop lay in darkness, so she stepped outside and crept down to the bank.

Half-hidden in the shadows of the old Victorian Bridge, someone was sitting in a boat. She couldn't make out who it was, but she recognised the vessel at once. It was the old clinker she and Brett had capsized last year.

It was motionless in the gloom, its oars resting on the surface, and awful memories came flooding back. The sudden lurch as the boat crabbed, the sickening thud of wood against bone, the shock of cold water as she sank beneath the surface and the overwhelming sense of hopelessness as the darkness closed in.

Annabel shook her head, trying to banish the image, but the creak of timber and splash of blades brought her back to the present. Beneath the bridge, the boat was beginning to move. She couldn't tell whether the rower had seen her, but he was paddling hard, the red blades cutting through the water as the boat picked up speed.

Only when the clinker emerged on the far side of the bridge did the pools of light cast by the old Victorian lamps reveal the faded cap she knew too well.

"Blades?" she murmured, her voice lost in the thrum of oars as the boat disappeared towards Jesus Lock.

Annabel set off after him, crossing the bridge and descending the steps on the far side. As she ran past the canal, boats moored along the bank, all she could hear was the regular splash of oars and the occasional grunt of the Boatman.

Then, everything went silent, and she saw him, hands stationary on the oars, staring at the boat's wake as the clinker glided towards the weir.

What's he doing? Annabel thought, slowing to a walk.

She was about to call over to him when Blades did something her father had taught her never to do in a small vessel. He stood up.

Annabel stopped walking as the Boatman raised his arms, the moonlight reflecting off a long metal object pointing at the river. That was when she noticed the line of bubbles racing across the surface towards the stationary boat. Just before they reached the stern, Blades hurled the harpoon, and the river erupted.

A dark shape breached the surface, the metal shaft embedded in its writhing head. Then, it dived beneath the boat, the wave lifting the stern of the clinker like it was driftwood. Thrown off-balance, the old deckhand toppled backwards, landing in the bow section on his backside. A stream of obscenities followed that would have made even the most grizzled Porter blush.

Then, the boat began to move, its prow edging towards the weir as Blades struggled to get upright. Annabel spotted the thin sliver of line, taut as piano wire, dragging them closer to the roaring falls. The Boatman strained against whatever was pulling them, but it was useless. The bow disappeared into the stream, and the clinker dipped under the weight of water.

"Blades!" Annabel cried, running again.

When the vessel was about to be swamped, the Boatman let go of the line. At once, the boat slewed around, shipping even more water as he scrambled back to the oars. Ignoring the spray, he brought its head around and, arching his back, hauled away until the heavy clinker moved ponderously into the stream.

"Blades! Over here!" Annabel shouted from the bank.

The look of surprise on his drenched face was almost comical. Adjusting direction, he paddled towards her, the boat sluggish and unresponsive. Annabel waited until the bow ball was within reach before grabbing it and pulling him alongside the bank. Panting, the Boatman stowed the oars.

"Are you all right?"

"A bit damp," he said, "but otherwise fine."

This wasn't entirely true. As he clambered onto the bank, blood dripped from his fingers where the line had cut into the palm of his hand.

"Here." Taking a handkerchief from her pocket, Annabel offered it to him.

He hesitated before taking it. "Cheers."

There was still water sloshing around in the boat.

"I thought you were going under for a moment."

"It takes more than a bit of water to sink one of these." He patted the wooden hull.

"Or capsize one," she said.

He stiffened, just a fraction, but it was enough.

"Does this have anything to do with that?" Annabel asked.

"With what?"

"My accident. Under the bridge with Brett."

Blades shifted. "I don't know what you mean."

"I saw the harpoon, Blades."

"Oh, you did, did you?"

"What was it? You know, the thing you were hunting?"

He shook his head. "Dunno. A pike, maybe."

"Must be quite a pike," she said, "to drag a boat against the current."

"Yeah, well, it won't be doing that anymore," he said, his expression grim. "Got him plumb to rights. Ain't nothing going to survive a head strike like that."

Annabel checked the river. But there was nothing floating on the surface. No torso and no line of bubbles. "I don't see anything."

He followed her gaze. "Maybe not now, but it'll wash up somewhere. You mark my words."

"Well, let me know when it does," she said. "It would be good to know it's gone."

"Aye, that I will." Then, almost as an afterthought, he said, "I'd be grateful if we kept this between ourselves. You know, the harpoon and everything."

"Of course."

"And thanks for this." He held up his bandaged hand. "I'll let you have it back tomorrow."

She was about to tell him there was no hurry when they were interrupted by hurried footsteps.

"There you are," called Nick, approaching along the towpath. "I went to the Boathouse but couldn't find you."

"Blades and I were just chatting," she said. "About fishing."

If Nick found this odd, he gave no indication. Nor did he appear to notice the clinker was ankle deep in water. Instead, he only had eyes for her. "Listen, I wanted to ask you something."

"Oh, OK? What, now, you mean?"

"Yeah, if you've got time."

"You go," the Boatman said to her. "I think we're about finished here."

"What about the boat?" she asked.

"It can keep. I'll tie it up here and deal with it in the morning. When it's light."

"Good idea," she agreed. "In that case, I'll see you tomorrow."

"On time, remember."

"Got it." She gave him a brief smile and climbed up the bank to where Nick waited for her.

"Sorry," he said as they walked towards Jesus Green. "This couldn't wait."

"No problem," she said, distracted.

"Only, I've just been to the May Ball Security briefing and…"

Nick continued talking as they walked back to College, Annabel doing her best to listen. But by the time they reached their staircase, she'd barely taken any of it in, still reeling from what she had witnessed on the river.

"Anyway," Nick said. "I wondered if you wanted to work security with me at the May Ball?"

"Security?" She shrugged. "Sure, OK."

"You do? Great!"

He sounded both happy and relieved, but all Annabel could feel was exhaustion. Not just physical but emotional too.

"Listen, I'm pretty tired," she said. "I'm going to head off to bed, if that's OK?"

"Right, of course." His smile faded a fraction.

"I'll see you tomorrow."

"Yeah. Sleep well."

As she trudged up the stairs, all Annabel could think about was that menacing shape lunging from the water. The same one she had seen moments before her boat had capsized all those months ago. When she returned to her room, she remembered what Blades had said about not believing in Jonahs.

Maybe not, she thought, as she closed the door behind her. *But that doesn't mean there can't be monsters in the deep.*

Chapter Seventeen

Dusk was falling as Giles led Alfonso along the shoreline, their feet kicking up red sand as they ran. They had set off at a steady pace from the bottom of the Matriarchy, keen to put as much distance as possible between them and pursuit before nightfall. They barely spoke for the rest of the afternoon, conserving their energy, but the soft sand and intense heat had taken their toll by the time the second sun dipped towards the mountains.

Though he never complained, Alfonso's breathing was laboured, and his skin glistened with sweat. Giles wondered what else he'd had to endure during his time in captivity. Slowing to a walk, Giles took out his canteen and splashed water over his face.

"Here." He handed it to Alfonso, who took a couple of mouthfuls.

"*Gracias.*"

Mist was rising over the falls at the end of the lake, no more than a mile away. But behind them, the shadows of the mountains cast the lower slopes of the Citadel into darkness. As the towers merged into the gloom, there came the unsettling screech of waking harpies.

"That doesn't sound good."

Alfonso handed back the canteen. "We need to get undercover."

"There's a cave at the bottom of the falls."

"You know this how?"

"Your friend, Katya, showed me."

Alfonso stiffened. "Katya?"

"She's the one who brought me here."

"She did?"

"That's why she drew her sister away. To buy us time to get clear."

Alfonso nodded slowly as he digested this. But a distant shriek echoing over the water from the Citadel ended his contemplation.

"Hello, what is that?" Giles asked

At first, he thought it might be a trick of the fading light, but the Matriarchy had all but disappeared in the gloom. As he looked closer, he realised it was hidden by a dark cloud around its peak. A cloud formed not by any weather phenomenon but by hundreds of airborne harpies circling under the shadow of the nearby mountains.

"*Merda*!" Alfonso breathed as the cloud began to unfurl towards them.

"Time to get going," Giles said, stuffing the canteen into his pack.

"*Si*."

They ran for the falls. Behind them, the distant cries rose to a crescendo, but Giles didn't look back.

Sometimes it's best not to know, he thought.

He focused on the ridge where he and Katya had crouched that morning. He could anchor the rope to abseil down the cliff if they could make it to those boulders. He hoped that any circling harpies would struggle to spot them among the rising clouds of spray in the fading light. Once they made it to the cave, the wall of water would keep them hidden until dawn.

As they ran, the shadows of evening overtook them, the darkness obscuring the head of the falls. Still, the roar of the water was clearly audible, and it grew louder as they drew nearer, drowning out the ominous sounds of pursuit. Giles was beginning to believe they might make it when Alfonso skidded to a halt.

"Why are we…?"

Alfonso held up a hand and pointed at the rocky outcrop. It was less than a hundred yards away, but it took Giles a moment or two to see what had brought him up short in the gathering gloom.

Statues. The same group he'd stumbled across earlier that day. Only now, their misshapen forms were not stiff and inert. They were stirring in readiness for the approaching night.

"That's not good," Giles muttered. Over his shoulder, the dark cloud of flyers stretched across the lake. "Not good at all."

Alfonso grabbed his arm. "The trees! We need to get undercover."

Giles remembered what had happened the last time he

and Raquel had taken refuge in the trees.

"I'm not sure that's a good idea."

"To stay here is death!"

Caught between the two groups of harpies, Giles had to admit Alfonso had a point.

"Fine, but we stick together, OK?"

A piercing shriek rose over the sound of the falls. The approaching cloud was halfway across the lake and making straight for them.

"Hurry!" Alfonso yelled.

Giles needed no more persuading. They sprinted up the slope, but the male harpies on their right shrieked in alarm. They, too, must have spotted the approaching flyers and were also scrambling for the woods.

Great, Giles thought. He was about to shout a warning to Alfonso when his feet sunk into the softer sand and he stumbled to his knees. When he looked up, Alfonso had already disappeared into the trees.

Giles hurried after him. He almost made it, too. But as he dipped his head beneath the outlying branches, a heavy object slammed into his back, knocking him face first into the dirt.

A dreadful howl rang out, so loud and piercing that he had to cover his ears. His head was still ringing when the leaves and sand began to stir from the downdraft of flapping wings. Then, the straps of his backpack bit into his armpits as he was hauled into the air.

He had only moments to react. Struggling with the straps, he managed to yank one arm free, and suddenly he was falling. He landed on his back as the harpy lurched skywards with his pack still grasped in its claws.

Giles seized his chance. Rolling onto his hands and knees, he crawled under the cover of the branches as more harpies swooped. There were angry screeches as they fought to get at him, but he kept crawling, expecting at any moment to feel a taloned claw rake him from above.

When the cries behind him grew louder, he turned to see a host of crooked harpies crash through the trees. For a moment, he thought they were pursuing him, but their anguished faces allayed his fears. A shadow descended, and a female plucked one of them into the air. The poor creature was still screaming and thrashing as it disappeared through the foliage.

After that, the fleeing males were so intent on getting clear that they paid little or no attention to his prone form on the ground. Giles looked around for Alfonso. How far into the trees had he gone?

Then, with a terrible creaking noise, a harpy landed on the swaying branches above him. He fumbled for his ice axe, but a hand clamped over his mouth and hauled him back into cover.

"Quiet," Alfonso breathed in his ear. "We are not alone."

Giles went still and heard it. Louder than the frantic thrashing of branches overhead, something was charging through the trees. Whatever it was, it was moving fast, the rapid hoofbeats making the ground shake.

Moments later, a stag-like creature burst through the undergrowth. Alfonso gasped and threw himself flat as the animal leapt over them. It landed without breaking stride and continued its headlong flight. Giles caught a fleeting glimpse of long, curved horns, powerful hindquarters and a tufted tail before it disappeared into the trees. He stared after it in amazement.

"Was that a Yale?"

Before Alfonso could reply, another creature staggered into view. The male harpy was clutching its stomach, doing its best to hold back its intestines, which were oozing from a deep rent across its midriff. It took a few more faltering steps before collapsing on the ground nearby. Its dazed eyes settled on Giles. Though mortally wounded, it emitted an angry hiss that ended with dark blood bubbling from its maw. More cries erupted overhead, the females perhaps catching the scent of the dying creature.

"We need to get out of here!" Giles said, horrified.

"And go where?"

"We need to get to the cave!"

"Are you mad? We'd never make it."

Alfonso was right. The females were clawing at the trees to get at them. The cave was close, but the circling hunters would be on them in seconds if they broke cover and made for the falls. They needed a distraction, something to draw the harpies away and make them think twice before coming after them.

"Fire!" he said.

Alfonso cocked his head.

"We start a fire! Drive them off long enough to make a break for it."

Giles patted his pockets before remembering he'd tossed the lighter to Mary on the tower. But Alfonso was already fishing a leather pouch from his pocket.

"Cover my back."

Alfonso gathered dry leaves into a pile and began striking what looked like a pair of flints while Giles stood guard. Over the rhythmical chipping sound, he heard a twig snap and the unmistakable sound of sniffing. Seconds later, the branches parted, and a crooked figure lurched into view.

It was one of the statues he'd encountered earlier. The new arrival was very much awake, its hunched body bent low to the ground following the trail of blood. Alfonso chose that moment to utter a flurry of expletives in Catalan as he struggled to light the fire. The harpy saw Giles crouching near its fallen brother. It let out a long, menacing hiss, and another immediately appeared at its side.

"How are you doing back there, Alfonso?" Giles muttered, gripping his axe. "Only, we have company."

There was the frantic sound of flints being struck together. "Almost there!"

"Now would be a good time," Giles added as the first harpy rose to its full height and extended a claw.

"Hah!" Alfonso cried as an orange glow lit up the trees around them. Both harpies flinched, their expressions changing from hostility to alarm. Then, with a fearful hiss, they blundered back into the forest.

Working quickly, Alfonso had managed to get a small fire going. Soon, flames began spreading over the tinder-dry leaves strewn across the floor, sending smoke and sparks into the air.

Above them came a strangled squawk from a female harpy a few yards away. It must have given up trying to break through the canopy. Instead, it had been creeping down the tree trunk undetected.

Now it hung there, terror-stricken in the flickering orange light. At a pop of burning sap, fear gave way to panic, and the creature began clawing its way back up the trunk to get clear. As it did so, it came across other harpies still struggling to force their way down through the branches.

In the ensuing altercation, sparks in the rising smoke alighted on the feathers of one of the creatures. When the threat became apparent to their erstwhile attackers, a cacophony of howls erupted. Those highest began flapping their wings, which worsened matters as the downdraft fanned the rapidly spreading flames.

As the conflagration took hold, fire spread towards the dismembered body on the floor. Giles remembered what had happened when he'd burned the creature in the New Court cellar, and he yelled, "Come on! It's going to blow!"

Alfonso needed no persuading. Together, they fled through the trees, passing other beings milling around in confusion and panic. They'd covered no more than a dozen yards before a searing blue light lit up the forest. Giles threw himself against Alfonso, knocking him to the ground moments before the shockwave hit.

A burning cloud of debris whipped through the trees, accompanied by a roar of super-heated air that singed his hair. Only when it finally passed did Giles dare to lift his head.

The surrounding trees – those that had survived – were well and truly on fire. Crackling flames danced over their trunks, throwing off waves of heat. Alfonso sat up and shook ash from his hair.

"Are you OK?" Giles asked.

"*Si*, I think so."

There was a terrible scream behind them; two blazing male harpies stumbled through the trees towards them, their stunted wings torching everything they touched.

"Holy crap!"

Alfonso grabbed Giles's arm and dragged him to his feet. "Quick! This way!"

They set off through the inferno, Alfonso leading the way, ducking under burning boughs and leaping over fallen trees. The heat was intense, and the smoke made it hard to breathe. Soon Giles was struggling to keep up.

"Wait up," he gasped, the sound catching in his throat.

His guide appeared not to hear him, speeding up if anything.

"Alfonso!" Giles cried, worried he might lose him.

Raquel's brother turned. He opened his mouth to say something when his face was lit by an incandescent glow.

The explosion was so bright it turned night into day. Whether it was caused by the blazing creatures they had seen earlier or something else, it set off a chain reaction that shook the forest and sent multiple shockwaves through the trees, flattening everything in their path.

The force slammed into Giles's back, lifting him off his feet and hurling him headlong through the burning branches. He landed hard and rolled down a slope before coming to a stop a few yards from the lake. Behind him, the forest burned, thick black smoke rising to obscure the sky and the harpies circling above.

Giles struggled to his feet. Then, he murmured, "Oh no."

Raquel's brother was standing by the water's edge, and his back was ablaze.

Chapter Eighteen

Alfonso knew he was on fire, though he couldn't see the flames. He couldn't see anything, not since the bright flash in the forest had turned his world black. But he could feel the heat on his back, spreading over his carapace armour and crisping his hair.

It was the molevin gut, he realised. The long strands of oily leather binding the chitinous plates to his body had acted as a wick for the flames. If he didn't get the armour off soon, the fire would wrap around his torso and roast him alive.

Stumbling down the slope, he started tearing at the bindings, crying out in fear and pain. But above his cries and the roar of the nearby falls he heard someone call his name.

"Alfonso! I'm coming."

Turning towards the voice, he screamed, "No, don't, I'm–"

Something barrelled into his midriff, driving him backwards. For a brief moment, he flew through the air. Then, he hit the surface of the lake and went under.

Water gushed over his nose and mouth, and he gagged,

struggling to free himself from the tangle of arms and legs. With a desperate lunge, his head finally broke the surface, and he managed a sobbing breath before a wave washed over him. When he surfaced again, he heard Giles's voice over the roar of the falls, which was getting ever louder as they were swept along.

"Alfonso? Are you all right?"

The intense heat from his armour had gone, doused in the frigid lake water. Of more concern was the darkness that continued to cloud his vision. "*Si*, only… I cannot see."

"What?"

"My eyes, Giles."

"You've got to be kidding… Aaah!"

He heard frantic splashing. "Giles?" Then, something slammed into his carapace plate, and a long, sinewy limb wrapped around his leg. Alfonso felt himself being dragged under even as Giles began hacking at the water, sending spray everywhere.

"Get off, you slimy…!"

The creature shuddered and the grip on his leg loosened. Thrashing in panic, he kicked it free. The water continued to boil around him, though this might have been the current, which was growing stronger, as was the noise of the falls.

"Giles! Are you OK?"

"I… I think so."

"The hydra," he gasped, "we must get ashore."

"No time! We're going over."

"What?"

"The falls," Giles yelled. "Brace yourself!"

"No, we can't! It's too..."

But the roar now was deafening, and he could barely hear himself, let alone Giles, as his stomach lurched, and the water fell away beneath him. Alfonso plummeted, the sound of the rapids briefly replaced by rushing air before a thunderous noise rose to greet them. He just had time to clamp his feet together before hitting the water.

The impact sent a shockwave through his body, compressing his spine. Whatever armour sections remained were ripped free as he plunged through a cascade of bubbles. Water was forced up his nostrils as he descended, causing painful popping in his ears.

Gradually his downward momentum slowed, and the rush of bubbles eased. When they finally ceased, Alfonso found himself floating in the dark, too stunned to register the oppressive silence. But the growing pain in his chest and lungs stirred him into action.

He reached up with his arms and drew them down in long, powerful strokes while kicking steadily with his legs.

When his head broke the surface, the deep, pounding roar was deafening. After a few gasping breaths, Alfonso turned his head this way and that but could not discern anything in the all-consuming darkness.

"Giles?" he spluttered. "Giles?"

Had his sister's friend survived the drop? Was his body floating nearby, face down in the water? Then another, darker thought occurred to him. Had the hydra come over with them?

Suddenly, he was aware of his legs kicking back and forth below him, so he swam towards the main cascade, hoping its churning waters might disguise his movements. When he neared the boiling, frothing wake, he thought he heard a muffled voice. Alfonso tried calling Giles's name, but he only succeeded in swallowing more water.

When he stopped coughing, there was the voice again, nearer this time. Though he couldn't be sure, it seemed to come from somewhere beyond the pounding wall of water. He tried skirting around the main cascade, careful to keep within the confusion of choppy waves.

A hefty downpour drove him under, and this time when he surfaced, the sound of the falls had changed. The roar had a different quality, bouncing off the cliff face like an echo chamber. After a few more tired strokes, his fingers brushed wet rock.

Panting, he clung to the slippery cliff face. Was this where the cave was? Was Giles already here?

"Giles?"

The response was immediate: a shrill cry that chilled him to the bone.

"There he is!"

An image of Mary glaring down at him formed in his mind, and he pushed himself clear of the wall. How had she got here ahead of them? A powerful claw gripped him and hoisted him from the water, and for a few dizzying moments, he hung upside down as he was swung through the air. Then, he was dumped on a wet, stony floor.

Almost at once, footsteps approached. He rolled away,

but his back collided with the cave wall. Alfonso raised his hands above his head to protect himself from the blow he knew was coming.

The footsteps stopped.

"Alfonso! *Ésta bien*!"

He froze, his mind transported to a light, airy bedroom overlooking Alcudia Bay. The childhood bedroom he had shared with his sister.

"R… Raquel?"

"*Si*, Alfonso," she replied. "It is me."

Then, she was hugging him, her cheek against his and her sobs ringing in his ear. For some time, they remained like that, Alfonso too overwhelmed to do or say anything. It wasn't until he heard the scrape of a claw nearby that he remembered they were not alone.

"Who is there?" he said, staring into the darkness.

Raquel released him and hesitated. "Alfonso, you cannot see him?"

He turned towards her voice, willing his sight to clear. But everything remained dark.

"No."

He heard her sharp intake of breath. "When did this happen?"

"With Giles, in the forest. We were trapped and…" The white light had obliterated the burning harpies… and his retinas. "Wait. Is Giles not here?"

"No," she said.

"But he went with me over the falls."

"He has not returned."

"We have to find him!" He began getting up, but she grabbed his arm.

"Wait, Alfonso!"

He was about to shrug her off when something wet thudded to the floor and rolled against his leg. He heard the harpy's startled hiss and his sister's horrified gasp.

"Sorry I'm late," said Giles from the entrance. "Couldn't shake this fella off."

"Giles!" Raquel let go of Alfonso's arm and hurried across the cave.

Alfonso reached down and felt the thing lying next to him, his hands tracing the sinewy torso. The others joined him.

"What is that thing?" Raquel asked.

"A hydra," he murmured. "A juvenile, I think."

"Well, it's a clingy little tike," Giles said. "Broke my fall, along with most of its vertebrae. But you made it, I see."

He patted Alfonso's shoulder, and he winced at his touch.

"Careful!" Raquel said. "I need to get you out of these wet things. Giles has some spare clothing in my bag."

"What about Giles?"

"I'm fine. I'll keep an eye on old misery guts over there."

It was then that Alfonso remembered the harpy.

"What is he doing here?"

"Katya sent him to watch over me," Raquel explained. "Come, you need to lie down."

"You need a hand?" Giles offered.

"No, is OK, Giles," she said. "I have him now."

There was a possessive tone in her voice that jarred somehow. But Alfonso was so weary all of a sudden that he allowed himself to be led to the back of the cave, where Raquel changed him and dressed his wounds. By the time he laid down on a rolled-out sleeping bag, he could manage no more than a murmur of thanks.

"Sleep well, my brother," was the last thing he heard before he drifted into a dreamless sleep.

Chapter Nineteen

Whatever joy Giles had hoped he might bring Raquel by reuniting her with her brother had disappeared by the following morning.

When the pale dawn light filtered through the curtain of water screening the cave entrance, the full extent of Alfonso's injuries became apparent. Much of the long beard and hair from his months of captivity had burned away, leaving patches of scorched and blistered skin. His emaciated body was covered in scars; though many were old, there were numerous sores and weals from his rescue.

Raquel used their rudimentary first aid kit to dress them as best she could. And though he never complained, her brother couldn't suppress a grimace as she bandaged the livid bruises on his ribs.

Of most concern was his loss of sight. Giles had hoped that the effects of the dazzle-blindness might have worn off by the morning, but it became clear from Alfonso's glassy-eyed expression that he could not make out his sister kneeling before him to tie his shoes. The only blessing was that he couldn't see the anguish on her face as she did so.

Giles could see how close their bond was. It made him wonder what room Raquel had in her heart for him now that she had her brother to care for. Immediately, he was ashamed. Given what Alfonso had been through, why should his sister spare a thought for anyone else right now?

"Pathetic," he muttered to himself, the word coming out louder than he intended.

Raquel raised her head and glared at him. Giles's cheeks flushed with heat. He was about to explain what he'd meant when Katya's father emitted a hiss from the entrance.

"We go. Now."

Raquel turned away from Giles, and the moment was lost.

A few minutes later, she helped her brother rise stiffly from the floor. Giles's borrowed clothes fitted Alfonso pretty well and hid the worst of his injuries. These and the bandages made him look less like a castaway and more like a wounded veteran from a POW camp, which, in many ways, he was.

"All set?"

"*Si*, Giles, thank you," Alfonso replied, but his sister said nothing.

They emerged from the cave to find dirty grey smoke drifting above the waterfall, adding a murky gloom to the damp morning air. The first sun had yet to rise above the surrounding cliffs, leaving the pool in deep shadow.

The old harpy led them around the edge of the water, Raquel instructing Alfonso where to place his feet and Giles bringing up the rear. He kept a wary eye on the surface for the tell-tale sign of moving bubbles, but none appeared.

His only scare came when he saw a half-submerged object tracking their progress. Then, he realised it was a charred tree trunk drifting along with the current, and there were others floating downstream or nestled among the rocks. How many of the forest's inhabitants had survived the firestorm?

Once clear of the plunge pool, they made for the shelter of the trees below the cliffs. Mercifully, this narrow ribbon of woodland that followed the river's course had been unaffected by the fires of the night before. Its leafy canopy would allow their guide to press on free from the calcifying effects of the suns' rays. Giles also hoped it would keep their escape from last night's inferno secret until they were far from the Citadel.

"Hurry!" Katya's father said.

Alfonso stumbled as he tried to speed up, prompting Raquel to swear at the disappearing harpy.

"Here," Giles said, hurrying to take her brother's free arm.

Alfonso sighed. "*Gracias.*"

Hoisting him between them, they made it to the trees before the first shafts of sunlight broke through the thinning grey mist. Even at this distance, the falls looked impossibly high. That they had both survived the drop was still hard to believe. He hoped any pursuers would think the same.

That was when Mary appeared at the top of the falls.

"She look for him," muttered Katya's father from beside Giles. In the dim light, his gruesome features were more grim than usual.

Blind and scarred, Alfonso stood a little way back, a bandaged hand resting on his sister's shoulder as he stared blankly into the woods. Whether they had heard, Giles couldn't tell, but he hoped not. The thought of what would happen to him if Mary's other daughter caught up with them didn't bear thinking about.

"We go," the harpy hissed.

Though they were hidden among the trees, Giles couldn't shake the feeling that Mary was staring right back at him. With an involuntary shudder, he joined the others, hoping he was wrong.

For the rest of that morning, they pressed on, making better progress than Giles had expected. Katya's father led them back beneath the trees that he and Raquel must have passed under to reach the falls. Thankfully, this well-worn track was largely clear of roots or other trip hazards, making the going easier for Alfonso.

Giles suspected the path had been formed by renegade harpies to travel undetected along the valley's upper reaches. Now and again, he caught glimpses of the creatures lurking in the shadows. Though unsettling, the watchers made no attempt to intervene, allowing them to pass unmolested. But later that day, when he paused to tie a bootlace, Giles heard leaves rustling, and several misshapen figures slipped behind the trees.

I see you, he thought.

He made a point of unfastening the clasp of his ice axe and nodding at the hidden trackers before rejoining the others. He suspected Katya's father knew of their presence because the harpy glanced back down the track now and again. But Raquel was preoccupied with guiding her brother safely along the route, something the pair became more adept at as the day wore on.

Raquel developed a simple set of commands in Catalan to warn Alfonso of dips or rises in the path. This allowed him to follow in her footsteps, only slowing for the steeper or more treacherous sections. Here, she would pause for him to put a hand on her shoulder and follow her detailed guidance on where to place his feet.

These necessary delays became less frequent the further they travelled down the valley. Not only were there fewer rocks to clamber over or around, but the forest encroached less and less on the path. By the afternoon, the trees were far enough apart for Raquel to walk side by side with her brother, linking her arm in his as they hurried along the track.

Following them, Giles caught snatches of their murmured conversation, conducted entirely in Catalan and all but incomprehensible to him. Indeed, the pair seemed oblivious to his presence, lost in their own familial world – one that was as alien to him as the land they were travelling through.

"Just so you know," Giles said in a low voice, "we've picked up a few followers."

Raquel eyed him. "You're sure? Where?"

"A little way back," her brother said. "I heard them."

"You did?" she asked, surprised.

"Flushing out molevin from tunnels improves your sense of hearing."

Giles wasn't sure what molevin were, but Raquel was clearly horrified that her brother had been used this way. And his matter-of-fact tone made his disclosure all the more chilling.

"Well, glad you're on the case, anyway," Giles said. "I'll find out what old hop-along has to say and report back."

Katya's father greeted him with little more than a cursory scowl.

"Afternoon." Giles fell in step as the harpy limped down the track with his strange, lopsided gait. "So, what is it with your friends in the woods?"

This earned him a sharp look.

"Sorry, but they're hard to miss. Are they here to help or hinder us?"

"Make sure you go," the harpy said, before adding, "*I* make sure."

"I see," Giles said. "That's good of you."

"Not me. Katya."

"Right, of course."

The old harpy had looked mutinous when Katya had commanded him back at the clearing, but he had complied with her requests so far. Indeed, since returning from the Citadel, Giles had sensed a change in Katya's father's mood, particularly around Alfonso. There had been a thoughtful glance when Raquel dressed her brother's wound or a pause while they navigated the trickier sections of the route.

Could the creature be feeling empathy for another disfigured by the Matriarch's brutal regime? The harpy had clearly been disgusted when they'd seen Mary at the top of the falls. Perhaps helping the three of them escape was his way of exacting some measure of revenge for what she had done to him.

Either way, the old harpy and the threat of Katya were the only things holding back the watchers in the trees. If anything were to happen to either of these guardians, he doubted the lurkers would hold back.

"So, what's the plan?" he asked.

"Plan?"

"Well, yes. We're making good progress under cover from the suns, but what about when these trees run out?"

"Is night. We go on. No stop."

"I got that bit. I was thinking about tomorrow. By my reckoning, we still have another day to the portal."

"You go. Follow river."

"What about you? What are you going to do then?"

The harpy considered him for a moment, as if surprised by the question or that Giles would care.

"Find my Katya."

The response was like a slap to the face. His daughter was out there, either fleeing for her life or already dead. Giles looked away. For the first time, he contemplated what their presence here had cost the harpies.

"Well, when you do," he said, "be sure to thank her from me. From all of us."

They continued down the track, the woods quiet save for the occasional murmur from their companions.

"She cannot have him." Katya's father broke the silence.

"Sorry? Katya, you mean?"

His face grew dark. "Olga."

"Well, no, of course not," he said. "I'm not going to let that happen."

The harpy glanced briefly at the ice axe on his belt. "Never. You understand?"

Giles did understand, but he had no intention of doing what the creature implied, no matter how dire the circumstances.

"I will not let your daughter have him," he said. "You have my word on that."

Giles meant it, though not the way the creature intended. He wondered if her father suspected as much. Either way, he kept his hand close to the axe, conscious of its handle brushing against his leg as they walked.

As the afternoon wore on, the woods began to thin, the trunks becoming further apart. Soon, he could see the river through the trees and hear the gurgling and splashing of waves. Occasionally, a shaft of sunlight penetrated the canopy of leaves overhead, causing Katya's father to step cautiously around it.

If they reached the limits of the woodland before dusk, they would have to stop and wait for the shadows to spread across the valley floor before the harpy could continue. Giles was about to raise this issue when the footfalls behind them stopped.

Alfonso was gripping Raquel's arm.

"What is it?" she asked.

Her brother had his eyes closed, his head cocked to one side. They all stood very still. There was a faint whispering somewhere ahead of them. The strange noise grew until

Giles recognised it: a sequence of hisses, one after the other, getting louder and more insistent the closer they came.

Katya's father thrust a tattered wing out and said, "Down."

They all left the path and squatted under the trees. Giles peered through the gaps in the branches and heard a bone-chilling shriek echo down the valley. Moments later, a dark shape swept overhead, its fleeting shadow blotting out the light of the twin suns before it was gone.

"What was that?" Raquel asked their guide.

But it was Alfonso who answered, his face ghostly pale in the shadows.

"That was Olga," he said, his voice dull and lifeless. "She has... returned."

The anguish on Katya's father's face said it all.

"I'm sorry," Giles said. "Truly sorry."

The harpy said nothing. The woods were unnaturally still, as if a shroud had been laid over them. Then, the silence gave way to another sound, low but harsh.

Behind Giles, Alfonso stirred.

"What is it?" Raquel asked.

"They are coming."

"You go!" Katya's father said as the woods came alive.

Giles reached for the ice axe strapped to his belt.

"No!" the creature hissed. "Go to river."

Through the trees, sunlight reflected off the distant stream. The harpy was right. That was their only hope.

Already, Raquel had hold of her brother's arm and was half dragging him through the trees, issuing hurried instructions in Catalan.

“What about you?” Giles asked the harpy.

“I stay,” he said, placing a gnarled claw on his arm. “Remember. She cannot have him.”

Giles nodded as a chorus of hisses erupted behind them.

“Go!” the harpy said, thrusting him towards the river.

Giles ran as Katya's father lurched at their pursuers, his mangled wing spread wide, screeching his challenge.

Chapter Twenty

The sun was setting when Ravi stepped from his staircase into Second Court. The fresh air was a welcome relief after an afternoon spent clearing his desk and rescheduling his academic commitments.

The one consolation was that, with exams only a week away, his Tutees were too busy revising to bother him with domestic concerns. This meant he now had a brief window of time to follow through on his commitment to Rose, the Bedder, and to track down the elusive Giles and Raquel.

If they were still together. Or alive.

Pushing this uncomfortable thought aside, he walked to the Forecourt Porters' Lodge, where he was greeted by the taciturn Shirley.

"Evening, Professor."

"Good evening. I was wondering if Bert is about by any chance?"

"Afraid not. He's taking his missus out for dinner this evening. Can I help?"

Ravi hadn't anticipated this. He was so used to finding

the Head Porter here that he often forgot Bert had a life outside College.

It would be tonight, he thought, *just when I need a favour.* Still, there was nothing for it.

"I hope so. I wonder if I might borrow the keys to the New Court cellars? I have some items I wish to store there."

The Porter frowned. "You're the second one to ask me that this evening."

"I… Sorry?"

"Dr Dutour was around here not long ago asking the same."

Ravi's stomach shifted. "Gabrielle?"

"That's the one. Anyway, I'll give you the same answer I gave her. You can't have them, I'm afraid."

Ravi blinked. "Why not?"

"Master's orders. He left specific instructions those keys are not to be let out without his express permission."

"You're not serious?"

The Porter visibly stiffened. "Those are our orders, Professor. If you're unhappy with them, you'll have to take it up with the Master. After Dr Dutour, of course; she's gone over to see him right away."

Ravi was speechless. He'd known the Master had beefed up security since last term's cellar incident. Still, he'd never imagined that his carefully planned expedition would be cut short like this.

Before he could protest, the lodge doors swung open and a phalanx of Choir members, resplendent in their red robes and white surplices, began filing through to Evensong.

Conscious that the Porter was still watching him, and not wanting to make a scene, he nodded.

"Thank you, Shirley. I shall make an appointment to see him in the morning."

He stepped outside and paused in the relative quiet of Chapel Court to gather his thoughts.

Even if the Master refused Gabrielle's request for the keys, there was no way he could then ask for them without arousing suspicion. Lester would assign Jane to watch his every move, if she wasn't doing so already. If that were to happen, it would make it almost impossible for him to slip through the portal unnoticed.

Ravi was wondering if he might have better luck waiting until the morning to persuade Bert to give him the key when a voice behind him disturbed his thoughts.

"Evening, Ravi. Are you joining us for Evensong?"

The College Chaplain stood by the Chapel entrance, greeting the last of his evening's worshippers as they filed inside.

"Sorry, Matthew, I didn't see you there."

"Things on your mind, perhaps?"

"One or two."

"Come and join us, then. I've always found that a half hour of quiet contemplation, accompanied by the finest choral music in Cambridge, helps unburden the mind."

Ravi doubted even these would be sufficient in his case. If Giles and Raquel were marooned on Gemini, nothing short of divine intervention would be required to bring them safely back.

He was about to decline the Chaplain's kind offer when he spotted Gabrielle Dutour emerging from the archway to the Master's Lodge. Even from the other side of the square, her cheeks were visibly flushed and her eyes were wild with outrage as she strode towards the passageway to Second Court.

"You know what, Matthew?" Ravi turned his back on the court. "That's an excellent suggestion."

"Wonderful. Go and find yourself a pew, and I'll be with you all shortly."

The Chaplain's advice proved remarkably prescient. Though there by necessity rather than conviction, Ravi found the quiet solemnity of the service and the heavenly music both calming and uplifting in equal measure.

What could he do now that the Gemini Passage had been all but barred to him? Sitting in his pew, he ran through his options:

I'd need to steal the keys, disarm the security systems… Oh, and then there's the small matter of giving Jane the slip long enough to pass through…

He struggled to see how he could access the portal without drawing unwanted attention to his clandestine mission.

By the time the Chaplain stood to deliver his sermon on remaining true to one's faith during the challenges of exam week, Ravi was gazing despondently at the sunlight streaming through the stained-glass windows above him. The windows' intricate designs projected on the Chapel walls reminded him of the glowing sigils surrounding John Dee's arcane portal.

How many hours had he spent practising those symbols, he wondered? Most of last term, he realised, hidden away in the disused Librarian's Office. At times, its tiny wall had been all but covered in chalk…

"For so it is said from Matthew, Chapter 7, Verse 13," the Chaplain concluded, "Enter in by the narrow gate; for wide is the gate and broad is the way that leads to *destruction*, and many are those who enter in by it." His voice rose over the heads of his congregation. "How narrow is the gate and restricted is the way that leads to *life*." His gaze settled on Ravi. "Few are those who find it. Amen."

"Amen," Ravi murmured as the spark of an idea flickered into life.

The Chapel organ struck up, and the Choir bowed at the altar in unison to signal the end of Evensong. Then, in time-honoured tradition, the choristers filed out of the stalls and followed the Chapel Clerk, who was resplendent in gilded robes and carrying an eagle-tipped staff, back down the aisle.

Ravi barely saw them go, his mind occupied by possibilities.

There could be another way after all.

Rising from his pew, he bowed to the altar. Woven into the rich tapestry, the eagle of St John the Evangelist stared back at him, wings flared in warning. But Ravi's mind was set.

Averting his gaze, he set off after the procession, his hurried footsteps resounding off the marble tiles. However, when he reached the antechapel, he slowed at the sight of Dominic Lester standing alongside the Chaplain, offering praise and thanks to the departing choristers and Director of Music. The Master's smile was strained and didn't extend to his eyes, which were fixed on Ravi as he approached.

"Good to see you again, Ravi," said Lester. "I was telling Matthew how much I enjoy his words of wisdom."

"One does what one can," said the Chaplain. "Though I fear it went over the heads of some of our congregation." He indicated a rear pew where an elderly Fellow sat with his chin resting on his gently rising chest.

"Is that Henry Winterbottom, again?" the Master asked. "Dear me, he gets more like his beloved dormice every term."

The retired Veterinary Professor's head was beginning to loll to one side.

"Don't worry. The Chapel Clerk will see to him shortly," said the Chaplain. "We wouldn't want Henry missing his supper."

"Are you joining us for dinner, Ravi? It would be good to catch up on various matters."

"I'm afraid that won't be possible this evening, Master. I made other plans."

"A pity. I wanted to update you on a conversation I had earlier with Dr Dutour, who is rather vexed about some new rules."

"I see. Well, I'm a little busy over the next couple of days. Can it wait until next week?"

"Better still, perhaps you can have a word with Gabrielle

yourself. I know how much she confides in you."

Ravi could tell by his tone this was more than a suggestion.

"Very well, Master."

"Excellent. Well, I'd best be off. I'm hosting the Master of Trinity tonight. Be sure to let me know how you get on."

"Of course, Master."

Ravi watched him go, relieved he'd not put his name down for dinner.

"Feeling better, Ravi?" The Chaplain was studying him.

"Sorry?"

"You said you had a lot on your mind earlier."

"Oh, you know. This and that." He sighed. "If I'm honest, there's a particular student I'm concerned about."

"Exams?"

"Not as such. More a tendency to stray from the path. In this case, rather a long way, I fear."

"I see. A prodigal son."

"Something like that."

The Chaplain nodded. "As a young man, I struggled with that particular parable."

"How so?"

"I remember thinking how unfair it was that a boy who so clearly defied his father's will would be welcomed home with open arms. It was only later, as I struggled with my own demons, that I realised we all take the wrong path now and again."

"How true."

"The important thing is to keep a light burning for him."

"A light, you say?"

"After all, how else will he find his way home?"

Ravi nodded. "How else indeed, Matthew."

"Will I see you at tomorrow's Evensong?"

"I expect not. I plan to be away for a day or two."

"Anywhere nice?"

"A remote spot I used to visit many years ago."

"Well, I wish you a safe journey." He smiled and turned to the recumbent academic snoring in the Fellows' pews. "It looks like Henry has missed his supper after all. If you'll forgive me, Ravi."

"Of course. Good night, Matthew."

He left the Chaplain to wake the dozing member of his congregation and headed outside. Chapel Court was quiet, its occupants either dining in Hall or hard at work in their rooms. On the far side of the square, the Library was lit up like a Christmas tree, its windows filled with students hunched over desks. Their ghostly pale faces, lit by the glow of their laptop screens, reminded Ravi of the parable of the prodigal son and the Chaplain's parting words.

"Ensure a light is kept burning for those seeking a way home," Ravi murmured. "So be it."

Chapter Twenty-One

The following morning, Ravi left his home in Newnham and made his way along the Backs, careful not to rush, his sturdy leather walking brogues crunching on the gravel path.

Though the sky was clear, he had eschewed his light summer blazer for his waxed Barbour jacket. Tucked inside its capacious pockets were his metal ruler, a canteen, an LED flashlight, a toothbrush, spare socks and a box of chalk.

In all other respects, he appeared his usual shabby self. Overdressed perhaps for what promised to be a sunny day, but nothing that would attract undue attention in the sartorial eccentricity of Cambridge.

Still, by the time he'd crossed the Kitchen Bridge and opened the door to the Buttery, perspiration had soaked his shirt. This discomfort was accentuated as he approached the person standing behind the servery.

"Good morning, Aurelia," he said.

"Good morning, Professor. The usual?"

"Yes, please." While Aurelia prepared his cooked breakfast and Earl Grey tea, Ravi added a couple of energy bars and a bottle of water to his tray. He looked long and hard at a carton of fresh milk but decided against it. There was only so much room in his pockets, after all.

The waitress raised an eyebrow at his additional purchases as she ran them through the till. "Hungry today, Professor?"

It took him a moment to think of what to say. "Oh, just expecting a long day in the Library." He swiped his card over the reader, and she nodded.

"Well, have a good one."

"Thank you."

Without another word, she returned to the servery, where her next customers were waiting, and Ravi felt unaccountably sad for the lie.

With a heavy heart, he made his way to a table at the far end of the Buttery. He removed his jacket and stowed the bars and water bottle into its remaining pocket, then settled down to what he expected would be his last good meal for a while.

As he finished, the Buttery door swung open and Jane entered. She gave him a weary smile and headed over to the servery, where Aurelia greeted her former colleague with a hug. After loading her tray with coffee and pastries, Jane approached his table.

"Mind if I join you?"

"Please."

"Thought I'd catch you here," she said, settling into a chair affording her a view of the other tables. There were dark rings under her eyes.

"I'm that predictable, am I?"

She glanced at his empty plate. "Poached eggs and Earl Grey tea?"

Ravi inclined his head. "Point taken."

While she tucked into a *pain au chocolat*, he asked, "Long night?"

"You could say that. Dominic asked me to keep an eye on some cellars."

"I see."

"All part of the service."

"And what service would that be exactly?"

She smiled and began depressing the cafetière's plunger. "Did you find her?"

"Sorry, who?"

"The last person to speak with Giles?"

"What makes you think it was a woman?"

"Bedders generally are."

"Ah, yes. I thought you'd get there in the end."

"You really do cosset your students here, don't you?"

"As you say, all part of the service."

She raised her cup. "Fair enough."

They both sipped their drinks.

"So, what did you discover?" Jane asked.

"From Rose?" He sighed. "That she had no idea where Giles is, other than the fact that the last person she saw him with was Raquel."

"That's unfortunate."

Ravi wasn't sure if she was referring to Giles's whereabouts or his choice of companion. "Rose doesn't have a very high opinion of Alfonso's sister."

"Oh yeah?"

"Doubts her motives. A view you share, perhaps?"

"What makes you say that?"

"Your colleague, Cummings, once told me the Vidals were part of the Catalan separatist movement." When Jane didn't acknowledge this, he continued. "Jack was under the impression that Raquel had recruited her brother into her cell. Possibly even become its leader."

A couple of students entered the Buttery and glanced their way. Jane put down her cup. "If that was the case, Professor, you'll understand why we're anxious to locate them."

"We? Is Jack on operational duty again?"

Again the smile, before taking another bite of her pastry. "Tell me, where do you think Giles is?"

"Beyond our help, for the moment," he said truthfully. "But if anyone can get themselves out of a fix, that young man can."

"You really think that?"

"I have to."

Jane pushed her plate away.

"I hope you're right, Professor. I really do."

Ravi thought she meant it, too. As she ran a finger around the rim of her cup, he wondered if this intelligence officer's interest in Giles's safe return was more than professional. Jane took a final sip of coffee and rose from her chair.

"Well, I'd best get back. Good to catch up, Professor. Keep me posted, and if there's anything you need, let me know."

For a moment, Ravi was tempted to involve her in his plan. Here was a trained intelligence officer, undoubtedly resourceful, quite possibly armed and, like him, desperate to get Giles back. But then he remembered how many people had been hurt already.

"When you next see Jack, give him my best."

She snorted. "Have a good day, Professor."

"Goodbye, Jane."

She walked towards the Kitchen Bridge, passing under the stone Yales guarding the crossing. Ravi waited until she had disappeared before rising and heading for the door.

Following his usual routine, Ravi left the Buttery and made his way to the College Library. It was a daily pilgrimage he'd established decades ago when the Library entrance had moved from his staircase to its new one in Chapel Court. And though he had attracted a certain notoriety among the College community, it now afforded him the perfect cover for what was about to happen.

Ravi pushed through the revolving door of the Library as the Trinity clock struck nine. At first sight, the lobby was deserted, but as he headed for an archway in the corner, he heard a familiar voice.

"Good morning, Professor."

Behind the counter, the Librarian's balding head was bent over a stack of returned books.

"Good morning, Mr Weston."

All too conscious of his bulging pockets, Ravi continued through the connecting passageway to the Old Library foyer. As expected, the Archivist was sitting at her desk overlooking the reading tables. She gave him a brief smile.

"Good morning, Professor."

"Good morning, Andrea."

Accustomed to his daily visits, she returned to her computer without further comment, leaving Ravi to cross to the side table where the visitors' register was kept. Keeping his back to her desk, Ravi stooped over the old ledger and picked up the pen resting alongside its cover.

Instead of recording his name, date and time of arrival, he made a show of writing the required information while making sure the pen never touched the paper. Then, the misdeed done, he put the pen down and crossed to the Lower Library entrance. Only when he opened the glass door did Ravi risk a glance at the raised desk. Andrea sat staring at her screen, oblivious to the breach of protocol he'd committed under her nose.

Being predictable has its advantages, he thought as he closed the door and set off along the narrow walkway between bookcases towards the magnificent Oriel window overlooking the river. He took the spiral staircase to the upper level, barely noticing the view of the Bridge of Sighs and New Court beyond, their sandstone surfaces gleaming in the morning sun.

The Upper Library, by contrast, was cast in a dull, sombre light thanks to the UV screens covering its arched windows. These lent a murky feel to the place that added to the clandestine nature of his purpose there.

Ravi crossed to a little-visited bookcase in the North wall, whose shelves were hidden in shadow. He located a large leather-bound volume, which he eased from its neighbours. With great care, he removed the manilla envelope nestled between its leaves.

Inside were two sheets of parchment, which he laid flat on the book's surface so their torn edges were aligned. Then, as he had done half a century earlier, he studied the completed design. The arcane glyphs and Gemini symbol slotted into his memory like a key in a lock. Below was the incantation, the Latin so familiar he barely needed this reminder. Still, it was too important to make a mistake now.

After imprinting the ancient spell in his mind, he returned the sheets to their envelope, which he slipped inside the almanac. Then, he replaced the book on the shelf.

On the far side of the Library was the nook above the corner bookcase where Giles must have hidden his camera. Though now empty, it provided the perfect vantage spot for tracking the movement of anyone perusing the bookshelves – or hiding fragments of parchment among their 32,000 volumes.

Ravi's admiration for the boy's ingenuity was tempered by embarrassment at being outwitted. Still, there was nothing for it now but to do what he could to save his acolyte, and himself, from his own foolishness.

Ignoring the creak of ancient timbers underfoot, he made his way over the carpeted floor to the disused Librarian's office at the far end of the hall. The discreet wooden door with its brass handle was unlocked, and inside it was much the same as he'd left it last term. The stone fireplace and bookshelves were empty, as was the reading table in the centre of the small room. Indeed, the only item of interest, and the one crucial to his plan, was the large canvas scroll hanging from the far wall: a copy of the Mappa Mundi, the medieval map of the known world.

Closing the door, Ravi lowered the blinds over the panelled window and the other windows on either side of the fireplace. Then, he turned to the map, which was mounted on a roller set high on the wall. Drawing down on a loop of string, he began furling it up to reveal the plaster behind, its surface discoloured to a dirty yellow.

Even now, he could make out the smudges of chalk dust, faint deposits from the glyphs he had practised drawing here weeks ago. He decided it should be possible to recreate the complete design and still cover it with the map once he stepped through. Of course, it would be smaller than the Gemini Passage he'd created in the New Court cellars. But he and Raquel should be able to stand up in it, even if Giles were forced to crouch.

Ravi shook his head. "Don't get ahead of yourself, you old fool. First, you have to find them."

He retrieved the box of chalk from his jacket and selected a fresh piece. He could scarcely believe he was planning to create a second portal after spending a lifetime trying to bury the existence of the first.

Then, he thought about the two young people he was doing this for. How they'd stood with him on the Chapel Tower the night he'd confronted the harpy. And visited him in his hospital bed after surviving the New Court cellars. If they were still alive, he couldn't abandon them on Gemini.

He'd done that with someone once before and wouldn't do so again.

With a final sigh, Ravi began to draw.

Chapter Twenty-Two

Jane was standing by the Eagle Gate when the alarm went off. Her first thought was that it must be coming from one of the sensors they'd set up in the New Court cellars. But as she hurried along the cloisters, she saw a couple of Bedders stop on the Bridge of Sighs and look back towards Third Court.

Jane stopped abruptly and speed-dialled a number.

"I hear an alarm."

There was a brief pause before the response. "Confirm that. It's a fire alarm."

"Where?"

"The Old Library."

She began to move again. "Have you got eyes there?"

"Negative. No cameras are allowed there."

Jane broke into a run. When she arrived in Chapel Court, students and staff were already streaming from the Library to gather in groups on the lawn. Pushing through the crowd, she approached the entrance, where the imposing figure of the Head Porter held up a hand.

"Sorry, Miss, you can't go in there."

"Bert, it's me, Jane."

His expression changed to one of surprise.

"Jane? What are you doing here?"

"It's a long story. What's going on?"

"Fire alarm. We're clearing the building. Ah, here's the College Librarian... Is that everyone, Mr Weston?"

The small, balding man turned to his female colleague. "We've checked everywhere, haven't we, Andrea?"

The woman gave him a doubtful nod.

"And there's no sign of what might have set it off?" Bert asked.

The Librarian shook his head. "None."

"In that case, I'd best notify the fire service. Don't want them coming out unnecessarily. Can you ask everyone to stay here for the moment? I'll let you know when you're clear to return."

"Of course."

The two men dispersed, leaving Jane with the subdued Archivist.

"Are you all right?"

"What? Oh, yes." Andrea smiled. "I think so."

"You don't sound very sure."

"I... It's nothing. I was a bit worried, that's all."

"About what?"

She hesitated. "I thought we were missing someone."

Jane tried to keep her voice level. "Missing? Who exactly?"

"One of our Fellows – Professor Gupta. I could have sworn I saw him come in this morning." She frowned. "But I checked the register and..."

"We were mistaken," said Mr Weston.

The Librarian had reappeared alongside the Archivist and was watching Jane over his half-moon spectacles. "I thought the same as Andrea at first," he explained. "The Professor comes in most mornings, you see."

"So I understand."

"Unfortunately, not this morning," Mr Weston said.

"Why unfortunate?"

"He'll be disappointed to have missed all the excitement, of course."

"Of course," Jane said.

The sound of the alarm stopped and the Porter reappeared from the lodge.

"All clear, Mr Weston!"

The Librarian raised a hand in acknowledgement before turning to his colleague. "In that case, Andrea, shall we get everyone back inside?" He smiled. "Nice meeting you... Jane, was it?"

"And you, Mr Weston."

The Librarian inclined his head before accompanying Andrea and the others back through the entrance, leaving Jane alone. The phone started vibrating in her pocket and she put it to her ear.

"Jane? Are you still there?"

"Yes."

"What's going on?"

The Library's wooden door closed long after, she suspected, a wily old horse had already bolted.

"False alarm," she replied.

"You're sure?"

"Yes." A wry smile tugged at the corners of her mouth. "Oh, and Jack? Professor Gupta sends his best regards."

There was a snort from the other end, and the line went dead. Still smiling, Jane wandered back to the Eagle Gate as the sun rose high above the now tranquil courts.

Chapter Twenty-Three

Sweat ran down Alfonso's back as he hurried along at Raquel's side. His sister barely needed to guide him now they had reached the lower river where the ground was level and the going easier. But with no trees to offer cover, the heat was oppressive, radiating from the dusty earth and leaving his lips dry and cracked.

Conversation had all but dried up, too. Giles's earlier attempts at keeping their spirits up had waned as the suns had begun to dip. Now, the Englishman was quiet, save for his laboured breathing ahead of them. Even the river had fallen silent as it widened into a broader, meandering stream, the crash and roar of the falls a distant memory.

But the peace was an uneasy one, and at the next water break, Alfonso began to understand why. Leaning on a fallen stone column, he overheard his sister talking in a hushed tone to Giles, who had returned from refilling their canteen.

"Giles, you see the cliffs?"

"They're kind of hard to miss."

"Those patches of grey."

"What about them?"

"Are there more of them now?"

There was a brief pause.

"Yes, I think so."

Alfonso didn't need eyes to know what this meant. Dormant harpies, perhaps stragglers from Mary's raid on the Hive, were spread along the valley's length. As soon as the suns set, they would become active, taking to the night skies to hunt. And what better prey than the three of them, hurrying along the valley floor, vulnerable to their swooping assaults?

"Shouldn't we find a cave?" Raquel asked.

"Not a good idea," Giles replied.

"We can't stay out here. Not with my brother" – she lowered her voice – "injured."

"We're almost there. A few hours and we should be within sight of the portal."

"But it will be dark before then!" she hissed. "Besides, you've seen him? He's exhausted."

"We can't stop, Raquel. We'll be trapped."

"How so?"

"We'll have to light a fire to hold off these harpies. That's as good as putting up a sign to any pursuers saying 'We're over here!'"

"You said back at the falls there was so much smoke from the fire that none of the harpies saw you escape."

"True, but..."

"You don't know Mary," Alfonso cut in. "She will not rest until she's sure."

"What do you mean?" Raquel asked, speaking at a normal volume.

"When she can't find our remains among those in the forest or floating below the falls, she and Olga will head downriver. If they capture Katya's father or one of his followers, it won't take them long to discover we're still alive."

Though his sister didn't argue, he could tell she wasn't happy.

"Come on, we've waited long enough," Giles said, needing no further encouragement. "We must press on while there's still light."

The next few hours in the dying rays of the suns were more challenging than any of Alfonso's trials since arriving on Gemini. His blistered skin had become unbearable to touch, preventing his sister from supporting him. And there wasn't a part of his battered body that didn't protest every time he stumbled, which in his exhausted state happened more frequently, despite the level ground.

This made Raquel curse Giles more for his unrelenting pace. However, the thought of what would happen if they were caught in the open by Mary and Olga was such that Alfonso never offered a word of complaint. Instead, he concentrated on putting one foot in front of the other in a shambling jog.

In the end, though, it was Raquel who undid him. Perhaps turning to glance back up the valley, or simply missing her footing in the lengthening shadows, she bumped against his arm. It was enough to send him sprawling. He bounced painfully against the ground and lay in a cloud of choking dust.

"Alfonso!" Raquel cried, dropping down next to him.

He was barely able to breathe, let alone speak.

Giles swore and ran back to them. "Are you all right?"

"He fell," Raquel said.

Giles was panting. "Come on, we need to keep going."

"Give him some time!"

"There is no time, Raquel. The shadows… They're at the cliffs."

Above their breathless voices, Alfonso thought he heard the faint flapping of wings.

"He has to rest, Giles!"

"He can't. Not here. Not when we're so close."

Alfonso struggled to his knees.

"Giles… is right," he gasped.

"But Alfonso…"

He grabbed her arms.

"Raquel!" he snarled. "I… will not… be taken… again."

In the silence that followed, Alfonso realised he had bared his teeth, and his fingers were like claws digging into her flesh. Appalled, he let go, relieved for once that he couldn't see her expression.

"OK," Giles said, his voice level. "Hopefully, it won't come to that. But we have to move now."

Raquel said nothing, and Alfonso wondered if his bestial response had repulsed her as much as it had him. He held out his hand.

"Come, Sister, I cannot do this without you."

For a moment, she didn't take it. But he felt for her arm and, trying not to wince from his blistered skin, gave what he hoped was a reassuring squeeze. "*Gracias.*"

"Is OK," she murmured. The hurt in her voice made him sick. But apologies would have to come later.

"Giles, you know the way?"

"Yes, it's just over…"

Raquel gasped. "*Deu Meu*!"

"What is it?" Alfonso imagined a swooping harpy. "Tell me!"

"Well, unless I'm mistaken," Giles said, his voice full of wonder, "someone over there has left a light on."

Chapter Twenty-Four

Ravi took a sip of water from his canteen. Across the valley, stars were emerging in the darkening sky. The unfamiliar patterns reminded him of those heady days when he and Robert had first ventured into this new world, embarking on their voyage of discovery. Now, the wonder at his surroundings was replaced by a gnawing fear for Giles and Raquel.

Earlier that day, his new portal had brought him back to the same cave he'd arrived at all those years before. The scene had barely changed. The same rust-coloured valley lay before him, with its green river snaking around tall columns of rock, and the twin suns blazed overhead. That the arcane hieroglyphs had led him like an astronomical compass to the same spot had come as a relief.

However, there had been no sign of Giles or Raquel, save for what might have been a sand-filled footprint on the scree slope. Ravi had spent the rest of his time exploring the valley, searching for any indication they had passed that way. But if there had been any tracks on the hard-packed ground, they had long since disappeared. He had even resorted to calling their names, but the only response had been the forlorn echo of his voice off the sheer-sided walls.

After hours of fruitless searching, and with his throat parched and raw, he'd returned to the sanctuary of the cave to prepare for the night ahead. For he knew he wasn't alone. He had seen the clusters of harpies clinging limpet-like to the cliffs, calcified wings curled over their inert raptor bodies, waiting for the approaching dark.

As he sat near the entrance to his cave, his flashlight shining out along the valley, Ravi thought back to the harpy he had encountered on the Chapel Tower. She had ventured into his world to recover the egg Robert had stolen from her, and he and his students had tracked, cornered and ultimately destroyed her. He regretted that. Now he was in her world, recovering those precious to him, and it would be a bitter irony if he suffered the same fate at the hands of her kind. Perhaps Giles and Raquel had already fallen victim to avenging harpies, their bodies broken at the foot of a tower like the harpy's egg in Chapel Court.

"Stop it," he muttered, closing his eyes to blank out the image.

That was when the harpies started screeching and cawing at the bottom of the slope. Reaching for his ruler and flashlight, Ravi rose to his feet as the harsh cries became more febrile.

Were they fighting over a kill? Or had one of their number been injured and was being set upon by the others?

Whatever it was, they were getting nearer, and he shone his flashlight towards the clamour. Panning the beam across the slope, Ravi glimpsed a wing as a harpy swerved away from the light, squawking in alarm. More cries erupted from the circling flyers as Ravi swung his torch back and forth. There was also movement on the ground, among the rocks. Whatever crouched there was using the brief respite to scramble up the incline.

"Damn," he muttered. What new menace was heading his way?

Before he could train his torch there, particles of fine red dust floated down in front of the entrance. Ravi swung the beam up in time to catch a pair of outstretched claws reaching for him.

"Aaah!" he yelled, springing back.

A split second later, the harpy landed in the mouth of the cave, the downdraft from its wings throwing up dust. Spluttering, Ravi staggered backwards, caught his heel and sprawled on the floor.

Had it not been for the confines of the cave, that might have been his end. But in its eagerness to get at him, the harpy's wings snagged on the walls, slowing it long enough for Ravi to lash out with his ruler. The creature screeched and leapt back, buying him precious seconds to raise his torch and direct the beam into the creature's face. The cry died in its maw, and a grey patina spread over its wide eyes.

Then, there was a loud crack, and a fissure appeared down the centre of its forehead. Ravi just had time to register the axe blade protruding from the gap before the calcified face exploded into dust with the rest of the body.

Coughing, he backed into the cave. Beyond the slowly

settling cloud, a ghostly apparition stood in the entrance.

"Evening, Professor. Sorry about the mess. Can't abide cold callers."

"Giles?"

Two more figures staggered into view.

"Raquel!" he cried, almost laughing with relief until he saw the hideously scarred man on her shoulder.

"Oh, my…!"

"Torch, please, Professor," Giles said, grabbing it from his hand and directing it at the opening. Not a moment too soon. A pair of harpies, jostling to enter the cave, were caught in the beam. They recoiled at once, shrieking in anguish as they tumbled out of sight. More of the creatures veered away as soon as Giles swept the beam across the sky.

"Professor," panted Raquel, "can you give me a hand?"

"Of course." He got to his feet and helped her lead her invalid to the back of the cave, where they set him down gently against the wall.

"*Gracias,*" he murmured, and Ravi finally understood.

"Alfonso? Alfonso Vidal?"

"*Si,*" he panted.

It was like looking at a corpse brought back to life. Ravi and almost everyone else had long since given up Alfonso for dead. Not so his sister squatting beside him or Giles guarding the entrance to the cave. "My name is Ravi," he said, offering his hand. "Professor Ravi Gupta."

Ignoring the gesture, Alfonso replied, "Hello, Ravi. Thank you for coming back for me."

Ravi withdrew his hand. The anguish in Raquel's eyes

told him her brother hadn't seen it.

"Professor?" Giles called from the entrance. He had his axe in hand and was directing the torch into the night sky. "We'll need you to open that portal pretty soon."

"Of course. How long can you hold them off?"

"It's not these I'm worried about. There's a Matriarch and her daughter on their way."

"A what?"

"He means Mary," Alfonso said.

Ravi stared into the boy's sightless eyes.

"Who did you say?"

"Mary. She is coming for me. With her daughter, Olga."

"No," Ravi murmured. "That's not possible."

But further discussion was cut short by a distant screech, deeper and longer than the others.

"Oh crap!" Giles muttered. "I think they're here."

"No!" Raquel cried. "Professor, quick, please. We can't let her take him!"

Her terror stung him into action.

"I'll need some light," he said.

"Take the torch." Giles hurried over and handed it to him. "It won't do any good against Olga anyway."

If they were right, the woman Ravi had last seen almost half a century ago could step through the opening at any minute.

"Please, Professor!" Raquel said, helping her poor brother to his feet. "The gate!"

"Of course," he said, leading them to the section of wall where the new gate had opened.

"Are you sure this is right, Professor? I thought it was further along."

"Trust me, Giles, this is the way I came."

Ravi started to recite the Latin, slowly at first, then increasing the tempo. The glyphs on the wall appeared, their glow casting a pale light across the cave. Finally, the archway materialised, revealing the passageway beyond.

"Come on!" Giles said.

The three of them guided Alfonso across the threshold. Once on the other side, Ravi turned and began reciting the closing spell. The screech rang out again, now ominously close, but Ravi didn't dare to stop reciting the Latin.

Behind him, Alfonso cried out, "It's her! She's come for me!"

"Alfonso, come on!" Raquel said.

"What the hell's got into him?" Giles asked.

Ravi continued, ignoring the struggle behind him. But as he uttered the final words – *"bibliotheca ostium"* – Raquel yelled.

"Giles, I can't hold him!"

"Oh, for heaven's sake," Giles muttered as her brother pushed past Ravi towards the portal.

"Be careful!" Ravi said, grabbing the boy's arm. "The gate is closing."

Alfonso turned towards him, his face wild – not with fear, he realised.

Could it be joy?

Then, he broke free of Ravi's grip with disarming ease, but not before Giles had managed to get between him and the portal.

"Alfonso!" Giles yelled. "Behind you!"

Raquel's brother hesitated for a fraction of a second – long enough for Giles to pull back his fist and punch him square in the face.

Raquel screamed as Alfonso's head flew back, blood spurting from his nose. Somehow, Ravi caught him, and together they dragged him clear of the portal. Raquel directed a stream of Catalan expletives at Giles as they lowered her brother's limp body to the ground.

"Sorry, it was the only way," he said before a gust of air ruffled his hair.

The wall was beginning to reform, obscuring the archway. But on the other side of the narrowing aperture, an enormous harpy landed in the mouth of the cave. It wasn't just the size of the creature that surprised Ravi. It was the fact that she strode towards the portal.

The harpy made no attempt to rush them. She halted a few feet from the gate, her massive presence filling the dwindling opening. Large amber eyes looked at each of them before resting on Alfonso, taking in his scarred and bloody features.

Whether Alfonso sensed the gaze, Ravi would never know, but the boy stirred and his sightless eyes opened. And as the gate between the worlds finally closed, he uttered a single word.

"Katya!"

Chapter Twenty-Five

The return journey from Gemini had been very different from the first time Giles had passed through the portal. Back then, Raquel and he had marvelled at the breathtaking starscape as they travelled along the passageway. Giles had been excited at the prospect of exploring an alien world with this woman, hoping it would bring them closer.

Now, as Giles tramped along behind the others, that memory seemed a distant and unrealistic pipe dream. Though they had succeeded in recovering Alfonso, the mood among the travellers was sombre, and Professor Gupta appeared lost in his thoughts, head down and shoulders hunched.

Alfonso hadn't spoken a word since calling Katya's name. He'd withdrawn into himself, and nothing Raquel said or did elicited a response. Giles wondered if he should try, but he doubted she'd let him near her brother after his sucker punch to get Alfonso away from the portal.

Preoccupied with these thoughts, Giles was surprised at how fast they reached the other end of the tunnel.

"We are here," the Professor said, indicating the archway, which was much smaller than Giles remembered. "It is important that we all remain quiet when we return through the gate. I don't want us drawing attention to the portal's location."

Giles thought it unlikely that anyone would be around the New Court cellars to hear them, but Raquel had other concerns.

"We need to get Alfonso to the hospital."

"We will do, of course," Ravi assured her. "As soon as we are clear of the gate. But no one must know where we came from. Is that understood?"

They nodded.

"Good," said the Professor. "Follow me."

He approached the archway, which had some sort of screen over the opening. The Professor pressed a finger to his lips before lifting the cover and stepping through.

Instead of emerging into a darkened cellar, Giles found himself in an oak-panelled room, with leaded windows set high in the walls. A sliver of morning sunlight escaped the drawn blinds, illuminating a reading table and empty bookcases that he recognised at once. He'd been here before: it was the Old Librarian's Office.

The Professor murmured the closing spell again, and the archway faded, leaving chalk glyphs that he wiped away with his sleeve. Then, he lowered the Mappa Mundi and faced them.

"So, this is what you were doing last term," Giles said.

"I had to be sure I could still perform the spell."

Giles had to admit the Professor was a much better poker player than he let on.

"The hospital, Professor?" Raquel said.

"Yes, of course." He crossed to the door. "Not a word, remember."

The Old Library, with its carved bookcases and tall leaded windows, felt almost as unreal to Giles as the world he'd escaped. The musty air, with the smell of old leather, paper and parchment, couldn't have been more different from the harsh, arid atmosphere they'd endured these past weeks. Raquel also seemed affected by it, glancing at the cabinets of old books and manuscripts as she guided her brother towards the Oriel window overlooking the river.

Head up and shoulders unwound, the Professor strode to the head of the spiral staircase and swung open the metal gate before descending the steps. Raquel followed, taking care of her brother as he made his tentative way down the stairs. Giles waited until they'd reached the bottom before shutting the gate and following them through the deserted Lower Library.

When they arrived at the glass partition to the reading area, it wasn't the College Archivist sitting at the desk but another familiar face.

"Good morning, Mr Weston," said the Professor.

"Good morning, Professor. I wondered if that was you upstairs..."

The College Librarian raised his head but froze when he saw the four of them.

"I see you have some guests with you."

"Ah yes, some visitors from Spain. I've been showing them some of the hidden wonders of the Old Library."

Over his steel-rimmed glasses, the Librarian took in their dishevelled and sunburnt appearance, his gaze lingering on Alfonso's ravaged features.

"And how did you find them?" Weston asked.

The Professor stiffened. "Sorry?"

"The hidden wonders," the Librarian said, considering the others,

"Captivating," Giles replied, meeting his gaze. "Though some of the original handwritten indexes might need updating."

"Is that so, Mr Chamberlain?"

"Absolutely, Mr Weston. Took us ages to find some of the items."

"Clearly," the Librarian said, "as you appear to have been up there some time." He hesitated, peering down at the leather-bound register. "Although I can't seem to find an entry here."

"Really?" said the Professor. "That's not like me."

"It surprised me too," Weston agreed.

There was an awkward silence, and Giles wondered if he should say something. But then the Librarian closed the ledger and set it to one side.

"These things happen, Professor. Let's keep it between ourselves, shall we?"

"I think that's probably wise, Mr Weston."

We look after our own, Giles thought, considering the pair.

"Though, I would ask you to remember, Mr Chamberlain," the Librarian indicated the backpack over Giles's shoulder with the ice axe protruding from the flap, "that bags are not allowed upstairs."

"*Mea culpa,* Mr Weston. I'll try to remember next time."

The Librarian nodded. "Now that's all settled, don't let me detain you." He smiled at the Vidals. "It was nice to meet you both."

The Professor ushered Raquel and her brother through the exit and Giles hurried after them.

"Oh, and Mr Chamberlain?"

Giles paused in the doorway.

"It's good to have you back."

"Thanks, Mr Weston."

The Librarian returned to his books, leaving Giles to catch up with the others.

Once outside, they headed straight for the Forecourt Lodge, ignoring looks from a couple of College gardeners tending the lawns.

"Good morning, Bert," said the Professor as he entered the lodge.

"Morning, Professor." The old Porter looked up and dropped his newspaper. "My goodness! Is that…?"

"I'd be grateful if you could order a taxi to Addenbrooke's hospital," the Professor said. "As soon as possible, please."

"Right, Professor. Of course. Taxi for four."

"No! Just two," Raquel corrected him.

"Raquel, are you sure you don't want us to…?"

"*Si*, I am sure, Professor."

As Bert picked up the phone, Giles asked, "Shall I get you some things from my room? Some clothes for Alfonso?"

"There is no need. I think we can manage now."

It was clear she hadn't forgiven him for punching her brother.

"Taxi's on its way," Bert said.

Giles looked from Raquel to Alfonso. "In that case, I'll say goodbye."

"Goodbye, Giles," Raquel replied. Her brother showed no sign of having heard him, but when Giles turned to go, a hand grasped his arm.

"Giles." Alfonso's grip was strong, despite his blistered skin. They stood facing each other. No words were said; none were needed. When he finally let go, there were tears in Alfonso's glassy eyes. Not trusting himself to say anything, he patted Alfonso on the arm and walked out of the lodge without looking back.

If he attracted strange looks walking through the courts, Giles neither knew nor cared. He found himself outside his room with no recollection of climbing the stairs. His spare key was behind the fire extinguisher, and he unlocked both doors, dumped the backpack on the neatly made bed and slumped into the armchair.

How long he remained there, Giles couldn't tell. Time absented itself as he stared into a fireplace as empty as himself. Footsteps on the stairs didn't register until the door swung open. Then, Ying was there, eyes widening as she took in his dishevelled appearance.

"Giles!" She crossed the room and threw her arms around his neck. "You gorgeous, bloody, sweaty idiot! Where have you been?"

Behind her, Trevor appeared, a broad smile on his bearded face.

"Leave him alone, Ying. You'll suffocate the poor man."

She squeezed him one more time before letting go.

"Thank goodness you're back," she said. "This place is so damn boring without you!"

Giles looked at them both.

"That's good to know," he said, and for the first time since returning through the portal, he smiled.

Chapter Twenty-Six

Three weeks after his return from Gemini, Professor Ravi Gupta slipped out the back of College and walked along Madingley Road. The evening sky was blessedly free of clouds, the perfect conditions for a long overdue spell of stargazing after many late nights marking examination papers.

The Cavendish Observatory was located just past Churchill College, the fifteen-minute walk so familiar to him that he could do it in his sleep. Indeed, some mornings he'd returned to College with almost no memory of the journey, his exhausted brain on autopilot to see him safely back to his room.

Tonight, however, his mind was preoccupied with the precarious state of his Fellowship since his latest run-in with the Master in the aftermath of his return from Gemini. To say Lester had been unhappy about his illicit journey through the portal to rescue Giles and the others would be an understatement. The man had been apoplectic.

******

"What the hell did you think you were doing?" Lester yelled. "Can you imagine what would have happened if you had not made it back? There would have been the most almighty uproar, not to mention the fact that the police would have launched an investigation into your disappearance!"

Though shocked by this outburst, Ravi stood his ground.

"One of our students was missing, Master, and I had reason to believe he had passed through the Gemini Passage."

"And who might have given him that idea? Ye gads, man! We all know Chamberlain is a maverick. You might as well have given the boy a corkscrew and told him no one had ever broken into the Fellows' wine cellar!"

It was one thing to be reprimanded for his own behaviour, but Ravi wasn't going to stand by and let the Master disparage what Giles had done for the Vidals.

"Might I point out, Master, that Giles almost certainly saved Alfonso Vidal from a long and painful death?"

"From what I understand, the unfortunate wretch might have welcomed that, given the state he was in. Reports from the hospital suggest he will never recover his sight. As for the burns, well, there was only so much the plastic surgeons could do."

"I can assure you, Master," Ravi said, his voice level, "the Vidal family were overjoyed to have their son back, whatever his injuries. That is down to Giles, particularly since everybody else had given Alfonso up for dead."

This rebuke did something to quell Lester's tirade.

"Well, it seems to have ensured their silence on the

matter, at any rate – something for which we must be thankful. That we managed to keep a lid on this thing is nothing short of a miracle."

This was true. There had been rumours among the Fellowship that one of their brightest scholars had almost missed his exams. But the Master's well-timed slip at High Table that this was due to an ill-fated fling with a Spanish beauty had done much to distract his colleagues from the real reason for Giles's absence.

Their dramatic reappearance in the Library was known only to Mr Weston, who rarely dined with the Fellows in Hall. And Ravi's donation of a new leather-bound register had ensured that the Librarian's legendary discretion was more than assured.

"One thing is for certain," Lester went on. "I'm going to prevent this sort of thing from ever happening again. You mark my words, Ravi, that area of the New Court cellars will be out of bounds to anyone, be they student, staff or Fellow, whatever their standing in College. I don't care whether young Chamberlain is tipped to become the next Stephen Hawking. If he so much as sniffs around those cellars, he'll find his academic career cut shorter than the College lawns – something you would do well to pass on next time you speak with him."

"If I see him, Master, I shall. Although I think that unlikely."

"Meaning?"

"Exams, Master. I expect he'll be sitting them about now."

Lester glared at him. "Exams or not, I have marked that boy's card, and I'll be watching him like a hawk from now on."

As if that will deter Giles, Ravi thought. But he decided not to share this insight when the Master was in such a volatile mood.

"Will that be all?"

"I suppose so," Lester replied, scowling. "But if you had any doubts whether your card was marked, I can assure you there's a bloody great cross on it."

******

Even now, Ravi was unsettled by what the Master had said. Not so much the thinly veiled threat to himself – he was far too long in the tooth to worry about that. What disturbed him were Lester's comments about Giles.

Admittedly, what the boy had done had been foolhardy. But his rescue of Alfonso Vidal had been nothing short of heroic. In any other circumstances, he would have received a special award of some description. Instead, all the boy had to show for his remarkable endeavour were painful physical scars to his arms and legs and an irretrievably broken relationship with Raquel.

The latter appeared to have affected Giles the most, an impression confirmed by Rose, who had been briefing Ravi on her student's mental state since his return.

"Never goes out, not even the rooftops at night, from what I can make out. That's not like him at all."

On the few occasions Ravi had spotted the familiar mop of blonde hair on the other side of Second Court, there had been no theatrical wave or cheerful "Halloo" across the lawns. Instead, Giles had kept his head down, barely making eye contact as he made his way to and from the Archaeology Faculty in town.

As far as exams were concerned, Ravi doubted Giles had much to worry about. His Director of Studies had greeted the prodigy's reappearance with the sort of ecstatic relief that a coach might show when a star player returned from injury. It was Giles's emotional well-being that concerned Ravi. He hoped he had friends who would rally around him and cheer him up.

Perhaps I should have a quiet word with Annabel and Nick, he thought. *Ask them to go and see him.* If Giles could open up to anyone about what had happened, it would be them.

Ravi arrived at a squat conical tower nestled among the lawns of the Cavendish campus. Taking a set of keys from his pocket, he unlocked the door and made his way up the well-worn steps to the observation platform on the upper level. Settling into his usual routine, he made himself a cup of tea and sat in his observation chair before wrapping Robert's tartan blanket around him.

Like all the old observatories at the Cavendish, this one was open to the elements to avoid internal and external temperature changes distorting light waves. Which is why Ravi looked like he was about to explore the Arctic Poles rather than the starry skies.

He patted the frigid surface of the Thorogood telescope, its cylindrical array of lenses pointing through the dome's vertical aperture.

"Just you and me tonight, old friend," he murmured.

Ravi was about to use the sighting scope when unwelcome footsteps brought him up short. He waited, hoping they would continue past, but they stopped. A match was struck, and a plume of smoke drifted into view.

Jane, he thought.

After giving the intelligence officer the slip before departing to Gemini, Ravi had been wondering when she'd come to see him. He hoped she'd be more understanding than the Master had been.

The observatory door rattled.

"I'm coming," he called, making his way back down the stairs.

The visitor's outline in the frosted glass window warned him too late that it wasn't Jane after all.

"Allo? Ravi? Is that you?" The door rattled again.

With a sinking heart, he opened the door for Gabrielle Dutour. Wearing a long dark cloak and a beret pulled down over her severe bob, Gabrielle looked like she had walked out of a 1930s' film noir.

"Ah, there you are," she said, taking a final drag of her cigarette before crushing it underfoot.

"Gabrielle. What are you doing here?"

"Getting lost. Are there no streetlights in this place?"

"I'm afraid not. As you can imagine, light pollution is something of an issue here."

"Well, some better signage would have helped."

"Perhaps, although most of us know our way around by now."

Her oversized glasses gave her a strangely alien look.

"Are you going to invite me in?"

"Oh, yes, of course, forgive me."

Ravi led her to the observation platform, aware of how old and shabby it must look.

"Would you like tea? I've just boiled the kettle."

"You don't have coffee?"

"No, I'm afraid not. I don't get many guests here."

"I'm not surprised. It's freezing!"

"Ah, yes. Comes with the job. Here, this might help." He handed her Robert's blanket. "Please, take a seat."

She perched on his well-worn desk chair, the wheels squeaking as she unfolded the blanket over her legs.

"So, Ravi, this is where you have been hiding from me."

"I'm not sure hiding is how I would describe it."

"I have hardly seen you."

"Oh, you know how it is, what with exams and troubled Tutees."

"Ah *oui*. Some of the lawyers were stressed. I cannot think why. If they had done the work, there would have been no problem." She waved a hand at Ravi's expression. "It was a joke, Ravi. I do remember what it was like to be a student."

"I see." He smiled.

"I never realised how time-consuming it is being a Tutor," she went on. "Is it always like this?"

"Occupational hazard, I'm afraid," he said, though he wasn't sure she heard him. She appeared preoccupied with examining the weave of the blanket.

"What brings you out here, Gabrielle?"

He expected the inevitable barrage of questions about his early research. However, she surprised him.

"The May Ball is tomorrow night, is it not?"

"Why yes. You're going, I take it?"

"*Oui*. I received an invitation."

"Ah, yes," he smiled. "It's one of the perks of living in College. Resident Fellows tend to pop along, if only for the fireworks."

"On their own?"

"Well, yes, as most are… single."

She nodded. "I see."

Ravi was trying to work out where this was going when Gabrielle raised her head, her wide eyes magnified by her lenses.

"Would you like to take me, Ravi?"

"Sorry?"

"It is a masked ball. Angels and demons. As I have no friends to speak of among the Fellowship, I am asking you to be my guardian angel."

Ravi was so astonished he didn't know what to say.

"Oh, I see." She blushed, misreading his hesitation. "You already have a partner."

"No," he admitted, "I don't."

"But you do not wish to take me?"

"No, I mean… It's not that. It's that, well, I hadn't planned on going." He almost added, *without Robert.*

"Then, will you… go with me?"

Her vulnerability struck him. Gabrielle had trekked here in the middle of the night to ask him to take her to a ball. If he refused, she would have that same long walk back on her own. Whatever her association with Julian Schiller, Ravi couldn't do that to her.

"I would be delighted."

Her smile was so genuine he found himself reciprocating.

"*Bon.* That is settled then." She rose from the chair. "I'll leave you to your observations, Ravi."

"Oh, right, of course."

She held up the blanket. "This was in your room, no?"

"For a while, yes."

"I like the design. What is it called?"

Ravi hesitated. "It is the Mackenzie tartan."

"Robert's?"

"Yes."

She nodded. "Like the trunk."

Ravi went very still.

"In your room. I saw it. Robert's initials were on the side."

"That's right," Ravi said, wary.

She shrugged. "A good idea, putting the blanket over it. That old trunk was ugly, but this... It added a nice touch of colour." She handed it back to him. "*Merci*, Ravi. And goodnight."

"Good night, Gabrielle."

After she'd closed the door, Ravi sat and draped the blanket over his knees, idly tracing a finger over the tartan squares. Had he just made a terrible mistake?

Chapter Twenty-Seven

"Pens down, please!"

Annabel did as instructed by the gown-clad invigilator whose commanding voice had broken the hushed silence. For a fraction of a second, the hundred or so bodies around her remained still. Then, with a collective sigh and scraping of chairs, the examination hall stirred into life. Students lifted their heads, arched their backs and stretched aching shoulders.

"Please, no talking until we have collected all your papers," came the belated reminder as quiet conversations rose and then fell to a residual, furtive murmur.

Annabel couldn't blame them. With so many topics to cover, first-year Natural Scientists had endured one of the longest timetables of all subjects, with today's exam taking place after the May Bumps, much to her annoyance.

Two nights earlier, she'd attended a boisterous Boat Club dinner to celebrate Brett's M1 crew going Head of the River. The evening had ended with the ritual burning of the Headship boat on the lawn in front of New Court. And once the victorious crew had leapt over the flames, Annabel,

Clarissa and the rest of W3 had done the same to celebrate winning their oars after bumping Newnham on the final day. It should have been the perfect celebration of her first rowing campaign. But the need to revise for her final exam and Blades's absence had cast a shadow over the event.

Since that fateful night by Jesus Lock, there had been no further sightings of the creature Blades claimed to have speared. But neither had any remains been recovered. And though the Boatman had assured Annabel there was nothing to be concerned about, she suspected from his haggard appearance that he was continuing to patrol the banks at night.

These unsettling thoughts were interrupted by an arm waving from the far side of the examination hall. Ash, practically standing on his chair, was grinning at her over the heads of his bemused neighbours. He gave her a double thumbs-up sign and an outrageous wink. Whether he thought the exam had gone well or he was just happy it was over, she couldn't tell.

Probably both, knowing him, she thought.

Ash stopped waving and began gesticulating at Brian, who was sitting a few rows away. They appeared to be using some secret sign language. Either that or they were playing one of the most complicated games of rock–paper–scissors she had ever seen.

An examiner walked past Annabel's desk and collected her paper, then continued along the row to the front of the hall, where she joined the other invigilators. Once all the stacks were complete, the lead examiner addressed the room.

"Well done, everyone. You have completed Part 1 of the Natural Sciences Tripos. You are free to go. Enjoy May Week!"

The last words were almost drowned out by the clamour of noise. There were a good few whoops as the liberated students rose to their feet. Already, she could see Ash bounding towards her, Brian a few feet behind as they weaved between desks.

"How'd it go?" he asked, grinning.

"What did you think about the question on..." Brian began, but Annabel held up her hands.

"Guys. I want to enjoy this moment and not worry about which questions I got wrong."

"Oh," Ash said, his smile faltering. "OK."

Annabel realised she was putting a dampener on what should have been a joyous occasion. "Come on," she said. "Why don't we celebrate with a pot of tea and a Chelsea bun at Fitzbillies. What do you say?"

Their obvious disappointment was unexpected.

"Um, isn't it a bit hot for tea?" Ash frowned.

"It is rather warm," Brian agreed.

"Or a cold drink. Whatever your fancy. My treat."

Again, the pregnant pause.

"How about an ice cream?" Brian suggested.

Ash's face lit up. "Ice cream! Great idea!"

Annabel frowned. "I'm not sure Fitzbillies does those."

"There's often a vendor down at the Mill Pond," Brian replied.

"That's right," agreed Ash. "We can get one there!"

She shrugged. "Ice cream it is, then. As long as mine has a chocolate flake, I don't mind."

They headed to the river and arrived at a cheery collection of pubs and restaurants clustered around the punt stations at the bottom of Mill Lane. The place was busy with punt touts plying their trade to the many tourists gathered there, though they wisely left the penniless students alone.

"Guys, I don't see anyone selling ice cream," Annabel said.

"Oh, I think there's one along here." Ash strode over the stone crossing to the picturesque stretch of meadow on the other side. He led them past the slipway between the lower and upper river, peering with exaggerated interest at the almost cloudless sky.

"Lovely day, isn't it?"

"Certainly is," Brian agreed without raising his head.

Though Annabel couldn't argue, she still couldn't see where they would get an ice cream.

"Guys, are you sure there's somewhere to…?"

At that moment, they stopped and parted.

Nick stood on the path ahead, wearing shorts and a white shirt with rolled-up sleeves revealing surprisingly tanned forearms. Alongside him, nestled against the bank, was a punt with the distinctive St John's College red trim.

"Hi," he said. "All done then?"

"Nick? What are you doing here?"

"I made you a promise, remember? To take you punting."

"But you don't…?"

Nick stepped onto the punt and hoisted the punt pole

with practised ease. Annabel stared from him to the others.

"You two were in on this?"

Ash beamed. "Now you know why we couldn't go to Fitzbillies."

"We didn't want to spoil your appetite," Brian explained.

In the punt, a bulging backpack was stowed between the seats.

"Come on," Nick said. "It's a fair old trek to Grantchester."

"One hour and eleven minutes," said Brian.

"At least, that's Nick's best time to date," Ash added.

Shaking her head, Annabel stepped on board the punt and settled into her seat. When the others made no move to join her, she asked, "Aren't you coming?"

"We have other plans, don't we, Brian?"

The other shifted uncomfortably. "Yes, but we're not supposed to say."

"True." Ash lowered his voice so that only a dozen or so people could hear. "It's for the May Ball, very hush hush."

"I see," Annabel said, trying not to smile.

"Anyway, have a good trip," Ash said, waving. "Make sure you bring the punt back in one piece."

"Will do," Nick said before turning to Annabel. "Shall we?"

She laughed. "Definitely!"

The punt ride to Grantchester was everything Annabel could have wished for. The sun shone down from a cloudless sky, its hot rays fanned by a gentle breeze that sent water lapping against the hull. The heady scent of waterlilies and meadow grass wafted on pollen-laden air from the surrounding meadows. And the quavering buzz of insects first softened and then displaced the lingering sounds of the city as they glided beyond its thinning borders.

However, as she followed the dragonflies flitting among the reeds, her gaze was drawn to the willow trees lining the banks, casting dark shadows across the water. Unable to help herself, Annabel scanned the surface for signs of movement. Was that a line of bubbles under one drooping branch…?

"Are you OK?"

Startled, she raised a hand to shield her eyes. Water had run down Nick's arms, soaking the shirt that clung to his shoulders and chest. His once sandy hair, bleached blonde by hours spent practising punting, framed his rugged face, and his thoughtful eyes were steady and unwavering.

She hesitated. Then, she remembered how much effort Nick had put into this trip. Was she really going to let some irrational paranoia spoil it?

Get a grip, girl, she thought and smiled. "Just a bit of PESD."

"PESD?"

"Post-exam stress disorder. You know, when you're worried that you messed things up."

"Right," he said, though he didn't sound convinced.

It took them another half hour to make it to Grantchester, and the only incident of note came in a shadowy stretch under overhanging trees where the local Cambridge Naturist club was located. Fortunately, Nick had warned Annabel in advance, so she wasn't completely shocked when an elderly gentleman emerged from the bushes wearing nothing more than a swimming cap.

"Nice weather for it!" he called out, arching his back and shaking his arms.

"Certainly is," Nick replied as Annabel stared fixedly at the horizon. Moments later, a similarly attired woman with a silk headscarf over her coiffured hair emerged from the bushes.

"George, have you seen Muffy anywhere?"

The old man frowned. "Could have sworn I saw the damn thing earlier!"

"Probably chasing voles again," the woman said.

"He'll turn up, don't you worry." George turned to Annabel. "If you spot a Spaniel on the towpath, give us a shout. Damned fella is as mad as a badger."

Not trusting herself to speak, Annabel nodded her agreement. Nick, his face rigid, propelled them around the next bend before collapsing in silent laughter as she dissolved into convulsive giggles.

When they finally reached Grantchester Meadows, Annabel had recovered sufficiently to reach for the backpack while Nick moored them alongside the bank.

"So, what have you got in here?" she asked before lifting the flap. She found it stuffed with packets of crisps, sandwiches wrapped in tinfoil, pork pies, a box of Mr Kipling cakes, a punnet of strawberries and a pair of plastic glasses. "Wow! You really went to town!"

"I thought you might be hungry."

She was and immediately popped a strawberry in her mouth. "Hmm, delicious."

"They're for the Champagne," Nick said. "To bring out the flavour."

Annabel almost choked. "Says who?"

"Dr Dutour. Told us in our last Tutorial."

"You're joking?"

"Said it was essential preparation for May Week."

Annabel rolled her eyes before poking around at the bottom of the bag. "That's all very well," she said. "Only one problem."

"What's that?"

"You forgot the Champagne."

"Ah, but did I?"

He nodded at the bow where the boat chain hung over the side of the punt.

"You're kidding, right?"

"Well, you can't drink warm Champagne, can you?"

"Don't tell me that was Dutour's idea too?"

"No, Brian's," Nick replied, stepping over her seat. "It was in the Punt Society Handbook."

"Well, I'm impressed."

Nick hauled on the chain, and it came up so suddenly he almost tipped backwards.

"What the hell!"

"Nick? Is everything all right?"

He pulled it clear of the water. If a bottle had been attached to the end, it wasn't there now. Instead, the galvanised steel links had been severed in half.

In the distance, they heard a scream.

Chapter Twenty-Eight

Any thoughts Nick had entertained of an idyllic picnic together disappeared with that scream.

"Come on!" he said. "Grab the paddle."

He pushed them off, and they journeyed back down the river, him punting and Annabel paddling from the bow. Rounding a bend, they saw the stretch of woodland ahead of them, its discreet privacy hedge running along the bank.

"There she is!" Annabel cried, pointing at the woman staring at something in the water.

Her partner was splashing a few yards offshore.

"It's the old man," Nick said. "I think he's in trouble!"

He leaned on the punt pole, and they approached the overhanging trees.

"George?" The woman was frantic. "For goodness' sake, save him."

The old man gasped and disappeared below the surface.

"Shit!" Nick steered towards the expanding circle of ripples. "Can you see him?"

Annabel stopped paddling. "No, I… There!"

The swimming cap emerged right by the punt. Nick let

go of the pole and dropped to his knees.

"It's OK, I've got you!" He hooked his hands under the man's arms.

"What are you doing?" the woman yelled from the bank. "Leave him alone!"

"Get off me, you idiot!" the old man roared.

Annabel reflected Nick's surprise back at him.

"OK, sorry," he said, letting go.

As the man swam back to shore, the woman cried, "Now look what you've done!"

"Sorry, we thought he was in trouble," Annabel explained.

"Not George. Muffy!"

"The dog?" Nick asked.

"Of course the dog," the man spluttered, reaching the bank. "A ruddy great pike took him! Just like that!"

"Muffy never stood a chance." The woman's tears began to flow.

Annabel's face was also pale. Not with shock, though, Nick thought. With dread.

The journey back was a subdued affair, neither of them speaking much. The old couple had clearly been devastated by the loss of their dog. Nick wished they could have done more, but he hadn't known how to console a pair of naked octogenarians. Annabel too had seemed at a loss, offering little more than words of sympathy as she'd repeatedly glanced at the water.

By the time they made it back to the Mill Pond, the conversation had all but dried up, and Nick decided it was time to get to the bottom of what was troubling her.

"Are you OK?"

Her face was still pale. "Yeah... A bit shocked, that's all."

Nick steered them beneath the wooden spars of the Mathematical Bridge.

"That must have been a big pike," he said. "I mean, a Spaniel's not a small dog, is it?"

"No," she agreed. "It's not."

As they approached King's College, Nick steeled himself. "You're very quiet, Annabel. Is it something I've done?"

"What? No, of course not. It's..." She hesitated. "There's something you need to know."

Here we go, he thought.

"I think I have a stalker."

Of all the things Nick had suspected might be bothering her, this was not one of them. He gripped the punt pole. "Who is it?"

"It's not so much a who as a *what*."

He felt a creeping sensation as understanding dawned.

"Not again," he said. "Where?"

"There," she gestured over the side of the punt.

"The river?"

She nodded. "Listen, I know it sounds crazy..."

"Like flying monsters and climbing statues, you mean? Annabel, after what we've seen this year, do you really think I'm going to find a river monster hard to believe?"

His smile dissolved the tension in her jaw. Indeed, the way she regarded him at that moment made the whole punt trip worthwhile.

"You remember my accident in Freshers' Week?" She spoke faster now. "You know when Brett and I almost drowned?"

"Not something I'm likely to forget in a hurry."

"Well, Blades thinks it started then. He reckons something tipped us over."

"I thought he said you hit a swan?"

"That's because he didn't want anyone to think it was my fault, what with Brett getting injured and everything. The truth is it all happened so fast that neither of us really saw what it was. It was dark under the bridge, you see.

"Then there was our accident in the Bumps. Blades found damage to the boat that wasn't caused by the crash. He thinks it must have happened during our early-morning outings, and the rudder only sheared off later when we went for our bump."

Nick remembered Annabel tugging uselessly on the rudder lines as they'd veered into the bank.

"Anyway, since then, he's been watching the river," she said, "particularly by the Boathouse. He freaks out when he finds anyone standing by the edge of the slipway. It's why he won't let boats go out after dark. That's when he goes hunting for it."

Nick stared at her. "You're not serious?"

"The night you found us out there, he thought he'd killed it. There have been no sightings since. But now…" Annabel grimaced at the river. "What do you think? Am I going crazy?"

"No," he replied. "I think it would explain the geese."

"What geese?"

"Exactly. They used to be all along the Backs." They glided past Trinity's riverbank. "This was covered in their..."

"Crap," she finished for him. "I remember the Professor calling it an avian latrine."

"Well, not anymore."

Annabel shook her head. "But Blades was so sure he'd got the creature that night."

"Maybe he did. But what if there was more than one?"

This obviously wasn't what Annabel wanted to hear. Behind her grimace, the distinctive profile of New Court came into view, its Paddock covered in contractors and students finalising preparations for the May Ball.

"Perhaps we should speak to Blades," Annabel said. "See what he thinks."

"Makes sense," Nick replied. "Though there's somebody else we might want to speak to first."

"The Professor, you mean?"

"No, not yet, anyway. I was thinking of someone who might have an even better idea of what we're up against."

"Who?"

Nick nodded at the Kitchen Bridge, where a solitary student lounged against the railing, a drink in hand. Annabel swivelled in her seat.

"Giles!" she cried.

"Hello, love birds!" He smiled, raising a glass. "Long time, no see."

"Hey, are you doing anything right now?" Nick asked.

"As you can see, I'm at my leisure."

"That's good, because we need to talk."

Chapter Twenty-Nine

After the punt had passed under the bridge, Giles resumed watching the May Ball preparations in front of New Court. Areas were marked out for fireworks, dodgems, fairground rides, food stalls and the temporary toilets tucked discreetly behind the West wing.

In previous years, he'd enjoyed the spectacle, the frantic activity adding a sense of anticipation to one of the best nights of the year. Now it felt rather pointless, after all that had happened on Gemini. The same had been true of the exams he'd dutifully sat to distract himself from his melancholy after Raquel's summary dismissal of his services. Since then, he'd had no word from her: no text, message, phone call… nothing.

It had been the Professor who'd informed him that Alfonso had been transferred back to Mallorca for treatment there. After that, the only communication Giles had received from the Vidals had come from Raquel's father. His formal letter, in perfect English, had thanked him on the family's behalf for returning their son to them. But, while Giles appreciated the gesture from a man who had barely acknowledged him before, it did little to alleviate his growing sense of emptiness.

He'd been foolish to think that rescuing her brother would have brought them closer. In reality, it had driven a wedge between them. Raquel had been consumed by her brother's care and had held Giles in some way accountable for his injuries.

But another part of him knew there was a deeper reason for his present malaise: the fear that the adventure of a lifetime was over and nothing else would match the daunting, terrifying and frankly exhilarating experience of venturing into an alien world and making it back alive.

Was that how it had been for old Mackenzie? Is that why he'd finally succumbed and looked for an excuse to return? To relive what he and his friend Ravi had experienced and be recognised by his peers for their discovery? Giles had more empathy for the old Scot after experiencing it himself.

He was also beginning to understand Professor Ravi Gupta. To have carried that burden steadfastly over the years said a lot about his strength of will. To never go back had almost become an act of faith. Yet he'd put it all at risk to return for Giles and Raquel, saving their lives and Alfonso's in the process.

Without the Professor driving off the harpies with his torch, they'd never have made it up the slope to the cave during that last desperate sprint along the valley as the light faded. Even if they had, Giles wasn't sure he'd have been able to conjure the portal and get Raquel and her brother through in time.

So, although Raquel's treatment of him had felt harsh, he did not hold it against her. Or for devoting herself to her brother's care. After what Alfonso had been through, Giles was glad his sister would be there for him. As for Giles? Well…

"Crap happens," he muttered and drained his glass.

"Hey, mopey! Has someone died?"

Ying, clipboard in hand, was striding towards him. She had a "No excuses or else" expression that made him glad he wasn't part of the May Ball set-up crew.

"My, Ying, you're looking officious this evening."

"It's working then," she said, giving him a kiss on the cheek. "What are you up to?"

"Not a lot. Then again, I've always found that watching others work is good for the soul."

"Well, you're welcome to lend a hand. Some of this year's crew are hopeless. Brains the size of planets but smarts the size of peas!"

"That's what happens when you hire Fellows to do the work."

"I wish!" She scoffed. "As for that Punt Society lot, we ordered ten punts for the courts, and they've only delivered nine."

"I think I might have seen the last one just now."

"Finally! Let's hope the ice arrives tomorrow." She shook her head. "We could have done with you on logistics, Giles. Instead, we've got some first-year numpty who spent more time selecting Champagne than scheduling deliveries."

"I'm sure it will all be fine on the night."

"Yeah, well, it had better be." She wiped a strand of hair from her forehead and looked at him. "I hear you've returned your tickets. Raquel's not coming?"

"Family commitments."

"Well, they were snapped up. You wouldn't believe some of the black-market prices this year. It's going to be a nightmare on security."

"Nothing you can't handle, Ying. Trevor always said you were great with handcuffs."

The buzz of her walkie-talkie saved him from a good kicking.

"Ying here. What? The punt's back? Great! I'll get the Redboys on it now. Out."

"Gotta run," she said to Giles, then hesitated. "Listen, you sure you don't want to tag along with me on the night? I could do with a runner who can think on his feet. But in the absence of that, you'll do."

She winked, but there was concern in her eyes.

"I'll be fine. I could do with a quiet night in with a good book and a cup of tea."

"You said that before crashing the Trinity Ball in our first year."

"It was an inordinately dull book, as I recall."

"Yeah, well, I'll see you around."

"Only if I let you, my dear."

Ying hurried off, and Giles leant against the wall of the bridge, while a team of contractors erected security fencing along the river. He had no intention of crashing this or any other ball. He might head to the roof to watch the fireworks, but that was about it. This made him even more depressed.

"Giles!"

Annabel and Nick were hurrying across the New Court lawn.

"Ah, the tardy punters. Seeing as you still have all your limbs attached, I guess you haven't bumped into Ying yet."

"No, was she looking for us?" Nick asked.

"For your sakes, I hope not."

"There's something more worrying we need to talk to you about," Annabel said, piquing his interest.

"I find that hard to believe."

"We think we might have another unwelcome visitor," she said in a low tone.

"From the other place," Nick added.

"I take it we're not talking Oxford."

Annabel shook her head, and Giles straightened up.

"One of our feathered friends?"

"More scaly than that."

She indicated the river, and nightmarish images of twin-headed serpents sprang to his mind.

"You've seen one?" he asked, trying to suppress his excitement.

"Not clearly. But we know someone who did."

Half an hour later, they entered the Waterman pub, a favourite drinking haunt of college Boatmen. On a balmy summer evening like this, the place was packed with town and gown alike, its patrons either relaxing after work or celebrating the holidays to come.

All the tables were full, save for one in the corner, where a dour man sat alone with his pint, his heavily tattooed arms crossed before him. His grim demeanour and hostile glare ensured that most customers were giving him a wide berth. But Annabel showed no such reluctance, crossing to the table and pulling up a chair.

"Hi, Blades."

"Evening, Annabel. What brings you here?"

"We wanted to ask your advice."

"Oh, yeah. You've come mob-handed, I see," he said as the others took the remaining stools.

"You know Nick, and this is Giles."

"You from John's as well, are you?"

"For my sins."

The Boatman took in the scars covering Giles's forearms and grunted. "What's this about then?"

Annabel checked that no one nearby was listening. "Our fishing expedition."

The Boatman gave her a sharp look. "We agreed we weren't going to discuss it again."

"I know, but something's come up."

Blades placed his hands on the table, and Giles noticed the letters HOLD FAST in faded ink across his knuckles.

"Come up how?"

Nick produced the severed chain from the College punt and placed it on the table.

"What did you use, a bolt cutter?"

"It was hanging over the side of the punt."

"Might have snagged on something."

"A dog was taken a hundred yards away," Annabel said, "by what its owner described as a large pike."

"Possible, I suppose. We've had thirty-pounders before."

"It was a Spaniel, Blades."

"And then there are the geese on the upper river," Nick added. "All gone."

"No… All of them?"

"Every one."

The Boatman frowned. "How long has this been going on?"

"I began noticing it four weeks ago."

"After he saw us that night on the river," Annabel said.

Blades leaned forwards, his voice low. "It can't be the same one, Annabel. I told you I got it plum to rights."

"They're not that easy to kill," Giles said.

Blades narrowed his eyes. "And what would you know about that?"

Giles rolled up his trouser leg to show the crescent scar on his calf.

"You get that on the Cam?"

"On a research expedition. The locals there know them as hydra."

"How'd one get back here then?"

Giles shrugged. "You know what academics are like for bringing back samples."

Blades grunted, then raised a calloused finger and tapped between two bushy eyebrows. "No skull is going to survive thirty-six inches of barbed steel between the eyes."

"True." Giles thought that might have come in handy at

the falls. "Or an ice axe blade."

The Boatman snorted. "You're joking, right?"

"Eighteen inches of stainless steel with a serrated edge."

"Seriously?"

Giles nodded, his gaze steady. The old sailor's frown softened, and he raised his glass. "Good on you, matey."

Giles waited until he'd drained his pint before asking his next question. "What about the other one?"

"What other one?"

"The other skull."

"What are you talking about?"

"If it was a hydra, it would have at least two heads."

They all looked at him.

"You know, like in Greek mythology? Hercules had to cut off each head, otherwise…?"

"They grow back," Blades said, absentmindedly touching his arm, which had a ship's anchor tattooed on it. Coiled around the neck was a serpent with twin heads leering back at him.

In the silence that followed, Annabel said, "We've got a problem, haven't we?"

"If we're lucky," Giles replied. "If not, we could well have more than one."

Chapter Thirty

Ravi stood before the mirror and considered the figure staring back at him. In recent years, he had attended the Ball with Robert, and Gabrielle's unexpected invitation had caused him to cast a more critical eye over his appearance.

The black-tie suit had, like its owner, seen better days. The cuffs were worn and the trousers baggy, giving him a Chaplin-esque appearance.

He should have asked Bert's wife if she could do something with them. But it was too late now; she would be busy in her temporary workshop in the Housekeeping Department, preparing for a long night of ballgown repairs.

"It will have to do," he said to his reflection, hoping his partner would be too wrapped up in the occasion to notice.

Not that he had any pretensions of sweeping her off her feet. Gabrielle was young enough to have been his daughter. But the least he could do was be a charming companion for the evening.

The Master had been delighted when Ravi had reported what had happened at the Observatory.

"A chance for you to redeem yourself, Ravi," he'd said,

"and discover the extent of Dutour's relationship with the Schiller Foundation. I don't want any nasty surprises coming out at the trial."

While Ravi saw the sense in finding out what Gabrielle knew, to prevent Julian Schiller from ever stepping through the College gates again, he was uncomfortable doing so. Nevertheless, he was looking forward to his unexpected assignment. The courts were stunning, the entertainment would be spectacular, and the guests, including his partner, would no doubt be enthralled. And with Alfonso safely back with his family, and Robert's Gemini papers hidden away in the School of Pythagoras, the immediate threat had passed. When was the last time he'd been in a position to relax and enjoy himself like this?

He knew when, of course, with perfect clarity.

As a much younger man, he had accompanied another spirited partner to the same event. Only then, he had been hoping for far more than the disclosure of confidential information.

******

The final fireworks lit the sky and the guests around Ravi burst into enthusiastic applause.

"Wonderful!" Mary exclaimed.

Tearing his eyes away from the display, Ravi admired the woman standing next to him. In an emerald-green ballgown, her face was no less captivating than the glittering trails above her, and her eyes sparkled.

"So, Ravi, what next?"

"How does dinner sound?"

She offered him a white-gloved hand. "Perfect!"

Finishing their Champagne flutes, they strolled arm in arm across the Kitchen Bridge. Ravi was all too aware of the other couples watching them. No doubt they were wondering why this vision in green had chosen a shabby little academic as her companion. He had asked himself the same question when dressing that evening.

The truth was that her usual partner, Robert, had other priorities. As President of the May Ball Committee, he would be occupied throughout the night, addressing the issues that always arose during such a complex and ambitious event.

Ravi suspected his friend had deliberately held back from inviting Mary, giving Ravi a clear run instead. If she had been disappointed, she'd given no indication, although he had been somewhat flustered at the time. She had accepted at once, and Ravi's emotions had veered between euphoria and panic.

Robert had seemed genuinely thrilled for his friend, though this might have been relief at being saved from an unfortunate conflict of interests. Whatever the truth, Ravi was now on the arm of the most beautiful woman at the Ball with a night in her delightful company to look forward to.

"Robert said we should head straight to Hall to get a good table for dinner," Ravi explained. "He'll meet us there to welcome us personally to the Ball."

"Wonderful!"

The sixteenth-century dining hall had been decked out

in the theme of the evening, which was "A Space Odyssey". Tiny blue, magenta and violet fairy lights hung across the ceiling to create an effect reminiscent of the Milky Way floating above their heads. Mary's face lit up on entering, and Ravi's heart soared at the joy in her eyes.

"You made it!"

It took Ravi a moment to register that her words were not directed at him. Robert was striding towards them, resplendent in tails. The scarlet sash across his chest accentuated his muscular frame, and he looked like a fiery comet blazing across the sky.

"Of course I did!" Without breaking stride, Robert picked Mary up in his arms. She laughed as he swung her in the air before depositing her neatly on the ground.

"My dear, you look a picture this evening."

"Why thank you," she said, breathless.

For a brief moment, conversation around them faltered, heads turning to witness these two otherworldly beings. The magnificent setting paled by comparison, and even the ensemble of musicians playing in the minstrel gallery stuttered, a harsh jarring note echoing across the Hall. This, more than anything, broke the spell the couple had cast.

Robert finally dragged his eyes away from Mary's.

"Ravi!" he boomed, his voice magnified in the faltering silence.

Aware that most people in the Hall were watching him, Ravi tried to respond, but a gag reflex rose in his throat. He retched, lurching forwards as he did so and splattering Robert's feet. Before he could apologise, another spasm gripped him, and he defiled the pristine tablecloth of a nearby table, its occupants leaping clear just in time.

Unable to speak, Ravi peered through watery eyes at the glistening tendrils hanging from his nose and mouth. In the horror of that moment, he felt Robert's reassuring hand pat his back.

"There now, Ravi, take it easy. I've got you."

He waved his hand to indicate he was all right, though clearly he wasn't, and something soft touched his palm.

"Here, take this."

Mary was pressing a handkerchief into his shaking fingers. Without thinking, he took it to wipe his mouth and nose.

The ensemble struck up again, perhaps attempting to restore the harmony his shocking upheaval had so spectacularly interrupted. A murmur of conversation began around them, followed by the scraping of chairs as guests evacuated the immediate area.

"Are you all right, old man?" Robert's voice was full of concern.

Ravi's convulsive breaths began to ease as he fought to control his contractions.

"I… I think so."

"Poor you," Mary said. "Was it the Champagne?"

"I… I don't know," he gasped, blinking away tears. "Oh no," he moaned. "Your dress!"

The emerald-green taffeta was now flecked with dark stains.

"And Robert, your shoes!"

The big Scot's patent leather brogues were splattered with the contents of Ravi's stomach.

"Oh, don't worry about that, old man. That'll wipe off in no time. I'm more worried about you. You look like death."

Ravi thought death might be preferable. He was mortified, not only by the devastation he had wrought but also by the sight of the two lovers that had triggered it. All he wanted to do was get away.

"I'm not feeling too good," he said. "I think I'd better go."

"The College Nurse is in Chapel Court," Robert said.

"No, please. I'll just head back to my room."

Mary took his arm. "Come on then. I'll go with you."

Unable to bear her touch, Ravi pulled free. "No, there's no need."

The mix of concern and pity on their faces was hard to bear.

"Please, you both go on and enjoy yourselves. I'll be fine. As you say, it must have been a reaction" – he paused, framing the lie – "to something I ate."

"I am so sorry, Ravi," Robert said. "I'll skin the chef alive for this."

"No one's fault." He backed away and glanced at Mary. "Please, stay. I'm sure Robert will take care of you." And to his friend, he said, "Promise you will."

"Of course, laddie," Robert assured him, taking her arm. "Consider it done."

His eyes burning, Ravi hurried from the Hall, horrified

guests parting as he clutched Mary's stained handkerchief to his mouth.

******

Even now, all these years later, the memory sickened Ravi. He still had her handkerchief, salvaged from the ruins of that night. Neatly pressed, the thin sliver of white material protruded from the top pocket of his jacket and served as a timely reminder of the importance of his mission this evening. To ensure that the consequences of Robert and Mary coming together could never be repeated.

Ravi reached inside his jacket for the ticket beside his old metal ruler. Then, he picked up the golden mask resting on the side table and, after adjusting the band, placed it over his head. The angelic face staring back at him could not have better suited the evening's purposes.

"Time to dance with the devil."

Chapter Thirty-One

Annabel adjusted the bust of her sister's ballgown and showed her grandmother.

"How does it look?" she asked.

"Like it was made for you."

The old woman had travelled from Yorkshire that day with the dress in her overnight bag. Annabel had a photograph of Serena wearing it for her first ball at Oxford. It was Annabel's favourite memory of her, and it felt strange to be wearing the same gown today. The two women looked at each other and Annabel felt the tears coming.

"Now then, don't do that," Gran said, reaching for her. "You'll set me off."

They stood holding each other, Annabel consumed with guilt. As if reading her thoughts, her grandmother whispered, "I'm sure she would be thrilled that you're wearing it."

Not trusting her voice, Annabel gave her a squeeze of thanks before wiping her cheeks.

"Sorry about that."

"Nonsense. The only thing to be sorry for is if you don't go and enjoy tonight. I expect it's going to be a magical evening."

There was a knock on the door.

"That will be Nick!" Annabel said. "Will you get it, Gran? I must look a mess."

While Annabel fixed her eyeliner in the mirror above the sink, her Gran greeted Nick on the landing.

"Nick, dear. My, you're looking very dashing this evening!"

"Thanks, Mrs Hamilton."

"Annabel, your chaperone has arrived."

Tucking a stray strand of hair behind her ear, Annabel straightened and turned.

She had only ever known Nick in jeans and trainers, and she gasped on seeing him in black tie with a green sash over his broad chest.

"Well, young man," Gran said, "aren't you going to say something to your partner for the evening?"

"What?" Nick blinked, breaking eye contact with Annabel for the first time since entering the room. "Oh... yes. You look great, Annabel."

"Thanks, you don't look so bad yourself."

Gran handed Annabel's sash to Nick. "Would you do the honours, dear, as you're taller than me?"

Annabel felt a thrill of excitement as Nick leaned in close and placed it over her shoulder.

"There," Mrs Hamilton said, smiling. "You two look the perfect couple."

Stop it, Gran, Annabel thought pointedly. But she couldn't help hoping that her grandmother was right.

"I suppose the only thing we have to decide," he said,

holding up the red and golden masks, “is which of these you'd like to be this evening.”

“Playing rugby, I’m guessing you'd prefer the red one?”

“I'd not really thought about it.”

Annabel snorted. “Yeah right,” she said, taking the gold one. “I’ll be an angel this evening.”

“There's always a first time,” her grandmother murmured.

“Gran!”

“Listen, we’d better go,” Nick said. “We’re being briefed shortly.”

Annabel picked up her phone. “You're right! And we still need to get our bracelets.”

“They should be at the Cripps Lodge. I’ve told Aden we’ll meet him there.”

Nick stepped into the corridor, and Annabel was about to follow when her grandmother said, “Before you go, I have a final present for you.”

Rifling through her suitcase, she produced a compact handbag in the same pale blue as Serena's gown.

“Gran, what’s this?”

“I thought it would go well with the dress.”

Annabel gave her another hug and was about to slip her phone inside when she noticed another object there.

“What's this?” She held up the canister.

“Pepper spray, dear. You're working security, aren't you?”

“I can't take that.”

“Why not? It always pays to be prepared. Now, be off with you before that handsome fellow gets propositioned by someone else.”

There was no point arguing. Annabel kissed her and said, "You're sure you're going to be OK?"

"I'll be fine. Your charming Porter Bert has arranged a special spot for me to see the fireworks."

"Really, where?"

"That would be telling." She winked. "Have a wonderful evening, my dear."

Annabel was ushered out of the room and onto the landing. Nick was standing at the top of the stairs, just as he had done on their first day here.

Was that really only eight months ago?

Back then, she'd mistaken him for a Porter, laden with bags and soaked to the skin. Now he was resplendent in black tie, sash and mask, she had to admit that he was devilishly handsome.

"All set?" he asked.

"Yes, I think so."

"In that case, my lady," he said, affecting a stiff bow, "after you."

"My, you Porters really are polite."

"We do our best."

Annabel restrained herself from skipping down the stairs, an act that the hem of her ballgown would almost certainly have rendered a disaster. Reaching the bottom without mishap, they walked to the Cripps Lodge. Desks had been set up there to process the support crews and acts performing that evening. Among those milling around, Naomi stood tall next to Aden, whose bulky frame was squeezed into a tuxedo.

"Wow, Annabel!" Aden looked her up and down. "You're smoking, girl."

"You don't look so bad yourself."

"Yeah, well, I'm in good company," he replied.

Next to him, Naomi wore a scarlet gown with a side slit revealing an impossibly long leg and a designer shoe that probably cost as much as Annabel's entire wardrobe.

"Hi, Annabel," she said before giving Nick a radiant smile. "Nick."

"What's the score here then?" Nick asked.

"We're waiting for Trevor to issue instructions," Aden explained.

"Speak of the devil," Annabel said as the Redboy Captain hurried towards them, his face almost as ruddy as his mask.

"Evening, all. Thanks for being here on time. I'm glad somebody is."

"Problems?" Annabel asked.

"The other security teams are in place but Bert's in a bit of a flap. He's short-staffed in the Forecourt Lodge, where all the VIP guests are checking in – including the Master. But hey, not much we can do about it now." He clapped his hands together. "Let's get you signed in and issue you with your bracelets. Purple for security, OK?"

"I'm not sure that goes with my eyes," Aden murmured under his breath, prompting a nervous smile from Naomi. After they'd collected their bracelets, Trevor briefed the Cripps team, before leading the four of them through to New Court.

The nineteenth-century square had been transformed

into a cauldron of fire and flame. Glowing braziers were positioned in a line along the cloister roof, their flickering flames dancing above the parapet. Great bolts of red silk hung from the surrounding walls, their gently swaying folds adding to the fiery effect.

On the East Lawn was a food court complete with spit roast and tequila bar. On the West Lawn, coal-black carpets had been laid over the grass leading to the main stage. This domed structure filled the entire side of the court, its cavernous interior illuminated by a massive rig of lights.

"This is mental!" Aden said.

"Wait until 2 a.m.," Trevor said. "That's when Stormzy is playing."

Nick's mouth fell open. "You're not serious? Here, tonight?"

"Yep. And once word gets out, any crashers worth their salt will be trying to get in."

The others exchanged looks as Trevor led them to the Eagle Gate, beyond which the Paddock had been transformed into something like Barnum's Circus. A whole array of fairground rides filled the main lawn, ranging from swings to dodgems and even a merry-go-round, all festooned with flickering lights. Food stalls serving ice cream, candy floss, toffee apples, hot dogs, mini burgers and kebabs ran around the perimeter, interspersed with punts filled with iced bottles of beer and soft drinks. And over to the right, adjacent to the Fellows' Garden, was a roped-off area with warning signs: FIREWORKS, KEEP CLEAR.

"OK, listen up," Trevor said. "The guests will be arriving

shortly from over there." He pointed towards the Queen's Road Gate. "They've been queueing along the Backs since 8 p.m. We're holding the early-bird ticketholders in the Scholars' and Fellows' Gardens."

He waved his hand at the hedges lining the far side of the lawns.

"That's two thousand guests who will flood across this Paddock in less than half an hour. You can expect the first gatecrashers in that rush, so be on your guard. If they get on the other side of the river, it will be a nightmare tracking them down in the old courts. So, I need two of you on the Bridge of Sighs and another two on the Kitchen Bridge."

"We'll take the Kitchen Bridge," Annabel said at once, knowing this gave the best view of the river. Addressing Aden's and Naomi's obvious surprise, she added, "That way you two can catch some of the main act from inside New Court."

"You're sure?" Aden asked.

"Fine," Nick said, though they all knew he was a massive Stormzy fan. "Knock yourselves out."

"OK," Trevor said. "I'd better go. I'm supervising the Queen's Road operation. We'll open the gates shortly. Good luck."

He gave them a big thumbs up and hurried off to where the partygoers were corralled like cattle before a stampede.

"Well, I guess that covers it," Nick said. "You guys good?"

"It's like all my birthdays have come at once," Aden replied. Turning to Naomi, he added, "That's the fourteenth of September, in case you were wondering."

"Well, now I know," she replied, smiling.

"We'd better go," Annabel said, keen to get to the bridge in good time. "We'll catch you guys later."

"Yeah, have a good one," said Aden.

The heady aroma of cooked food filled the air as Nick and Annabel headed to the river, and the braziers crackled, their burning sparks rising into the darkening sky.

"So, Annabel, are you ready for this?" Nick's red mask glowed in the flickering firelight as he strode alongside her.

"Right now," she said, "I think I'm ready for anything."

Chapter Thirty-Two

Nick arrived with Annabel at the Kitchen Bridge, which was adorned with a canopy of hanging lights mimicking the roof of the Bridge of Sighs a few yards downriver. That better-known gothic superstructure had also been transformed by the May Ball scenery team, and it was illuminated by a moving image of billowing clouds projected onto the stonework.

"I don't believe it!" Annabel said.

"Yeah, it's pretty impressive."

"Not that." Annabel pointed at a punt gliding underneath the bridge. "It's Gran!"

The trim little woman was sat with a blanket over her legs, holding a glass of Champagne and chatting excitedly to her neighbour.

"So that's what she meant!" Annabel said.

"Sorry?"

"Before I left, Gran said Bert had organised somewhere special for her to see the fireworks."

The other passengers on the heavily laden vessel were craning their necks or reaching for smartphones to take photos of the spectacular display. All except the punt guide. He stared directly at Nick, who recognised him immediately.

It wasn't just the lank hair and goatee beard that triggered the memory – or the roll-up hanging from his curled lip. It was the shock of recognition in his eyes. Nick had seen the same look all those months ago when he'd tackled him and his drunken friends harassing Raquel outside the College gates.

"Jez," he breathed before the punt disappeared from view beneath them.

"Come on," Annabel said, crossing to the other side of the bridge. But they both stopped short at the sight that greeted them. "Oh my word. Look!"

The entire river was covered in punts, each filled with guests chatting and laughing in anticipation of the display to come. They were so tightly packed together it would have been possible to walk from one side to the other without setting foot on the water.

Nick thought back to Ying's security briefing, when she had warned them about spectator punts gathering here. But he couldn't have imagined this many, all wedged bow to stern from the walled garden of Trinity to the security fencing along the St John's perimeter.

"Like sardines," he muttered, then immediately regretted the phrase, knowing Annabel's grandmother would shortly be joining them.

"We'd better let the others know we're here," he said, reaching for his phone. "I'll call Giles."

She nodded.

After their meeting, Blades had suggested he station himself upstream by Trinity while Giles watched the river below John's. Their night-climbing friend had been coy in front of the College Boatman about where he would position himself, but Nick had a pretty good idea. Peering up at the rooftops, he dialled the number and heard Giles's cultured voice after a couple of rings.

"Chamberlain Pest Control. Press one for Containment, two for Removal and three for Termination."

"It's Nick. We're in position. The river's pretty packed down here."

"Usually is. People can always rely on John's to put on a show."

"What about you? Seen anything yet?"

"A couple of rooftop smokers."

"I was talking about the river."

"No. The last punts just went by."

"Yeah, we saw them. Annabel's grandmother is on one of them."

"Is she indeed?" Giles chuckled. "I wondered where Annabel got it from."

Mrs Hamilton's punt was stationed alongside the bridge. Jez raised a fist and extended a finger, which Nick ignored.

"Call me if you see anything," he said.

"Roger that. Oh, and I must say that mask suits you. A definite improvement."

Nick scanned the roofs as the call ended, but it was impossible to see where the night climber was hiding. He pocketed his phone at the same time as Annabel stuffed hers into her bag.

"Blades says it's all clear at his end."

"Yeah, Giles too."

She cast an anxious look at her grandmother. "Well, nothing we can do for now."

There was a distant cheer, and the first influx of guests appeared on the far side of the Paddock.

"Looks like they've opened the gates."

A wave of guests poured through the gap and began spreading across the grass. They washed up against the Champagne stalls before continuing onto the fairground rides.

At first, it was hard to make out individual couples, but the vibrant colours of the dresses became visible when they reached the glow of the New Court lights. Two students detached themselves from the front of the main body and strode towards them, one waving an arm enthusiastically over his head.

"Someone's excited," Nick said.

"Oh my," Annabel murmured. "What are they wearing?"

The invitation had said black tie, but Ash and Brian had clearly taken the Angels and Demons theme to heart. The former wore an all-white outfit, including a pair of spats over his polished leather shoes. Brian had done the opposite, dressed entirely in black except for a red bow tie to match his mask.

"Leave this to me," Nick said, stepping forwards. "Passes, gentlemen, please!"

Ash suddenly stopped, and Brian did well to avoid bumping into his legs.

"Oh? Right, of course." He held up his wrist, and his partner did the same.

Nick grinned. "It's OK, guys. You're good."

"Ha, you had us there for a moment." Ash snorted, while Brian emitted his strange gurgling chuckle.

"Guys, you look… incredible," Annabel said.

"Thanks! We got them in Vegas last year. You know, for the Esports Awards."

"Naturally," Annabel said, glancing at Nick. "So, are you excited about tonight?"

"Absolutely! Are you going to tell them, Brian, or am I?"

"I don't know if we're allowed."

"Oh, it'll be all right now." Ash grinned. "We've been keeping it quiet for weeks, but Brian designed the software for tonight's laser show! It's pretty spectacular, I can tell you."

"Brian, that's amazing!" Annabel said.

"Not really," he said. "I adapted an AI program from a first-person shooter simulator I've been developing…"

And before Annabel could stop him, Brian launched into a detailed technical explanation that had her glazing over in bemused silence.

Shaking his head, Nick noticed a group of guests hurrying across the lawn. Something about the way they were checking over their shoulders struck him as odd. Then, when the couples merged into a queue for one of the food stalls, he realised they were all wearing black masks.

"Sorry, guys." He interrupted Brian mid-flow. "I'm going to have to stop you there. Duty calls."

"Of course," Ash said. "We need to go anyway, don't we, Brian? They told us we could watch the fireworks from the control tower. How cool is that?"

After saying their goodbyes, they headed towards a fenced-off structure on the far side of the lawns.

"What is it?" Annabel asked Nick.

"I think we have some gatecrashers."

"Where?"

"Over there, by the ice-cream stall."

It took her a moment to catch on. "The black masks, you mean?"

"Yeah, that's them."

"Uh oh, they've spotted us."

She was right. The intruders were looking at the bridge, no doubt working out how easy it would be to cross.

"I think we'd better call for back-up."

But even as he said it, there was a shout in the distance. Trevor, accompanied by a security team, was hurrying towards the stall. Unfortunately, the crashers saw them too. They left the queue and started running for the bridge.

"Great," Nick said. "That's just what we need."

"What do we do?" Annabel asked.

For a fraction of a second, Nick thought about letting them through. What with the hydra, the punts and Annabel's grandmother, they had more than enough to worry about. But he couldn't do it.

"We stop them," he said.

Nick held up his hand for the second time that night, but now there was no smile on his face.

"Passes, please!"

He didn't expect them to listen and wasn't surprised when they kept coming. Annabel reached for something in her bag, but then a tall figure stepped in front of her.

"Hiya folks," said Brett, his smile almost as dazzling as his mask. "Need a hand?"

Next to him stood another colossus, the red mask matching his fiery red hair.

"Hello, boyo." Gareth flexed his tree trunk of a neck. "Shall I take the one on the left?"

"Help yourself," Nick said. As he faced the gatecrashers, the familiar adrenaline rush coursed through his veins, distracting him from his phone's urgent buzzing in his pocket.

Chapter Thirty-Three

Perched on the Old Library roof, Giles lowered his binoculars as the last punt disappeared under the Kitchen Bridge.

Cutting it fine, he thought. The fireworks would be starting in a few minutes.

Deciding to make himself comfortable, he removed his dinner jacket and unhooked the ice axe from his cummerbund, then laid them on the roof within easy reach. The last time he'd been up here, Giles had come face to face with a psychotic statue – so, hydra or not, he'd come prepared.

Over the rampart, down in the Master's Garden, the first VIP guests were arriving for pre-Ball drinks. Mr Weston was among them, talking to the Master. Of Professor Gupta there was no sign, and Giles wondered if he'd been invited. Possibly not, given the hot water he was in over their latest Gemini adventure. It probably hadn't done Giles's own prospects of returning next year any good either. If so, his parents' dream of a career in the City for him loomed large.

Not wanting to think about that depressing outcome, Giles raised his binoculars. He followed the river's course back towards New Court, pausing over the doorway they'd used to gain access to the cellars last term. The replacement door looked a lot sturdier and was no doubt fitted with a new lock and alarm system.

Something to keep him occupied while waiting for his results, perhaps?

But his plans were interrupted by a voice behind him.

"Reminiscing, are we?"

Giles spun around, his hand straying to the axe. The masked woman stood a few yards away, head cocked to one side. She wore a black ballgown with a slit down the side, revealing a finely toned leg and what might have been a garter. The effect was somewhat distracting. So much so that it took him a moment or two to place the smiling face.

"Jane?"

The intelligence officer eyed the axe.

"Expecting someone else, were you?"

Giles folded the flap of his jacket over it, wondering how she had managed to get so close undetected.

"Let's just say it can be surprising who you bump into up here."

"I didn't know smokers were dangerous."

Giles looked towards the rooftops of Third Court.

"Don't worry. I scared them off," she said.

"Why, thank you, Jane. Very considerate of you."

"Mind if I join you? You seem to have bagged a good spot." She peered down at the river before adding, "For the fireworks, right?"

"Naturally," he said, making room. "Be my guest."

Jane leant against the parapet. "Lovely night for it."

"Certainly is."

"So, how does it feel being back?"

"Back?"

"From your vacation. That's what it was, wasn't it?"

"More of a field trip."

"I see. Well, you certainly left it late. We were beginning to get worried."

"We?"

"The Professor and I. We didn't want you to miss your finals."

"Heaven forbid."

"Did you manage to get any revision done in the end?"

"Oh, you know, one can over-prepare for exams. No point in peaking too early."

"True," Jane said. "But I understand the trip was successful."

"That depends on how you measure success."

Jane paused. When she answered, her tone was serious. "I'd say finding Alfonso Vidal was a pretty good result. Most people had given him up for dead."

"Not you, though." Giles remembered their conversation at the Maypole.

She switched to her cheeky Essex accent. "I knew Alfie, remember? In another life, so to speak."

"Of course. The waitress."

"Good mates, we were."

"Well, it came at quite a cost."

"He's responding well to treatment."

Giles tilted his head, wondering how she knew this.

"I have my sources," she said.

"And what about his…?" He indicated his eyes.

"Not much change there, I'm afraid. Still, it's early days. He's in good hands."

Across the water, the Wedding Cake's golden wind vane reflected the flames from the braziers in the court below. Alfonso appeared, back ablaze, staggering blindly towards the water's edge. Giles closed his eyes, but the vision remained. Would it ever leave him?

"So, what are your plans for next year?" Jane asked, her tone conversational once more.

Giles shook his head. "I don't know. Depends on my results, I suppose."

"You're thinking of staying on then?"

"Maybe. A PhD perhaps."

"Interesting."

"How so?"

"I was thinking of doing the same."

Giles studied her expression. "Really?"

"Don't think you're the only one who can write an essay."

"Well, no, of course not," he said.

"Yes, I thought four years here might prove instructive, with some fieldwork thrown in."

"Fieldwork? I thought you read Classics at the Other Place."

"Oh, I wasn't planning on studying Classics."

"No?"

"I was thinking of a new field."

Giles snorted. "Not one of these newfangled 'ologies or programmes ending in 'studies'?"

"I'm not sure they're planning to give it a name. At least, not officially."

What is she going on about? Giles thought.

"What university worth its salt creates a subject with no name? The whole point of academia is to give yourself the most indecipherable name imaginable. How else do you expect to secure funding? Besides, which PhD student would want to work here if they couldn't add a string of letters after their name?"

She caught his eye. "I was rather hoping you would."

"Me? What in the world am I going to study?"

"Who said anything about it being in this world?" She turned back to the river, and her words hung in the air a moment before she continued, "Anyway, I thought you should be aware these opportunities exist before you go off and do something less… fulfilling."

"Hold on," Giles said, trying to get his head around this revelation. "You're telling me that the University authorities are considering setting up… what? An 'Otherworld' Faculty?"

She didn't respond.

"Come on, Jane. Tell me."

"What's that?" she muttered.

"This new department! You can't…."

"No, Giles!" She pointed. "What's that in the river?"

A line of bubbles was snaking across the surface towards the Bridge of Sighs and the punts beyond.

"Oh crap!"

"What is it?" Jane asked.

"Fieldwork's starting early," he said and reached for his axe.

Chapter Thirty-Four

Ravi stood in the queue of guests waiting to enter the Master's Garden, his head tilted back. A moment ago, he'd seen movement on the Old Library roof.

"Is it those smokers again?" asked Gabrielle. "I see them most evenings."

She was also staring up at the distant rooftop, oblivious to the looks they were getting from those around them. Ravi wasn't surprised; they were perhaps the most ill-matched couple on the guest list.

In contrast to the shabbiness of his old dinner suit, Gabrielle's magnificent gown could have come straight from a Paris catwalk. Its shades of scarlet and black shimmered in the glow of the paper lanterns hanging from the trees. As did the ruby-encrusted band that held her hair back from a face now devoid of glasses. These had been replaced by what he suspected were powerful contact lenses to accommodate the devilish mask that perfectly complemented her crimson lipstick.

The effect was striking. So much so that Ravi had felt a momentary thrill of surprise when collecting her from her room. And he was not the only one to be taken aback by Gabrielle's appearance. Dominic Lester all but gawked at her transformation.

"Dear me, Dr Dutour, is that you?" he asked. "For a moment, I thought Ravi had found himself a femme fatale!"

Gabrielle peered down at him.

"Why would you think that? We are not lovers."

Lester blinked, his smile fading as the conversation around them went quiet.

"No, of course not," he said, recovering. "Well, I hope you both have a lovely evening."

"I intend to. Tell me, Master, is that Champagne or Prosecco you are serving?"

"Champagne, naturally."

"*Bon*. Shall we, Ravi? I wouldn't want it to get warm."

"Heaven forbid," he said, taking her arm and leading her past their bemused host, whose eyes bored into the back of Ravi's head.

Goodness me, he thought. *This might be more entertaining than I expected.*

But Ravi had little time to enjoy the moment. On approaching the drinks station on the lawn, the waitress standing behind the trestle table stiffened slightly at the sight of Gabrielle and him together.

"Good evening, Aurelia," he said as they arrived.

"Professor." She held out two fine-stemmed flutes. "Champagne?"

Gabrielle took one. "*Merci*."

Ravi did the same. "Many thanks."

The waitress gave him a curt nod before serving the next guest. Wishing to escape Aurelia's implicit disapproval, Ravi led Gabrielle to the far side of the garden, where they stood by the large plane tree overlooking the river. With their backs to the water, they observed the other guests spreading across the lawn.

Lester welcomed the Master of Trinity, whose event the night before had lit up the sky with a spectacular display that even students watching from John's had applauded. Not to be outdone, a truck had arrived at John's earlier that day with an additional shipment of pyrotechnics courtesy of an anonymous donor rumoured to be residing at the Master's Lodge.

And that wasn't the only ordinance on show. The Fellowship were out in force, no doubt incentivised by the best Champagne the College could offer – which must be very fine indeed, given Gabrielle's lack of adverse comments. From what Ravi could tell, she was warming to the occasion, gazing around the garden with an air of complacency she rarely displayed.

"This is charming, Ravi. I am grateful for your invitation."

"On the contrary, Gabrielle; if I remember rightly, you invited me."

"I did, didn't I. Was I too forward? *Maman* always said I took after my father in that regard. He was an impulsive man. A force of nature, she used to say."

"Well, I'm delighted you did. I'm sure we will have a memorable evening."

"It is the least I can do. I will never forget that evening you saved me up there."

Ravi followed her gaze to the low parapet wall outside her window at the top of the building opposite, where she had tripped and nearly fallen.

"Oh, it was as much my fault for startling you."

"Either way, we lived to fight another day." She raised her drink. "*Salut*, Ravi." They clinked glasses, the sound causing one or two heads to turn their way, including that of the distant waitress.

"I have given up, you know."

Ravi tore his eyes away from Aurelia. "What was that?"

"Smoking. I decided it was time to quit. As you said, it can be hazardous to one's health."

"I see. And how is that going?"

"Awful! It is like I have lost a lover. A secret one at that. They are always the hardest to give up."

"Right," he said, not quite sure how to respond. "I'm sorry to hear it."

"I don't blame you for it. It was my decision in the end. My mother always said it was better that way."

"She gave up smoking too?"

Gabrielle snorted. "No, Ravi. Her lover. My father."

Perhaps it was the Champagne, but Ravi was struggling to keep up with Gabrielle's train of thought.

"Of course. Forgive me."

She sighed. "In the end, it is why I came here. To find out more about him."

"Here, as in Cambridge?"

"*Oui*, his College, St John's."

Ravi wondered if he'd heard correctly.

"Your father is here?"

"Not anymore," she said, shaking her head. "He died. Last year."

The ground shifted beneath his feet.

"You must know, Ravi; you were his oldest friend."

Her eyes betrayed the truth of her sadness.

"Robert was my father."

The garden, guests and surrounding conversation faded into the background. Until that moment, Ravi had feared this masked woman might be as she appeared – a demon seeking to bring about his downfall. Now, he doubted everything.

Gabrielle studied him. "You did not know?"

"No, I... He never told me."

"I thought that was why you were so distant."

"Sorry?"

"When I arrived in College, I hoped to learn more about him. That is why I wished to discuss his research with you. The research you worked on together."

Ravi remembered their first awkward conversation in the Green Room when the President had introduced them. Her questions about his early work had immediately put him on edge.

"When you avoided me, I assumed you disapproved of my connection with Robert."

The layers began to peel away as Ravi replayed their various encounters in his mind.

"I thought if I could spend some time with you, perhaps at dinner or even in that dreadful Buttery..." She suppressed a shudder. "Well, I thought you might decide my unfortunate past should not count against me.

"Robert always said you were a man of honour. It was one of the many things he admired about you. I came to believe that my existence was an affront to everything you held dear."

How had his avoidance appeared to her? The appalling realisation of what she must have felt began to hit home.

"I had almost given up on you ever sharing your knowledge of my father when you came to my room that evening."

She glanced once again at the rampart.

"I am unsure whether I would have had the courage to take the final step? I spent many nights there wondering if I could do it."

He remembered the pile of cigarette butts where she had been standing.

"And then, there you were! In my shock, I almost did it by accident. Until you saved me, and not just from falling. You gave me hope that I could one day truly know my father – through the eyes of his closest friend."

Her words were not intended to hurt him, but Ravi felt torn apart piece by piece. He had all but shunned Robert's daughter in the months after her father's death, to the point of her almost taking her own life.

"I had no idea," he said.

"No?"

"None at all."

Tears formed in her eyes.

"So, he never acknowledged my existence, even to you?"

"Gabrielle, I…"

She blinked, and the tears formed under her mask.

"Here." He took Mary's handkerchief from his top pocket and offered it to her.

She dabbed at her eyes, dark streaks of mascara staining the material. "I am sorry, Ravi. I was hoping we could put our differences aside and speak openly about my father."

Despite his shame, there was something Ravi needed to know.

"Gabrielle, forgive me, but I must ask you… What is your association with the Schiller Foundation?"

"Sorry?"

"The Schiller Foundation. They have been funding your research."

"Well, of course. They were funding Robert's research. That is why the grant extended to my research too."

Ravi remembered the photograph on her computer. "So, you know Julian Schiller?"

She frowned, dabbing at her eyes. "I think he once attended a PR event for my research group. Near CERN."

"Did Robert tell him about your… connection?"

She scoffed. "When he wouldn't even tell you?"

No, of course not, Ravi thought. *I've got this all wrong.*

"I'm sorry to have spoilt your evening, Ravi," she said, her tears flowing again. "I think I should go to the bathroom."

Before he could protest, she handed the handkerchief

back and hurried across the lawn, leaving him alone. Several guests glanced at him, their looks ranging from surprise to disapproval. Ravi registered the Master's quizzical expression but didn't respond, still reeling from Gabrielle's revelation.

Lester had been convinced Schiller had planted a mole in College after Robert's death. Ravi had agreed that Gabrielle, newly arrived from Paris, had been the obvious suspect – particularly with her interest in her father's research. It was clear now they had both been mistaken.

But if the mole wasn't Gabrielle, who else had arrived that term to do Schiller's bidding? Before he could give it any thought, the sky lit up with a series of thunderous detonations.

Chapter Thirty-Five

On the other side of the river from the Master's Garden, Shirley the Porter walked through the labyrinth of passageways below New Court, flashlight in hand and backpack slung over her shoulder. The bag contained the old leather journals she'd retrieved from the School of Pythagoras and studied at length.

That no alarms or security cameras marked her progress came as no surprise. With May Ball contractors hooking up rigs, sound systems and laser arrays, there had been several power outages over the previous twenty-four hours, both planned and unplanned. The latter included one that Shirley had engineered to disable the security systems operating in the New Court cellars. Now she could complete the last stage of her mission unseen and undisturbed.

At the end of the corridor, she retrieved a set of keys from her pocket, unlocked the sturdy door and switched on the lights. The room was just as she'd left it on her early-morning rounds, bare except for the far wall. This was covered in the pattern of arcane symbols transcribed in meticulous detail from the diagrams in the late Professor

Mackenzie's journal. Ensuring all the glyphs were set out as described had taken her a good hour and several stubs of chalk.

She set up the video camera and adjusted the viewfinder to make sure everything was in frame. No video meant no fee, and she wasn't about to lose out on one of her most lucrative paydays for an easily avoidable mistake.

Once happy, she checked her watch. The firework display would start at any moment. Thirty minutes of loud explosions and glittering lights would be the perfect distraction to cover the ritual she was about to record.

Not that she expected it would come to anything. This sort of mystical spell-casting was a fanciful charade. And when the whole thing turned out to be a complete hoax, she wanted the video evidence to prove she'd done everything by the book – or journal, in this case.

What her client did with it afterwards was not her concern. As long as she got paid, she didn't care. She'd be lying on a beach somewhere a lot warmer than Cambridge, with a healthy bank balance and plenty of time to enjoy it. That was the great thing about Schiller and his cabal of environmental fundamentalists. Funding was virtually limitless, as were the lengths they would go to in order to "save the planet".

It was only a matter of time before they'd come calling again for her particular set of skills. Hopefully the next organisation she'd have to infiltrate wouldn't be so dull. A bit of action, preferably short and violent, was long overdue. Like that climate-denying scientist she'd once been tasked to cancel

– quite literally in that case – or the protest march where…

A distant thump brought her back to the present, and Shirley listened at the open doorway. There was another muffled thump, followed by more in quick succession. The fireworks had begun.

Right on time, she thought, closing the door. Retrieving the journal from her backpack, she turned to the page with the Latin incantation.

"OK, let's see what this hocus-pocus is all about."

Pressing the RECORD button on the camera, she began the chant.

For someone who had never believed in God, spirits or anything beyond the absolute reality of death, what happened next was a revelation. The forces conjured by the spell were beyond anything Shirley had ever imagined.

The words seemed to have a will of their own, tumbling from her mouth with ever-increasing clarity, her pronunciation more assured the further she read. She was barely aware of reading the last few lines, wrapped up in the magical transformation they wrought.

The chalk symbols changed from crude markings to pulsing lines that cut through the reality of her world as it joined with another. When she fell silent, she watched, bewildered, as Mackenzie's Gemini Passage opened up before her.

At first, all Shirley saw in the shifting tunnel were faint glowing dots swirling in the gloom. Gradually, these become larger and brighter, like glow-worms shining in the darkness. By the time she realised they were eyes – many pairs of eyes – it was too late.

Chapter Thirty-Six

When the gatecrashers reached the bridge, Annabel's fingers were already closing around the pepper spray in her bag. But she didn't need it. Nick and Gareth took out the leading men, dropping their shoulders to lift and dump them like tackle bags onto the ground. As for their partners, Brett intercepted them before they reached her.

"Sorry, Mam, can't let you pass," he said, enveloping one in his arms. Seeing this, her colleague hesitated for a split second before throwing herself at him as well.

Typical, Annabel thought, but before she could intervene, her phone vibrated in her bag.

"Giles?"

"Annabel?" His voice was breathless over the sound of running footsteps.

"What is it?"

"The river," Giles panted. "Hydra heading your wa–!"

At that moment, the sky lit up, and the air was filled with explosions. Annabel didn't care. She had only one thought.

"Gran!"

She began pushing through the mesmerised spectators.

"Security, coming through!"

She reached the handrail as the next fireworks burst overhead. Gran was staring skywards among a sea of spectators, entranced.

Beyond the punts, towards Trinity, a weeping willow overhung the river, and the clinker was completely hidden beneath its drooping leaves. She dialled the Boatman, and he answered immediately.

"Annabel?"

"Blades, it's here!"

"The hydra? Where?"

"I'm not sure. Giles said he'd..."

Then, Annabel heard the cry. It came from Gran's punt alongside the bridge. One moment the guide was leaning on his punt pole, and the next he was thrown to the deck as the aluminium rod disappeared under the arch. It all happened so fast, she doubted anyone else had noticed, all eyes glued to the fireworks.

But a moment later, the adjacent punt bucked, causing its occupants to yell in alarm. The same happened to the next punt, and then another, each vessel rising as if a wave were passing underneath. A ripple of consternation spread through the floating spectators, their drinks spilled and plates dropped.

"It's probing for a weakness," she murmured.

"What was that?" The voice at the end of the phone sounded alarmed.

"You'd better get over here, Blades. Now!"

"On my way!"

Annabel waited for movement among the hanging fronds of the distant tree. Instead, splashing below alerted her to the punt guide slapping the water with a paddle as he tried to retrieve the punt pole.

"Don't do that," she fretted, too quiet for him to hear.

But already cries were coming from the furthest punts as the ominous Mexican wave began moving back towards the prone punter.

"Leave it!" she cried, but he couldn't hear her warning over the fireworks erupting.

However, someone did. Annabel's grandmother looked up at her just as the wave reached her vessel.

"Got it!" the punter cried, moments before the stern surged upwards, throwing him into the air. Arms and legs flailing, he hit the bridge's underside and flopped into the water.

Annabel didn't hesitate. She hoisted up the hem of her dress and swung her legs over the parapet. Then, kicking off her shoes, she dropped onto the pitching deck six feet below.

Had her dress not billowed out around her, Annabel might have made a better job of nailing the landing. Instead, her bare feet slipped on the wet surface and she collapsed on all fours, stifling a cry. The punter's body was a few yards away under the span of the bridge. For a terrible moment, Annabel thought of Brett unconscious under the bridge by the Boathouse. But then she heard the guide's weak voice, magnified by the archway.

"Help me..."

"I'm coming!"

He was too far away to reach, but the punt pole was bobbing up and down in the water. Reaching out, Annabel grabbed it, surprised at how light it was. Then, she realised why. Half was missing, the aluminium shaft torn – or bitten – in two.

Careful to avoid cutting herself on the jagged edge, she held the handle out towards him.

"Quick! Get hold of this!"

The guide flailed an arm, knocking against the outstretched pole.

"That's it, grab hold!"

As soon as he closed his fingers over the end, Annabel began hauling him in. When she had him alongside, she let go of the pole and was about to grab hold of him when a shout came from above.

"Annabel!"

Nick was swinging his legs over the stone railing.

Annabel shouted, "Nick, no!" but she was too late; he'd already let go. The deck dipped under his weight, and Annabel overbalanced. She would have tipped into the water had a hand not grabbed the back of her dress.

"Now, now. Don't go ruining that gown," her grandmother said, dragging her back.

"Thanks, Gran," she gasped.

Then, Nick was squatting next to her.

"I didn't know where you'd got to," he said, breathless. "You should have told me!"

"I'm sorry… I was worried about Gran."

Nick grabbed hold of the punter as Annabel scanned the

water. Between the two bridges, the splintered remains of the paddle were being torn to pieces in a fountain of foam and spray.

"Hurry," she said.

"Come on, Jez," Nick grunted, adjusting his grip and heaving the punter up. Almost at once, the distant thrashing stopped. A line of bubbles emerged from the disturbed water and began snaking back towards them.

"Quick! We need to get him out!"

"Easier said than done," Nick muttered as the punter sagged against the punt's side, his legs hanging in the water. "Come on, you big lump!"

"Here, let me help," Gran said, reaching down. The bubbles adjusted course and sped towards her instead.

No, Annabel thought, horrified. *I'm not letting that happen.*

Ripping the flap of her satchel open, she tugged the pepper spray out as a dark shape surged beneath the bridge. She had a fleeting glimpse of glistening tentacles and rows of serrated teeth breaking the surface. Then, the creature disappeared in a cloud of choking gas.

Something heavy slammed into the side of the punt. Nick and Gran tumbled backwards, their momentum dragging the punter's body clear of the water. The sudden movement caught Annabel unawares, and she dropped the spray and grabbed the heaving deck. That was when she saw the creature properly for the first time.

The long sinewy torso writhed beneath the bridge, the two stubby heads whipping back and forth just feet from her own. One of the heads had what looked like Blades's rusting harpoon protruding from its rotting skull. The other was still very much alive, thrashing from side to side.

While Annabel desperately searched for the lost canister, the shattered punt pole floated by the hull, scraping against the wooden side. She grabbed the handle as the hydra's remaining head shook itself free of the spray and turned its gaping maw towards her. She just had time to hoist the broken shaft up before it lunged.

The impact drove Annabel back against the duckboards as the mangled end of the pole disappeared between rows of teeth and lodged in the top of the hydra's throat. Razor-sharp shards of metal punched through the back of its skull as the creature speared itself on her makeshift pike. For a few dreadful seconds, the tentacles writhed inches from her face. Then, they slowed and stilled.

Annabel clung to the pole until the monster began sliding back into the water. Its deadweight might have dragged her. But strong hands grabbed her shoulders and hauled her back.

"Let it go, lass! Let it go!"

She registered Blades's sweating face inches from hers.

"It's OK," he said. "It's over."

She held on for a moment longer, then released her grip. The lifeless torso sank beneath the surface, taking the bent and battered punt pole with it.

Annabel sagged against the Boatman as the others struggled upright. Her grandmother immediately began tending to the dazed punter while Nick stared warily at the water. But no line of bubbles broke the surface.

"Thanks, Blades," Annabel murmured.

"No need," he replied. "Sorry I wasn't here sooner. Not as agile as I used to be."

Annabel imagined him leaping from punt to punt.

"Anyway, seems like you two had it in hand."

She and Nick exchanged a look but said nothing, knowing how close they'd come to disaster.

"It was lucky for this chap they did," Gran said, eyes shining with what might have been pride.

A quick succession of detonations boomed overhead as the tempo of the display increased. Annabel spotted movement on the bridge, and a pair of anxious, breathless faces appeared over the balustrade.

"Better late than never," Blades muttered.

"You… guys… all right?" Giles asked.

"We're fine," Annabel called back.

Giles sagged against the railing. "That's good," he panted. "So what's the plan?"

Annabel's grandmother nudged her. "Go on. I think Mr Blades and I have got this. You two have a good time."

Nick held out a hand and helped Annabel to her feet. "Come on, we'd better get back."

Together, they stepped onto the stern, and she felt a warm glow as he gripped her waist.

"Ready?" he asked.

"Yes."

Annabel was lifted into the air as red and white stars burst overhead.

Chapter Thirty-Seven

Nick reached for Giles's hand and hoisted himself over the railing onto the bridge.

"Cheers," he said, relieved to be back on solid ground.

"Any time," Giles replied, clapping him on the shoulder. "I hear you've been fishing."

"Not me. Annabel."

"Has she indeed?" Giles regarded her. "I always said, Nick, if you don't marry that girl, I will."

Annabel snorted.

"You'd think his May Ball partner wasn't here," quipped the woman next to Giles, and Nick realised he knew her.

"Jane?"

"I wondered when you'd recognise me."

"What are you doing here?"

"Keeping an eye on him." She nodded at Giles.

"In your dreams," Giles scoffed. "The truth is we bumped into each other earlier, and she's proving remarkably difficult to shake off."

Nick was about to ask what he meant when he noticed a stream of dark objects rising from New Court. For a moment, Nick fancied they were some lighting effect similar to the clouds that had been projected onto the Bridge of Sighs. These ones looked like animated bats escaping from the fiery hellscape of the gothic courtyard. But as they flew over the cloisters, the braziers glowed and flickered in the downdraft of their wings, scattering clouds of burning ash along the ramparts.

"That's not good," he murmured.

"What?" Annabel asked. Then, she gripped his arm. "Oh my word."

The others must have followed their gaze because Giles said, "Oh crap!"

"What are those things?" Jane asked. "Display drones?"

It was easy to understand why she might think so as the dark cloud swept up past the Wedding Cake and over the entranced crowd. From the excited buzz around them, Nick suspected other guests thought the same. But Giles wasn't fooled.

"They're harpies!" He muttered. "Someone must have opened the gate."

Before any of them could react, the glowing tails of a pair of rockets disappeared into the cluster of rising creatures. Then, two vast spheres of light appeared, one red, the other gold. These were followed by a double detonation so loud that the revellers around them flinched.

For a few seconds, there was stunned silence as red and gold tracer trails shot through the cloud. Like a chain reaction spreading across the sky, vast swathes of hapless creatures burst into incandescent light. The resulting supernova prompted cheers and applause from the partygoers.

"What's happening?" Jane asked.

"They're igniting," said Giles, his face grim as more rockets shot into the air, adding to the conflagration.

"That's horrible," Annabel cried, barely audible above the explosions, which were coming so fast it was impossible to tell them apart. When they ceased, a vast mushroom cloud of pale dust hung over the College. Someone over by the dodgems cheered, and then applause broke out, sweeping across the lawns as guests reacted to the spectacular and shocking finale.

But Nick spotted a few fluttering shapes whirling within the cloud.

"Some are still alive."

A few of the guests noticed, too, pointing at the distant objects.

"This could get ugly," Giles muttered.

Suddenly, techno dance music blasted from speakers set around the grounds, and an oscillating wave of red light lanced over the Paddock to light up the New Court walls. People around them started dancing, and the party mood kicked in as the laser show began.

"There!" Annabel cried as a pulsing white light caught one of the flyers in its beam. Nick stared in horror at the familiar raptor-like outline. Then, the frozen creature exploded in a flare of sparkling dust.

"The lasers," Giles yelled above the din, his eyes shining in the reflected light. "Remember the statue?"

How could Nick forget that grey hand tightening around

his neck as the torch beam lit its calcifying features?

"Can you two make sure they keep the display going while I deal with the gate?"

"Don't you need someone with you?" Annabel asked. Nick wondered if she was also mentally reliving the horror of the cellars.

"I'll go with him," Jane said, nudging Giles. "Like I said, someone's got to keep an eye on you."

"Fine. We'll close the gate if you two cover the guests."

"Got it," Nick agreed.

For a moment, they all looked at one another.

"In that case, we'll see you later," Giles said with a wink. "Be good."

He and Jane crossed back over the bridge and disappeared between the watching Yales.

"You OK?" Nick asked Annabel.

She nodded before what might have been a screech cut through the thumping bass.

"Come on!" he said, and they set off through the dancing crowd.

Chapter Thirty-Eight

Annabel followed Nick as he weaved between the dancing couples like a winger carving through a disorganised defence. As the crowds thinned beyond the carousel and fairground rides, Annabel noticed a fine grey dust settling on the lawns. By the time they made it to the fenced-off tower, Nick's shoes were kicking up clouds of the stuff.

Ahead of them, two burly security guards stood before the access gate, their black tee shirts dusted with a thin patina of grey. There was no mistaking their heavily muscled forearms, which they crossed as Nick approached.

"You can't come through here, mate," one of them called above the heavy thumping of the music. "It's off limits!"

"We need to speak to someone in the tower."

"No can do, sunshine, sorry!"

"Please, this is really important," Annabel said. "There's been a change of programme."

"Sorry, Miss. Orders is orders."

Annabel worried that Nick's palpable frustration might lead him to take matters into his own hands. But then a terrible, keening screech cut through the air, so close that both guards looked up.

"What the f–!"

A dark shape swooped towards them, and a pulsing green laser swept over their heads. The shadow veered away, the downdraft throwing up a cloud of choking dust.

Coughing, she cried, "Nick, now!"

Blinking back tears, she felt rather than saw him dart forwards, swerve past the distracted pair and rush for the tower.

"Oi! You!"

Annabel ran after the three of them, lasers whipping back and forth over her head.

By the time she caught up, Nick was hammering at the door of a raised portacabin while the two guards were trying to drag him back down the steps. Their angry voices were clearly audible over the loud music.

"Come on, you! Out of here!"

"Sorry, this can't wait!"

"I don't give a flying–!"

The door swung open, almost knocking them down the stairs.

"What's going on?" Ash asked the three clinging to the handrail. Then, he spotted Annabel at the foot of the steps and waved. "Hi, Annabel! You made it!"

"Ash," she cried. "We need to speak to you."

"Oh, really?" He hesitated. "We're a bit busy right now."

"That's what we told them," said one of the guards, grabbing Nick. "Now come on, you. You're out of here."

"They're with us!" said another voice, so commanding

that Nick and the guards stopped their struggles at once. "Nick and Annabel are with the May Ball team," Brian stated, stepping out from behind Ash. "They have our permission to stay, don't they?"

Ash recovered from his surprise. "Absolutely."

"That's the first we've heard about it."

"That's because there's been a change of plan," Annabel said.

"Oh yeah, what's that then?"

"We need the laser show to run on longer."

"Longer?"

"That's right. Something's come up, and... we need these guys to cover for us."

The guard looked with obvious scepticism from Annabel to the figures on the gantry. "And you two can do that, can you?"

Ash blinked. "Well, yes, it's a fairly simple sequence, isn't it, Brian?"

"Elementary," the other replied, his voice returning to the nasal monotone Annabel knew so well. "I should be able to do it using some C++ and standard library functions that..."

"OK, OK," the guard said, letting go of Nick. "I get it. Just make sure this doesn't come back on us, OK? We were only following orders."

"Of course," Annabel said. "No one need know. Probably best that way."

He nodded. "Yeah, well." He turned to his colleague. "Come on, let's leave them to it."

Annabel waited for them to leave before thanking Ash and Brian.

"No problem," Ash said. "We–" But he was interrupted by another screech overhead.

The harpy that swept out of the sky in that instant might have taken one of them had a laser not caught the diving creature in its beam. The nightmarish vision of wings, claws and wide eyes froze in mid-air before ploughing into the trees of the Fellows' Garden. A dreadful splintering crash was followed by an explosion of dust that billowed out through the branches.

In the eerie silence, the smiles on her friends' faces disappeared.

"Tell me that didn't happen," Ash said, his voice unusually subdued.

"It did, I'm afraid," Annabel said. "That's why we came to find you."

Ash was still staring at the trees, now coated with a layer of powder. "What... what was that thing?"

"It looked like a gargoyle," Brian said.

"Sort of..." Annabel hesitated, not sure how to begin and worried about how far she should go. "It's hard to explain..."

Nick though cut to the chase. "Guys, there's no time for that now. Those things... those gargoyles, are circling above the crowd. The only thing keeping them at bay are your lasers."

"The lasers?" Ash said. "How?"

"It's the light." Nick indicated the cloud of dust rising from the trees. "It turns them back to stone."

Annabel picked up the thread. "That's why we need you to keep the light show running."

For a moment the others said nothing, and she wondered if it was all too much to take in. *Perhaps they won't be able to help after all.*

Then, Brian spoke. "Is that all?"

"Sorry?"

"Is a protective shield all you want?"

"What do you mean?"

"We could hunt them too."

Ash's bemused expression changed to one of piqued interest. "Offence and defence, you mean?"

Brian shrugged. "Stops them probing for weaknesses."

"But we'll need spotters," Ash continued.

"We can help," Nick said. "Just tell us what to do."

A distant shriek, just audible over the pulsing music, sealed the deal.

"Brian," Ash said, holding up a hand, "I think it's time to lock…"

"…and load," the other said, slapping it.

Ash turned to Nick and Annabel. "Come on! We'll need you watching the screens while we do the coding."

"No problem," Annabel agreed.

Nick nodded. But as they followed the others into the control room, he murmured, "I hope these guys are as good as you say they are."

"I guess we'll find out," she said.

Chapter Thirty-Nine

Giles led Jane through the balloon-covered Third Court, their feet tapping over the flashing disco floor, while a DJ performed sound checks on his microphone and speakers.

"Where are we heading?" Jane asked as Giles veered left towards the Bridge of Sighs.

"The New Court cellars."

"That's where this gate is then?"

"It was, the last time I looked."

"You seriously think you can stop those things with nothing but that axe of yours?"

It was one of those annoyingly sensible questions that someone like Ying would ask. But the fact that Jane was running alongside him suggested she was open to plausible answers. Unfortunately, he couldn't think of any.

"I'll improvise!"

As they crested the rise, Giles saw that guests returning from the laser display were being checked by a security couple, one of whom was the burly prop from the rugby team.

"Crap," he said, slowing to a halt.

There was no way they'd let him through, maskless and without a wristband. There again…

"Quick," he said. "I've got an idea."

"What?"

"Give me your mask."

Frowning, she removed it, and Giles slipped it over his face. Then, taking her hand, he pulled her close, his face inches from hers. Jane's eyes were surprisingly bright. *Must be the absence of Goth make-up*, he thought.

"What are you playing at?" she asked.

"The gallant hero. Listen, can you play dead?"

"Sorry?"

Reaching down, he hooked one arm behind her legs and swept her off her feet.

"Hey! Mind the dress!"

"Here's the deal," he said. "You've fainted – and given my devilish good looks, who can blame you – so I'm taking you to the first aid station."

"You're kidding, right?"

"You have a better plan?" She frowned but said nothing. "That's settled then." He headed for the archway. "And see if you can look helpless for once."

"You wish," she muttered. Nonetheless, she sagged against him as he descended the ramp, one of her arms flopping in a pleasingly convincing manner.

At the sound of his footsteps, the security couple glanced back, the tall girl's mouth dropping open when she saw Jane's limp form. "Aden, look!"

The Redboy, though, was having none of it. "Wristbands, please."

"I'd love to," Giles replied, hurrying forwards, "but I need to get my friend here to the First Aid Centre. Someone said there's one in the Fisher Building?"

"What happened?" the girl asked.

"All a bit much, I'm afraid. Up from Oxford, you see. Bless her. She's never seen anything like this over there."

Jane gave a pathetic moan, using the opportunity to jab him in the ribs.

"Poor thing," the girl said, though her colleague seemed less impressed.

However, more guests were arriving now, keen to get to dinner.

"Listen, I don't want to cause a hold-up," Giles said, making sure to block the gap with his listless invalid, "and she's not as light as she looks."

Jane moaned again, her elbow catching him painfully in the kidneys.

"Of course," the girl said, stepping to one side. "Do you want me to come with you?"

"No, no. That's very kind of you, but I'll manage. Here, let me get out of your way."

Slipping past, he carried her along the line of queuing guests while Jane checked behind them.

"We're clear!" she whispered, and Giles swung her legs down without breaking stride and deposited her neatly on the carpeted lawn.

Jane straightened her dress. "Next time, I'm carrying you."

"Promises, promises."

Above them, the laser show was in full swing. Dazzling beams of light swept over the cloisters, illuminating the Gothic facade of the Wedding Cake. There was no sign of the airborne harpies, hidden from the guests by the constantly evolving canopy of light. Giles wondered how long that would last, even with Nick on the case. Not that he could do much about that. His job was to ensure that no more joined them.

"Do you have any matches?" he asked.

"What for?" she asked, removing a pack from her clutch bag.

"And you couldn't get us a couple of shots of vodka as well?"

"Now? Are you serious?"

"Trust me, there's method in my madness."

Jane hurried over to the nearby drinks stall while Giles headed for one of the iron sconces lining the wall. Unhooking a pair of the flame-effect torches, he squatted down, removed his cummerbund and used the serrated blade of the axe to tear the silk into long strips. By the time Jane had returned, he'd tied them in a tight bundle around the end of each baton.

"What are you doing?" she asked.

"Improvising," he said, taking the drinks from her and dunking the tightly bound material in the neat alcohol. "Our feathered friends don't like fire."

Lighting the ends, he waited until each one was burning with a pale-blue flame before returning the matches to her.

"They teach you all this in Archaeology, do they?"

"Naturally," he said, straightening up and handing her a torch. "Can't go tomb raiding without one."

Tucking the axe inside his jacket, Giles glanced around, but people were too busy dancing or queuing at the food and drink stalls to pay them any attention.

"OK." He turned for the staircase entrance. "I've dealt with these creatures before, so I'll lead. Make sure nothing gets behind us, OK?"

"Got it." No protest, no question, nothing.

"Good," he said, trying to hide his surprise.

"And when we get to the portal?"

When and not *if*, he noticed. "You hold them off while I close it."

She nodded. "You're making this up as you go along, aren't you?"

"Would I do that?"

They reached the staircase entrance and Giles held up a hand. The door had been all but ripped from its hinges. Reaching inside his jacket, he unhooked his axe.

"Ready?"

She nodded. "Go."

Holding the torch in one hand and the axe in the other, Giles stepped inside the staircase lobby.

The first thing he noticed was that the lights were out, all except for the emergency exit sign glowing dully above the door. Then, there was the smell – a musty mix of baked earth and feral creatures. Scanning the stairwell above them, he crossed the lobby, Jane a few steps behind, keeping her torch clear of his back.

The door leading to the cellar had been smashed from its hinges, its splintered timbers scattered across the floor. Though it must have been one hell of a crash, he doubted any of the staircase's remaining residents would have noticed – just one more bang among all the others from the fireworks.

But now there was another sound over the heavy thump of the music outside. The click and scrape of something at the bottom of the stone steps. Giles tensed, wondering if it was coming or going. Either way, he didn't want to take the chance it might get past them into the lobby. Glancing briefly at Jane, he held the torch before him and stepped in front of the doorway.

Like the lobby, the cellar was in darkness. However, there was no mistaking the creature caught in the flickering glow of the torch's flames. A harpy squatted at the foot of the stairs, bent over a dark shape on the floor.

For one dreadful moment, Giles wondered if a guest had inadvertently stumbled into the path of the harpies or been plucked from the crowd and brought down here to be consumed. But when the creature raised its head, he saw blood-soaked feathers protruding from its maw.

Its eyes widened in alarm, and it screeched at the sight of the flames. But it held its ground, refusing to give up its cannibalised kill.

"Bad call, I'm afraid," Giles said, lobbing the torch at it.

Trapped in the narrow stairwell, it tried backing away, but as soon as the burning brand touched its feathers, they burst into flames. Its cries rose in pitch as it thrashed, making matters worse as fire spread over its wings. Giles didn't wait to see what happened next. He dragged Jane away from the opening and flattened her against the wall.

"Look away!"

Moments later, a bright light lit up the lobby and hot air rushed up the stairwell, ruffling their hair and making Jane's torch dance and splutter. Finally, the dreadful screeching fell silent, and Giles opened his eyes.

"Does that happen every time?" Jane asked, her face close to his. "The light?"

"Yeah. You don't want to look directly at it."

"Like Alfonso, you mean?"

He nodded, releasing her. "Still, it should have cleared away any lurkers."

"Or warned them we are coming."

"There's only one way to find out."

They descended the stairs, now covered in drifts of pale dust, and Giles retrieved the extinguished torch. Holding it to hers, he waited for the end to catch, and though it eventually did, the flame sputtered and flickered feebly.

"I've got this," she said, taking the lead.

"You're sure?"

She raised a finely arched eyebrow.

"Fair enough," he replied. "Age before beauty."

Jane held the torch before her and led him through the archway into the labyrinth of tunnels.

Chapter Forty

Ravi was still in the Master's Garden when a gong sounded, its deep tone rising above the music from the laser show. The Fellows' Butler stood at the top of the patio steps.

"Please be advised that dinner will be served in the Senior Combination Room in Second Court. For those wishing to use the facilities at the Master's Lodge, feel free to do so now. The Master's party will depart from the garden gate shortly."

There was a buzz of excited chatter as guests finished their drinks and headed for the toilets. Gabrielle hadn't returned from the lodge, and Ravi wondered if he should go and find her. But the College Librarian was crossing the lawn towards him, the trim lines of his black-tie outfit perfectly matching his moustache.

"Evening, Professor. I wondered if I might have a word."

"Of course, Mr Weston." He affected a smile while scanning the crowd for Gabrielle.

"My wife asked me to tell you that she bumped into Dr Dutour in the ladies' room."

Ravi started. "Is she all right?"

"Ann wanted to reassure you that Gabrielle is fine. She

has been a little unwell but is on the mend and hopes to join you shortly."

"Thank goodness," Ravi said. "I was beginning to worry."

"You and me both. It seems they rather hit it off. I'm not sure if you are aware, but Ann is a sommelier and knows many of the vineyards that Dr Dutour favours."

Ravi hadn't even known the man was married. In fact, he was starting to think he knew very little about Mr Weston.

"Well, I'm both relieved and grateful to her."

"Between you and me, Professor, Ann was thrilled to find someone who wasn't only interested in books."

"I see," he said, smiling. "A happy coincidence, then."

"Indeed. Speaking of which, Professor, did you find the journals useful?"

"Sorry?"

"The journals you requested."

"I don't understand."

"We opened the School of Pythagoras especially. She said you wanted them urgently."

"Who, Gabrielle?"

"No, Professor, the Porter you sent."

"Porter?"

"Yes, that new one. Shirley, is it?"

Ravi's chest tightened.

"Is everything all right, Professor?" Concern marred the Librarian's usually placid features.

"I'm not sure," he replied, his mind racing. "Mr Weston, could I ask you to wait here for Gabrielle? I'm afraid I have to check on something."

"Of course."

Ravi began striding across the lawn.

"And where should I say you've gone, Professor?"

"I need to speak to the Head Porter."

When Ravi stepped into the Forecourt Lodge a few minutes later, the place resembled an emergency control room.

A harassed looking student wearing a red committee sash was speaking into a walkie-talkie, while two of her security detail escorted a gatecrasher out through the doors. On a nearby seat, an elderly guest with a pallid face was being assessed by a paramedic. Next to him, a pretty student in tears showed the torn train of her dress to the College seamstress as her guilt-ridden partner looked on.

Amid the organised chaos, the Head Porter stood behind the counter, a phone to his ear, making notes on a pad. Bert spotted Ravi and held up a finger to indicate he'd be with him in a minute. Outside, lasers continued to strobe across the sky, and the Porter had to raise his voice over the loud music.

"What's that? Oh, he's in A&E now, is he? That's good. Yes, we are trying to get an incident report. That's right. I've got Ying Li, Head of Security, here."

He looked at the girl with the sash, who nodded while talking into her radio.

"We'll have it ready for you in the morning. Right you are, Officer. I'll expect to see you then."

As soon as he put the phone down, it began ringing again, but Bert ignored it.

"Sorry about that, Professor. How can I help you?"

"I was wondering if Shirley was around? I'd like to have a word with her."

"You're not the only one. It's why we're run off our feet. Shirley called in sick."

Ravi's stomach contracted.

"Yes, I wasn't too impressed either," the Porter added, mistaking his expression.

"Tell me, Bert, could you check the security cameras for the New Court cellars?"

The Porter looked surprised. "You know they've been sealed off, Professor. No one's allowed access, least of all tonight."

"I realise that, Bert, but it's urgent."

"Very well, Professor. As it's you."

While Bert checked the display panel, Ravi heard Ying exclaim, "Chamberlain? In New Court?"

The knot in his stomach tightened further.

"And where is he now?" she asked the walkie-talkie, rolling her eyes. "Well, if he shows up again, I want you to let me know, OK?"

Before Ravi could ask her what was going on, Bert muttered, "Would you believe it? The cameras are down."

"Sorry?"

"In the cellars, Professor." The Porter frowned at the screen. "I had Shirley check them only yesterday. In fact, it looks like everything's out there, lights included."

Ravi ran for the door.

Chapel Court was lit by scarlet lasers sweeping over the

ramparts, but he paid them no attention. Instead, he hurried past the mesmerised guests as glowing comets blazed across the scarlet sky.

******

Through the fine mist of blood – her blood – Shirley saw a pair of wings arched over her. For an all too brief moment, she thought an angel had come to save her. Then, the monster leaned close, its raptor's head inches from hers.

It was the perfect opportunity to strike or drive a knee into the creature's midriff. But Shirley had no weapon, and she'd lost the feeling in her legs. Moreover, one of her arms was a bloody stump, and it was only a matter of time before blood loss and shock would finish her off.

"Not the boy, then?" Another being drifted into view, a woman, hooded and holding what looked like a staff.

"No, Mother," hissed the creature.

The woman reached down and picked up something lying by Shirley's face.

"She used this, by the looks of things." The woman held up what remained of the old journal, its pages shredded. An unbearable pain spiked through Shirley's chest as the staff dug into her broken ribs.

"Where did you get this?"

She wanted to tell the woman to shove it, but all she managed was a wheezing groan.

"I'll make this quick if you tell me. Where did you get it?"

The woman's face was so beautiful.

Some bitches have all the luck, Shirley thought and remained silent.

"For the last time…?"

Agony wracked her chest as something inside her splintered, and she gasped.

"What was that?"

The pain came in waves, so overwhelming it was hard to identify the origin. Shirley blinked. Darkness was closing in. She opened her bloody lips, and her torturer leaned in.

"Speak up. I can't hear you."

Another gasping breath, and the face came closer. Oh so close. *Those eyes really are stunning,* she thought.

"Yes?"

Marshalling the pooling blood in her mouth, she spat, sending a gobbet of crimson phlegm onto the woman's startled face.

Her look of surprise made Shirley want to laugh, but that was beyond her now. As her vision faded, a voice laden with scorn said, "Over to you, Olga, my dear. But don't take long. I think we have company."

Chapter Forty-One

Giles had never seen a professional execute a room-to-room clearance operation before. Jane moved with purpose and precision, relying on the harpies' pathological fear of fire to send the shadowy creatures scrabbling away, their anxious screeches echoing through the cellars.

Meanwhile, Giles covered her flank, drawing on his knowledge of the cellar layout to alert her to blind spots. As they drove the terrified creatures back, he began to believe they might actually succeed in making it to the portal – and possibly even hold them off long enough for him to seal it.

When they reached a four-way junction, Jane thrust her torch into the two side passages, listening for noises of alarm from any harpies lurking within. When none cried out, she stepped across the junction, holding the torch in front of her. Giles was about to follow when a shadow dropped from the ceiling and slammed her to the ground.

There was no shout, no cry, just a surprised gasp as she hit the floor and her torch was snuffed out.

"Jane!" he cried, leaping forwards and raising his axe.

Too late, Giles saw movement in his peripheral vision.

Something pale swung through the air and struck his wrist with shocking force, sending the axe spinning from his hand. Another blow to his midriff cut short his cry, driving the wind from his body. Then, a third sent him sprawling into the opening opposite. His back hit the ground hard, the torch rolling from his hand.

While he gasped for breath, someone stepped into the passageway and stood over him. There was a metallic clink, and a flame flickered into life. A hooded figure was framed in the archway. For one terrible moment, he thought the statue of Lady Margaret had been revived. Then, he recognised the long wooden staff in one hand and the lighter in the other.

"You again," she said. Then, louder, "Olga! Leave that one and come here. I have something for you."

There was a sickening thud, and a giant appeared behind Mary. Giles had thought Katya was big, but her sister was monstrous in every sense of the word.

"Mother?"

"This is the one I told you about."

"The one who stole my mate?" Olga hissed, her eyes brimming with undisguised malice.

"The very same." She jabbed the staff into Giles's midriff, making him gasp. "Perhaps you'd like to tell my daughter where he is."

The thought of what she would do to Alfonso, or Raquel, if she ever caught up with them sent a chill through him.

"Bad news, I'm afraid. Alfonso's dead."

The harpy bent down, and her fetid breath washed over him.

"Dead?"

"I killed him and his sister."

The hiss turned into a shriek of rage that lanced through his skull, making his head ring. Then, a massive claw slammed down on his chest, pinning him to the floor.

"Olga! Be still."

Giles had no doubt that Olga would have eviscerated him if her mother had not been there. The grip on his chest tightened, and he whimpered in pain.

"It matters not. If anything, it simplifies things," the mother said. "If this one has bested your mate, he has proven himself worthy."

Olga's wild, undisguised hatred morphed into something more unsettling.

"We take this one, then?"

"Why not?"

Giles did his best to meet the harpy's eyes as he fought for breath.

"Very well," she hissed, and the pressure on his chest eased.

Gasping, he was vaguely aware of Mary leaning on her staff.

"Take this one back. I have one more loose end to tie up."

"Your former mate?"

Mary shook her head. "No, the gatekeeper."

Even in the flickering light of the flame, her murderous intent was visible.

"Gupta's gone," Giles wheezed.

Mary stopped.

"What did you say, boy?"

"Went... to Oxford."

Her face froze for a moment. Then, she began to laugh – or cackle. It wasn't a pleasant sound.

"Good try," she said, "but we both know that would never happen." She prodded him again with her staff. "He's probably in that same old room, isn't he? Above the Library?"

Giles said nothing.

"So predictable. I will enjoy telling Ravi what we have planned for you."

"You seem to be under the mistaken impression I give a crap."

"Oh, but you do." Her eyes flashed maliciously. "I can tell." She addressed Olga, her voice no longer playful, "Take him to the gate, and wait for me there. This won't take long."

The flame of her lighter retreated down the passageway, and darkness returned to the cellars. The air shifted as the enormous harpy bent down. Her breath was warm on his face, and there was a strange hissing sound as she inhaled his scent. Giles's skin turned to gooseflesh. Still, he resisted crying out, using the opportunity to feel around in vain for his extinguished torch.

"Get up."

Even if he'd wanted to, Giles wasn't sure his legs would obey.

"Now, this minute? Don't you want to chat and get to know each other...?"

Claws hooked into his jacket and yanked him to his feet. Stars exploded behind his closed eyes as he was slammed against the cellar wall, his head cracking painfully against the brickwork. He blinked, and two glowing amber rings filled his vision.

"When I tell you to do something, boy, you do it."

Giles sensed the barely restrained violence below the surface, like a powder keg in a furnace waiting to blow. The hate radiated from her dim outline like an aura. But the glow around her head was no illusion: a light was flickering from the passageway behind her.

"Now, that's no way to begin a relationship, is it?" he said, willing himself to gaze into her eyes. "It wouldn't hurt to say please and thank you, would it? Or did your mother forget to teach you that when you were growing up?"

"Shut up."

The glow was coming from the flame of a match.

"That's the trouble with parents nowadays," he continued. "Too busy conquering the world to focus on common decency. Honestly, I'll have words with your mother when she's back..."

Even though Olga's eyes were incandescent with rage, something – a fleeting shadow on the wall, perhaps – alerted her to Giles's saviour. She jerked her head around and screeched at the hovering flame.

"Run!" Giles yelled, throwing himself at Jane.

The giant harpy shrugged him off, sending him tumbling to the floor as she lunged for the flame. A shot rang out, the sharp bang shocking in the confines of the cellar. Then, two more followed in quick succession, the muzzle flashes illuminating Jane, framed in the doorway.

The harpy staggered and dropped to the floor. She remained there, head bowed to her chest as if in prayer, as three patches of grey spread across her ruffled plumage. Then, she raised her head, the motion already stiff and laboured. She stared at Jane, who was leaning against the cellar wall with a match in one hand and a compact automatic in the other.

The harpy opened her mouth wide, but no sound came out as the grey patina spread over her startled face. She began to sway, the weight of her arched wings toppling her forwards like a felled tree, and Giles just had time to avert his gaze before Mary's eldest daughter hit the cellar floor and exploded.

The backdraft of hot ash tugged at his clothes and ruffled his hair. When everything stilled, he found himself lying in a drift of dust. Something sharp dug into his ribs, and Giles found the discarded torch trapped beneath him. Easing himself to his feet, he retrieved the still-warm piece of wood and limped along the passageway.

Jane too was slumped on the floor covered in dust. She was trying to light another match, but her fingers were shaking too much to get a clean strike.

"Here," he said, taking the box from her and lighting the torch.

In its spluttering flame, her face had a deathly grey pallor, and there was an ugly red line that ran across her forehead. But the eyes were steady – as was her voice.

"You made it then," she said.

"You know me," he replied. "Like a bad penny."

She snorted, a puff of dust rising from her parched lips. Then, from the direction of the Gemini Passage, there came the distant screeching of harpies.

"Sounds like we've got company," he said.

"That's a bummer." She retrieved the gun from her lap.

The other torch was lying nearby. Giles lit it before handing it to her. By now, claws were scrabbling down the corridor, and eyes peered out of the darkness.

"This lot just don't know when to quit," he muttered. "You want me to deal with them?"

"What, and miss out on all the fun?"

She held up a hand, and Giles helped her to her feet. Holding the flaming torches in front of them, they limped towards the waiting harpies, their angry screeches rising to greet them.

Chapter Forty-Two

Ravi hurried through Second Court, which had been transformed into a heavenly realm of pale pavilions, with matching carpets and cushions covering the lawns. Scattered around the outside were dry-ice machines blowing cloudy vapour between food tents and ice-filled punts overflowing with bottles of beer and spirits.

Already, the place was filling with partygoers, streaming back from the firework and laser displays, eager to tuck into the dishes on offer. Ravi swam against the human tide pouring through the archway under the Shrewsbury Tower.

And that was when he saw her.

Mary, or a young woman who looked exactly like her, peeled off from the crowd towards his staircase. As she walked up to the wooden room indicator and ran a finger over the names listed there, he stood still, mesmerised. He was about to call her name when a wave of excited guests surged past, blocking his view. And when Ravi looked again, the staircase was empty.

Thoughts of finding Shirley were forgotten as he crossed the court and climbed the staircase. On the first floor, two waiters holding trays of drinks outside the Combination Room were staring wide-eyed up the stairs, from where a loud banging noise had originated.

Ravi gave them what he hoped was a reassuring smile before continuing to the top floor. When he arrived on the landing, he stopped. She was hammering at his door with a wooden staff, the old oak panels creaking under the blows.

"Mary?"

She whirled around, and any doubts Ravi had had about the woman he'd seen earlier vanished. There before him was his former May Ball partner. Her bright, intelligent eyes, her smooth, unblemished face, and even her lustrous hair were as he remembered them from half a century ago. Recognition spread across Mary's face, and she cast the stick aside.

"Ravi," she said, hurrying along the corridor.

He did the same, his feet obeying an impulse he was powerless to control. When they came together, Mary took his face in her hands, her eyes never leaving his.

"You bastard!" she said, bringing her knee up into his groin.

The pain was unlike anything Ravi had experienced before. It blotted out everything. His senses momentarily overwhelmed, he wasn't even aware of hitting the landing, the thump of his head against the floorboards barely registering above his agony.

How long he lay there, unable to move or speak, was difficult to say. Eventually, something tucked under his chin and raised his head. She had retrieved her wooden staff and now stood over him, her hood raised.

"Oh, Ravi, you have no idea how long I have waited for that."

Her cold, flat voice was so different to the one he remembered.

"How I wish Robert were here too. I had something special planned for him. Still, you are here, and that will have to do."

Ravi tensed, expecting another blow. Instead, her breath fanned his cheek as she bent low to murmur in his ear.

"Don't worry, Ravi dear. While I would love to draw this out, I don't have much time. Which means, I'm afraid, neither do you."

She reminded him of a cat watching a trapped mouse.

"Not all pain is physical," she said, tracing her fingers over his sweat-soaked brow. "Wounds of the heart run much deeper, lasting long after a body has healed. Believe me, I know." She gripped his hair and yanked his head back.

"Tell me, Ravi, did you believe Robert's stories about going off for 'rugby training'?"

He said nothing.

"All those times, he was with me." She smiled humourlessly. "And what do you think we were doing?" She jabbed the staff into his abdomen. "Again and again and again!"

Ravi was curled on the floor, gasping for breath, when she finally stopped.

"Your best friend, Ravi, and all the time he was screwing me behind your back. Is that why he decided to abandon me? Because I had come between you – the dynamic duo who were going to save the world. Or did Robert become bored? Another conquest, and time to move on."

Ravi's words came out as a gasping moan.

"Speak up. I can't hear you."

"Robert… loved you."

She laughed, shrill and bitter.

"The only person that oaf ever loved was himself."

"You're wrong," Ravi murmured. "He kept your letter."

"Letter?"

"From Grantchester."

There was a flicker of doubt in her eyes. "A trophy, that's all."

"It was folded inside the blanket."

This time she didn't hide her surprise. When she spoke, her voice was softer, like an echo of the one he remembered.

"Then, why did he leave me there?"

"He didn't," he said. "I did."

The landing went very still. Even though the May Ball was in full swing, Ravi heard only his laboured breathing.

"You?" Her eyes locked on his, and he couldn't look away. She needed to know. He owed her that.

"I saw your tracks in the sand that day, not Robert."

"And you didn't tell him?"

"No."

"Why not?"

"Because I knew he'd come back for you, and I couldn't let that happen."

"Why not?"

"Because I knew who you were working for."

"What are you talking about?"

But the haunted look in her eyes betrayed her.

"Moscow," he said.

Mary's mouth was a thin line. When she didn't reply, he went on.

"It was a honey trap, wasn't it? The beautiful agent seduces the hapless academic. I'd heard about them, of course." He added with bitter humour, "It was practically a rite of passage at Trinity."

She remained silent.

"Until then, no one at John's had been turned, had they? But then these two young physicists began working on something very hush-hush. And Cambridge being what it is, word got around. I assume your handlers suggested you contact me first. The lonely and impressionable oddball. But then I introduced you to Robert, and you realised how… keen he was to impress you."

"When did you know?" Her tone was almost conversational, but slight creases had appeared on her forehead.

"I'd had my suspicions from the outset. Why would a woman as beautiful and talented as you be interested in me? It didn't make sense. When you switched your attention to Robert, I became more concerned. Not just for our research but for him. I'd never seen Robert like that before. And by the time the May Ball came around, I could see he'd fallen for you."

Mary was quiet, her face a mask.

"But then you gave me this."

Ravi eased himself up, ignoring the pain, and removed

the folded handkerchief from his top pocket. Mary's eyes widened in recognition.

"I meant to return it after the Ball. But then I noticed the embroidery."

He indicated the corner with its finely woven star circled by the letters M A S H A.

"I thought at first they were initials. Then, I realised they were a name. Your name, Mary. Or, as a Russian would say, Masha."

After a moment, a faint smile appeared on her lips. "Yuri always said you were the smarter of the two."

"Yuri? Your case officer?"

"What does it matter? No doubt he's dead by now." She considered him. "So, Ravi, I take it you informed the authorities?"

"I did. There were channels in John's. As it turns out, the spy catchers were already closing in. It was only a matter of time. But then, well, you stepped through the portal. After that..."

"I knew too much," she said.

He nodded.

"British Intelligence would never have let you share what you'd seen. What the Kremlin would have done with that information was unthinkable."

"So, you decided to leave me there."

"To come back was a death sentence. At least on Gemini, your fate was in your hands."

Her eyes took on a cold, hard edge again.

"And Robert agreed to this?"

"He never knew. When you disappeared, I told him about Moscow. I wanted him to believe you had returned there."

"And he believed you?"

"Not at first. Robert made enquiries, of course, and our people confirmed much of what I had said. Everyone thought Moscow had pulled you out before the net closed in. The fact that no trace of you was ever found was unsurprising. It was well known what happened to blown agents on their return."

"You never told him the truth."

"I couldn't. Robert would have gone back for you. And we'd agreed the gate should never be opened again, its existence kept secret."

"Along with mine," she said.

"Yes, along with yours."

He half expected her to attack him again, to vent her rage for what he had done to her. Instead, Mary laughed.

"You think you've been so clever, don't you, Ravi? Keeping your secret safe all these years. Well, no more."

Mary reached into the folds of her cloak and removed a tattered, leather-bound object: Robert's journal.

"I found this in your old clubroom just now," she continued, chilling Ravi's heart. "You remember, the one in the cellars you showed me that time. How careless of you to leave this lying around. Why, anyone could pick it up..." She turned the book over in her hands. It was bloodstained. "Sadly for her, someone did."

Ravi clutched his stomach and rolled onto his front.

"Oh dear, someone you cared about, was she? Another victim of your foolishness?"

Ravi moaned as if in pain. She leaned in, goading him, and he slipped his hand inside his jacket pocket.

"Call yourself a gatekeeper? Believe me, Ravi, I shall not be so careless with his key. I know its true value and will use it in a way you were never–"

Ravi didn't wait for her to finish. Whipping around, he slashed at her arm with his metal ruler. Her speed, though, was incredible, and she blocked his strike with the journal. Still, the blade's sharpened edge caught her hand, slicing the back of it open.

With a cry, Mary dropped the journal, and he lunged for her again. But she dodged his clumsy blow and brought her staff down on his wrist. A numbing pain shot up his arm, and the ruler went flying.

Ravi rolled as she swung again, the staff slamming into the floorboards inches from where his head had been. There was a splintering crack, and she was left holding the broken shaft in her trembling hands.

Seizing his chance, he scrambled for the journal, but Mary was too quick for him, wielding the wooden stump like a club and knocking the journal across the landing. She slammed his face into the floor and spun him over, pinning him to the ground.

"Is that the best you can do?" she sneered, kneeling on top of him, the shattered staff held like a stake. "Let me show you how it should be done."

Mary raised the jagged stump over her head, and Ravi

saw her now for what she was. Not the beautiful young woman he had once loved but a monster. A monster with a shadow that loomed up behind her and wrapped an arm around her neck.

There was a horrible, wet thud, and Mary's eyes bulged, pained surprise filling her face as she toppled forwards onto the floorboards next to him. Above her stood Dominic Lester, Ravi's old metal ruler in his hand, its blade a glistening scarlet.

A gurgling wheeze disturbed the shocked silence, and Ravi turned to see blood bubble from her mouth. More seeped from under her body, staining her cloak and pooling between the old floorboards. Mary's face was deathly pale, her eyes wide and staring. Then, they blinked and gazed past Ravi. Her lips twitched, and he leant closer. Her final word was little more than a whisper of air against his cheek.

"Yuri..."

Ravi lifted his head, half-expecting her long lashes to blink again. However, they never flickered, even when he passed his hand over them. He followed their sightless gaze and looked up at Dominic Lester, his mind reeling. In his shock and confusion, a stream of questions clouded Ravi's thoughts. In the end, all he could manage was one.

"Why?"

The man's expression was grim. "She would have killed you."

"I... I know, but she–"

Before he could finish, Lester's mouth fell open, and he gasped. "Ravi, look!"

Ravi turned and recoiled at once. Mary's youthful face was changing, the skin wrinkling and shrinking over the bones beneath. Then, her hair whitened and withered like frosted cobwebs, and her eyes misted, the radiant colours fading to a milky sheen. Finally, her body began to shrink, the flowing robes sagging as the smooth curves beneath deflated.

The glimmer was barely noticeable at first, a pale flicker beneath the translucent skin. But when the gleam intensified, Ravi realised what was about to happen.

"Close your eyes," he said.

"What?"

"Close them!" Ravi repeated, following his own advice.

Moments later, a bright flare of light was followed by a rush of air that sent him tumbling across the landing. When he looked back, Mary's body was still glowing. Then, there was a sound – not so much a gasp as a release of something into the ether, some essence that was no longer beholden to the mortal body in which it had been held.

Ravi had a fleeting vision of tall towers, red plains and a green meandering river. Then, the image was gone, and he was kneeling beside an outline of smouldering grey ash.

"Is it over?" Lester asked.

"Yes." Ravi reached for a small rectangular lump in the centre of the pile. It was a tarnished metal lighter, the surface still warm to the touch. Brushing the dust clear, he read the inscription.

"What is it?" Lester had moved closer, his face set.

Before Ravi could reply, a voice called up from the stairwell.

"Dominic?" It was Gabrielle Dutour. "The Master of Trinity wonders if you will be joining us for dinner?"

Lester held up a finger to Ravi before replying.

"I shall be down presently."

"The Fellows' Butler wanted to know if you preferred red or white wine with your meal."

The Master's eyes bored into Ravi's, but his voice was as cheery as ever.

"It's a Bordeaux, is it not?"

"*Oui*, Master."

"Red then, obviously."

"*Bien*," she replied. "I shall tell him."

Lester waited until her footsteps had disappeared. Then, he indicated the pile of dust.

"Did Gabrielle have anything to do with tonight's incursion?"

"No, Master. If I'm not mistaken, it was Shirley Blake."

"The Porter?"

It was gratifying that even Lester was shocked by this.

"I believe so, yes." Ravi retrieved the journal and stuffed it in his pocket.

"I thought for sure it was that Chamberlain boy of yours..."

Giles! Ravi thought, suddenly remembering where he'd been heading before seeing Mary.

"I have to go, Master."

Lester stepped between him and the stairwell.

"Nothing that happened here goes beyond this staircase, Ravi. You understand that, don't you?"

The man's expression was unreadable, but the metal ruler was still in his hand.

"Only too well," Ravi said, keeping his voice level. "But I'm the only one who can close the gate."

For a moment, he wasn't sure what Lester would do. Then, with a deft movement, the Master wiped the blade clean and offered Ravi the handle.

"As long as we understand each other. Go on, while I sort out this mess."

Ravi paused at the top of the stairs. The former spy was examining the pile of ashes that had once been Mary. Or would he say Masha?

"Dominic?" The other man raised his head. "Thank you for coming when you did."

Lester nodded and there was a rare sadness in his eyes. "We look after our own, remember?"

"Indeed, we do, Master."

"Now go and shut that damn gate, once and for all."

Chapter Forty-Three

"Watch out!" Giles yelled, shoving Jane to one side and then ducking beneath a claw that would have taken her head off. Before the harpy could recover, he thrust the burning torch into its face.

Screeching, it reared up, flames racing over its neck and torso. It collided with another trying to force its way through the portal, and soon both were ablaze, thrashing like crazed marionettes beneath the glowing archway.

"Come on," he said. "They're going to blow!"

He hoisted Jane up, and they stumbled clear of the portal and crouched with their backs against the wall. A blinding flash and a cloud of hot ash swept over them.

"You OK?" Giles asked when it had passed.

Through the swirling dust, she appeared dazed. "I think so."

Getting to his feet, Giles took in the scene of carnage inside the portal, his eyes watering as the smell hit him and made him gag. With nowhere to run, the creatures caught in the blast had suffered terribly. Those not incinerated in the initial explosion now lay sprawled on the floor. Above their mewling, Giles heard screeches in the distance. Not of panic but of… battle?

"What's going on?" Jane asked.

"I'm not sure." He helped her up. "But I'm not waiting to find out."

Giles stepped in front of the portal. "I might need you to buy me some time."

"Now you tell me!" she muttered, fingering her empty gun.

While Jane retrieved his torch, Giles composed himself and tried to recall the Latin incantation, murmuring the words aloud.

"I thought you'd done this before," she said.

"Well, yes, but it's not like reciting Grace in Hall."

Blotting out the distant clamour, Giles formed the spell in his head while Jane held the flickering torch aloft in front of him. Then, just as he was about to speak, the tunnel fell silent. They stood still, neither of them daring to move.

There came a low, rumbling sound.

"What's that?" Jane asked as the noise grew louder.

Something was coming from Gemini. No, not something, many things. So many that their footfalls combined into one thundering mass.

"Get behind me," Giles said. "It will only take a few minutes."

"I'm not sure we're going to have that long."

She was right. A dark shadow was approaching from the tunnel, individual shapes becoming clear: harpies, both male and female, some limping and others carrying wounds from whatever confrontation had occurred at the other end of the passageway. At their head was a huge figure, her broad wings bunched as she strode towards the gate.

"Typical," Jane said, tossing the torch aside and thrusting her hand down the front of her dress.

"What are you doing?"

"Always keep one for emergencies," she said, retrieving a bullet and inserting it into the chamber of her gun. "Looks like that's now."

Racking the slide, she trained the weapon on the monster leading the charge. "This one's almost as big as that last bitch," she muttered. "Still, hard to miss."

The harpy loping towards them locked her amber eyes on his.

"Wait!" Giles yelled, grabbing Jane's arm.

"What are you doing?"

"It's OK! She's with us!"

Jane's muscles remained tense.

"Trust me," he said, stepping between her and the approaching creatures.

The giant harpy halted a few yards from him, fanning her wings out wide to hold back her followers. Though a good many hissed in surprise, none tried to pass. When she lowered her wings, Giles recognised the lopsided old male at her side.

"Hello, Katya. It's good to see you again."

Instead of a warm greeting from the towering female, he received a sharp question. "Where is she?"

"Who?"

"My sister, Olga."

Giles hesitated. "Why do you want to know?"

She glared at him. "Because we are here to ensure she never returns to Gemini."

"I see. Well, she's not going to. Ever."

Her father let out a startled hiss that was echoed by others in the horde.

After a beat of silence, Katya asked, "And my mother?"

Giles didn't know what to say.

"She… won't be coming back… either," a breathless voice said behind him.

The Professor stood in the cellar doorway, his crumpled suit covered in dust and his dress shirt stained with blood. Bruised and battered, the old academic limped forwards to stand alongside Giles and Jane. Despite his dishevelled appearance, he met the harpy's gaze without flinching.

"Mary is dead."

Katya's father let out a long hiss that was picked up by the other harpies, the sound spreading back along the tunnel.

"Did you kill her?" Katya asked, her face unreadable.

Giles felt a tingle of alarm and wondered if Jane did too. She still had the gun in her hand, and he prayed she wouldn't have to use it. Katya's face never flickered as she stared into the Professor's eyes.

"No," he said. "She died in my arms."

Katya bowed her head. "Then her spirit has returned home."

Ravi nodded. "It has."

The tension eased throughout the passageway, harpies shuffling and murmuring. Katya stood with her head bowed as if in contemplation. Then, she addressed Giles.

"Where is Alfonso?"

"He is home with his family."

"And his injuries?"

"Healing. But… he will never see again."

She considered this silently. Then, she looked at the glowing archway above them.

"This gate has brought much suffering."

"It has," Ravi agreed. He reached under his arm and held out a filthy object. "Which is why I bring you this."

It was an old journal, its cover scorched and spattered with dried blood.

"This book was used to open the gate, first by my friend Robert Mackenzie and tonight by another." He indicated a smouldering pile of rags by the Gemini Passage entrance. "Both paid the ultimate price for their foolishness. As did your mother and sister."

To Giles's astonishment, Ravi then produced Robert's lighter. The same one Giles had tossed to Mary in the Matriarchy.

"I propose we close the gate now and destroy the journal to prevent it ever being used again."

Katya nodded. "So be it. But I warn you, the tunnel will remain guarded. If any try to pass this way again, they do so on pain of death."

"So be it," the Professor agreed.

Holding the lighter's flickering flame over the journal,

Ravi started to read. The others stepped back as the old man stood before the glowing portal reciting the incantation. The Latin rolled off his lips without doubt or hesitation, the energy flowing from him into the glyphs around the opening.

When he'd completed the spell, he lowered the lighter and held it under the torn and tattered pages. They caught at once, flames spreading over the journal as he placed it on the floor. They watched it burn until all that remained of Robert Mackenzie's legacy was a pile of blackened ashes.

"Remember my promise," Katya said to Giles through the closing aperture as the cellar wall began to reform. "None may pass this way again. I shall be watching."

As the thrum of dark matter filled the void between the worlds, it blotted out all sight or sound of the great harpy. But Giles never forgot those eyes or her words.

Chapter Forty-Four

On the far side of the Paddock, Nick stood in front of an array of screens monitoring the sky above College.

"Was that the last of them?"

"Pretty much," Ash said.

Annabel leaned over Brian's shoulder and pointed at his screen. "There! Is that one?"

Brian's hand was a blur over the tracking pad, moving a red dot towards a dark shape circling above the pulsing lights of the laser show. He hit the ENTER key and a bright beam lanced at the object, which disappeared in a puff of white.

"Not anymore," he said, scanning the cameras back and forth across the empty sky. "Clear."

Nick could scarcely believe it. The screens had been swarming with shadowy dots when they'd first arrived. Now all that remained was a mist of fine dust drifting to earth.

"What now?" Ash asked.

It was hard to think above the constant banging on the door. This had begun soon after the scheduled end of the laser show and had grown increasingly frantic over the past hour.

"What do you think?" Nick asked Annabel.

"Some could be hiding on the rooftops, like last time."

"True. I guess we won't know for certain until dawn."

Ash's eyes lit up. "They're like the trolls in *The Hobbit*, you mean?"

"'Dawn take you all, and be stone to you'," Brian said in a deep voice.

"Something like that, yes."

"So cool!" Ash said. "In that case, we're happy to stay on watch throughout the night, aren't we, Brian?"

"It's what we do on gaming tournaments."

The banging was becoming even louder.

"I'm not sure they're going to let you do that. They'll be pulling the plug on us soon."

"What if I gave them something special?" Brian suggested. "Like an *Aurora Borealis*?"

"A what?"

But Ash understood. "Like the Northern Lights, you mean? Yes, that could work!"

"We could program a randomised wave pattern with a kaleidoscope of low-intensity colours."

"That should keep them from returning," Ash agreed.

"And if we flush any out..."

"I can take them down with a laser!"

"OK, I'm on it." Brian bent over his keyboard and began tapping away.

"So, that's all good, then?" Nick asked their hunched backs.

"Absolutely!" Ash replied. "We've got it covered."

"And the music?"

"Oh, no, we don't need that. Unless you have any mindfulness tracks we could download."

"No. Not really."

"In that case, we'll do without," Ash said, typing away. "Just make sure they don't cut the power."

"OK," Nick said. "We'll see what we can do."

Nick and Annabel left them frantically tapping at their keyboards and approached the door, which was shaking from the force of the blows.

"Any idea what they're talking about?" Nick asked.

"Sort of."

"OK, I'll hold the door if you do the talking."

She nodded, and Nick gripped the handle.

"Coming out!" he shouted and shoved it open.

The banging stopped immediately and was replaced by a startled cry. Darius, Nick's fellow first year, was sprawled in the arms of the security guards. The young lawyer's face was as scarlet as his sash.

"Nick! What the hell is going on? The lasers should have finished half an hour ago!"

"Yeah, sorry about that." On the lawns, plenty of guests were still partying under the strobing lights. "Seems to be going down well, though."

"That's not the point!" Darius yelled, pulling himself upright. "We've got guests late for dinner, and the warm-up band's playing to an empty court."

Annabel stepped in front of Nick. "The guys are setting up the final special effect. It's going to be pretty spectacular."

"I don't give a flying–"

"Darius," Nick interrupted, closing the door behind him. "You have to trust us on this."

"Trust you? What makes you…?"

But before he could finish, the music fell silent.

"Blow me, will you look at that!" said one of the security guards.

Darius followed their gaze upwards, his mouth falling open.

The dazzling laser show had been replaced by a series of mesmerising waves, drifting across the night sky and washing over the College rooftops. The dancing couples slowed and stopped, admiring the weaving canopy of colour. Spontaneous applause sprang up everywhere.

"What did I tell you?" Annabel said.

"Yeah," Darius murmured. "That's… pretty good."

As if on cue, Stormzy's distinctive vocals boomed out from the main stage.

"Dammit," Darius said. "I'm supposed to be marshalling over there." He hurried down the steps.

"What about the control tower?" one of the guards asked.

"Oh, I don't know. Just… let them do their thing!"

Then, he ran across the lawn as the bemused security team looked on. Nick was about to apologise when a beam of light shot out from the tower, illuminating a distant speck rising above the College. For a few brief seconds the dot glowed like a comet before disintegrating in a shower of sparks.

"Come on," he said to Annabel, setting off towards the Eagle Gate. "We're needed elsewhere."

Chapter Forty-Five

When Annabel arrived with Nick at the staircase in the corner of New Court, it was clear that something terrible had happened. The door had been all but torn from its frame, the sturdy brass hinges bent and twisted out of shape. Then, there was the smell, an acrid mix of sulphur and cooked meat that had nothing to do with the crowded food stalls nearby.

But as they crossed the lobby to the entrance to the cellars, nothing could have prepared them for the ghastly apparition that emerged from the doorway. Ghostly grey and covered in gore, it was like a ghoul rising from a crypt. For one wild moment, Annabel thought of the statue they'd destroyed last term, wondering if its soul had come back to haunt them. But then the figure raised its head, the eyes widening in recognition.

"Annabel? Nick? What are you doing here?"

"Professor!" She hurried forwards and hugged him. "Are you all right?"

"A little grubby perhaps, but otherwise in one piece."

"Where are the others?" Nick asked.

"They're coming," he said. "The stairs were a bit narrow for all three of us."

Giles emerged then, axe in one hand as he helped Jane onto the landing. A sleeve from his dress shirt had been torn off and fashioned into a dressing to stem the blood from a nasty wound on Jane's forehead. They, too, were covered in dust and soot, their clothes singed in places.

"Oh my goodness," Annabel cried. "What happened?"

"Forgot to duck," Jane murmured.

"We need to get her to hospital," Giles said.

"I'm fine," she protested. "I'm… a bit woozy, that's all."

"We'll be the judge of that," said a voice from the staircase entrance.

Bert was standing in the doorway, flanked by Ying and Trevor.

"Giles!" Ying cried. "Trevor, quick!"

They crossed the lobby, easing Jane from Giles's grip.

"What have you two been doing?"

"Would you believe we ran into some gatecrashers? And… well, things got a bit heated."

"Crashers? Where?" Trevor asked.

"It's OK, Trev," Giles sagged against the wall. "We showed them the door."

"Giles did," Jane murmured. "Not as useless as he looks."

"I find that hard to believe," Ying replied, though not unkindly.

Trevor was eyeing Jane's head wound. "Come on, we need to get you an ambulance."

Giles pushed himself off the wall. "I'll come with you."

"You're not going anywhere. Trevor and I have got this," Ying said, taking Jane's other arm. "Besides, you don't have a ticket, remember?"

"Seriously?"

Ying ignored him. "Annabel, I want you and Nick to escort Giles to the Wilberforce Room."

"The Wilberforce Room? But–"

Ying held up a hand. "None of you have eaten anything yet, I take it?"

"Well, no, not as such," Annabel said. "We've been a bit... distracted."

"In that case, you'll find port and cheese in the Wilberforce Room."

Annabel gaped at her. "What? I don't understand."

"We laid it out for the Master and his guest, but he was a no-show."

The Professor coughed. "Ah, yes, that may be because... he was assisting me with another matter."

"Well, it's a pity to waste it," Ying continued. "If I'm honest, I'd rather have you in there than out and about scaring the guests. No disrespect, but you all look like death." She turned to the Head Porter. "What do you think, Bert?"

"You're not wrong. Leave them with me. I've got it in hand."

"In that case, I'll see you lot later." She began guiding an unprotesting Jane towards the door. "The Survivors' Photo is at dawn, remember."

When they were gone, Bert said, "Well, you heard the

young lady. I suggest you get some food inside you, and I daresay a stiff drink wouldn't go amiss either."

"I don't suppose it would do any harm," Annabel said to the others.

Nick shrugged, and Giles said, "You had me at port."

"We also have various matters to discuss," the Professor added meaningfully, "while we have the chance."

"If you do that, I'll sort things out here," Bert said, approaching the splintered cellar door. "Make sure everything's secure."

The Professor paused at this. "Tell me, Bert, did you manage to fix the CCTV at all?"

"Afraid not, Professor. The screens are completely blank."

"So, there's no video footage of what happened down there."

"Not a frame, Professor. Which is a pity, really."

"Why?"

"Because I'd love to get my hands on who did all this." He indicated the state of the lobby.

"I'm not sure you would," Giles said, and the Porter gave him a sharp look.

"Listen, I don't know about you," Annabel said quickly, "but I wouldn't mind having that food now."

"Agreed," said Nick.

Annabel held out her arm for the Professor, and after wishing the Head Porter a good night, the four of them limped from the staircase into the dancing crowds.

Chapter Forty-Six

Ravi had attended many private dinners in the Wilberforce Room, but this was undoubtedly the most astounding. By the time the others had finished relaying what had happened to them that evening, the candles had burned low in the sixteenth-century dining room. Ravi had barely touched the food while he listened in rapt attention to their accounts, shocked at how close they had come to disaster.

Occasionally, he glanced at the portrait of Sir William Wilberforce and wondered what the great Abolitionist would have made of these young Johnians. Though none of their deeds matched those of pioneering the abolition of slavery across the globe, their actions had undoubtedly saved many lives, both here and on Gemini.

Not that you would know that from their demeanour. Annabel and Nick had lost much of the wide-eyed wonder he remembered from their first weeks in Cambridge. Even Giles was sombre as he described the carnage of the cellars and Olga's demise.

"If it weren't for Jane, I'd be back with the delightful Olga on Gemini, becoming acquainted." The room went quiet at this, and Giles added, "I know, to think Jane graduated from the Other Place… I'll never live it down."

Nick lobbed a walnut shell at him, which he batted away.

"Pass one of those chocolates, Annabel," Giles said, "before you turn into one."

Handing him the plate, she asked, "What I don't understand is what Shirley thought she was doing? And how did she get hold of Professor Mackenzie's journal?"

"I may be able to help there," Ravi replied, deciding it was his turn to share some uncomfortable truths. "After Roberts's death, the Master believed we might have a mole in College."

"A mole?" Nick asked.

"Placed here by the Schiller Foundation to discover what happened to Robert's missing papers. For some time, we thought it might be your Tutor."

"Dr Dutour?"

"Even for a physicist, she seemed unusually interested in Robert's work. But, as it turned out, we were wrong to suspect her. We should have realised they'd want someone with access to all parts of the College."

"A Porter," Annabel said.

Ravi nodded. "It was obvious when you think about it. What better person than a member of staff whose job was to know every nook and cranny in College and monitor all the security systems?"

There was a brief silence as the logic of this sank in.

"It was Shirley who showed me the New Court cellars," Nick said. "That time I discovered Professor Mackenzie's trunk."

"And now that I think about it," Annabel added, "I was pretty sure Shirley spotted me stealing the punt that night we entered the cellars."

Ravi remembered the curious look on the Porter's face when he'd handed in Robert's keys to the New Court cellars. The more he thought about it, the more ashamed he was for not identifying her as the real threat.

"Either way," he continued, "I think Shirley was beginning to realise the importance of that trunk. Which is why she came to investigate Mr Weston and me when we relocated it to the School of Pythagoras."

"Ah, so that's where you hid it," Giles said. "Smart move."

"Not smart enough, it would appear. But for Mr Weston's vigilance, she might have got clean away."

"Still, why did Shirley try to open the portal?" Annabel asked.

"I've been wondering that myself. We may never know. Perhaps it was in her brief, or it was personal curiosity. I doubt she would have attempted it if she'd understood what was waiting on the other side."

"Where's the journal now?" Nick asked.

"I destroyed it in the cellar. I should have done it earlier, but…", he picked up the lighter sitting on the table in front of him and fiddled with it, "sentiment got in the way."

"And there are no other copies?" Nick asked.

"Not as far as I am aware." Ravi looked across the table at Giles, who shook his head.

"No, I didn't make any."

Ravi wondered if that was because he didn't need to.

"So, that's it?" Nick asked. "The Gemini Passage is shut for good?"

"Katya made it pretty clear she wasn't going to let anyone through from their end," Giles said.

"Yes," Ravi agreed. "I think we can safely say no one will be opening it again."

"Good," Nick said. "One less thing to worry about next year."

Ravi supposed it was, though some part of him doubted he would ever be free of it.

"Professor?" Annabel asked. "Who was Mary?"

Ravi paused, but after what they had all faced this evening, he felt he owed them some honesty.

"An old work colleague."

"And how did she end up on Gemini?"

"She followed Robert and me through the portal and became trapped there. I thought she was dead, but clearly not."

"Is that why she came looking for you?"

"Revenge, you mean?" He sighed. "Yes, partly. But also because she knew I could open the portal. And she couldn't take that risk."

"So, what happened?"

Ravi had anticipated someone would ask this, but he had no intention of sharing what had happened on the landing outside his room.

"She was killed by one of her own, as is often the way with tyrants."

And spies, he thought.

The room went quiet, each lost in their thoughts, until a distant wailing noise cut through the silence and a sliver of light filtered through the gap between the curtains. Moments later, a lone bagpiper struck up with the *Dawning of the Day*, the tune swirling over the College grounds.

Ravi eased back in his chair, relief and tiredness washing over him. Annabel, though, sat up tall.

"The Survivors' Photograph!"

"Well, I think we qualify for that," said Giles, removing his dripping hand from a bucket whose ice had long since melted. "What say you, Professor?"

"I think I'm a bit old for that sort of thing."

"Nonsense. I saw you with that femme fatale at the Master's reception. You and Dr Dutour make quite the dashing couple."

"Come on, Professor," said Annabel. "The four of us."

"We're not going without you," Nick said.

He knew it was foolish, but Ravi was touched that they wanted him with them.

"Oh, very well, but I won't be saying 'Cheese'."

The others rose and began filing out of the room. Ravi eased himself to his feet, his body stiff and sore from the blows Mary had rained down on him. He was about to follow when he heard floorboards creak behind him.

Ravi spun around. A door at the back of the room led to the College Kitchen. It swung open, and Aurelia appeared carrying an empty tray. He wasn't sure who looked more surprised.

"Sorry, Professor. I didn't know you were here."

"We have just finished."

He indicated the table, but she ignored the gesture, her eyes never leaving his face.

"You are injured."

"What?"

"Your cheek. It is bruised."

"Oh?" Ravi winced when his fingers found the lump that had formed there. "Nothing to worry about. I had a fall at the top of my staircase."

She crossed the room, stopping a few feet away to examine him.

"A fall, you say?"

She leaned in closer, her face a few inches from his own.

"Er, yes, I knocked my head against the handrail."

Her eyebrows arched with suspicion, dislodging specks of grey dust lodged within the dark hair.

"And how is that woman you were with?" Ravi felt his stomach tighten. "She looked upset," she added. "Like she was crying."

It took him a moment to realise who she meant.

"Dr Dutour, you mean? She is fine, as far as I know. I haven't seen her since the garden party. I believe she may have joined the Master and his guest for dinner."

Aurelia considered this, her eyes never leaving his. Finally, she nodded. "I'm glad… that she had a nice evening."

"Yes," he replied. "So am I."

Then, to his astonishment, she raised her hand and laid it against the side of his face, careful to avoid the bruise.

"You are a good man, Professor."

Ravi didn't know what to say. All he could focus on was the touch of her skin against his and her shallow breathing matching his own. He never knew what he would have done next because, at that moment, Annabel stuck her head around the door.

"Professor, are you coming?" She stopped short when she saw them standing there, their faces inches apart. "Oh, sorry, I didn't know you were… together."

Ravi didn't dare move, not wanting to break the moment. To his surprise, neither did Aurelia.

"Will I see you at breakfast tomorrow, Professor?"

"I expect so, yes," he said, thinking it would take nothing short of a flock of harpies to prevent him from making that appointment.

"Good," she said. "I look forward to it."

Aurelia turned for the kitchen and left Ravi wondering if he had just experienced a remarkably lucid but fatigue-induced dream.

"Professor?"

Annabel was still in the doorway, her eyes shining.

No dream, he thought.

"Professor," she said, "if we hurry, we can still make the Survivors' Photograph."

"Of course," he replied as reality reasserted itself, and he followed her outside.

When they emerged, Second Court was deserted except for a few exhausted bar staff sharing a cigarette. They made their way through Third Court, which was now open to the heavens, the canopy of balloons floating somewhere over the city.

Ravi paused briefly on the Bridge of Sighs, appreciating how still the river was, before descending into the cloisters behind Annabel, who was on Nick's arm. In the distance, the College Choir's a cappella group, the Gents of St John's, were leaving the stage after their signature closing gig. A few good-natured "Halloos" were directed at Giles, who acknowledged them with a princely wave of his uninjured hand.

They were some of the last to arrive at the Eagle Gate. Several hundred guests stood with their backs to the College, facing what looked like dew-covered lawns. It was only when a dust cloud was thrown up by Ash and Brian hurrying across the Paddock to cheers from an appreciative crowd that Ravi realised its true nature.

Many of the young gentlemen waiting for the photo had given up their jackets to their partners, whose ballgowns offered scant protection from the chill morning air. Dotted among the guests, Ravi spotted the red sashes of the May Ball Committee, whose tired but happy faces suggested no one knew how close they had all come to disaster.

"There's a gap over there," Nick said, leading them around the back of the crowd to a patch of lawn relatively clear of guests, a few yards from where the College gardeners had discovered Robert's lifeless body all those months ago. A generous planting of White Heather now covered the spot, a thoughtful touch from the Gardens Committee that Ravi was sure his friend would have appreciated.

"Professor?" Annabel asked. "They're about to take the photograph."

Ying Li was standing in front of the temporary scaffolding tower erected on the lawn. From its summit, the official photographer gave her a thumbs-up.

"OK. Quiet, you lot!" she shouted, and, despite the high spirits of those present, the voices fell silent.

Dominic Lester stepped forwards, almost as dapper as when he had greeted his guests the previous evening, though Ravi thought he was a little paler than before.

"Good morning, everyone!" he cried.

A chorus of cheers rang out, followed by a very American whoop from Brett standing alongside Gareth in the middle of the throng.

"May I commend you all on your survival!"

More cheers followed as Lester beamed at his audience, his gaze lingering on Ravi for a moment.

"May I also congratulate the committee for what I'm sure my honoured guest here would agree has been the most spectacular May Ball in living memory!"

The Master of Trinity acknowledged the good-natured whistles this provoked.

"As I'm sure, like me, you will be keen to get back to the Library," he said, pausing for the laughter to die down, "I shall bring proceedings to a close in the traditional manner."

He produced a Champagne flute out of nowhere and raised it to his students, staff, Fellows and guests.

"My compliments to you all, this year's irrepressible survivors!"

To thunderous applause, Dominic Lester strode back to his place in the front row.

"Always the showman," Ravi said to Annabel.

But his Tutee wasn't listening. Indeed, he suspected that neither she nor Nick had heard a word that had been said. They were wrapped in each other's arms, oblivious to him, the Master or anyone else.

Better late than never, he thought.

"OK, everyone," the photographer called from behind his camera lens. "Big smiles, please. On the count of three."

"One!"

"Two!"

"Three!"

"Stilton!" Giles yelled, and Ravi smiled.

Epilogue

Alfonso sat in his favourite chair on the veranda overlooking Alcudia Bay. Though the night air was still warm, the evening's promenaders had long since retired to bed, their cheerful voices a distant memory replaced by the faint creak of little boats moored just off the beach.

He imagined the moon's reflection on the gently lapping waters. But the image shifted as a line of ripples appeared in his mind, morphing into a V that picked up speed across the water towards him.

"No," he murmured. "Stop it."

Alfonso closed his eyes to blank out the recurring nightmare.

Next to him, Raquel stirred.

"Alfonso? What is it?"

"Nothing," he said, calming his breathing. "It was... a mosquito."

There was a rustle of cushions as she sat up, yawning.

"I must have dropped off. Maybe we should go to bed."

With the image still fresh in his mind, that was the last thing Alfonso wanted.

"No, I'd like to sit here a little longer." He needed to find some measure of peace before venturing into the perilous world of dreams. "You go. I'll follow later."

"You want me to get you something to drink? Tea, perhaps, or something cold?"

"No, thank you. I'm fine."

She hesitated as she always did when he used that phrase. Because in her mind, he wasn't fine at all and hadn't been since the day the consultant ophthalmologist had confirmed the test results. The ones that confirmed Alfonso would never see again.

Raquel had taken the news badly, railing at the specialist until her mother had led her away. His father, having himself lost an eye, was the one member of the family who'd understood.

"It's different," he'd said as they'd sat alone in the ward. "But life goes on."

It did, of course, but not how Alfonso had expected after his time on Gemini. Gone were the beatings, the threats and the constant risk of a terrible, painful death. But gone, too, was the simple relief of seeing a sunrise to mark his survival from another night of horror. Now there was no respite from the darkness that followed him everywhere, with all the monsters that lurked there.

"In that case," Raquel said, bringing him back to the present, "I will say good night."

Her voice betrayed her hurt. Still, she kissed the patch of hair on the top of his head, taking care to avoid the stretched and puckered skin surrounding it. Alfonso raised his hand to reassure her, but she was already walking away, the gentle slap of her feet fading into the distance.

For a while, he sat alone, regretting his words. *Just another wound to heal*, he thought as he waited for his next carer to join him. Sure enough, the gentle pad of paws soon approached, and the dog's warm muzzle rested on his thigh.

"Hello, Chara." He ran his fingers through the dog's fur. "Come to keep me company, have you?"

She nuzzled his hand.

"I know. I could have handled that better. But don't worry, I will make amends in the morning."

Apparently satisfied, the big German Shepherd settled down, no doubt exhausted by a long day watching over her boisterous brothers now sleeping in the kennel nearby.

"Family, eh," he said, reaching down and scratching her ear. "Can't live with them, can't live without them."

Then, the hackles rose on Chara's neck, and she lifted her head, her body falling still. Moments later, a gust of wind rustled the leaves of the trees in the compound. The warm air fanned Alfonso's face, carrying a smell that sent his nerves tingling, and Chara emitted a low growl and crossed to the steps of the veranda.

Alfonso leaned forwards. "What is it, girl?"

The dog growled again, longer this time and more menacing.

"Chara?"

Alfonso could imagine her ears pricked, listening. He did the same, straining to hear anything as the breeze died away.

A twig snapped somewhere in the distance, and Chara

was off, leaping from the steps and dashing across the yard. Alfonso struggled to his feet, expecting to hear her bark or growl at any moment. Instead, her running faded until it was gone too. He called after her.

"Chara?"

In the silence that followed, the senses he'd refined in the tunnels of Gemini returned. Opening his mouth, Alfonso cocked his head to one side and quieted his heart. Instinctively, one hand drifted to a pocket that was no longer there, his fingers searching in vain for the stylus that had saved him so often.

Then, Chara barked, and the padding of paws returned. Only this time, she was not alone. The footsteps of what he thought might be two people made their way through the trees. Scampering up the steps, the dog rubbed her head against his leg, her tail thumping in greeting.

"Who is it?" Alfonso asked when the footsteps stopped below the veranda.

"Evening, Alfonso," said a cheery voice. "Glad to see Chara's looking after you."

"Giles?"

"Afraid so. Forgive our creeping around in the dark. We didn't want to wake the family."

"Who is that with you?"

"An old work colleague of yours."

Alfonso heard the other person step forwards.

"Hello, Alfie-mate. Long time, no see."

"Jane?"

"There you go. I knew you'd remember me."

"But… but what are you doing here?"

"Keeping Giles out of trouble, of course. Someone has to."

Alfonso wasn't sure why a waitress would need to watch over Giles, but he was too stunned by their arrival to ask.

"How are you doing, Alfonso?" Giles asked.

"I am OK. It has been difficult at times, but Raquel has been looking after me."

"That's good to know. How is Raquel?"

"My sister finds it hard, you know, to see me like this."

The others were silent, and he wondered how much they could see of his injuries.

"That's why we're here, Alfie-mate," Jane said. "Giles knows someone who can help you."

"I have a doctor here, a specialist. There is nothing more you can do."

"It's not exactly a traditional approach," Giles explained. "More of an alternative remedy."

Then, Alfonso felt it again. The breeze, closer now, ruffled his shirt, and the aroma became more intense and distinctive. Next to him, Chara growled, and he reached down to put a calming hand on her collar.

"It's OK," he said, but the air buffeted them again, and the dog started barking, setting off her brothers in the kennels. Soon he could feel the percussive beat of wings, and he dropped to his knees, gripping the dog's collar as terrible memories returned.

The veranda shuddered as something heavy landed a few feet away. Frantic now, Chara lunged, and it was all Alfonso could do to restrain her. Then came the hiss, long and slow, blanking out all other sounds. When it stopped, the dogs, the crickets and even the trees had fallen silent as if waiting for the new arrival to speak.

"Hello, Alfonso," said Katya.

Alfonso gasped. Her voice transported him back to another world of valleys and towers with rivers flowing beneath them, the images burned into his memory by the relentless twin suns overhead.

"Katya?" he said. "How did–"

But he was interrupted by footsteps running from the villa.

"Alfonso? I heard the dogs and…" Raquel's voice trailed off. "What is she doing here?"

"I brought her," Giles said, stepping onto the veranda.

"You!"

"She's here to help your brother."

"Help?" Her voice rose. "Don't you think you have all done enough?"

"Let him speak, Raquel," Alfonso said.

"But Alfonso–"

"Raquel," he raised his voice. "I said, let him speak."

His sister fell silent, and after a moment, Giles continued.

"Katya has brought something that may be able to restore your sight."

"Impossible," Raquel said, but Alfonso held up a hand.

"Sister, take the dog inside if you cannot be quiet."

"What?"

"Here, take Chara, and be still. I mean it!"

There was a brief pause before she came and took the collar. "This is madness," she muttered before retreating to the house.

Alfonso turned back to the harpy.

"You have brought something for me?"

"I have. Hold out your hands."

Alfonso did as she requested, and a large oval object, similar to the egg he'd once stolen from the Hive, was placed in his hands.

"Take it," she said.

"Where did you get it?"

"It is mine to give."

Alfonso frowned. "No, you cannot. It is too much."

"Alfonso. There can be no others like me. I am the last of my kind."

The enormity of what she was saying was too much for him.

"You cannot do this for me."

"I can and I must."

"But why?"

"I stood by while my mother and sister did terrible things to my world. Then, you came, and all that began to change. With their passing, it is left to me to heal those scars, both on Gemini and here."

Alfonso was humbled. During their time together, he remembered how Katya had watched her mother and sister, those sharp eyes following every action and consequence, her expression unreadable. Now he understood why. She was learning not how to mimic them but how they were wrong.

"You know what to do," she said, stepping back.

Alfonso cradled the egg in his hands. It wasn't as heavy as the one he'd stolen from the Hive. Perhaps it had only recently been laid. But he was all too aware of what was within that smooth shell.

Alfonso thought back to that moment on top of the tower when he'd first seen this ritual performed. Olga had held the stolen egg over Mary's wounded body, surrounded by the circle of stone harpies.

"Everyone, stand back," he said.

Giles and Jane withdrew to the trees, but Raquel remained.

"Alfonso? What is going on?"

"Take Chara inside the house and stay there. Please, Raquel, it's the only way."

The dog whined as Raquel led her back to the house, leaving Alfonso alone with Katya once more.

"I don't remember the words," he said.

"When you are ready, I will begin."

Squaring his shoulders, Alfonso raised the egg above his head. There was a brief rustle of feathers, and he imagined Katya spreading her broad wings above him. Then, she spoke in a solemn voice.

"From death to life!"

He took a deep breath and repeated, "From death to life!"

The air stilled as he accepted what he was about to do. He might not have done it if the egg had twitched. But it didn't. It felt cold and inert in his hands.

Alfonso closed his eyes and hurled it down.

The egg smashed on the veranda's tiled floor. There was no blinding light – or none that Alfonso could see. Instead, there was a surge of energy so intense he wondered if a bolt of lightning had escaped from the heavens to discharge itself through his body.

Then, his world went white. Not the pale, lacklustre white of the sun at noon or a car's headlights on full beam. No, it was more brilliant than that, as if all things, actual or remembered, had been atomised. Alfonso stood at the epicentre, incapable of any response other than to endure the forces unleashed within him.

When it was over, the light receded in an instant, and darkness descended again. Alfonso's knees buckled, and he collapsed to the ground, his face resting against the cool, hard tiles as the air swirled around him. How long he lay there, he couldn't tell, but eventually the cries of his sister and parents brought him back to his senses.

"What the hell is going on?"

"Alfonso!"

Chara barked close by, and a warm, wet tongue slobbered over his face,

"Hey! Chara, stop it," he said, looking up at Raquel. "Give me a hand here, will you? She's…"

And then he stopped. His sister's shocked expression was mirrored on the faces of his mother and father. The dog barked and dropped down next to him, her tail thumping against his legs. Alfonso reached down and ruffled her ears, marvelling at his arms, the skin unblemished by burns or scars.

Raquel dropped to her knees and took hold of his head, her hands running through his thick, dark hair.

"Your face, it's... healed." She hesitated. "But your eyes, they... they are different."

"They are fine," he said, beaming. "I can see you, all of you, perfectly."

He looked around, revelling in his restored sight, which was, if anything, better than he remembered. Then, across the terrace he saw his reflection in the windows of the house and understood why.

"*Deu meu*!"

Next to him, Chara's ears pricked up, and she sprang to her feet. Somewhere far off, Alfonso thought he could hear chanting. The dog barked and leapt from the veranda.

"Chara?"

But she was already running through the trees towards a strange, glowing shape in the distance. He set off after her, his old injuries forgotten.

"Alfonso, wait!" Raquel cried, but he had no time to explain.

The glow was coming from the perimeter wall, where the trio stepped beneath an archway of pulsing symbols. Chara pulled up short and sat on the ground, her tail wagging as Giles and Jane disappeared inside.

The harpy, however, glanced back when Alfonso emerged from the trees and skidded to a stop. Katya's beautiful, proud features were exactly as he remembered them. But the wall began to coalesce in front of her. They were almost out of time.

"Thank you," he said.

"No, thank you, Alfonso."

The gap grew smaller as he struggled to find the words.

"I'll never forget you."

A smile crept across her face.

"No, I don't believe you will."

"Goodbye, Katya," he said moments before the final stone fell into place.

The last thing Alfonso saw of the creature who had given him back his life were two amber eyes. The same alien colour as his own.

The End

DID YOU ENJOY THIS BOOK?

I hope you enjoyed *Legacy of Shadows*. If so, could I trouble you to spend a few minutes leaving a review (it can be as short as you like) on the book's Amazon page.

Honest reviews help to bring my books to the attention of other readers who might enjoy the series. Just click on the link below and it will take you to relevant page on Amazon.

Many thanks,
Mark

GET YOUR FREE COPY OF *CAMBRIDGE SHADOWS*

CAMBRIDGE GOTHIC SHORT STORY COLLECTION

If you enjoyed *Legacy of Shadows* and would like to learn more about the fantasy world of Cambridge Gothic, sign up to my mailing list at www.marknwells.com.

In addition to regular updates from the author on future books, offers and promotions, you will also receive a free copy of my short-story collection, *Cambridge Shadows*.

COLLEGE OF SHADOWS

CAMBRIDGE GOTHIC BOOK ONE

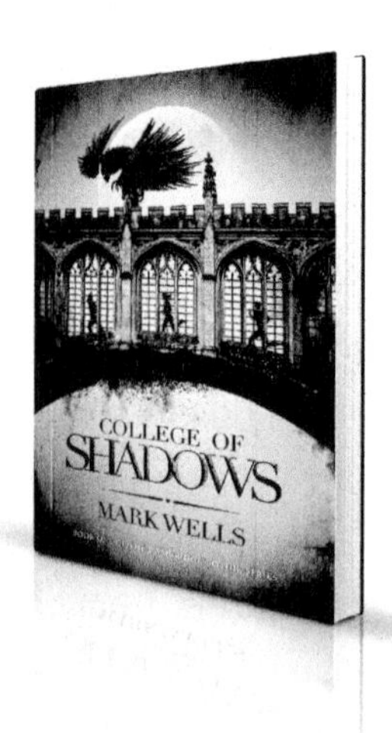

Cambridge is home to the brightest minds... and the deadliest monsters.

Working-class rugby player Nick feels out of place at University. The hallowed halls of Cambridge seem impossibly huge and far beyond the Mansfield of his youth. But Nick has much more to fear than fitting in when he is attacked by a creature straight out of his worst nightmares...

Emotionally scarred by the sudden death of her parents, Annabel buries her feelings deep in her studies. But after barely surviving another freak accident, the shy girl begins to fear she's cursed. And when her new friends nearly fall prey to a monstrous beast that shouldn't exist, she's terrified that her bad luck could bring about their demise.

As Nick and Annabel plan to trap the creature, they stumble upon a long-held Cambridge secret. And the otherworldly truth is less pass–fail than do-or-die.

Can Nick and Annabel banish the beast before Freshers' Week becomes their last?

College of Shadows is the engrossing first novel in the Cambridge Gothic YA urban fantasy series. If you like haunted heroes, unspeakable horrors and mystical magic, then you'll love Mark Wells's atmospheric tale.

Buy *College of Shadows* to watch students school the supernatural today!

GATE OF SHADOWS

CAMBRIDGE GOTHIC BOOK TWO

A mystic portal lies open. A chilling predator stalks the night. Can an undaunted student stop the darkness from spreading?

Giles Chamberlain returns to a snowbound Cambridge after Christmas spent with his girlfriend. Determined to prove himself to her family, he sets out to discover what became of her missing brother. But when he encounters a sinister figure prowling the College's rooftops, he suspects last semester's creature was not the only entity to cross into our world.

After the tight-lipped Professor Gupta refuses his plea for help, Giles enlists his feuding friends to locate the otherworldly passage. As hunters and hunted converge on the portal, the students discover just how far the old academic will go to keep his secret safe.

Faced with forces beyond his imagination, can Giles conjure up the key to save them all?

Gate of Shadows is the spine-tingling second book in the Cambridge Gothic fantasy trilogy. If you like resourceful heroes, nail-biting action and atmospheric settings, then you'll love Mark Wells's page-turning tale.

Buy *Gate of Shadows* to ward off the darkness today!

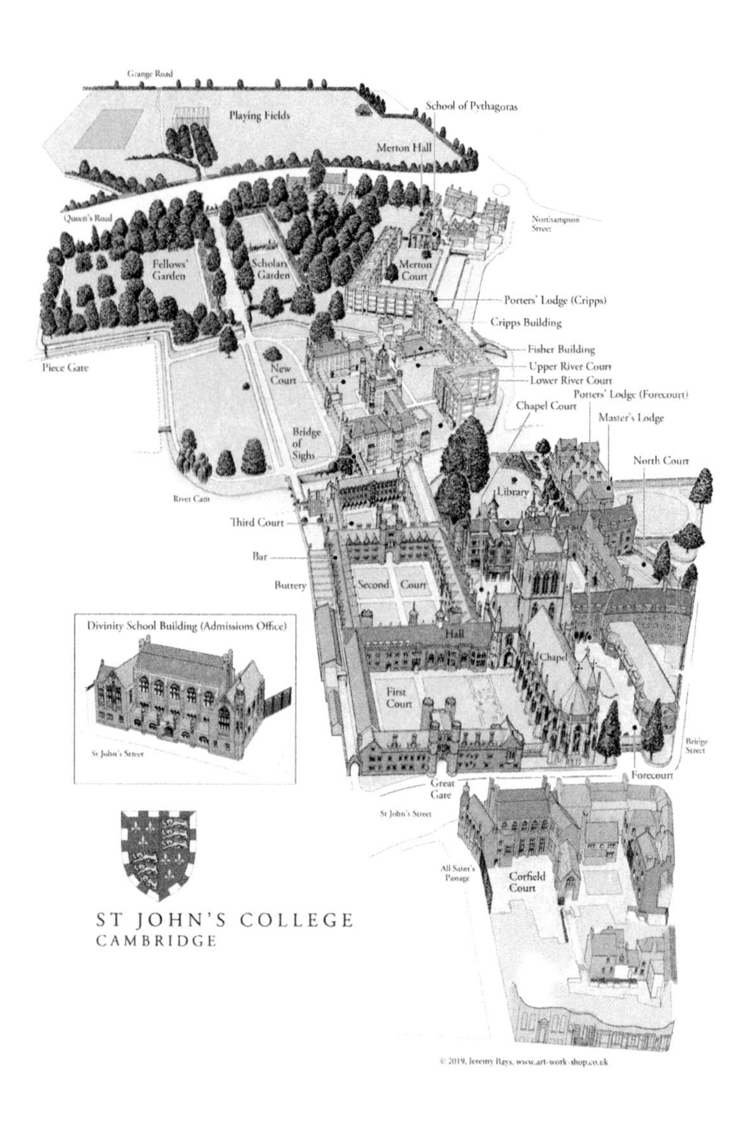

For an interactive map of St John's College visit:
www.marknwells.com/maps

ABOUT THE AUTHOR

Mark Wells read Law at Cambridge University and, after a career in business, returned to his old College as a Bursar and Fellow. He has published fantasy short stories for Black Library and a children's adventure book for the Arts Council of England. But he is best known for Cambridge Gothic, the bestselling urban fantasy series set in the ancient University: www.marknwells.com.

Mark lives in Cambridge with his family and can be found wandering its ancient courts and passageways, plotting…

You can follow Mark on:

Facebook www.facebook.com/markwellsauthor/
Instagram www.instagram.com/marknwells/
TikTok www.tiktok.com/@markwellsauthor
Or you can email him at mark@marknwells.com

Printed in Great Britain
by Amazon